The

LITTLEST
LIBRARY

Also by Poppy Alexander

25 Days 'Til Christmas

The

LITTLEST
LIBRARY

A NOVEL

POPPY ALEXANDER

AVON
An Imprint of HarperCollinsPublishers

Originally published as *The Littlest Library* in Great Britain in 2021 by the Orion Publishing Group.

FIRST U.S. EDITION

Library of Congress Cataloging-in-Publication Data has been applied for.

ISBN: 978-0-06-321693-8

22 23 24 25 26 LBC 8 7 6 5 4

For Nyx, who loves stories too

The
LITTLEST LIBRARY

Chapter One

"You're free!"

"That's one way of looking at it."

"Oh, come on," said Hannah. "You were buried alive in that place. How long's it been? Ten years?"

"Eleven. Since we both graduated. And I was very lucky to get that job."

"But ask yourself honestly—will you keep in touch with any of them?"

Jess sighed. She had worked daily with the unlikely ragbag of personalities in Bourton-on-the-Marsh Library. But even on the day it closed its doors for the last time she knew, beyond the fondness of familiarity, she had nothing in common with any of them. Not really.

"Exactly," said Hannah, smug in victory. "You've lost nothing."

"What? I've lost my job."

"Sure, but it's just a job—and a boring one at that—and it's not like you've . . ." Hannah faltered.

"It's not like I've got anyone to support," Jess finished for her. It was true, she didn't. Not anymore. It had been a year of crushing losses, as her friend knew better than anyone.

"You know you've always got me," said Hannah, stoutly, shoveling another spoonful of mush into her baby's face and then turning back to face the screen, seeking eye contact.

This was their near-daily ritual, with Hannah on the screen

propped on the dresser in the kitchen and Jess sitting at the scrubbed pine table having her pre-supper glass of wine.

"It was so lovely having you at the funeral," Jess remembered, wistfully. "Such an amazing surprise."

"Where did you think I'd be?"

"I thought you'd be eleven thousand miles away. Seeing as you are."

"Thank God for airlines and the internet," said Hannah, raising her mug of coffee in acknowledgment of Jess raising her glass. "I do feel virtuous drinking coffee while you're knocking back the vino."

"Oi, less of the value judgments. When I start drinking wine for breakfast you have my permission to be officially concerned."

"So, what will you do? Nothing keeping you in Bourton-on-the-Marsh now, is there? It's about time . . ."

"It's my home. I've got the house."

"It's time to move on," said Hannah resolutely. "What would Mimi say? 'Home is where you lay your hat.' She always wanted you to go off and explore the world. Now's the time."

"'Pastures new,'" agreed Jess, doubtfully. "That's what she used to say."

"Exactly. 'Pastures new.'"

Jess was what her grandmother Mimi had always called a home-grown lass; Bourton-on-the-Marsh born and bred. Mimi was from France originally and Papa had always proudly declared that you could take the lass out of Paris, but you couldn't take Paris out of the lass. "Mimi" wasn't her name really, but it was the closest a two-year-old Jess could get to Mémé—French for Granny—and, in the end, it was what everyone called her. Mimi had settled in the UK without a backward glance after falling in love with Papa all those years ago. Her grasp of English became near perfect and her French accent almost consumed by flat middle England vowels. That said, Mimi may have submitted to life in a small market-town far from home, but she certainly didn't capitulate. Her sometimes humdrum life was enlivened—as were the lives of all around her—by her relentlessly Parisian attitude; no outfit was complete without a jaunty scarf, no supper, however light and casual, was presented without a single bloom in a slim vase and a glass of good red wine. She was never without a slick of her signature bright-red lipstick and she had the permanently exciting—unsettling—tendency to give the impression she was just about to embark on a huge adventure.

Jess's life, on the other hand—with one, huge exception—had followed a pre-ordained path from local school to local college to local university and then, straight from there, to a local job in the local library: all safe, safe, safe. God, she was boring. Predictable.

As usual, Jess and Mimi did everything they could to avoid dangerous introspection over "that point" in her life: the event, just before her fourth birthday, which was so terrible it still had the power—nearly thirty years on—to stop a conversation in its tracks. This was why none of her colleagues in the library had known. She had barely any memory of her parents now, relying instead on the stories Mimi told her throughout her childhood. These stories were never about the car crash, of course. Instead, they were about when her mother was a little girl and how very like her mother she—Jess—was. The stories would generally finish with a rhapsody about what an extraordinary blessing it was for Mimi to have the privilege and pleasure of raising her daughter's child. To turn such a cataclysmic event into an opportunity for something good was typical of Mimi's relentlessly positive outlook. Despite Mimi's best efforts, though, these tragic events scarred Jess's impressionable four-year-old psyche, teaching the tiny girl that devastation inevitably followed joy just as night followed day.

As the years passed, there came a time when only Mimi, Jess, and Hannah—Jess's close friend from school—knew the crash story. Now, it was just Hannah and Jess.

Unlike Jess, Hannah had pulled herself free from the cloying mud of Bourton-on-the-Marsh four years ago; first, heading off backpacking and then staying to set up a brand-new life with her handsome New Zealand vet husband, leaving Jess becalmed in what Hannah referred to as Nowheresville.

At that point, Jess still had Mimi, of course.

Most people would have despaired at Mimi's terminal diagnosis. Jess did; it confirmed her theory of disaster growing out of happiness. Mimi didn't. She wouldn't, and—thanks to her relentlessly positive attitude—even Jess found moments of pure joy in Mimi's final months. There were weeks, days, sometimes just minutes, when the older woman's intense euphoria at being alive had infected Jess with a courageous optimism. At other times, the thought of facing the future without Mimi at her side filled her with stark terror. She did her best to put that to one side, to live in the moment, savoring the intensity of the time they had left together. Freed from the grueling treatments that had become futile, Mimi felt better than she had in an age. She made use of the renewed bursts of energy, using the time to clear steadily through decades of collecting, the silting-up with possessions that human beings do, without thought, whenever they live their lives in one place.

Every day Jess arrived home from work to two piles inside the front door, one for the charity shop and one for the dump. Occasionally she protested at Mimi expending her strength on such things, but her grandmother had been adamant.

"The last thing I want is for you to deal with this when I'm gone," she said repeatedly. But when it came to the books, Jess tried to put her foot down.

"You always told me books were sacred," she insisted, the first day she came home and found them by the door. Her voice wobbled only very slightly as she fought back sudden tears.

Mimi noticed, of course. She put out her hands and cupped Jess's face lovingly. In that moment, the tears Jess had kept hidden inside welled up and ran as if they would never stop, making rivers down her cheeks. Mimi cooed words of comfort, kissing her forehead and wiping away the tears with her thumbs.

"Don't worry, *ma chérie*," she had said. "All the books that matter are still here. They are yours to keep, and to take with you wherever you go."

"But I'm not going anywhere," Jess protested.

"Not now, but you will, and when you do—when you are ready—you will unpack these boxes and it will be like I am standing there beside you; all our memories, all our precious times together, wrapped up in these books . . . Trust me. You'll see."

But Jess did not see. She could not see how nearly thirty precious years spent with Mimi by her side could possibly be contained in the ten smallish boxes, each with *Books* in Mimi's distinctive copperplate handwriting on the sealed lids. How could any inanimate object possibly compensate her for the absence of the woman she had centered her life around? God knows she'd learned when she was four that people who constituted your whole life could be ripped away from you in an instant. At thirty-two she should be so much more able than her four-year-old self to make her way in the world alone. Some days—most days—it didn't feel like it.

Since Mimi died, the ten boxes had remained untouched,

crouching in the corner of the newly decluttered sitting room in the little house they had shared for all those years. Jess allowed her grief at the loss to surface only in tiny increments. It was like a caged animal liable to consume her if she gave it too much freedom; and this, her own form of grief management, definitely didn't include exploring any of the ten boxes—simultaneously her most precious and most distressing possessions.

After the comforting rituals of her lonely evening were done, Jess lay in her cozy, deeply familiar little bedroom, staring at the vast night sky through the skylight. She could have moved into the big room at the front of the house, but she didn't. She couldn't. And now she never would, because Mimi was right. There was nothing keeping her here. Being a librarian in Bourton-on-the-Marsh was no longer an option and being a librarian anywhere else was a doubtful ambition; council funding cuts and the digital age were making traditional librarian skills increasingly obsolete. It was a case of evolve or die.

What would she do? And where would she go?

The hours of the night ticked by as she turned the problem this way and that, like a puzzle box, needing examination from every angle, hoping for the nudge or prod that would make it spring open.

By dawn, she knew.

The wait for nine o'clock seemed to last forever. By the time she could legitimately leave, she had polished the old range, done a load of washing, emptied the dishwasher, and swept the kitchen floor, even getting the little brush out to go under the dresser. A fitted kitchen would be easier to keep clean but not nearly as cozy, she and Mimi had always agreed.

Finally, the radio announced the nine o'clock news and

Jess—her head muzzy with lack of sleep—was off down the high street to the estate agents.

She agreed to get the sale off to a flying start with an open house that Saturday. When slick Dave, the manager who wore a shiny suit and a large gold signet ring, proudly announced there would be at least six couples attending, she decided to absent herself rather than see strangers peering critically at her home. She couldn't bear to think of them turning up their noses at the solid deal furniture, the worn kitchen table where she and Mimi had sat to cook, eat, and do homework over the years, where Mimi had taught her how to knit and sew—Jess had been terrible at both—and where she and Mimi had just sat to talk, cradling mugs of tea, on rainy afternoons or late into the night. These potential buyers might dismiss her life together with Mimi, and that was fine, but she wasn't going to stay and watch them do it.

For a change Betsy, the battered old scarlet Mini Cooper that Mimi had adored, started immediately and by the time the first viewers arrived, Jess was miles away, driving with no purpose in mind other than to spend the day enjoying her thoughts and the glorious late winter sunshine, with its promise of spring.

Her instinct took her toward the West Country.

She had such happy memories of holidays there with Mimi, eating fish and chips on the seafront, watching as the seagulls regarded them beadily with their sharp yellow eyes and wheeled above and around them with menacing intent. When Mimi became ill, the camping holidays had stopped. There were plenty of great places you could get to and back in a day. When Mimi became too frail to walk the world shrank again, this time to places providing an easy drive, a nice garden with level access, and an on-site tea room serving a decent cup of tea.

That was then. Freedom beckoned today. Within a couple of hours, she was passing Bristol and then continuing on down to Exeter, wending her way through Dartmoor toward the little fishing villages on the south coast, shedding care and responsibility as she went. The weather was ominous now, though; the scudding clouds were crowding together, blotting out the light in the thin, blue February sky. Jess came to the brow of the hill she and Mimi loved for the spectacular view, but today she climbed to the peak, the engine laboring; and then she groaned. There was a tailback going right into the valley and beyond. It wasn't just slow, it was stationary. In a reflex action, Jess indicated left and swooped into a side turning she had never noticed before.

Chapter Two

Middlemass 1 mile, Portneath 5 miles, read the sign as she whizzed past it.

"Right," said Jess aloud. "We're going to Middlemass until that mess sorts itself out."

Quickly the road narrowed, and she found herself bowling along a lane with passing places, bounded by a steep bank and hedge either side. Hopefully, there would be a café or a pub. She could do with a coffee after her early start.

She turned a corner in the narrow lane, coming unexpectedly across a village in the valley below. Initially it looked unhelpfully small—nothing more than a hamlet—but then the road widened, scattered houses became cheek-by-jowl, and she found herself at a terrace of pretty Georgian buildings; the first three housing a launderette, a dentist's, and a strange-looking shop selling metal detectors, each with its own bay window. The shop next door, which proclaimed itself the post office with its bold white lettering on a red background, was closed and empty. There was a large *For Sale* sign fixed in the window.

In contrast to its emptiness, right at the end of the parade there was a general-purpose shop with a metal rack of potted plants outside, hyacinths and cyclamens, the only plants to welcome—or at least tolerate—the chilly February wind. The shop window was packed high with boxes of soap powder, tins of soup, and—randomly—a tangle of shrimping nets.

There was a double buggy, parked outside the door, with an older child at the front and a baby sleeping in the back. The older child—a boy of perhaps two years old—was completely absorbed in trying to work out how to undo his harness. He looked like he might succeed at any moment, Jess noted with mild concern as she crawled past, checking her mirrors anxiously.

On the opposite side, Jess noticed, there was a pair of tiny, semi-detached cottages crouched on the edge of the road, their pale green–painted front doors no more than five feet high. They were like doll's houses, she thought, each with dinky and impressively tidy front gardens, planted with serried rows of crocuses and the first green shoots of daffodils already pushing their way up past them.

Jess wondered whether to stop and inquire about a café, but the two older women in headscarves, coming almost simultaneously out of the neighboring doors, looked fierce and she didn't dare.

Rather than reaching some vibrant epicenter with the facilities Jess wanted, the settlement then petered out, until, rounding another corner, she arrived at an enchantingly pretty duck pond, edged with rushes. It was inhabited by a surprisingly large number of ducks, some of them snowy white, and two of them apparently just about to launch themselves kamikaze-style into the road.

Worried about running them over, Jess slammed on the brakes, fumbled a gear change, and stalled, right on top of a branch in the road which took it either side of the pond.

She couldn't be worse placed, with the little car straddling the junction. She tried the ignition, which spluttered encouragingly and then died. So close. She tried again, getting a more half-hearted splutter this time, and again, nothing. *Damn.* She must have flooded the engine or whatever that thing was, she vaguely knew about. She was pretty sure you had to wait a few minutes and then try again. It would be fine.

She got out and contemplated pushing the car to the side of the road, but—at barely five feet tall and under eight stone— she had no chance of moving it on her own. It couldn't matter, surely? This was such a tiny place and the houses clustered around the pond all had a blank, closed air.

Forcing herself to quell the anxiety rising in her chest, she looked around her.

She hadn't seen a red telephone box for years in Bourton-on-the-Marsh. This one, on the grassy verge studded with primroses, had a *For Sale* sign lashed to it. For sale to who, exactly? Surely, even in this rural backwater, they were no longer in use? Everyone used smartphones, even Mimi. Especially Mimi.

Out of curiosity she pulled open the phone box's heavy door.

The stench of stale urine hit her like a punch in the face. She reeled back, letting go of the handle to cover her nose and mouth.

"Ugh, grim," she said aloud faintly, gasping for a lungful of clean air as—thankfully—the door slowly closed.

Backing away, her feet pitching her off-balance on the boggy earth, she nearly fell backward up the steep verge.

Regaining her balance, she climbed up the primrose-studded bank, which was verdant with grass and definitely squelchy. Great. Her shoes were now rimed with mud. A bit of additional height improved the view further, though, and despite her cold, wet feet Jess was enchanted. The pond, with its weeping willow and bulrushes, was surrounded by an extraordinarily picturesque array of houses; she admired a handsome Victorian villa, with a grand porch and stained glass in its front door. It stood proud, its formal symmetry marred by an overgrown lawn littered with a scooter and a discarded bike. Next to it she could see a sweet little red-brick house with a charming cottage garden and frilly green-painted bargeboards outlining its eaves. Beside that was a rambling, gnarled old cottage with blackened beams, wonky windows, and a shaggy thatch that had seen better days. Inside, she could hear a small dog barking insistently and metronomically. He might have been barking at Jess, but she suspected he had been barking for longer than that. He had probably forgotten what started him off and now he had forgotten to stop.

Completing her circle of observations, she turned to look at the house behind the wall she was leaning on and her heart skipped a beat.

The cottage was ridiculously picture-postcard cute and neglected, all at the same time. It sat at a comfortable distance from the telephone box. Like a child's drawing in its simplicity, the whitewashed cottage had a low wooden front door in the middle with two pretty casement windows either side and two more directly above. Jess was breathing fast. It was magical. Mesmerizing. The garden was overgrown but already, delicate snowdrops and crocuses bejeweled the overgrown grass in a circle under the naked magnolia tree. A bare rosebush was splaying inelegantly with a sagging stem, leaning gratefully on the stone wall, much like Jess was doing. She felt the sharp flint and the rough mortar beneath her fingers, noticing the rose had hooked her with its thorns as if it were drawing her in. Easing herself free and looking around guiltily to see if anyone was watching, she pushed open the peeling wooden gate, letting loose a screech of protest from the rusty hinges. She was drawn, as if compelled, down a narrow brick path, green with moss.

Her jeans bottoms and shoes were quickly soaked by the

long grass collapsing defeated onto the path, and she squelched slightly as she arrived at the stone slab steps leading to the front door. It was sheltered from the weather by a simple wooden canopy with a leaded roof but, even so, the heavy wrought-iron knocker was rusted, leaving fox-red tears streaking the peeling green paintwork. She raised a hand to knock, and then noticed the door was ajar.

Without thinking, she pushed. It opened with a creak and a young woman standing leaning on the wall inside visibly started.

"Yikes! Hi!" she said, brightly, springing upright, her hands flying to smooth precisely cut bobbed blonde hair, framing a sweet, wide, childlike face.

Jess's initial impressions were of a low-ceilinged, oak-beamed room with an unlit wood-burning stove in the fireplace. There was a worn, pink carpet on the floor and the whole room smelled noticeably of damp. Behind the woman was a doorway to another room which seemed to be the kitchen, and beyond that, a window giving a glimpse of the back garden.

"I'm Lottie," the young woman said, coming forward, hand outstretched. "Do you not have a brochure?" She glanced down at Jess's empty hands as if puzzled.

"A brochure for what?"

"The sales details for the house," said Lottie, putting her head on one side.

The *For Sale* sign on the phone box at the front made a lot more sense now.

"Is it yours?" asked Jess.

"God no," said Lottie, with a shudder. "I wouldn't be seen dead . . . It's in a right state."

"So, you're the estate agent?" said Jess.

"I am!" Lottie agreed, happily. "Uh-oh, hang on, I wasn't

supposed to say that—the bit about it being in a right state."

"It's refreshingly candid," Jess said, her lips quirking up in a quick smile.

"This is my first open house," admitted Lottie. "Actually, it's my first week in the job. Things haven't been going that well, if I'm honest." Lottie had a faraway look on her face. Jess guessed there might have been a few unfortunate examples of Lottie's straight-talking that week.

"I thought it was the phone box for sale," Jess said.

"I know! Right? Actually, that might explain why no one's looked round the house . . ."

"No one?"

"Nope. Uh-oh, hang on, can we pretend I didn't say that either?" Lottie looked stricken.

"Don't worry, anyhow, I was just passing, but—the funny thing is—I *might* be looking for a house to buy."

"Perfect!" Lottie beamed. "Can I show you round?" she clasped her hands together pleadingly. "It'll be good practice."

"I probably can't afford it. I mean, I don't know what houses go for around here, but I doubt . . ." Jess took the proffered sales details and glanced at the price. "Hmm. Actually . . ." she said, looking around the little room they were standing in with renewed interest. "I kind of could, maybe . . . Go on then. A tour would be lovely."

Lottie looked thrilled and opened her mouth to reply.

"Is that your car?" came a deep voice, loaded with irritation, from beyond the open door.

The figure darkening the doorway was well built—actually, very well built—with broad shoulders and wavy, dark hair, silhouetted against the light.

"Ah," said Jess with a start. She had forgotten. "The Mini is mine," she admitted.

"So, what do you call that, exactly?" said the man, coming

into the room. "Does that pass for parking where you come from?"

"I—no—I'm not parked . . ."

"You're telling me. That's some rare talent, you've got there, blocking two roads simultaneously. Please tell me you're not considering moving in. I dread to think you'll be doing that all the time."

"I am thinking of moving in, actually," said Jess, who wasn't at all. Not until that moment, anyhow. "In fact, I am right in the middle of a viewing, if you don't mind."

"I do, rather," he said, mockingly echoing her tone. "Could you possibly park and then view—if it's not too much trouble?"

He had her there. "Actually, I might have broken down. I'm sure it's nothing serious. If you would be kind enough to give me a moment, I was just waiting for it to . . . get over itself," she finished lamely, giving Lottie a sheepish smile and then brushed past the man hurrying back to her car.

"You were waiting for your car to 'get over itself'?" he asked, incredulous as he followed her down the path.

She ignored him and unlocked the door, climbing in. Saying a silent prayer, she turned the ignition. Nothing.

"Let me," he said brusquely, holding the door open for her to get out.

Watching him climb in was like watching a clown riding one of those miniature bicycles. His knees had to go either side of the wheel, with the roof barely clearing the top of his head.

"You've run out of petrol," he observed, scathingly.

"Ha! That's where you're wrong," she snapped. "The petrol gauge is broken. It reads 'empty' when it's full."

"I'm guessing it reads 'empty' when it's empty too," he said.

There was no challenging his logic. Then she remembered: her routine was to fill the car at the same time as her Saturday trip to the supermarket. It was an unshakable habit of hers. She used to do it with Mimi. She would have done it today, only this time she had set off on her road trip without even stopping to think. How could she have been so idiotic? The uncommon spontaneity she had congratulated herself on this morning was punishing her now.

Aware of being watched by this frankly rather judgmental man, she suppressed the urge to strike her forehead with the palm of her hand, but his smug countenance made clear that her facial expressions had already told the story.

"Fine," she snapped. "Perhaps you could direct me to the nearest garage?"

"It's further than you'll want to walk," he said dismissively. "Wait."

She watched him go to the back of the filthy khaki Land Rover which had appeared behind her car. The Mini really was very in the way, she had to admit.

"Excuse me," he said witheringly, waiting for her to stand aside before efficiently glugging in the contents of the jerry can he had produced.

Before he had the chance to take over completely, she slipped back behind the wheel and turned the key. She didn't know whether to be disappointed or pleased when it still didn't work.

"So. Apparently not the petrol after all," she said, deciding to be thrilled he was wrong.

"Have you been attempting to start it with an empty tank?"

And then she remembered. She had. Several times.

"It looks like you've flattened the battery," he said, half to himself, before rummaging again in his boot and producing a set of jump leads.

He worked methodically and quickly, she had to confess.

When he had got the engine going again, he ushered her ceremoniously back behind the wheel. Fumbling in her phone case, she got out a ten pound note and went to hand it to him.

"For the petrol," she said, recoiling as his frown deepened further.

"We help each other out in Middlemass," he said tightly. "We don't pay each other. Now, the battery needs to charge so don't stop until you've gone at least seven miles," he advised. "That should be far enough," he muttered, deliberately loud enough for her to hear. "It's a start, anyhow."

Being furious and embarrassed didn't help Jess in the execution of a classic three-point turn. It might have been an eight- or ten-point turn before she finally managed to head back up the way she came, and it wasn't until she had rejoined the main road—the traffic jam now completely clear—that she noticed she still had the printout of the house details sitting on the passenger seat. Poor Lottie. She had been so thrilled to find someone to show the house to.

As the little car climbed out of the valley Jess's phone notifications pinged repeatedly. She was still hours from home; maybe she should stop and check her messages. There were three. They were all from slick Dave, the estate agent. She pulled into the layby to listen to them, but just then her phone rang.

It was slick Dave. "Jess? Jess! You're there. Where have you been?" he asked. "Down a well? The moon?"

"Devon," she told him repressively.

"Blimey, I didn't realize communications were so basic in the West Country. So, whaddayathink of that, for a day's work, if I say so myself . . ."

"Why, what have you done?"

"'What have I done?'!" he said, squeaking with disbelief,

"I've only got you an asking price offer, on the first day of marketing, that's all."

"Really?"

"Yes, really, and a cash offer too, no less."

"Right, so, that sounds good," hazarded Jess. "Actual cash, like in a briefcase in used notes?"

"No, not exactly," said Dave, sounding guarded, as if he had suddenly realized he was talking to an idiot. "'Cash,' as in nothing to sell, no mortgage to redeem or anything. Like—well—cash."

"Ah, right, good. And will it be quick, too?" she said, her spirits rising again.

"Yes—now—I'm glad you mentioned timescales. The offer depends on you being out by the beginning of March."

"But that's not even two weeks away!"

A heady rush of adrenaline coursed through her, firstly the familiar feeling of panic, but then quickly a germ of excitement. The little cottage had been imprinted on her inner eye since she drove away. There was, as far as Jess could see it, one way to avoid homelessness by next month, and—as she secretly admitted to herself—her heart swelled with excitement at the thought. As soon as she had managed to stop Dave congratulating himself long enough to end the call, she rang the number on the house details sitting beside her.

". . . So I would like to offer fifty thousand pounds under the asking price, please. Of course. Please let me know as soon as you can."

Later, just before five o'clock, with minutes to spare until the office closed, she stopped at a motorway services and dialed again.

"On second thoughts," she said, "I'm prepared to offer the

full asking price, but—did I say?—I need to be in by the beginning of March . . . I know, very soon . . . I'll ask my solicitor to contact you straightaway."

With shaking hands, she pulled out of the service station and headed for home.

Chapter Three

Home at last, Jess wearily slid the kettle onto the hotplate. Of course, it was ridiculous, buying a house she hadn't even looked around. She should phone again in the morning and withdraw her offer, no harm done. It had been a sudden rush of blood to the head. It had been an intoxicating day. The adrenaline was making her so giddy, she thought she might just levitate like a helium balloon at any minute, ending up pinned to the ceiling of the little, achingly familiar kitchen. The kettle whistled, but suddenly tea seemed inadequate, so she put the kettle aside and poured herself a large glass of wine.

"Go, you!" said Hannah excitedly after Jess had finished updating her on the day she'd had.

"That's not what you're supposed to say," complained Jess, suppressing a smile. "You're supposed to tell me to grow up, calm down, and generally get a grip."

"No chance," said Hannah, taking a bite of toast and Vegemite and then waving it expressively as she talked. "It's the next step, lovely. It was fate, taking you down that road."

"It was a traffic jam taking me down that road," corrected Jess. "An accident, probably."

There was a silence while they both remembered it wouldn't be the first time a traffic accident had caused a fundamental change of direction in her life. "Also, what would I do for work?" Jess went on. "What jobs could I do, in the middle of nowhere?"

"You wouldn't be. You'd be in the middle of a village community. It'd do you good. Bring you out of yourself. People are friendlier in villages."

"People are nosier in villages."

"That bloke who fixed the car sounds intriguing. What was he like? Was he single?"

"He was not intriguing. Only you could think he was intriguing. He was rude, that's what he was. And I do need to have a job."

"Not straightaway. You've got a bit to last you for a while."

"I have," admitted Jess. "Mimi left me a bit of money, bless her."

"There you go then," said Hannah stoutly. "Lovely," she added, addressing Jess, "I know you're scared." Only she and Mimi ever knew the fear that Jess lived with—the fear of change, the fear of devastating loss that growled and snapped at her heels—a fear of impending disaster that could, Jess knew very well, come true. Because it had.

"This is going to be okay," soothed Hannah, "I can feel it."

The waiting on Sunday was almost unbearable. In her mind, hordes of people had arrived to see around the little cottage within minutes of her departing, all of them richer, quicker, and more experienced in buying houses than her. She convinced herself one moment the cottage would be hers, and she was buoyed with excitement and trepidation; the next moment she was equally convinced it wouldn't, and she was cast into a pit of despair with a side order of relief. It was exhausting.

She slept fitfully on Sunday night—it seemed odd not to be setting her alarm for work on Monday—and, in the end, she overslept, being woken by her phone. Mimi had never let her sleep with it by the bed, so she turned the house upside down looking for it, eventually answering breathless with foreboding and excitement.

"Yes, hello, am I speaking to Miss Metcalfe?" said the caller promptly, when Jess gasped a greeting. "This is Adrian Holsworth from Pewsey & Hawes." He sounded loud, middle-aged, and tweed-suited. "I am calling about your offer to buy Ivy Cottage."

"Yes?"

"I am glad to tell you it has been accepted."

"Has it really? Have I really got the cottage?"

"Providing you're good for it, yes. You've got yourself a bargain."

"I'm good for it," she gasped. "I am." She didn't know what to say next. It seemed too momentous a conversation to be that short. "Have I really got a bargain?" she asked. "I did offer the full asking price."

"Nonetheless, yours wasn't the highest offer . . . I will never understand clients, but—there it is—you are the chosen one, as it were."

When he had gone, Jess put her hand on her chest, feeling her heart crashing against her ribs. Whatever this was—fate, kismet, witchcraft—she was doing it. And it was thrilling.

Jess lay awake on the night before moving day. The bed was dismantled and packed up. There was just a mattress on the floor of the bedroom, but it was uncomfortable and it was drafty at floor level. For hours her mind chattered and whirred, as she stared up at the sky through the skylight, chastising herself for her idiocy, buying a house in the middle of nowhere, giving up everything she had ever known, for an uncertain future alone among strangers. That said, she had to admit to herself that in Bourton-on-the-Marsh she was also now essentially alone among strangers. This dismal thought was allied with the certainty that with the library closed, she had no future there at all.

The alarm went at five o'clock—still dark—and she knew she must have slept at last because it woke her, dragging her up from a drowningly deep sleep that was reluctant to let her go. Head aching, she made herself a cup of tea with the provisions she had left out the night before. Everything else had been taken by the removal men the previous evening. Seeing her worldly possessions packed up and taken out of the only house she had ever remembered living in had been heart-wrenching but at least mercifully quick. Wandering through the empty, dusty rooms with her tea now, she was glad she was alone. This time the tears fell as she stood in the pretty drawing room they had repurposed. This was the room Mimi had latterly lived in and then died in. How could she have given up the chance to be in it, near her, every day for the rest of her life? How would she survive without being able to go back there ever again? To smell that dusty carpet smell, to see the sun rise through the bay window, to remember lying next to Mimi on top of the covers, reading one of Mimi's favorite books aloud after she had become too weary to read for herself? Jess had a physical pain in her chest at the thought of leaving that room, never to return.

Eventually, she took some deep breaths and marched out of the house, grabbing her bag on the way. It was like ripping off a plaster: better to do it quickly. She closed the door behind her, put the keys through the letterbox, and drove away without looking back.

*

Jess was glad to arrive at the cottage before the removal men. She had made incredibly good time. It was still only eight thirty in the morning, and she had been instructed to collect the keys from the previous owner in Quince Cottage at nine.

Here was Quince Cottage with its peeling painted sign fixed to the gate post. It was the beamed and thatched house on the other side of the pond she remembered from before. The one with the barking dog.

Hoping it wasn't too rudely early, she knocked, and immediately set the dog barking again. Then she heard footsteps.

"Carter, shut up," said a man roughly as he drew back the bolt and latch. It was a horribly familiar voice but before Jess had a chance to run away, the door flew open and there he stood.

"Oh God, it's you," he said. "I thought it might be."

"I could say the same," said Jess.

"I hope your parking has improved," he said, looking out, over Jess's shoulder. "My, my, Miss Metcalfe, how conventional you are," he said. "Fully on the verge, and everything."

"If I'd known it was you selling, I wouldn't have bought it."

"If I'd known it was you buying, I wouldn't have sold it."

"You just said you thought it might be me," said Jess, quickly.

"The other offer wasn't suitable," he conceded. "A second homer."

"Well, lucky old me," said Jess, sourly.

"Yeah, you were the least objectionable choice."

"High praise, thanks. What's the matter with a second homer anyway?"

He glowered and was silent for so long Jess wondered if she was going to get an answer at all.

"We've seen the second home brigade turn places like this into ghost-villages," he grunted, slightly less aggressively. "My grandfather was determined the house would go to someone who would contribute to the community."

"What if I don't?"

"I think you will," he said, softening slightly. He dangled in front of her face a large iron key tied to a luggage label. "Need some help?"

"No thanks," said Jess, swiping it out of his hand. "I think I can operate a key."

He seemed just about to close the door in her face when he changed tack disconcertingly, putting out a large hand instead.

"Aidan Foxworthy," he said, tersely.

"Jessica Metcalfe, as you know," she replied equally abruptly. She slipped her hand into his and shook it briefly, but for long enough to feel his rough, work-hardened skin and a tempered strength that could probably crush her hand to dust if he chose to.

"Welcome to Middlemass," he said.

She was sure the gate had not been quite so nearly off its hinges the last time she was there. In the bright sunshine, the flaking paint and the bent latch which wouldn't close were more obvious than before, but it didn't matter. She could imagine herself out there in the sun giving the gate a good lick of bright paint and the fastenings some oil. Of course, little things like that would have been overlooked by the former owner, she reassured herself; it was only to be expected.

The front door was firmly locked and initially looked as if it was going to stay that way. Jess pictured—with dread—having to return to Quince Cottage to take up the offer of help so sarcastically offered. She would rather chew her own arm off. Thankfully, after a few minutes of pushing and shoving while twiddling the key this way and that, it yielded, flying open so suddenly that Jess fell into the house and landed heavily on her knees. Inside, it looked and smelled even more derelict than ever, although the collapsed leather sofa she noticed last time had disappeared and someone had clearly dusted and hoovered the threadbare carpet. The Aga in the kitchen was belting out heat now and Jess—even though it was a crisp, bright early spring day—leaned briefly against it, taking comfort from its solidity and warmth.

Ever since her brief first visit she had been pining to explore the rest of the house, poring over the photos online and in the brochure, memorizing the room layouts, her imagination and every fragment of memory from her brief visit providing the rest.

Now, at last, she was here.

On proper examination, the little kitchen was disheartening. The fitted cupboards were beyond repair and the flagstone floor needed a thorough scrub, but the sink had a pretty window above it, with a view to the back garden, and the cupboards would have to do for now. She had Mimi's old Welsh dresser and painted sideboard that would just about fit at each end of the room, with a space in the middle for the little table and chairs she had brought from the old house.

The uncarpeted stairs echoed hollow underfoot. They led to a tiny landing with three doors. The middle one led to a spacious bedroom at the front of the cottage. Enchanted, Jess went in, her heart lifting at the wide oak floorboards that needed nothing but a lovingly applied coating of beeswax to bring out their beauty. There was a charming little Victorian fireplace and a small double casement window, opening to the front of the cottage, with a pair of painted wooden shutters folded back against the wall instead of curtains. Jess went over to the window and felt a surge of happiness at the view. The red telephone box rather dominated it, but beyond she could see the little green and the village pond, with the big white duck there again today, bossily quacking and rounding up his harem.

She sighed with pleasure, imagining herself reclining against many pillows in her high iron bedstead, enjoying the view with her early morning cup of tea.

The rest of the upstairs tour took no time at all. There were two more rooms, a narrower but still pretty room overlooking the back garden, and then the bathroom directly over the kitchen. It was all relatively dark and small, with low ceilings, although the bathroom looked as if it occupied a room meant originally as a third bedroom and was a decent enough size. In fact, unlike everything else, the bathroom looked better than the photos had indicated. It was perhaps fifteen or twenty years old, dating from a time when brilliant white gloss paint and mottled beige tiling was at the height of fashion. If it ever was.

She went gingerly down the narrow stairs, back into the kitchen, and on to explore the rest of the ground floor, which didn't take long. The door from the kitchen which she assumed went to the garden actually led to a small larder, empty except for a wide, cold slate shelf and some wooden painted shelves above it. Under the shelf there was a double socket. The fridge-freezer could go there. The narrow corridor also presented her with another ledge-and-brace door with a latch. She opened it to reveal a suspiciously old-looking boiler. The pilot light was lit and, as Jess regarded it doubtfully, it whoomphed into life. She had noticed no radiators, so presumably it was just heating water in some hidden-away tank. She was lucky the house even had a bathroom. She was lucky it had water and gas, come to that.

A sharp rapping sound made her jump. What could it be? Was it the plumbing? She froze. Replaying the noise in her head against her mental picture of the rusty iron knocker, she deduced it was the front door. The removal men had arrived at last.

The unloading—like the loading up—happened shockingly quickly. Mimi's ten boxes of books came in last. Jess got the men to put them down in stacks in the middle of the sitting room.

Ron the removal man looked around as he stood in the little sitting room. "Got your work cut out for you here, ain't ya? Gonna cost a pretty penny . . ." he sucked his teeth reflectively. "Five figures? Got to be."

"I hope not," said Jess. Five minutes before, she had been admiring the little room's beamed ceiling and peeling back the carpet to reveal some absolutely filthy flagstones that looked as if they would be great with a thorough scrub and a nice rug. Now she saw it through his more pessimistic eyes.

"See them?" he said, pointing at the beam in the corner of the room, so honeycombed with little boreholes that it tapered away to almost nothing in one part. "Deathwatch beetle, that is."

"Really? But probably not still alive, though? I mean, this house looks like it dates back to about 1700. If it's been standing this long, surely . . ."

"Can of worms," he proclaimed, depressingly. "Listed too, I'll be bound."

"It is," said Jess, deflated. In her excitement and certainty that the whole escapade was meant to be, she had put her reservations over dilapidation to one side. "I thought it was a good thing if your house was listed," she said. "That's a sign it's interesting, surely."

"Nice to look at, sure, lovely for everyone else. Nightmare for the owner though, innit. Restrictions an' that? Expensive repairs with all the right materials? Costs a bleedin' fortune."

Belatedly, he noticed Jess's crest had plummeted to her ankles. "Still, there's a nice view of the pond. Once you've got rid of that telephone box," he added kindly.

Despite the exhausting day, sleep eluded Jess again that night. She lay with eyes pinned open and trained on the ceiling. Surely it shouldn't be bowed down like that? The village was so much quieter than Mimi's townhouse, where the constant hum of other peoples' lives created a reassuringly familiar background to their own. Here in Middlemass, the noise levels were lower but more varied and intrusive. In time, she wondered if the ebb and flow of noises throughout the day and night would ever become, in its familiarity, a soothing soundtrack to her life. It was hard to imagine. Now for instance, her ears were trained to the slightest sound. She knew it was late. The village pub had long ago disgorged its customers, a group of lads shouting goodbye as they strolled past the pond and went their separate ways. She wondered if Aidan Foxworthy had been among them. She also wondered if this little pack of young men were the ones relieving themselves in the telephone box. That was going to have to stop. The removal man had been right, she should get rid of it entirely. That would solve the problem.

Now though, all the village was asleep. The street lamp outside her window—one of only a handful in the village— had gone off at one o'clock and still she lay there, eyes wide, limbs heavy with fatigue.

As she stared into the velvety-black darkness, newly certain she had made the biggest mistake of her life, the sudden keening of a fox made her jump, its howling raising the hairs on the back of her neck. When her heart had finally stopped thumping, she dozed briefly and miraculously until a sharp, scurrying, scratching noise yanked her out of sleep. And there was another. And another. Soon, there was a cacophony of scritching and scratching, and then, her ears hypersensitive, Jess picked up—what was it?—squeaking? Like a tiny squawking creature—only hundreds of them . . . Was it coming from the walls? The roof? She suddenly sat bolt upright in terror, her neck straining as she stared through the darkness at the bowed ceiling above her. They were too big-sounding to be mice.

Rats! In the attic!

She gasped.

What if the ceiling was about to collapse from the weight of them? Once the idea of a ton of rats landing in her lap along with the ceiling had entered her head there was no shaking it. Frantic, she shuffled to the edge of the bed and swung her legs out, feeling with her feet in the dark for her slippers. Then, she scampered to the spare room where the single mattress and a sleeping bag would suffice for the remainder of the night.

Chapter Four

In the watery sunshine of a fine, early March morning, Jess wondered if she had allowed her imagination to get the better of her. The skittering and scratching of the previous night seemed unlikely in the broad daylight. She might summon up her courage and take a look in the loft, assuming she could find a ladder. Using the last of the milk, Jess made herself a cup of tea and, without waiting to get dressed, carried out an analysis of the space upstairs.

The second bedroom—where she had eventually slept— was big enough for a double bed, provided there wasn't too much else. As a guest room, it would do very well with the little bedside table that could double as a dressing table. She needed a mirror above it, and a lamp too. There were already a couple of hooks on the back of the simple ledge-and-brace door; with some nice wooden coat hangers, they could serve in lieu of a wardrobe. Perhaps, by the window, there could be one of the Lloyd Loom chairs that formerly lived in the kitchen. There was wall space for a little bookshelf too, and she could easily imagine guests, or even herself, curled up in the chair, enjoying the afternoon sun, buried in a good book. Perhaps this room could be home for some of the precious books that she had brought with her. If she could ever bring herself to unpack them, that is.

"A guest room," she said aloud in the silent house. "For all my guests," she added, with irony. Her friends from the library? Probably not. Or maybe some old school friends? Apart from Hannah, on the other side of the world, who actually cared enough—who mattered enough—to be carried through from her old life to her new one? Anyone?

Mimi had helped with Jess's friendships when she was a child, organizing sleepovers and birthday treats, later listening with wisdom and calm as Jess navigated the treacherous waters of teen relationships. No, it wasn't Mimi's fault that Jess had neglected her few and fragile friendships. She had poured everything she had into her relationship with Mimi instead, especially when they both faced the truth that it would come to an end sooner than either of them wanted.

Anyhow, thought Jess briskly, it still needed to be a guest room, probably. Not a child's bedroom. Not that, because that would mean having someone else to share her life with. It was the most wonderful concept of course, but a distant one, like a daydream—something that might happen in other people's lives, but not her own. The mutual commitment of marriage and the noisy, joyful chaos of a family home seemed as remote as it ever had. No. Furnishing the room as a nursery was not an idea she would allow herself to take out and play with—the cot here, a mobile hanging over it, a chest of drawers with animals on it, a toy box perhaps . . . She couldn't be further away from that future if she had just moved to the moon.

She checked out the bathroom next; it was the only room where the men had not dumped random boxes. Surveying the layout of the large room, with a claw-foot bath right in the center, her practical head said the bare wall at one end could be a place for either a freestanding towel rail or a bookshelf. Jess was a committed fan of reading in the bath and thought a selection of fat bonkbuster paperbacks was an excellent addition to any bathroom. Again, unwillingly, she imagined herself unpacking the ten boxes of books downstairs. Tears sprang hot to her eyes at the thought and—rubbing them—she looked for a distraction.

There was a pretty window overlooking the wilderness which was the back garden. She would love to leave the window bare, so she could enjoy the view from the bath, but her neighbors might not share her enthusiasm. Just a simple voile panel—nothing frilly—would do the job. She added it to her growing mental list; but looking out of the window had provided her with too big a distraction. She couldn't wait to get out and explore. The estate agent's details had said hardly anything about the outside space, except to say it had "potential"—which was never good. She wasn't even sure where the garden ended.

Refilling her tea mug—with the milk all gone, it would have to be black—she stood barefoot on the bit of the stone floor that was heated by the Aga. Warming herself, she gazed out through the window where tendrils of ivy filtered the morning light into a green, underwater world.

She slipped on her wellies, put a coat over her pajamas, and took her tea out to the back garden.

There was a square of moss-covered brick patio directly outside the kitchen door. It was dotted with big, round terra-cotta pots, weathered to blend with the floor. The large pot by the door was planted with bright green spearmint leaves elbowing aside a woody, gray-green sage. A dead plant that might have been thyme filled the remainder of the space and she made a mental note to replant it. Herbs by the back door were a simple luxury. She and Mimi loved to cook with them; she could have chives, coriander, dill—a pot of rocket, even.

The brick terrace was a cool, shady space now, but the

sunlight would flood it in the afternoon, especially when the sun was riding high in the summertime. By June, this little spot would be crying out for a table and chairs and perhaps an umbrella too. With the shelter of brick walls warmed by the sun on two sides, it was the perfect place to eat on a summer's evening, or just to have a glass of wine at the end of the day.

Jess yanked away a few strands of the ivy over the window. Most of it snapped off short, but the tougher strands came away with dusty mats of root and dust from the mortar of the wall, showering down onto the brick veranda floor. She could do more later, but she noted a pretty honeysuckle fighting hard for space that would flourish given half a chance. A rose, growing up a trellis on the corner, was also battling against the odds. Tiny florets of scarlet and bright green were already starting to explode from tight buds but the blooms were going to be too high for anyone sitting down to appreciate. A good prune was needed before the rose got into its stride. Thanks to Mimi she knew a bit about gardening. Her ability to manage this one—or not—would be Mimi's legacy.

She retrieved her cooling mug and continued, shivering slightly in the morning chill. The bones of a much-loved and bountiful garden were there but it was clear to see Aidan's grandfather had neglected it for at least the last year of his life. The grass, still wet with dew, was long enough to reach her bare legs above the tops of her wellies. Dried stems showed her that bindweed had tracked its greedy, smothering path across a pair of large rectangular raised beds and would again this year unless she dug up its evil white roots. These beds must have been for vegetables, although there was little evidence now, just some wigwams of pea sticks at one end, straggled with dead tomato plants. A lopsided rhubarb forcer sat on top of a clump of slug-eaten rhubarb at the near end, but little else. She might find treasures when she cleared the weeds away, but digging would have to wait a few weeks so she could avoid uncovering anything sleeping beneath the surface of the dark brown soil.

The straight, brick-paved path led past the vegetable beds and under a rose arch. Ducking to go through, she was showered with dew. Brushing off the worst, she had arrived in a little orchard with a low, branching apple tree, its leaves just starting to erupt. There were other fruit trees too and in the corner was a deserted chicken house, its wood gray with age and in need of creosote. She and Mimi had always intended to get some chickens—ex-battery rescue hens—but they never had. Could now be the time, at last?

Bending to go under the low branches of the apple tree, swishing in her wellies through the long, wet grass, she came to a waist-high wooden gate and, on the far side, a wildflower meadow, flooded with thin, early spring sunshine. It stretched before her, the bright green grass promising a haze of summer color, on the way to a stream at the bottom of the hill. She leaned on the gate and sighed, tears pricking her eyes again. She dashed at them impatiently with the back of her hand. So many tears. So much sorrow. When would she dare to be happy without feeling she had invoked the curse of disaster following hot on happiness's heels?

At her feet, hugging the ground, there were cowslips and yellow celandine, optimistically studding the spring grass with gold. And the smell: a heady, hopeful mix of sap rising and the moist, brown earth after rain. She felt the delicate warmth of the sunshine bathing her skin. Turning her still-wet face to the sky, she felt a tentative rush of optimism, the constant fear and foreboding tempered with an emotion that felt like it might be joy.

*

It was full daylight when Jess eventually returned to the kitchen and she decided her first job was to get dressed, get the heck out, and buy some milk.

The ducks on the pond ignored her as she passed but a sinewy old man in a flat tweed cap—no sign of a helmet—cycled serenely past on his ancient black bicycle and wished her a good morning.

She had been so tightly wound over the past few months since Mimi died that on this bright, fresh morning, the stress of the move behind her, Jess felt her shoulders drop by inches. It might have been a ridiculously impulsive decision to move here, but the village was even prettier than she remembered, and Ivy Cottage could be brought up to scratch with a bit of paint and effort. There was enough money in the bank to see her through a few months without work, providing she didn't do anything madly extravagant. She allowed herself a little pat on the back as she walked. She had just begun to wonder if she had missed a turning when there, ahead of her, was the little parade of shops right at the bottom of the steep, narrow road which led down into the village. It was a bit further on foot than she remembered, but it was an acceptable walk for a pint of milk. In town there was a shop on every corner; but then in a village, surrounded by countryside, going out for a stroll was a lot more appealing.

As she drew near, it was eerily as if the clock had wound back to the day she stumbled across Middlemass for the first time. She had a snapshot memory of two figures coming out of the semi-detached cottages. They were now outside the shop, both reading the noticeboard while studiously ignoring each other. As she watched them walk into the shop, she saw the first rather obviously not hold open the door for the second. It seemed strangely out of step with the old-worldly charm she had seen in her own encounters. They could have been sisters, too; both women were in their sixties, she estimated; both with flowery dresses over solid, well-upholstered frames. The one with corrugated gray hair had clearly applied a startling shade of orangey-red lipstick and jammed on a straw hat in preparation for coming out. The other had a stiffly controlled bob in an unconvincing shade of dark brown.

Pushing open the door Jess activated a scratchy old bell, putting paid to any attempt to enter inconspicuously.

"Hello dear," said the first lady, turning to Jess. "Are you the girl who's moved into Ivy Cottage?"

"I am. Gosh, news travels fast."

"Some people don't miss much," said helmet-hair, sniffing dismissively.

"Some people take a polite interest," said the lady in the hat, turning away scowling.

Mortified at being the catalyst for such obvious enmity, Jess blushed. "It's lovely to meet you both. People have been so kind. I am sure I will settle in and get to know everyone." She smiled nervously at the two women in turn, who both carried out the extraordinarily practiced trick of acknowledging Jess while blanking each other. "I'm Jess," she said, turning from one to the other and back again, as if she were watching a tennis match in which the outcome relied entirely on how assiduously the audience could smile at the ball as it went back and forth.

"Muriel," said orange lipstick, with a smile.

"Joan," nodded the woman with the bad hair dye. "Delighted, I'm sure. So, what are you going to do with the telephone box? We're all wondering."

"You are?" said Jess. "I really don't know . . ."

Muriel huffed slightly, and Joan said, more understandingly, "Of course, dear, you've got a lot to sort out." At that, they both turned their backs before Jess had a chance to ask them what they meant.

She busied herself with examining a stack of soup tins, wondering whether the washing powder would eventually turn up in the packing boxes at home or whether she should buy some more. The milk she found easily, and it looked lovely, clearly from a local dairy. She felt bad buying a plastic carton of it though. She must ask if anyone knew about doorstep deliveries. Mimi had been ahead of the curve, insisting for years on proper, reusable glass bottles delivered each morning.

Neither of the women seemed to be doing a major shop. Jess suspected they came in at least daily. Comically, they both marched to the till simultaneously, each ignoring the other. Joan got there first, by a whisker, making Muriel scowl even more. Jess was sure she was then deliberately delaying, taking forever to buy her lottery ticket and engaging the shopkeeper in conversation about the weather with saccharine sweetness. Muriel, for her part, was standing behind Joan looking daggers at her as she waited to buy her pack of butter and two baking potatoes.

Jess hung back long after she had chosen her purchases, only daring to take them to the till after the women had left.

"Don't worry about them," said the man behind the counter in a soft Irish accent. "Their bark is worse than their bite."

"It's fine," said Jess. "I didn't get the impression they loathed and despised me, just each other." She pulled a face. "Did Muriel murder Joan's cat or something?"

"Worse," he said, simultaneously tapping numbers into the ancient-looking till, with its Bakelite buttons and noisy sprung drawer, which flew out when he pressed *total*. "Joan passed critical comment on Muriel's sweet peas."

"She did what?" gasped Jess, reeling backward in feigned shock.

"I know," he said, grinning. "Fair play to Muriel, she's been wanting to assassinate Joan ever since. They're neighbors too and I even heard a rumor they're sisters, but don't quote me on it. Sure, and I think the brick wall between them is not nearly enough to contain their discontent. It makes the Troubles look like a spat over a parking space."

"People have been killed over less," she said, remembering the chaos over inadequate parking in Bourton-on-the-Marsh as well as the embarrassing not-parked parking incident that marked her first visit to the village. "I haven't accidentally moved into one of those Agatha Christie sets, where the body count climbs relentlessly but there's always cucumber sandwiches for tea?"

"You'd think, wouldn't you?"

"You're from Ireland," said Jess after a pause.

"How can you tell," he replied, in mock amazement.

"That's not a local accent."

"Nor it isn't," he admitted. "And neither is yours."

"True enough," she conceded. "Jess Metcalfe, formerly of Bourton-on-the-Marsh, currently of Ivy Cottage, by the telephone box."

"Ah, *you're* the mystery buyer. Hence the question about the telephone box. We're all dying to know. What will you do?"

"I have literally no clue," said Jess, a little more sharply than she intended. "There's so much to think about, I don't even imagine . . ."

"Take your time," he said, soothingly. "Anyhow, Paddy, that's me—and no, we're not all called Paddy, although I'll grant you it's a cliché—formerly of Belfast, County Antrim, but been here for years."

"You'd never guess."

"I know, I know. I should come with subtitles. Anyhow, welcome to our world. Honestly, it's not as bad as it looks. I wouldn't have stayed if it was."

"How long have you been here?"

"Twenty years. More, actually . . . twenty-two now I think of it. I'm still the new boy, naturally."

"Naturally. Do you think I'll ever stop being the new girl?"

"Depends. Do you intend to spend the rest of your life here and be the first of a dynasty?"

"Possibly 'yes' to the first thing and 'unlikely' to the second."

"No kids?"

"No partner, even."

"Ah . . ."

"And how about you?"

"That's why I moved here. Lost my heart, so I did, to a local lass when I was on a fishing holiday with my lairy Irish mates, and the rest is history. Three kids at the village school and the eldest one at the high school in Portneath. It feels like yesterday he came along, and now he's a six-foot beanpole of grumpy, teenage eating-machine."

"Blimey, four kids," said Jess. "They must take some supporting."

"Ay, they do that."

She was turning to leave when she remembered.

"Slightly unusual question . . . I've got some sort of infestation in the loft," she admitted. "It sounds like rats or something," she shuddered, remembering. "What do I do?"

"Depends," said Paddy. "If it's really rats there's a pest controller guy in Portneath. But surely if it's the loft it'll more likely be bats, no?"

"Ugh. Even worse," said Jess.

"In which case, you'll want to talk to the bat warden."

"There are bat wardens?" said Jess, incredulously.

"Indeed, there are. We have our very own one, as it happens. He's a neighbor of yours. Quince Cottage, opposite the pond?"

"Oh great," said Jess, heavily.

"You know him?"

"Sadly, yes."

If Paddy was surprised, he didn't show it.

"Say it *is* bats," Jess went on, hopefully, "is there any way I could *not* call the bat warden and deal with them on my own?"

"Ah, now . . . I think it's all a bit strict what you can and can't do, but there's an old wives' tale you can lure them away with white noise from an untuned radio because they really like it. No—hang on—I think you put the radio where they already are, and they fly away because they *don't* like it? It's definitely one or the other. If there's anything in it at all, that is . . ."

Chapter Five

That evening before she went to bed, with no real confidence in the plan Jess put fresh batteries in her portable radio. Having tuned it between stations and turned it up full volume— she stood on a chair, opened the loft hatch a crack and popped it up there, slamming the hatch down again quickly to stop anything flying out.

The scritching and scratching was so loud that night it was even discernible over the noise of the radio. Clearly, they loved it.

By morning, Jess had had enough.

She weighed the trauma of knocking on the door of Quince Cottage to confess girlie hysterics about attic invaders versus the even greater trauma of spending another night imagining seething knots of bats falling onto her bed through holes in the bowed ceiling. It was a no-brainer.

Not able to do anything sensible with her hair, she pulled it back into a loose bun. She was so practiced at this she didn't need the mirror, twisting and pinning up her dark, curly hair—which had a distressing tendency to frizz—with the knot high on her head. She fondly imagined it made her look taller. Unlike Mimi's eternally chic, smooth, chin-length bob, which had faded elegantly from mahogany to steel gray as she aged, Jess accepted she would never acquire that Parisian savoir faire. But she was fairly clean and just about presentable. And why was she dolling herself up to go and see that rude man anyway? Taking deep breaths to calm her nerves, she skirted around the village pond and headed for Quince Cottage, this time knowing her enemy at least.

There was an extended scuffling sound after the echoes of her knock died away. Eventually the door creaked open a foot or so and a skinny, dark-haired girl appeared in the gap, bending to hold a little dog by its scruff to stop it escaping. She was perhaps eleven years old, with large, intelligent brown eyes.

"I'm so sorry to disturb you. I'm Jess," she said reaching out to shake the girl's hand.

"Maisie," she said with a shy smile, holding out a slim brown hand in return. "You're the new lady opposite. Dad sold you the house, it was my great-grandpop's."

"Your dad being Aidan?"

She nodded.

"Is he in?" Jess asked.

Maisie nodded again and shyly invited Jess in, showing her down the wide stone-flagged hall with its worn Indian carpet runner and into a capacious kitchen at the back of the house. There, she stood awkwardly, shuffling from foot to foot.

"So—um—where is your dad?" Jess asked.

"He's in the shower," said Maisie, and that was when she became aware of the thundering noise directly above her head.

Jess was mortified. He wouldn't be pleased to see her as it was. He was going to love her turning up in his house before he had even had breakfast. She thought about making her excuses and leaving, but it would be even worse to have this sweet girl think she had done the wrong thing. She was going to have to grit her teeth and stick it out.

"So where do you go to school, Maisie? Locally?"

"Middle school in Portneath now. On the bus." She paused. "I was in the village, just up there, when I was little." She pointed vaguely past the pond in a direction Jess had never gone. "But that's just a primary school."

"I imagine most of your primary school went on to the middle school with you, didn't they? It must have helped to be with some people you know? It's a big step."

Maisie nodded. "I've still got friends I was at preschool with," she agreed. "But my really best friend now's someone I only met when I got to Portneath, she's from—"

"What are *you* doing here?" said Aidan, as he came into the kitchen.

Startled, Jess felt a blush break out over her cheeks, "I just came round to ask a question. Sorry, I didn't realize . . ." She flustered, caught off balance by his ire.

Today, Aidan was in a white T-shirt and jeans, with bare feet and tousled wet hair. For the first time she could see just how much of his bulk was muscle. The man was seriously fit. And seriously pissed off to see her.

"Paddy at the shop says you're the bat man around here," she went on.

Aidan didn't reply, but just raised his eyes to heaven.

"So presumably you must be Robin," she joked lamely to Maisie. To her enormous credit, the child cracked a smile— which was more than her father did, Jess noticed. Getting over her awkwardness, she was starting to feel annoyed. Did he have to be so rude? Rolling his eyes like that?

"I'm not answering any questions about bats or anything else until I've had a coffee," he growled.

Jess nodded patiently. "Fine," she said.

"Want one?" he added, with apparent reluctance.

"Thank you, that is *so* kind of you. I would *love* a coffee," she said with quite unnecessary gratitude, just to emphasize his brusqueness. She was getting fed up with this man's boorish attitude.

"Sorry," Aidan grunted. "You've caught us having a slow start to the day."

It was an apology of sorts, Jess supposed.

And then, to Maisie, he said, "Why don't you grab some money from the dresser and go get some chocolate biscuits or something from Paddy?"

"Please don't just for me," Jess demurred.

"All right Maisie, stand down," Aidan told the girl, who in turn gave Jess an exasperated look.

"Actually," said Jess, "on reflection, I'd love a chocolate biscuit with my coffee."

Maisie grinned approvingly.

"You're back on," said Aidan, "and get some toothpaste while you're at it? We're nearly out."

And that seemed to be all Aidan could manage in the way of conversation. Jess leaned against the door frame as he rattled around with great efficiency of movement, gathering together a stove-top espresso maker, coffee, and a pint of milk. It was as if she weren't there as she watched him measuring the coffee and pouring the water with practiced ease.

As he worked, Jess looked about her. As well as the cooking space which occupied three sides of one end, the room was large enough for a scrubbed pine table with mismatched chairs and, at the far end, a saggy old sofa. It was this Aidan eventually waved her toward. She went as directed, tentatively picking up a pile of folded washing and putting it gently on one side so she could sit down.

Noticing, wordlessly, he came over and picked it up along with a discarded school bag, dumping both at the bottom of the stairs in the hall and putting a bag of gym kit in the basket on top of the washing machine.

The dog, a shaggy brown terrier, came to sniff at her feet.

"Get off, Carter," Aidan admonished sternly. The little dog ignored him.

"He's fine; I like dogs," she said, reaching down to pat him. He instantly rolled on his back and offered her his tummy. Wouldn't it be nice if Aidan was that friendly, she caught herself thinking.

"Why do you call him Carter?" she asked, rubbing the little dog's tummy obligingly.

"It seemed the obvious choice. It's after Howard Carter the Egyptologist."

"The Tutankhamun guy," said Jess, nodding. "But why?"

Aidan's mouth twitched into what might have been the beginning of a smile. "It's corny, but he's always digging up old bones."

"Ah. Got it. Is he a rescue dog?"

"Yes." He looked at her in surprise. "How do you know?"

"Only that you were naming him with bad habits already apparent. If he was a puppy when you got him, he would have been free of all sin."

"True enough," he said, begrudgingly. "Maisie's mother just turned up with him one day. Decided she should have a dog. He didn't answer to the name his previous owners gave him anyhow, so we thought we might as well start from scratch. He doesn't often answer to this one either, now I think of it."

"I love your house," she said after a pause, taking in her surroundings.

The space had clearly been carved out of more than one room in the past, with wide oak beams dividing the lines where the walls had been.

"It works," he said, looking around as if seeing it anew. "It's my family home—since the dawn of time—but this," he said, waving his arm to include the entire space they were in, "is Lucie's creation."

"That's your wife?"

"Ex-wife," he corrected.

It was presumably the ex-wife, then, who had chosen the painted kitchen cupboards in an impeccable shade of dove gray, with a tasteful eggshell finish. The large, central island was painted an intense and complex dark blue, reminding Jess of ink and stormy seas. It incorporated a sink and one of those pull-out, extending tap things that Jess didn't know how to use.

Aidan was by the stove, pouring the coffee into a pair of cobalt and turquoise shaded mugs and topping it up with hot, frothy milk. Looking around further, she noticed walking boots by the back door, muddy but tidily placed, along with neatly hung waxed jackets and serious feather-padded gilets that spoke of occupants who were used to being out in all weathers. There were no feminine embellishments, no jugs of flowers or pots of herbs, although the careful décor cried out for these things.

This was definitely a man's house now.

Just then, Maisie crashed in through the back door, brandishing a packet of chocolate chip cookies.

"Toothpaste?"

She looked stricken. "Oops."

Aidan sighed. "Fine," he said, "I'll pick some up myself. Just brush your teeth really well with water until then, okay?"

Maisie nodded.

"Brain like a sieve," Aidan muttered to no one in particular. But Maisie, having liberated a medium-sized fistful of biscuits, had wandered back out of the kitchen into the hall before disappearing into the room on the left and closing the door firmly. She didn't respond.

Jess wasn't looking forward to having to "make nice" with Aidan over the length of time it would take to drink a coffee.

He loped over, handed her a mug, waved at the sugar on the table, offered the depleted packet of biscuits, and pulled a wooden chair at the dining table around to face her.

"So . . . bats?" he asked with a perceptible effort at civility. Jess briefly explained.

"Fine," he replied after a few moments of thought. "I'll come and see. Tomorrow afternoon."

There was no choice of timing offered, Jess noticed, although luckily she had absolutely nothing in the diary. She nodded her acquiescence, taking a big gulp of her coffee so she could finish and get out as soon as possible.

But Aidan had more to say. "Has anyone told you about the parish council meeting tomorrow night?"

"Er, no, should they have done?"

"Yes. There are at least *some* people who have been keen to see you arrive. You're here now and they've been holding off on the telephone box until there was a new owner at Ivy Cottage."

"What do you mean 'holding off on the telephone box'? What have I got to do with it?" asked Jess, ignoring his quite unnecessary rudeness about people being keen to see her. Perhaps it was supposed to be funny. "An awful lot of people seem to think I know about this telephone box, but I don't."

"You should," he said shortly. "My grandfather made a specific stipulation that the new owner of the house would take responsibility."

"Fine," said Jess. "Since you ask, if it's my responsibility I'm probably going to get rid of it. It's blocking my view."

"Not an option," he said, quickly. "You should check your deeds."

Jess said nothing, taking another big gulp of coffee to hide her confusion. She certainly wasn't going to admit to him that in the rush to exchange and complete so fast, she had barely flicked through the documents and notes her solicitor provided. She just signed where he had indicated and passed them back. She had been in a hurry, she told herself in her defense. And it wasn't the only out-of-character thing she had done in recent weeks.

"The village hall at seven o'clock tomorrow," Aidan interrupted her thoughts.

"What is?"

"The parish council meeting," he repeated testily.

"Right. Sorry. Will you be there?"

"No."

Small mercies, thought Jess.

Glad to get home but reluctant to get back to work unpacking, Jess decided sorting out the little kitchen was a priority. A couple of sweaty, grimy hours later she had cleaned up, located the washing-up liquid, most of the crockery, and a few store-cupboard supplies to keep her going. Less usefully she found a fondue set she had never seen in her life before, a bread-maker rendered obsolete by the Aga, and a set of steak knives: Mimi had probably saved up petrol tokens for them decades ago and then never taken them out of their box. She was astonished all these things had been overlooked in the cull Mimi carried out in the months before her death.

Looking around the kitchen Jess was so grateful she had brought the old painted dresser. It took up the whole of one wall with the matching painted sideboard opposite; and together they immediately made the kitchen feel cozy, like home. Soon, she would take out the knackered kitchen cupboards under the window, but they were needed for now, if only because the heavily scratched and lime-scaled aluminium sink was built into them. She would love an old stone sink, a Belfast sink, like the one she had at home. Oops, Freudian slip. This was home now. As a woman in her early thirties, she knew she was lucky to own a house outright, although she would rather have Mimi with her any day.

She'd learned at school that being raised by a grandparent was unusual. Children were pretty direct about these things. It always made her wonder what would her life look like if her parents had lived longer? What if she had had brothers and sisters? She might be an auntie by now. Christmases would be like other peoples' Christmases, arguing over whether to watch the Queen's Speech and complaining about who should do the washing-up or mammoth present-buying responsibilities.

If her life had worked out differently she would not be alone.

Chapter Six

After a busy and dusty morning, Jess was just thinking about a cup of tea, and maybe lunch, when there was a knock on the front door.

Answering it as she brushed a tendril of hair off her shiny face with a distinctly grubby hand, she blushed to see Aidan on the doorstep, with Maisie loitering behind him. Of course, the bats. Damn, the last thing she wanted was for him to see her looking such a state.

"Batman," she declared, opening the door and sweeping him a theatrically mocking bow of welcome. "And Robin. Is it really afternoon already?" she looked at her watch and was astonished to see it was nearly two o'clock. No wonder she was hungry.

"You are both definitely my superheroes," she declared, determined to be polite and enthusiastic. In fact, the more forbidding Aidan was, the more committed she was to be overtly pleasant. "Whoever's in the loft, it sounded like they were playing football up there last night," she said—unnecessarily, as she still had dark circles under her eyes to tell the tale.

The awkward twosome shuffled in and stood either side of her, arms clamped to their sides to save space, in her cramped little sitting room.

"Tea?" she offered.

"No," said Aidan gruffly, "thank you."

She showed them upstairs, with Aidan ducking to go

through doorways. The house felt even smaller with him in it. On the upstairs landing, Aidan left Maisie holding the foot of the ladder and climbed nimbly up into the loft, holding a little torch in his teeth. The stepladder wasn't quite high enough to reach, but he quickly swung up using the strength of his arms. It was impressive, she would give him that. She found she couldn't tear her eyes away. Then she became aware she was staring after him into the black void of the roof space with her chin hanging down. "Right, well *I* want tea," she said briskly, going downstairs.

"What the hell was the deal with the radio all about?" said Aidan coming back down the stairs to the kitchen minutes later.

"Just an aversion thing I heard about," she muttered.

He shot her an incredulous glance. "Look," he said, proffering his hands. He was cradling something with just a bit of what looked like black bin liner poking out between his fingers.

Intrigued, Jess came closer as he slowly opened his fingers. In response the bin liner expanded like a tiny black umbrella being opened.

She jumped back with a screech. "What is it, what is it, don't let go . . ." she squawked. "It's a rat!"

"It's not a rat, it's a bat," he murmured. "Don't raise your voice, you're frightening it. I think it's injured, or it wouldn't have been on the floor."

"Injured's a start. Dead would be preferable."

Aidan ignored her. "There's a decent-sized colony up there," he said, "but we can't afford to lose this one if we can help it. They're protected."

"Does that mean we can't kill him?" asked Jess, hope of a peaceful night's sleep dying.

"Of course you can't kill him, or any of the others come to

that," he said, glowering at her, but keeping his voice down in deference to the bat's fine sensibilities.

"Can we just—you know—persuade them to leave?" she suggested.

"Nope. By the way, while I think about it, you've got zero insulation in your loft, did you know? I was always trying to convince my grandad to put some in, but he was tough. And contrary, with it."

"I am sure there was something about it in the survey, now you mention it," said Jess, trying to sound wise and canny. The truth was, she hadn't read the survey either and was now thinking she might go back—belatedly—through the paperwork to see what other pleasant little surprises the cottage had in store. "Anyhow," she said, feeling he might have been deliberately changing the subject, "back to the bats. How many are we talking about?"

"Couple of hundred, I'd say."

"How many?!" she squeaked. "Well, that's just great," she said, her voice heavy with sarcasm. She took a deep, steadying breath and then, steeling herself, she edged closer to Aidan and the bundle in his hands. "Okay, fine. If I'm stuck with them, can I see?" She was encouraged that he was now holding the creature gently but firmly in one hand, its wings contained and its head poking out at the end of his fist.

"A face only its mother could love," she observed, looking at the strange little ginger-furred visage with its tiny black, shiny eyes like chips of jet. It was moving its head from side to side, its pink nose whiffling as it sniffed the air.

"I'm deadly serious," Aidan counseled. "It's an offense to do anything to disturb a bat colony. I should report you for trying that little radio stunt. Which is ridiculous, by the way. I've taken it out and left it on the landing."

"So, their rights trump my right to have a good night's sleep without Dracula's little helpers tap-dancing on the ceiling above my head," grumbled Jess, calmer now.

"Yup," said Aidan.

"I just don't like seeing their wings," said Jess, with a shudder. "Without them they'd possibly be quite cute, I suppose. Is there really nothing I can do?"

"Nope. I'm the official bat warden for around here. I need to do a report now I've taken a look. I suggest we do a bat count in the summer, around dusk, so I can approximate numbers a bit more accurately."

"You knew they were there, didn't you?"

"I thought they probably were," he admitted. "We used to count them once a year, but not recently, so I wasn't certain. Regardless of what you think, it's genuinely good news to see them up there now."

"If you say so," said Jess, mentally dismissing her tentative idea of storing some of Mimi's books up in the loft.

"We'll take this one back home for now," he said, gently transferring the little creature to a silent Maisie's waiting hands, "and we can check it out for injuries. It might just be a bit shocked."

"Him and me both," said Jess to their retreating backs as she stood in the doorway. "How do I get a decent night's sleep now?"

"I've been stitched up," Jess complained to Hannah the following evening. "Thanks to your encouragement, I've bought a—granted—quite superficially pretty cottage with a resident population of creatures of the night, and some sort of mysterious responsibility for a defunct telephone box. Plus there's no loft insulation, which explains why I've been having to go to bed wearing all my clothes. And now I have to haul myself to some godforsaken council meeting tonight, which sounds like a right barrel of laughs. I completely blame you," she grumbled. "You were far too keen."

"Tell me more about the bat-man neighbor guy," said Hannah, unrepentant. "I'm liking that he's nice to small, furry animals. That's a seriously good sign."

"A seriously good sign of what, exactly?"

"I want to see him," said Hannah, ignoring her.

"Dream on," said Jess gruffly, as she forced herself to tug a brush through her hair and look mildly presentable. "Anyhow, I haven't got time to indulge your little romantic fantasies tonight, I've got a parish council meeting to go to."

The village hall was a green-painted wooden building, looking out over the village playing field. It had a large scoreboard fixed to its wall, with empty hooks where the number boards went so it clearly doubled as the village cricket pavilion too.

She went inside, straight into a large, brightly lit main room smelling of dust and beeswax floor polish. There was a table and chairs at one end, presumably for the committee members, and just two rows of chairs facing them.

Jess had never been to a parish council meeting before. She could hardly believe she was at one now.

She sat herself unobtrusively on the end of the back row. A tall, glamorous older woman and a man in scarlet trousers came in after her and went to the front of the room. They were bickering amiably and seemed not to notice she was there. The woman was perhaps in her mid-sixties. Jess was always attuned to meeting women the age her mother would have been if she had lived; however, this woman was anything but the cozy, motherly type. She looked carelessly glamorous in her slim, very dark jeans, high ankle boots, and a drapey smoke-gray top that seemed to be all different lengths, with wafting, full sleeves made of some sort of semi-transparent fabric. There was a silk scarf wound around her neck, the colors enriching the streaks in her artfully highlighted, wavy blonde hair. Her candelabra earrings swung nearly down to her collarbone. Her effortless elegance reminded Jess of Mimi, although Mimi had been tiny and dark. The man in the red trousers was taking a seat next to her and was perhaps a few years older, with a tweed jacket and an impeccably tied cravat.

"Water?" he asked, handing the woman a full glass from the jug on the table.

"I'd prefer gin," she replied.

"I know you would. In fact, given the time of day I'm surprised you don't have a hip flask."

"How do you know I haven't," she fired back. "And I'm going to need it if our esteemed clerk heckles every item on the agenda, like she usually does."

"Shh," he said urgently. "Speak of the devil."

The glamorous woman caught Jess's eye, clamping her mouth shut obediently, but her eyes were flashing with mischief.

A split second later the door opened, and Jess saw it was a formidable looking woman she had seen but never spoken to—partly because she emanated such fierce vibes. She bustled in holding a cardboard folder, her reading glasses perched on top of her dramatically peroxided hairdo.

"April, how charming," said the man. "Allow me," he added, drawing out a chair for her.

"Hello Mungo. Hello Diana," she said briskly, nodding at them both as she sat down and then taking out a sheaf of papers which she shuffled importantly.

"Are we all here then?" asked Diana. "Do we have an apology for absence from Becky?"

"No, she said she was coming," said Mungo. "I saw her at

Paddy's this morning, she'll be here but she can't get away until Rakesh gets back, so she said she might be late."

"Hm," said Diana. "She might not be here for hours if she's waiting for the lord and master to come home."

"Sorry," came a weary-sounding voice, from the doorway.

"Becky," said Mungo, sounding delighted. "No apology needed, you're just in time."

A pretty brunette in her late twenties or early thirties came into the hall and sat in the last empty chair at the end of the table. Her hair was tied in a simple, no-nonsense ponytail and she had on the young mum's uniform of jeans with a blue and white stripy top.

She pecked Diana on the cheek and waved an all-encompassing greeting at the rest of them, including Jess, who was still the only person in the audience. "Sorry I'm late, I dumped and ran as soon as he got back. Just in the middle of bath time, more's the pity—for Rak, that is, not me—I was waiting for their heads to spin around." She sighed. Her shoulders dropping a couple of inches as she relaxed.

"He's babysitting then?" asked Mungo, heartily. "Good man."

Becky gave Mungo a scathing look and he wilted visibly. "I'm not sure if babysitting is the correct term," she said tightly, only slightly mollified by Diana's patting her on the forearm. "He *is* their father, after all."

"Yes, no, absolutely," said Mungo, contrite. "Quite right too."

"Sorry," she said, shaking her head, "bad day. Now improving considerably, especially thinking of Rak up to his neck in bedtime tantrums. Although he probably isn't," she added bitterly. "That Isla's got him wrapped around her little finger. Butter wouldn't melt. She's been an absolute monster for *my* benefit all day."

"That's my girl," smiled Diana, with a wink at Becky to show she didn't mean it. "All the feminine wiles in place at a year old. She'll go far."

"She'll be the death of me in the process," said Becky, taking a sheet of paper from April who was handing them out and clearly keen for them all to get started.

"Right," said Diana, taking her cue, "let's hold our noses and dive in, then shall we? You," she said, pointing at Jess.

"Me?" Jess squeaked, sitting upright and putting her hand on her chest.

"You're the new girl in Ivy Cottage, aren't you?"

Jess nodded dumbly.

"Welcome," said Diana. "I think you had better come and sit with us, don't you?"

"Yes, m'dear, do," said Mungo, smiling at her and leaping up to position another chair at the table for her.

"I'm so sorry," Jess said, gathering herself together, awkwardly, "I didn't mean to invite myself. I was told to come, so I assumed it was open to the public."

"It is," said Diana. "You *are* the public. To be honest, your turning up has improved the audience turn-out by one hundred percent over the last PC meeting."

"So—everyone—this is Jess," said Mungo, who seemed extremely well briefed. It could only have been Aidan who had filled him in. Or perhaps Paddy in the shop that morning.

The others around the table nodded and smiled at her, including April, who slid a copy of the printed agenda to her.

"We always have the chairs out in hopeful expectation," explained Mungo, "but community participation is at a pretty low ebb in Middlemass nowadays. We don't even have a full contingent of councilors. There hasn't been an election in years, and we struggle to even co-opt people onto the committee."

"So I should watch out, if I were you," joked Becky. "I

volunteered to fill a gap just for a few months and that was nearly two years ago."

"On the other hand, Mungo is unelectable, and heaven knows how he would find ways to occupy himself otherwise," said Diana.

"I could always resign," he warned.

"God no, don't do that," said Diana, only slightly repentantly, "I'd have no one to delegate to."

April cleared her throat pointedly.

"Quite right, April," said Diana. "Now, shall we . . .?"

After that, there was at least half an hour of points raised, actions agreed, and discussions minuted, until Jess started to feel her eyelids droop.

"I propose poor Jess should be released from this nightmare as soon as possible, as there's only one agenda item she has the slightest interest in," interrupted Mungo, noticing her fatigue.

She sat upright immediately. "Oh, that's really kind but totally unnecessary, I'm fine, I'm fine," she gibbered, apologetically.

"Of course!" said Diana, striking her forehead with her palm. "Let's do that. I propose we discuss agenda item number twelve, the plan for the telephone box. Now, who's first?"

Jess wondered about admitting she had plans to get someone strong to chuck it in a dumpster. "Okay, well, I've been dying to know," she admitted timidly. "Am I in charge of the phone box? Only, people keep asking and it's becoming a bit weird. Is it mine, or something?"

"You're right about the 'or something,'" advised Mungo enigmatically. "I mean, it belongs to the parish council . . ." He paused.

"Sorry, so, the parish council are in charge of it?" Jess hazarded.

"Ah, yes, but it's on your land," said Mungo. "In fact, I was going through the history today to remind myself. The deal is, the phone box used to belong to the county council, but when it was decommissioned it was handed to the parish council. Actually, I think we paid a penny for it. Or a quid, or something. Anyway, it's no longer a phone box because—as we all know—people just don't use them nowadays. But it's there and the community gets to say what it's used for."

"The community decides then, not me?" clarified Jess, still puzzled. "Which is probably good, because, honestly, I don't have a clue."

"Don't worry," chipped in Diana. "I've got a brilliant idea," she beamed, looking around the room enthusiastically. "I think it should be a one-woman disco."

"What?" they all chorused.

"A tiny disco," explained Diana. "If I had a sound system, a glitter ball, and a few flashing lights in there, I'd be thrilled. It could be my own little club, and people could queue up outside to lend authenticity. I could have a hunky, muscly doorman . . . Actually, that could be Aidan," she said dreamily.

"Mm," said Becky, "I think you might be the only taker for that idea."

"Nonsense," said Diana, doggedly, "Mungo would have a go, wouldn't you, Mungo?"

"Now you're talking," said Becky, "I could see Mungo in tight white flares, giving it *Saturday Night Fever* in there."

"I could see me doing myself an injury," said Mungo repressively. "You'd have to have exceptionally short arms to do a full JT in a phone box."

"Erm, sorry," queried Jess, starting to feel she had stumbled into some bizarre Mad Hatter's tea party, although to look at the rest of them this was all perfectly normal. "What is a JT?"

"John Travolta, of course. The man's a legend."

"Anyway, April should minute that—please, April? We'll have a vote presently," said Diana.

April—with a mouth-pucker of disapproval—made a note.

"Okay, what else?" said Diana, looking around the table. "It could be a very small gin cocktail bar?" she proposed, hopefully. "Or a whisky bar for Becky, seeing as she's Scottish."

"A wee bar," proffered Becky in a thick Scottish accent, which took Jess by surprise.

"It's already a *wee* bar; that's a sore point," observed Jess, wondering, with growing alarm, where the discussion was going to end up.

"Yes, I do know what you mean," agreed Mungo. "We need to train the boys coming home from the pub not to do that."

"That's another argument against anything to do with alcohol," said Becky. "There's already a pub nearby and we don't want to undermine their trade. Also, why do I get the impression 'people' are indulging their niche interests at the expense of an idea that perhaps the whole community can get behind?" she said, looking pointedly at Diana. "I was at that council meeting where we took over the telephone box."

"I don't remember," said Diana.

"Well, I was there," she confirmed. "I had Rak 'babysitting,'" she added wryly, glancing at Mungo, who accepted the reproof with a humble duck of the head. "One idea that was mooted at that first meeting was to put a village defibrillator in it."

"Permission to speak, Madame Chairman," interjected April, putting up her hand.

"Out with it, April," said Diana, "you know you don't have to ask."

April nodded her thanks obsequiously. "The defibrillator. That was my idea. I was talking to my cousin in Wales and I understand a lot of communities have fundraised to buy a defibrillator and put it in the phone box because it's usually right in the middle of the community and people can run to get it if they need it."

"Ghastly idea," proclaimed Diana. "May I just say—for the record and in the presence of witnesses—that if I begin to die for any reason, I absolutely don't want people to rip off my clothes and electrocute me. Just let me slip away quietly, for heaven's sake."

"'Slip away quietly'?" teased Mungo. "That'd be a first."

Diana gave him a quelling look and only Jess noticed that April, looking very annoyed, made a note that nearly tore a hole through the paper she was writing on.

"Also," said Becky, ignoring them both, and focusing on April and Jess, "there was a suggestion it could be a sort of book swappy hub thing." She waved her hand vaguely. "Where people come and take books, or donate them—or both—not sure, something along those lines anyhow . . ."

Jess raised her hand. "You mean," she clarified, "a book swap where people come along and—say—borrow books and bring them back afterward, aka a library?"

"Yes, I hadn't thought but, I suppose so."

"Because libraries are something I know about," admitted Jess shyly.

"Amazing," exclaimed Diana, all thoughts of cocktail bars and discos forgotten. "A village library in a phone box. Superb."

"You're a librarian?" queried Mungo.

"I am literally an actual librarian," agreed Jess.

"Amazing," exclaimed Diana again. "It was meant."

"What about the books for it though," Becky pressed on doggedly. "Where would they come from?"

"Books?" said Jess, thinking of the ten untouched boxes in the cottage. "Books I have," she said, with masterful understatement.

"Shall we have a vote then? Hands up for a defibrillator?"

April's hand went up, but it was alone.

"Okay, the mini library thing?"

Diana's, Becky's, and Mungo's hands shot up. Jess wasn't sure if she was allowed to vote, so she just smiled politely. April's face was a ferocious scowl as Diana declared the results.

"That's that sorted then. The community gets its very own, tiny library," announced Diana. "Aidan can build the shelves for it and you can tell him what you need."

"Oh no!" exclaimed Jess, in horror and then, recovering herself, "I mean, won't he mind being volunteered?"

"Tough, if he does," said Diana. "Serves him right for not coming. People should know by now they get delegated to if they fail to turn up and defend themselves. Also," she added, slyly, "it'll be nice for you two young ones to get to know each other."

Chapter Seven

"Fortune favors the brave," said Hannah encouragingly a few days later, when Jess outlined the telephone box plan.

The setup was almost identical to their chats when Jess was in Bourton-on-the-Marsh, with the screen still propped up on the dresser and Jess at the kitchen table, a glass of wine in hand. They'd spoken a couple of times a week since she'd moved into Ivy Cottage, and Jess suspected—on the days in between—Hannah missed it less than Jess did.

"It's good to hear you're getting to know people," Hannah went on.

"I'm not really. I haven't properly met anyone apart from the parish council people, plus Paddy at the shop, who's sweet, and Aidan Foxworthy, who makes me feel like an idiot. His daughter Maisie seems like a nice kid, though. Shy." She kicked herself for mentioning Aidan again. She was developing mentionitis over him for some reason, and Hannah missed nothing.

"So, Aidan," Hannah pressed, predictably. "Tell me more?"

"He doesn't seem nearly as nice as his daughter," said Jess, discouragingly. "I don't know where she gets it from. Her mother, maybe? I haven't met her."

"Yeah, yeah, enough about the kid and her mother. Going back to Aidan, I want facts, not opinions."

"Like what?"

"Status. Married? Widowed? Divorced?"

"Divorced. But listen . . ."

"Ah, now you're talking," said Hannah, absently wiping the baby's face. Little Molly must be coming up to a year old now, and Jess thought guiltily how she had never seen her in real life.

"Listen," Jess insisted, "forget Aidan, there's nothing interesting about him—but it's a nice village, and the house is amazing, and—you're right, I need to go for it—the little library's going to be incredible. Come," she pleaded. "Come and stay. See for yourself."

"One day," said Hannah. "I will, I promise. But you don't need me."

"I do, though," Jess protested quietly after they hung up.

At first, having finished the main bits of unpacking was enough; but then, after a couple of weeks of settling in, Jess started to raise her sights. One morning, feeling energetic, she grabbed a pencil and pad to make a list of priorities for the house. She needed to make sure her efforts and budget were being allocated where they should be, and that spending was being kept to a minimum. She should think about paint. That didn't cost much and could make a world of difference. The sitting room, kitchen, and bedroom were the priorities there, she decided excitedly. She just needed to spend a little time and effort. The less it cost to do the place up, the longer she could go without having to take a proper job. The kitchen cabinets were an issue though. They needed something done to them, but ripping them out and replacing them just so she could have robust storage for the essential kitchen stuff—saucepans, utensils, and her huge collection of cake tins—that was an expensive proposition. Somewhere for the microwave to go, where she didn't need to look at it, would be great too.

It was splendid not to have to find storage for food actually in the kitchen itself. She loved having a separate larder, which was lovely, with its wide slate shelf and tiny north-facing window covered in fly-proof mesh. She was seeing ominous signs of mice though, with droppings on the floor near the fridge. It meant she had to store her loose packaged food, such as flour, rice, and pasta, in plastic mouse-proof containers, at least for now. She should get some mousetraps, but couldn't bear the thought of the violence, of having to dispose of the bodies, and she felt equally squeamish about poison.

Pushing this problem to the back of her mind, she continued her tour. Her main conclusion was that she would change as little as possible, because she adored the old-fashioned charm of what was already here. With Aidan's grandfather living in it, clearly the minimum had been spent repairing and updating it. And thankfully, that meant the character hadn't been ripped out over the years. There was the pretty fireplace in the bedroom; there were the exposed beams in the sitting room; and all the doors were the proper cottage ones, the simple ledge and brace with wrought-iron thumb latches that were presumably about three hundred years old. One day, she would love to get the doors stripped of their thickly repeated layers of white gloss, now tinged a dull, nicotine yellow. The window frames and surrounds featured the same discolored gloss paint. But Jess reveled in the deep windowsills—goodness, the walls were thick!—and she loved the quaint monkey-tail window latches.

Overall, Ivy Cottage was delivering in spades what she and Mimi had always daydreamed about—a picture-postcard-pretty cottage in the country, far removed from the 1930s suburbia of the house in Bourton-on-the-Marsh. Summer was coming, and already—with all of its oddity and decrepitude—Ivy Cottage was starting to feel like home.

*

A cup of tea and a cheese sandwich fueled an afternoon of focused unpacking. It was outrageous that there was still more to do but this was the last of it, and long overdue. Several hours on, she had emptied and flattened a good dozen or so large boxes upstairs, making floor space in the spare bedroom at last. All the rest of her clothes were finally decanted into the achingly familiar wardrobe and chest of drawers from Mimi's bedroom in the old house. Somehow moving these things into a different house had allowed Jess to start using them. Before, she would no more have taken them over than she would have moved into Mimi's bigger bedroom. The two pieces of furniture were huddled together in the corner, where the delivery men had put them. The chest of drawers would look much better on the other side of the window, she realized, too late. It was too heavy to move on her own. She needed serious muscle.

There was always Aidan, of course. But she would rather stick pins in her eyes than ask him.

Back down in the kitchen, she was just pondering over why, on God's green earth, she had four colanders and a set of sporks—still in their box—when there was a confident knock at the front door.

Her heart flipped. Perhaps her luck had run out and it was Aidan about the shelves. Hannah was away camping for the week and—admittedly—she had so missed their evening chats she was ready for any company at all. Even him.

It was nearly six o'clock already, she saw, glancing at her watch. Heavens, where had the day gone? She ought to offer him a glass of wine or beer . . . In fact, she should really take it as an opportunity to get their relationship on a more civil footing. He was her neighbor, after all.

"Hi," she said over-brightly as she opened the door, her noncommittal neighborly smile at the ready.

Diana was standing there with a basket full of bottles on her arm.

"Hi to you too," she exclaimed, flinging her free arm around Jess's neck and extravagantly air kissing both cheeks with loud *mwah, mwah* noises. "Me again," she said unnecessarily, standing back and pointing at her own face. "From the whole parish council fandango thing the other night. I thought you must be having such a nightmare—moving is ghastly, isn't it?—I decided I'd come and say hello. Plus, I've got this amazing new gin to try—look," she said, waving a large bottle. "I'll grant you it looks like a large urine sample, but it's actually saffron. What do you think? Elderflower tonic or Mediterranean herb?"

"Mediterranean herb," said Jess when she could get a word in. Diana had wafted her way into the sitting room as she spoke, plonking her basket down on top of a handy stack of book boxes and unpacking it onto the coffee table. She chattered as she worked. "Now, let's see . . . Glasses, obviously, because I do insist on these lovely, huge balloon-shaped things, and no one ever has the right ones. Mediterranean tonic, couldn't agree more. I'm thinking a slice of orange with that, although I'm a lime wedge woman usually . . ."

Jess was astonished to see she had even brought a selection of citrus fruit, a chopping board, and a knife. She watched, mesmerized, as the most perfect-looking gin and tonics she had ever seen started to materialize.

"Sorry, no ice; but this is chilled," said Diana, opening the bottle of tonic with a satisfying *shushhh* and pouring it on top of the fat, juicy orange slices and very decent-sized glugs of glowing yellow gin.

"This is so kind." Jess wasn't much of a gin drinker, and it really was an alarming color, but she badly wanted to know more about her fascinating new neighbor. Plus it seemed rude to refuse.

"Cheers," Jess said as she stepped forward decisively, claimed one of the glasses, and lifted it to touch Diana's.

"Up yours," agreed Diana, chinking the glasses together then taking a long pull. "Good grief, it tastes like a moldy dishcloth . . ."

Jess tried a sip. It wasn't what she was expecting. Along with the heady aromatic herbs in the tonic—reminding her of a sun-baked Greek garden—there was a subtle, almost musty, mushroom taste, which she assumed must be the saffron.

"I actually like it," she said, taking another sip, a larger one this time.

"Waste not, want not," Diana replied, gulping again. She had polished off nearly half her glass already.

"So: Middlemass. What do you think of it so far?" said Diana.

"It's lovely, I think. It's all been a bit of a rush. I've not been out much, there's been so much to do."

"The property's been on the market for a bit," said Diana. "Of course, it's been empty all the while too. Needed a good airing, I should think," she looked around. "I've always had a soft spot for this little cottage, but I suspect looking at it might be easier than living in it."

"Where do you live?" Jess asked, eager to change the subject.

"Other side of the pond." Diana pointed through the window.

"That's yours? The gorgeous little Victorian house with the amazing garden?"

"Mine," confirmed Diana. "Been there for donkey's years."

"I love your garden," said Jess, looking out of the window. It was everything she expected from a cottage garden, with a climbing rose over the pretty, latticed trellis that made up the porch, framing a smart green-painted door with brass polished to a bright gleam. The roof eaves were lined with matching painted bargeboards, the edges carved into curves and curls, for all the world like the decorative icing on a gingerbread house.

"Thank you for providing me with such a lovely view," said Jess.

"Likewise."

"I'll be tidying up a bit," replied Jess hastily. "The front garden's a bit wayward, as you'll notice."

"I'll give you a hand. That way I can nick cuttings and seeds. I covet your foxgloves."

"Help yourself."

"Don't worry, I will."

They both took a long, satisfying swig of their drinks. The saffron gin was growing on Jess and she wondered what others Diana had in her basket. It was probably the alcohol—or the company—but she was starting to feel adventurous.

Diana had made herself quite at home on the comfy low sofa, and was studying Jess thoughtfully, not shy of staring, it seemed. Jess squirmed mentally as she perched on the edge of the armchair. She had put on her shabbiest clothes that morning and her face must now be totally devoid of the slick of mascara and lip gloss she had given it first thing. She could even see her shiny nose out of the corner of her eye.

"So . . ." Diana said at last, in her charmingly husky, low voice, "who are you, and what are you doing here?"

Her china-blue eyes, with their expertly applied smoky lids and perfect eyeliner flick, rested frankly on Jess's face. Her whole demeanor expressed honesty and Jess tried to respond truthfully in kind.

"I had to make some big changes. I didn't want to. I was . . ." Jess shrugged, searching for the words. "I was content. But, unfortunately"—her voice wobbled but after a millisecond, she raised her chin and continued—"my grandmother died."

Diana considered Jess's words as if she was observing them, turning them this way and that, examining their meaning. "But people's grandmothers *do* die," she said gently, after a pause.

"No, but my grandmother—Mimi—she was everything," blurted Jess. "I've moved so far away from her now, from her grave."

"I am sure she is close by still," said Diana. "There's that poem. Scott Holland, I think. How does it go? I have only slipped away into the next room . . . or something. Yes:

'I have only slipped away into the next room
I am I, and you are you
Whatever we were to each other, that we are still . . .'"

She spoke the words with constrained longing and sorrow, her smoky voice mesmerizing. "And the ending is so lovely," she went on.

"'I am but waiting for you, for an interval, somewhere
    very near,
Just around the corner.
All is well.'"

Jess felt tears flood her eyes. She dabbed them dry and hoped the older woman hadn't noticed.

"That's beautiful." Jess went on, trying to steady her voice and failing. "So, she died, and I wasn't ready—would never be ready, really. But for her it was wonderful because she died in her own bed. She had had such a good day the day before, and I just went in with her tea that morning and she was gone."

"Wait, you mean she was living with you?"

"Technically, I was living with her. It was just us. It had been for as long as I can remember."

"God, I'm so sorry," said Diana, her face creased with concern. "Here's me saying 'Grandparents die'; it never occurred to me she raised you."

"She did. And she was brilliant. She used to say I was the world's most amazing consolation prize. The only thing that made losing her daughter and son-in-law bearable."

Goodness, thought Jess, astonished and a little embarrassed to find herself in the midst of such an intimate conversation with this woman she had only just met. It wasn't like her. It must come from going so long without talking to anyone. The sooner Hannah came back the better.

"You lost your parents too? How utterly ghastly."

"I was very young. It *was* nearly thirty years ago," she said. "I often stayed with Mimi when my parents were working and this time they just didn't come home, and she carried on caring for me. All my life."

"When did she die?"

"October last year. More than six months now . . . I don't know if I will ever be able to think of it without crying."

"It's really early days," said Diana, "and it's right that you cry for her, but—even without knowing her—I am sure she would want you to move on with your life too."

"And I have, haven't I?" announced Jess, looking around her. "It's been a heck of a year: I lost her, then I lost my job, then I sold her house and moved out of the town I've known since birth. Even though I really, really didn't want anything to change. And now I've moved to a near-derelict house miles away." She shrugged. "And I don't even know anyone."

"You know me now."

"I'll drink to that."

"L'chaim," answered Diana, draining her glass, and reaching for Jess's empty one. "Another?"

*

Diana seemed lovely, thought Jess woozily as she got ready for bed. She had a stab at brushing her teeth, but it seemed surprisingly difficult to avoid getting toothpaste all over her face, so she gave up and pledged to do better in the morning. Somehow, she felt slightly less anxious about the bats now she knew what the noise was, or maybe it was the Dutch courage from all that gin, but she decided to go back into the main bedroom at last, falling instantly and dreamlessly asleep.

It was amazing to be back in a proper bed after the mattress and sleeping bag in the spare room, but then after the amount of alcohol Jess had taken on board, she could probably have slept on a clothesline. She remembered waking at two in the morning, desperately thirsty and disorientated, staggering to the bathroom to drink straight from the tap, before crashing back down onto the bed and then—nothing. If the bats were having a party again, she didn't even notice.

When she finally awoke properly, she was horrified to see her watch said nearly ten o'clock. Her mouth felt like the bottom of a budgie's cage. She used the last of the milk for her tea, which revived her a little, after which she quickly had a bath and got dressed. Diana's unexpected arrival the previous night had pricked her conscience at not having got on with the telephone-box library. There was lots to do and this morning, hangover notwithstanding, she felt energized to get on with it.

Chapter Eight

"I need drain fluid," said Jess to Paddy. "And bleach. And a bucket."

"Blimey, you *are* dirty," joked Paddy as he efficiently picked out products for her from the groaning shelves in the shop.

"Not bad," said Jess. "Is there anything you don't sell?"

"Try me," said Paddy. "Come on, whaddaya want?"

"A torch."

"Too easy," he said, reaching behind him without even looking and grabbing a large, black torch in a plastic packet. It looked indestructible and would double as a useful weapon if an assailant was asking for a bop on the head.

"Okay, batteries."

"They're included, but here's a spare set," he said, plonking a packet of AA batteries on the counter alongside the cleaning products and torch.

"Small, sticky labels in lots of different colors."

"Also, too easy," he said, taking a packet off a hook and adding them to the torch and batteries.

"Impressive," said Jess, amazed. "Armadillo?"

"Fair enough, you win."

"Good, because I don't think a pet shop is what this community needs," said Jess, thoughtfully. "Talking of which, the post office closure was mentioned at the parish council meeting the other night."

"Get you! So, we've got the new girl turning up to parish council meetings. You're keen. You'll have been one of the few."

"I was the sole member of the audience. In fact, I might not have been entirely listening to the post office bit, but it certainly came up as an issue. What are your thoughts?"

"Ah well, in one way it's a boost having it shut," he admitted with a guilty look. "We were two shops next to each other fighting for the milk and newspaper sales. I've got a monopoly now. I could put my prices up and no one could stop me," he said, doing a pantomime villain laugh. "But I won't, obviously," he added, anxiously.

"Have other shops closed too?"

"Depends what period of time you're asking about. When I first got here, there was a good selection: we had this one, the post office as you say, which was another kind of general store and stationer's—wrapping paper, greetings cards, all that jazz—then a really good independent greengrocer shop, a bakery baking its own bread on site . . . You could basically live your whole life without venturing to Portneath. You can't do that now, that's for sure."

"But less competition now, as you say?"

"Yes, but it's more complicated than that. Bert, our postmaster, retired at Christmas so we've had no post office for more than two months and losing the service is really cutting deep. It's the older people I feel sorry for—the ones who still collect their pensions on a Friday. They struggle with online banking, and the bus service into Portneath is pretty terrible, so . . ."

"So, what about you? Could you take it on?"

"Don't you start." He smiled, but Jess noticed the faint exasperation in his voice. "I did look at it, honest to God I did. Space-wise, it's just about doable. I was thinking I could reduce the fruit and veg section maybe. Cut down on the numbers of magazines and fit a tiny cubicle in the corner there. I even thought about taking over the unit next door, but our rent and rates are horrendous as it is, and there's other stuff too."

"Like what?"

"The main thing being I can't be in two places at once. I've got to be on the till pretty much all the time. If there's a gap between customers I've got my work cut out just pricing and shelf-stacking. The other thing being, I couldn't provide a post office service without me having to go away to be trained and then who would run the shop? My wife Debbie can't cover for me. She already does the odd hour here and there, but she's got the little ones to look after. Even if I just did the post office side of things for a few hours a week, I would basically need another pair of hands in the shop for every hour I've got the post office open, and I can't afford to pay them. Who's going to work for free?" he sighed. "It's just not doable, however I look at it."

"It's a tricky one," agreed Jess. She noticed Paddy's genuine concern with sympathy. "But if you can't do it, you can't do it. I am sure people understand."

"Ah, you say that, but there's more . . ." He sighed heavily. "The bottom line is, if people are forced to go out of the village to do their post and banking and whatever, they'll pick up their daily bits and bobs elsewhere too. It's potentially enough of a loss of turnover to mean that this shop might just tip from being profitable to not profitable. It's not exactly a license to print money as it is."

Jess was preoccupied with the post office issue all the way back but—like Paddy—however she looked at it, the problem was insoluble.

As soon as she got home, she put all other problems to one side and hauled a bucket of steaming hot water, a chamois leather, a mop, some bleach, and the Jeyes Fluid out to the phone box. She hoped she had misremembered how bad it smelled. She hadn't. The sun had heated the tiny metal and glass space like a greenhouse and the urine stench was as pungent as ever.

Trying hard not to breathe too much, she set to work. At some point in the past, the telephone and its workings had been removed, leaving a well-attached sheet of black enameled metal which was at least washable and would be a good backdrop for shelves. She managed to prop the door open with the mop, which helped a bit, and then she set to with the chamois leather, washing the glass and the metal frame from top to ground level on each of the four sides. Being short, she needed to wedge her little stepladder inside for the top bit, which felt precarious. She then unpropped the door again to wash down the same four sides on the outside before slinging the now gray-brown water with its liberal dose of Jeyes and bleach all around the floor of the phone box, where it promptly ran out, making its way to the gutter in the road. A few more bucketloads like that and she might just be getting somewhere.

She was just lugging another full, soapy bucket from the kitchen sink when she saw Aidan bearing down on her from the opposite side of the road. She hadn't seen him for days, but it had been too good to last, she supposed. He was wearing a harness and had a helmet tucked under his arm. Was he a tree surgeon? Jess wondered. Hopefully he would be too preoccupied with work to want to talk for too long.

"I've been volunteered to do the shelves, I understand," he said when he arrived at her side.

"I know, I was at the meeting."

"I see," he said heavily, giving her an accusing look.

"Hey," she said, stung, "it wasn't my idea. In fact, it was the last thing I wanted, I can assure you." Damn. She was going to be politely distant when they next met and now, he had nettled her—again—into being unnecessarily rude. She took a deep breath. "Look," she said, "I feel we have got off on the wrong foot. Can I propose that we forget our previous encounters and start again from the beginning?"

He looked at her suspiciously and then nodded.

"Good," she said, summoning up a sweet smile. "Now. I am sorry you were volunteered to do the shelves, but I am really keen to do what I can for my new community and—" She swallowed; god, this was hard. "The fact is, I would be extremely grateful for your help."

Aidan stared at her. "You look rough," he observed.

"Charming. Thanks for that."

"You're welcome. Drinking alone?"

"I had Diana here last night actually."

"Ah, I see," he said, infuriatingly. "Feeling a bit fragile now, are we?"

"And what of it?"

"Ouch. Sensitive," he observed, clearly delighted at her discomfort. "Well, there's no escaping it, once that Diana's made her mind up . . . Let's just get it over with, shall we? I need to measure up and then I'll take a trip to Portneath B&Q for the materials."

"I can save you the bother of the trip," she said. "I was planning to go to the Portneath DIY place myself this morning, as it happens. Just give me the list and I'll bring you what you need."

"You're not going to get many planks in that," he said scathingly, pointing to Betsy. "I'll take the Land Rover."

"Fine. I'll probably see you there, then."

"Fine," he said, turning his back on her and getting out a tape measure.

*

Leaving him to measure up, Jess escaped to tidy herself up a bit. Damn. She had only had a vague plan of finding the DIY place that day. Why did she offer to get the materials? Now she would have to go, or it would look like he had put her off, which would be infuriating. Paddy had told her it was in Portneath, but he hadn't said where. If Aidan were less of an irritating, judgmental prat, she would have asked him for directions. Never mind, she would just busk it and hope for the best.

By the time she climbed into Betsy, Aidan and his Land Rover had already disappeared. The road out of the other end of the village toward Portneath took her over a bridge, past the school, then out onto what seemed like miles of windy, narrow lanes until quite unexpectedly it met a bigger road with white lines and two-way traffic. This took her through picture-postcard farmland before barreling over the brow of a hill and dramatically laying out the town in the valley below. Here was her first sight of Portneath, a higgledy-piggledy town of slate roofs and houses in every ice-cream shade. Then, beyond that, a stretch of coastline and the blue-green sea itself, reflecting the sky and twinkling in the sunshine. Her ill-tempered conversation with Aidan faded into the background and she couldn't help breaking into a smile. Just catching sight of the sea put her in holiday mood, as she and Betsy bowled happily along in the sunshine.

Luckily, the DIY place was unmissable, a huge, flat-roofed building at the top of the hill on the edge of town.

In no time, Jess was perusing some edible-sounding paint colors, each one more delectable than the last. There was Cooking Apple Green, in a washable paint ideal for the kitchen, and a fabulous-looking Rhubarb Crumble—a deep but subtle pink which would tone beautifully with her treasured patchwork quilt in the bedroom. The quilt was an heirloom and some of Jess's fondest memories were of Mimi hand-stitching it, evening after evening, as she supervised Jess's homework.

She was just trying to decide between Peach Cobbler and Salmon Belly for the sitting room—where a warm, glowing color would be cozy in the evenings with the fire burning—when a movement at the end of the aisle caught her eye.

There was no mistaking those broad shoulders.

There was a good chance Aidan hadn't yet seen her, as he was deep in conversation with the woman working the woodcutting machine, but Jess was damned if she was going to tiptoe off and risk having it look like she was avoiding him.

Instead, she marched straight up to him, a can of paint in each hand. "Give me a shout if you change your mind about getting this stuff back. I'm stronger than I look, and I can get plenty into my car."

"No, you're all right," he said. "Carry on with your fancy interior design and leave the proper DIY to me."

He made interior design sound like the most trivial, girlie occupation on the planet, which irritated her even more. She should have just snuck off and saved herself the high blood pressure.

"Forgive me if I want to paint my house," she said, nettled, "but it's been a bit neglected recently. It's just a shame you didn't keep a closer eye on the state of it yourself."

As soon as she spoke, she could have bitten her tongue. She certainly didn't mean to suggest that Aidan should have looked after his grandfather better, but clearly offense had been taken. He blanked her, turning back to the woman behind the counter and continuing his conversation as if Jess wasn't there.

She blushed, furious with herself. She would have hated anyone to suggest that she had not cared for Mimi's house— her home—and, by implication, not cared for Mimi. She slunk through the checkout and loaded the paint into the car, along with brushes, rollers, and a drop cloth. Anyhow, if Aidan wanted to be offended, there was nothing she could do, she decided. Choosing the paint had made her hungry, reminding her she had had no breakfast.

"If you're going into Portneath I suggest you leave your car here and walk," said Aidan from close behind, making her jump.

"Why?"

"The roads down to the quay are very narrow," he said shortly. "It's up to you, of course."

Jess dithered. It would be so humiliating if she drove down and—God forbid—damaged Betsy or got stuck. On the other hand, it was galling to be told what to do by him.

"Thanks for the advice, but I was going to walk anyhow," she lied.

Jess quickly found Aidan was right as she walked down an insanely steep and narrow hill culminating in a hairpin bend. The gouges and streaks of paint on the corner of the little white-painted cottage at the side of the road bore testament to how many vehicles hadn't quite made it around the corner.

The houses had clearly been around longer than cars had. It would have been a tiny fishing village when they were built, Jess thought. If she were in some of the little houses, she wasn't sure she would be able to sleep thinking a truck was going to take out a bedroom wall at any moment.

She suspected a large proportion of the houses in town were either rented out by the week or were second homes for the rich. With property prices so high, she doubted young local people would be able to buy. No wonder Aidan had been so determined not to sell Ivy Cottage as a holiday home.

Now she felt more ambivalent about enjoying the simple charm of the little houses clinging to the edges of the steep, cobbled road as she tramped down toward the sea. There were few front gardens. Mostly the houses fronted straight onto the road, with thick walls and little deep-set windows, one with a naive wooden model of a seagull on the windowsill, another with a pot of red geraniums in front of a net curtain. It was all delightful in the spring sunshine, but she could imagine the gray desolation in the winter months.

Where did the young people go? she wondered. There must be a huge amount of poorly paid work in shops, pubs, and restaurants during the holiday season, but what about the winter?

She was at the harbor now, with a broader road and pavement running alongside a narrow sandy beach. The sudden expansiveness was startling, with the wide ribbon of blue-green sea topped by an even bigger sky. Families strolled along the seafront, wrapped up warm in hats and gloves, enjoying the thin spring sunshine. Jess was glad of her jumper. Many of the children held drippy ice-creams, their parents following behind them laden with paraphernalia: shrimping nets, buckets and spades, beach balls, and capacious shoulder bags.

It occurred to Jess it would be Easter soon. Against all expectation, she had survived to the end of a long winter overshadowed by Mimi's death. The seasons had rolled on regardless of her loss, and she tentatively allowed herself to revel in an unexpected glimmer of optimism as she watched the sunshine playing on the wavelets, lending an impression of warmth which was stolen by the easterly wind.

She was astonished to notice there were palm trees at regular intervals along the promenade, incongruous but spirit-lifting. In the holiday brochures she and Mimi had pored over before their West Country summer trips, she remembered seeing public gardens filled with exotic plants. Mimi would have loved to have visited them, she realized in retrospect, but the itinerary had always been for her alone; visiting petting zoos, building sandcastles on the beach, eating fish and chips on the seafront. Her grandmother had completely dedicated her later life to raising her, and Jess wished she could live those years again—only maybe with more strolls around interesting public gardens—for Mimi.

As Jess walked, tears pricking her eyes as images from past holidays flooded her mind, she realized she was hungry. Really hungry. She headed toward the crab shack she could see on the parade just ahead. *Crab rolls a speciality*, it claimed in cheerful, curly red writing on its striped canopy. *Think about food*, she told herself frantically as memories of holidays with Mimi threatened to overwhelm her here in public. Heavens, there were even tears now, trailing down her cheeks as she tried to brush them unobtrusively away.

Joining the short queue, she kept her head down, hoping no one would notice.

"Are you all right?" came a gruff, familiar voice.

Damn! She was standing directly behind Aidan. How could she have not seen him?

"I'm perfectly fine," she snapped, dabbing the tears from her face. "It's the wind."

"Yeah, sure. Are you stalking me, by the way?"

"Absolutely not. In fact, I wish you'd stop popping up like this. It's making me nervous."

"What do you want?"

"Nothing," Jess replied sharply, sniffing the last of her tears away.

"I mean, what do you want to eat? I highly recommend the crab rolls," Aidan replied, his voice softening.

"I don't want you to buy me lunch."

"Oh, get a grip," he snapped wearily. "It's a crab roll, for heaven's sake."

Reproved, Jess reluctantly let him order and pay, thanking him as he handed it to her. God it looked good, a soft, chewy white roll, with oozing mayonnaise and crab meat, wrapped in a paper napkin.

They took their food to the harbor wall and sat beside one another, with Aidan positioning himself so he sheltered her from the worst of the biting wind.

She gave a moan of greed at the first mouthful.

"Told you, didn't I?" Aidan remarked, his mouth full. He had already eaten more than half of his, unselfconsciously stuffing it in in huge mouthfuls and chewing efficiently.

"I was rude to you up there," admitted Jess, swallowing another bite and licking mayonnaise off the corner of her mouth. "I didn't mean to suggest you hadn't looked after your grandfather. I'm sorry."

Aidan waved away her apology. "I'm a big boy," he said, "I can take a lot more abuse than that."

The little tethered boats bobbed gently against each other, their rigging cracking and jingling in the wind, providing a gentle musical accompaniment to the simple lunch. Jess felt surprisingly peaceful. Aidan was a man of few words, and she was grateful there was no need to talk. She couldn't quite remember the last time she'd felt so comfortable being silent with another person—since Mimi, that is. The nameless fear, that threatened to overtake her whenever contentment beckoned, briefly flared and then faded. For now.

"You want to watch those gulls," said Aidan as he swallowed his last mouthful. "I've known them take a whole pasty out of a person's hand."

"They'd have to fight me for this," said Jess, sadly stuffing the last bit in her mouth and brushing the crumbs off her hands. "Cornish pasties though," she added, "they're pretty good too. I remember Mimi and I eating them in places like this."

"Not Cornish if you don't mind. They're only worth eating in Devon."

"I'd love a Cornish person to hear you say that," teased Jess.

But Aidan wasn't listening anymore. His face had hardened as he stared at something, or someone, on the harbor road behind them. "What the—?" he said, as if to himself. "It can't be . . ."

He sighed. "Too late," he told Jess. "She's seen us. I apologize in advance."

"Who?" asked Jess, following his gaze. Standing among the crowd of holidaymakers on the quay—yet conspicuously apart from them—was a slim, fit-looking woman with a mass of artfully tousled blonde curls. Her hair was blowing away from her perfect cheekbones, emphasized by aviator sunglasses, her chin tilted up, her taut body bowed as if to perfectly display the flat abdomen and, doubtless, a tight, peachy little bottom. She looked as if she spent her entire life doing yoga, eating chia seeds, and having sports massages.

As Jess watched, the woman did a classic double-take and whipped off her sunglasses, revealing heavily mascaraed sapphire-blue eyes that were fixed directly onto Aidan.

"Darling!" she called, tripping lightly down the harbor steps toward him. "How lovely," she continued, throwing her arms around his neck and kissing him on the mouth. "I was about to drive up to Middlemass to find you, but I saw the Landy and now here you are."

She took a step back, her arms still around his neck. "You look tired, darling," she said, pouting and tilting her head to one side, pointedly ignoring Jess, who could only look from one to the other in confusion.

Aidan's face was stern and immobile, other than for a muscle ticking ominously in his jaw. He did not respond to the kiss, although—when the woman drew back—Jess could see she'd left a trace of her scarlet lipstick on his mouth. He was silent for a beat longer and then said, in measured tones, "Lucie—allow me to introduce you to my new neighbor, Jess."

Lucie turned and looked Jess up and down, clearly seeing nothing to impress her.

"Hello," she said blankly, turning back toward Aidan. "Aren't you pleased to see me?" she wheedled, in a little girl voice. "I've just come back to find out how my two favorite people are doing."

"We're doing just fine," replied Aidan.

Lucie clearly decided to ignore his rigid demeanor. "And my little Maisie, I can't wait to see her."

"You'll have to. She's with Charlotte until four thirty; they're working on some secret project together. Then, well, it's Thursday."

"I know, I know, Thursdays are riding, or computer club, or something." She waved a hand impatiently. "It's fine. I'll wait. I was just about to drive up to the house. My car's parked next to yours. I'll see you there."

Lucie sashayed off, her back eloquently speaking of her ire that Aidan was not being as obliging as she clearly felt he should be.

"So, that's your wife?" queried Jess.

"Ex-wife," he said, repressively.

*

By the time Jess climbed back up the hill to her little car, Aidan's Land Rover was already gone. Her drive back to the village was somber, and she felt curiously deflated that Lucie had interrupted the best and most relaxed interaction she and Aidan had ever managed. When she arrived back home, she glanced over at Quince Cottage to see a low, gray sports car parked insouciantly across both parking bays, forcing Aidan to leave the Land Rover on the narrow grass verge.

Chapter Nine

"This library is your raison d'être," declared Hannah.

"I think that's a bit grandiose," disagreed Jess as she sipped her evening glass of wine. "It's a bunch of old books in a phone box. Don't let's get carried away."

"No, it is, and shall I tell you something else?" Hannah pointed through the screen at her, for emphasis.

"Go on then, although I'm sure you're going to anyhow." Hannah always thought she was right. And she usually was.

"It's the key to your new life," she pronounced.

"That's definitely going too far," Jess replied, choking a little on her wine. "I'll be really pleased if it makes a difference to the community—that would be very nice—but it's not the solution to everything as far as I'm concerned. The house is still a bit of a wreck, and I still need a proper job that actually pays so that—you know—I can buy food and pay my bills. Stuff like that."

"It's a start," said Hannah, with an emphatic nod. "And Mimi would have totally loved it. Now tell me more about the wife turning up on your date."

Jess tried not to roll her eyes. "Like I said, not a date and not his wife," she insisted, knowing it was futile. "I'm sorry I even mentioned it now. I knew you'd make it into a big thing. He bought me a sandwich. He was just being polite—almost—which made a change . . . Anyhow, like I said, she was really, really beautiful. They're just recently divorced, by the looks of it. And it was weird, because he was completely detached, but from the way *she* was behaving you'd be forgiven for thinking they were still married, and I got the impression she wasn't quite ready to let him go. So, while you're constantly trying to shoehorn your salacious fantasies into a completely non-romantic situation between him and me, she seemed annoyed that he was having a perfectly innocent lunch with a strange woman."

"Mm. Awkward."

"Hardly. At least it shouldn't have been. We were just stuffing our faces with crab rolls, and I wouldn't exactly call that compromising. We weren't exactly in flagrante delicto. Although granted, it was a pretty lush crab roll."

Hannah barked with laughter, making Jess giggle, in spite of herself. "She doesn't look as if she eats that kind of thing very often herself," she observed.

"Like I said," insisted Hannah, "she was jealous."

"Like *I* said, not looking for anyone, remember? Actually—crushingly—she clearly didn't rate me as competition," Jess shrugged self-deprecatingly. "And that's fair enough, because I'm sure Aidan will have explained to her by now that I'm the most annoying person he's ever met. He's certainly made that obvious to me."

"The lady doth protest too much," said Hannah, blithely, and, blowing a kiss, she reached forward to switch off the screen.

Jess sat back in her kitchen chair and puzzled over her feelings. It wasn't as if she cared what Aidan told his ex-wife about her. He'd introduced her as his "new neighbor," so it was all quite clear cut. She just wished she could stop replaying that lovely moment of peace and contentment she had felt when they were just quietly together, eating lunch. Just before Lucie turned up and it all went weird.

*

It was a week later when Jess woke up early to the gentle cooing of the wood pigeons sitting on the chimney stack. The rest of the dawn chorus had begun to fade away as the blue morning light strengthened into another crisp, bright, sunny day with a fresh breeze blowing in through the open window.

Not wanting to waste a moment of the sunshine, she put on yesterday's clothes, quickly brushed her teeth, splashed water on her face, and headed out into the garden to drink in the dawn, brushing her hand lightly over the dew-drenched roses as she made her way, barefoot, to stand leaning on the gate leading into the meadow. It was something she had started to do most mornings, grounding herself and calming her anxieties by gazing, just for a few minutes, over to the horizon and the rising sun. It was a new habit—a ritual—something that belonged solely to Ivy Cottage and her new life.

Daydreaming there, she longed for the endless, languid days of high summer. This year, for the first time since childhood, the season would be hers to spend as she wished. Thanks to Mimi's nest egg, she need not think about getting a job until the autumn—and that felt like a world away this morning.

Returning from Paddy's with milk and bread, Jess saw a slight figure staring into the depths of the pond. Diverting toward the still, silent child, Jess wondered how to begin.

"Maisie?" she said quietly.

The figure turned.

"Hello, Jess," said Maisie politely, looking up with a brief smile that didn't quite reach her eyes.

Jess looked over to Quince Cottage. Both cars were still parked outside. "Is your mum here, still?" she asked.

Maisie nodded, "They're talking." She rolled her eyes so expressively Jess had to stifle a laugh.

"Grown-ups do that a lot, don't they?" she empathized. "Fancy coming and helping me plant some carrots?"

Maisie was silent for a moment.

"You'd be doing me a favor," Jess added.

"Sure," said Maisie, with another thin smile.

Bless her, thought Jess. The kid was so polite it was painful to watch. Jess genuinely hoped a bit of distraction might help—and maybe a chance to talk—but she wasn't confident. If anything she knew preschool and primary school kids best; but Maisie was treading the thin line between childhood and teenage. Jess didn't have the instruction manual for that. She was going to have to play it by ear.

She dropped the milk and bread into the kitchen and was following Maisie into the back garden when something occurred to her: "You'd better tell Mum and Dad where you are," she said. She didn't want Lucie or Aidan to accuse her of kidnapping.

"I don't need to," Maisie replied mulishly. "I said I was going for a walk, to see the ponies in the field by the church, but they won't mind if I'm here instead. I'm allowed to go out by myself as long as I stay in the village. I am twelve, you know?"

"If you're sure?"

Maisie nodded impatiently.

"Okay, so," Jess continued, "I was thinking of planting the carrots here. What do you reckon?"

Jess had dug over a small section of the raised bed, and now there was a wide strip down one side clear of weeds.

"That's where Great-Grandpops and me always planted them," said Maisie, with a slightly wobbly smile, pointing to the bare earth.

Jess's heart ached seeing the grief playing out on Maisie's young face. She knew all about recent bereavement. What a pair they were.

"Then that's definitely the spot," she replied, brightly. "Listen, I've not said how sorry I am that you lost your great-grandfather. That must have been really difficult for you."

Maisie's eyes began to swim with tears. She nodded and dashed them away with her sleeve, then turning away and sniffing she got herself back under control.

Instinctively, Jess wanted to sweep the little girl into a hug, but something held her back. Was it appropriate? Was it even wanted? Perhaps she would wait, until she knew Maisie better. She hoped she would get the chance to do that.

Once composed, Maisie and Jess went to work, with Maisie taking a surprising lead when Jess began to drop the seeds into the earth.

"Me and Great-Grandpops used to use the rake to break it up first," she explained. "Like this, see?" she grabbed the rake, turned it spokes up and began running it backward and forward over the soil to turn the clods into a fine tilth.

Maisie clearly knew her stuff, thought Jess. "So, Great-Grandpops taught you a lot about gardening, did he?"

"It wasn't teaching, really," Maisie explained. "We just did stuff together a lot. At the weekends. Or after school when Dad was working. And he's always working," she added wryly.

It couldn't be easy running a company and bringing up a child on your own, thought Jess as she raked over the next section while Maisie prepared the seeds for planting. Aidan had legitimate cause for being grumpy occasionally, she conceded.

"Whatever he taught you—or didn't teach you—I'm impressed," said Jess as she watched Maisie mix the seeds with a handful of sand before trickling them sparingly and evenly down the little trench she had created in the crumbly, dark soil.

"It must be nice having your mum here," Jess tried again, gently.

"She comes to see Dad," said Maisie.

"And you, too. Especially you. I would think."

"Mm," said Maisie, concentrating hard on spreading the seeds out evenly. "It's better when it's just Dad," she said at last, looking up and catching Jess's eye. "Can I tell you a secret?"

Jess nodded solemnly.

"I like it better when Mum's away," Maisie admitted. "When they're together, it's like—they don't notice me anyhow because they're too busy arguing."

"That must be awful, having to listen to them shouting."

"Oh no," explained Maisie, "they argue, really quietly but—like—really meanly. They think I can't hear them . . . And then, when I come into the room, they stop and they both give me this cheesy smile, like this." Maisie did an impression of a rictus grin, more of a grimace of pain than an expression of pleasure.

Jess laughed, although she thought she probably shouldn't. "I'm sure things will get better," she said. "Especially if they've not been divorced long. They've just got some sorting out to do." Jess amazed herself with how sure she sounded. Never having had a serious relationship herself, she basically had no clue. But it was up to the adults to be reassuring, wasn't it?

"And if you ever want to get away," she added, "just come here and hang out for a bit, you're more than welcome. I could use your expert gardening skills."

Maisie's face lit up, just for a moment, and Jess gave herself a virtual pat on the back. She must have got something right. Or at least she'd got through it.

She should know how to comfort a young girl who was grieving. It was something Mimi had always seemed to know instinctively. Jess had been so lucky to have her; she realized that now more than ever. What a responsibility the old woman had faced, coping with the grief of a four-year-old who had lost her parents. How did you even begin to know what to do in those circumstances? What she, Jess, knew for certain was that Mimi had always said—and done—the right things.

The one thing Mimi admitted to feeling helpless about was Jess's pessimism when things were going well. It was the monster that growled whenever life was good, warning that it could all be taken away in an instant, leaving Jess dangling over a precipice, never able to appreciate the good things in life for long. Nothing Mimi could do or say had ever been enough to silence that fear. It was Jess's constant companion—then and to this day.

Half an hour later Maisie politely thanked Jess and announced she would go home. Jess watched her go, making sure nothing terrible happened en route. She laughed at herself for thinking it, but she still watched. Just as the little figure opened the door of Quince Cottage, it turned to look back over the pond. Jess waved. Maisie gave a little wave back and then she was gone.

Jess hoped she would come back again.

Jess was sitting at the kitchen table the next afternoon, eating toast while running through her to-do list. It still included painting the living room the beautiful warm pink she had bought in Portneath. Paddy sold the most sublime granary bread from a baker in Portneath, who he had started using after the village bakery closed down. She knew she should make her own, and was looking forward to trying, but a slice of Paddy's bread, toasted and thickly buttered, along with a mug of strong tea, was her current favorite mid-afternoon snack.

As she ate, she heard some curious clanking and bumping. It sounded like it was coming from the front garden, but there was no knock on the door to reveal the cause or announce the arrival of whoever it was. Just as Jess decided to explore, it went quiet again. A couple of minutes later, similar noises began, and this time she scampered to the door, a laugh in her throat, and flung it open theatrically.

"Ha!" she shouted. "Caught you."

"Good grief, what's the matter with you, woman?" complained Aidan, who had nearly jumped out of his skin.

"Oops, sorry," she said, mortified. "I thought it must be Diana or someone."

"It is, in a way. As in, it's definitely Diana's fault I'm here," he complained, not meeting Jess's eye. "Shelves in the phone box? Ring a bell?"

Over his shoulder, Jess could see Lucie's sports car still hogging both car spaces on the drive of his and Maisie's cottage.

"I've been sorting out the books this morning," she said. "I'm ready when you are."

"Fine. I should be done by the end of day today. Also, I just wanted to say . . ." He scowled, and his brow knitted. "I appreciate the other day was a bit weird. When Lucie turned up, I mean."

"Oh, no, it's fine; really, it was fine. You don't need to apologize," said Jess, waving away the awkwardness, embarrassed.

"I wasn't apologizing."

"Oh."

"I just wanted to explain that Lucie isn't too happy at the moment. The divorce came through a few months ago and—well, she was expecting it but it shook her up. And, I know it's none of her business anyhow, but then, when she saw us together, she jumped to unhelpful conclusions . . ."

"Sure, yeah, no, unhelpful, sure," Jess floundered. "So, um,

I'll just get on while you do the shelving," she trailed off, pointing back into the house.

He nodded curtly and Jess shut the door as quickly as possible.

Jess was more than happy to leave him to it and within a couple of hours, true to his word, Aidan had efficiently measured, cut, and constructed some shelves for the telephone box. He had created shelves on three walls from floor to ceiling, leaving just enough room for one person to stand in front of them. It was basic, but it worked.

He didn't announce he had finished, and she hadn't noticed him leave while she'd been painting. Taking a break to allow the first coat to dry, she'd wandered down to the phone box to find it all finished. Checking out his work, she glanced over at Quince Cottage regretfully, not so much for his company but because she was looking for distractions, for reasons to delay having to fill the phone-box library with books. And now she had none.

Pulling the tape off the first box, she found it filled with children's books. All her old favorites had been perfectly curated by Mimi and it was almost too exquisitely painful to look. There was *The Velveteen Rabbit*; a couple of Dr. Seuss books, worn at the corners; and then there was her childhood copy of *Black Beauty*. She reached out a hand to stroke its well-worn spine and was transported to a vivid memory of reading it curled up in the kitchen rocking chair, rain thrashing against the window, keeping Mimi company while she kneaded dough for her famous farmhouse loaf. Setting the cherished copy aside, she found more . . . *The Magic Faraway Tree* had been her constant companion one summer, when she'd read it again and again with a torch under the covers. Sniffing, Jess blinked back the tears, but one escaped and ran down her face. All of these beloved stories, all these books; it was like the essence of her childhood had been packed up in a box.

And now she had the pleasure of sharing her books—her memories—with her new community. That was something Mimi would approve of.

Jess was in a reflective mood as she put the little colored stickers she had got from Paddy on the spines, carefully sticking a piece of clear sticky tape over the top to make sure they didn't come off. This was a self-service library and no matter how much she wanted to, she wasn't going to impose Dewey Decimal on anyone in the village. Her idea was simply to have a different color for each book type; yellow for children's books, purple for romance, red for crime, blue for sagas, green for cookbooks, and orange for autobiography and biography. There could be a shelf for each, although she might need more space for children's books and romance categories—those having been Mimi's and her favorites.

The library was Jess's gift to the community, a gesture to thank Middlemass for already taking her to its heart; although putting her precious books out to be shared—and perhaps damaged or lost—was the greatest leap of faith she had contemplated since deciding to move.

Driven to get the job done now, Jess continued with her task. The food-spattered cookery books, the well-thumbed romances, the armfuls of crime novels—out they all went, Jess marching to the phone box and back again, in a burst of nervous energy, until it was all done.

What had to be the littlest library ever was open for business.

Chapter Ten

She wasn't going to obsess, Jess told herself, but if she glanced out of the window once in a while—okay, every few minutes—was that unreasonable? Surely not.

At one point that first morning, she happened to be hovering by the window when she saw her elegant gentleman on the old black-framed bicycle take a second look at the phone box as he passed and then—excitingly—stop. He leaned his bike carefully against the wall and opening the heavy door, went in. She must have done a pretty reasonable job cleaning out all the wee—most people wouldn't have been able to stand being in there with the door closed a week ago.

Lurking behind the bedroom shutter, Jess watched eagerly to see what he would choose. Watching, she decided, was totally fine; she just didn't want to get caught doing it. Frustratingly, no matter at what angle she stood at, she couldn't see the moment he pulled out a book, but she was thrilled to see him carefully place something in his bicycle basket and slowly cycle off. Her first customer.

That evening, she ventured out to the phone box again, excited to notice some distinct gaps on the shelves. A few of her favorites were missing; the classics mainly: *Wuthering Heights*, *Mansfield Park*, and her treasured copy of *Black Beauty* . . .

Someone cleared their throat behind her, and she jumped. "Sorry," said a voice in the gloom. "Only me."

She turned to see Joan hovering awkwardly behind her,

an uncertain smile on her face. "I hope I'm not interrupting. I heard it was open, and look," she said, looking over Jess's shoulder at the tiny book-lined space. "It's beautiful." She pressed a hand to her top lip. "It's really beautiful."

Jess could see tears had come to the older woman's eyes.

"You've done a wonderful thing, my dear," Joan went on, pulling out a lace-lined handkerchief and dabbing at her eyes. "What a wonderful, generous, lovely thing to do . . . Now, what shall I choose?"

"What sort of thing do you enjoy?" asked Jess, feeling more on familiar ground for the first time in months.

"Well, since you're here—and I'm not expecting you to have everything—I'm looking forward to having a chance to reread some old favorites. It can be so consoling, can't it?"

Jess nodded.

"I've lived long enough now to start at the beginning again—since I lost my husband." Joan smiled sadly. "But you don't want to hear all this."

"I do," insisted Jess, shyly. "I'm so sorry for your loss. I've lost someone too. Books trigger memories, don't they?"

"They do," said Joan, reaching out and squeezing her arm. "They do."

"So, what sort of thing do you like?" Jess said, clearing her throat and attempting to put on her librarian voice, with limited success.

"The ones with really good heroes. I do love a Jane Austen when they put it on the telly. And—talking of heroes—how about Mr. Rochester. Now he's a funny one, as heroes go, but you can't not—"

"*Jane Eyre*," said Jess, delightedly. "Of course! I know that's here." She ran her hand confidently along the shelf where it belonged, but there was a gap where she remembered putting it.

"Oh, I'm so sorry," she said, mortified that she couldn't meet this modest request. "It looks as if it's already out. I'm amazed. We've only been open for a few hours."

"That's not surprising," said Joan. "Our old local library's been closed for nearly two years. We're book-starved here in Middlemass. Not to worry about *Jane Eyre* though. I'll get it when it comes back."

Jess managed to send her off satisfied with her precious copy of *Little Women* instead, certain that Joan would enjoy rereading another childhood favorite.

Going back into her little cottage, Jess gave a sigh of contentment. The little library's first day had been a success. Time for a celebratory glass of wine. Perhaps she could even ring up Diana for a cheeky gin and tonic? She smiled. Who knew that a wrong turn could end in such a wonderful adventure. Mimi would be proud that Jess had thrown caution to the wind and followed her heart. Jess felt closer to her that evening than she had since she had moved to Middlemass.

The next morning Jess wandered down to check on the library again—she couldn't seem to help herself—only to notice that Aidan had left his chisel on the top of Jess's garden wall. She'd obviously missed it in the gloom of the previous evening. She brought it inside to stop it rusting. She could just shove it in a drawer, but then he might come back over and ask for it at some point. Any point. Then, the thought that Aidan might just turn up out of the blue was so discomfiting that Jess grabbed the chisel and steeled herself to return it right away. With its worn wooden handle, it fitted pleasingly into her hand, making her think about Aidan's big, calloused hands, reigniting a memory of their shaking hands with each other on the day she moved in. She glanced over the road to his house.

The sports car was gone, she noticed with relief. She could do without Aidan's judgmental ex-wife giving her the once-over again.

Carter started barking even before she knocked, and she waited so long for a reply she thought they must be out, but eventually it was Maisie who opened the door.

"Would you like to come in?" she said shyly after Jess handed her the woodworking tool.

"Are you on your own?" Jess asked, peering behind Maisie to see for herself.

"Just for a bit," said Maisie. "Mum left this morning and Dad had an emergency call-out to clear a tree that's fallen onto the road on the way to Portneath. I'm old enough to be in charge, I'm just not allowed to turn on the cooker or let in any stray axe-murderers. But I saw you from the window and you're not an axe-murderer."

"I'm not," Jess smiled.

"So, what do you get up to at the weekends normally?" asked Jess, once Maisie had very efficiently made her a cup of tea.

"Anime, mostly," Maisie said shyly.

"Ah. Computer games? Cartoons?" Jess said. She had once been an avid reader of manga comic books, but her knowledge of the animated versions of the Japanese genre was limited.

"Both," Maisie admitted, "but not what you think. I've got this amazing anime game where you have to build a world and then you have to run the society, avoiding war and constructing settlements. Dad thinks I'm wasting my time but I'm not. At least I don't think I am. I've actually been . . ." she paused, considering Jess, and then—emboldened—went on, "I've been building something too. Would you like to see?"

"Yes, go on then." Jess smiled at her over the edge of her mug.

Maisie led her into the study, which was gloomy, with

thick curtains closed against the sunlight and no lights on at all. There was a huge screen on the desk, and a keyboard, glowing and pulsing in shades of red, then green, then blue.

"Amazing keyboard," Jess commented.

"Yeah. Dad hates it."

"I can see it's probably not ideal if you've got a migraine," she admitted, thinking secretly that if you didn't have a headache already you soon would.

"Anyhow, look," said Maisie, still polite but with a tiny whiff of impatience. "I'm just loading . . ." She tapped a few keys, waited, tapped a few more, and then stood back. "It's me and Laura, one of my friends from school. She's an even bigger nerd than me. Okay, so . . . it's not finished, obviously. I've just got this section done so far; here's my character." There on the screen was a young woman dressed in a cape and armor, like a superhero, standing in a cityscape, legs apart and hands on hips. "So, at this level, her challenge is to solve the riddle and save the city from being blown up by the evil mastermind. The player has a lot of freedom though. That's why it's so much work. There's dead ends and you have to have something behind all the options, see, so . . ."

"Sorry, hang on a minute," said Jess, understanding dawning, "you actually made this? You created this whole world, this character and so on?"

"Yeah, basically, I mean, it's classic anime style, I didn't invent that."

"Maisie, this is incredible," said Jess in awe, watching the character responding to Maisie's instructions, moving around the landscape, jumping from building to building and then finding treasure in an intricate, Japanese-style wooden box. "I can't believe . . . How on earth?"

"I've not coded it from scratch," she admitted. "There's this software that lets you do it. Provides you with blocks of code you can use to build your own game. It's not how I want to do it in the end 'cause it's not that flexible. I want something more—what's the word?"

"Bespoke?"

"Yeah, bespoke. I guess I'm going to code it myself."

"You've lost me but never mind, I'm just so astonished and impressed. Does your dad know this is what you've been working on?"

"Yes and no. He thinks it's all a bit of a waste of time, but he doesn't understand. My friends—most of them—don't understand either. It's what I want to do. For a living."

"Is that an actual job?"

"I'd be self-employed. Or I could go and work for a big games company or maybe work on anime for cartoons—they do these feature-length ones, in the UK and the States, not just Japan. I don't know, I haven't decided yet. But either way, I don't want to do A-levels in Portneath. I want to leave school and go to a college, like the one in Plymouth. They've got graphics and computer art qualifications. Learning about coding and animation. They've got teams building whole computer games too: the music, the artwork, everything. That's what I want to be doing one day."

"I think it's great you know what you want to be so young, Maisie. Most people don't have a clue, even when they're much older than you are. Good for you." Jess smiled.

Jess had never been without her library role, but she found that she was grateful for this chance to take a sabbatical from real life. Between checking on the library and ensuring things were still librarian smart, she'd developed a new routine to her days, scrubbing and painting every inch of the little cottage, bringing out its character as she cleaned the beams and scrubbed decades of dirt from the flagstone floors. On fine days she could be found bumbling contentedly around the garden, tending to her carrots and the growing vegetable patch Maisie had helped with. She'd retreated to the fireside on rainy days and during one extended cold, wet spell in April she'd dug out Mimi's old sewing machine. She ran up new cushion covers for the sofa and a heavy lined curtain to hang over the front door and keep out drafts, come winter.

She also got used to pottering around in Portneath, exploring the little independent shops that looked out over the water and getting to know the shopkeepers. For Easter, Jess bought two bags of little foil-wrapped chocolate eggs from the fudge shop on the promenade. They looked so pretty in their glinting jewel colors scattered on top of the books in the library like tiny treasures. They were just a little gift to make visitors to the library smile as they chose their books, and her heart was warmed by the surprised smiles of the library visitors that day. She was glad to see that by the end of the Easter weekend, the Easter eggs had all gone, along with a few more of her favorite books.

It took a while for Jess to notice but she felt her moments of swirling, bottomless terror receding in Middlemass too. The awful, deadening feeling that good would turn to bad at any moment, that light would turn to dark—the fear that would sweep over her whenever life seemed to be on the up—had loosened its grip, just a little. Maybe the antidote to terror was to do the very thing that frightened you; to dare to actively seek happiness. Who knew?

Hannah probably did.

"How are the nerves?" Hannah asked one evening.

"A bit better, actually," Jess admitted.

"Shows you're on the right track," she replied, contentedly. "It's what Mimi always wanted for you. She wanted you to take a few more risks because she knew that was the answer."

"The answer to what, exactly?"

"The answer to life, the universe and everything," Hannah said, simply. "The only answer to the fear of losing everything is to open up to the possibility of happiness and the possibility of loss. Two sides of the same coin, isn't it? Better that, than refusing to be happy just in case."

"Easy for you to say," muttered Jess, but maybe—just maybe—Hannah, and Mimi, were right.

Chapter Eleven

Jess stood back and looked at her work proudly. She had spent a long weekend cleaning and then painting the little sitting room. She was so pleased she had chosen the Salmon Belly, a beigey pink tone which looked fresh and pretty on a sunny day and cozy by firelight in the evenings, just as she hoped. The painting would have been achieved more quickly if she had not been distracted from it every time a new customer for the little phone-box library popped up at the door to say thank you and have a chat about this, that, and the other. And if they didn't come to her, Jess would pop out to them for no other reason than to satisfy her curiosity as to what they were borrowing. Providing it was a familiar face, that is. Jess had never been so sociable. Today, gratifyingly, there seemed to be a constant stream of visitors, standing in a queue along her garden wall, enjoying the bright spring sunshine and gossiping happily.

Today, she decided, was not going to be entirely spent twitching the curtains to see who was using the library. She'd been so focused on getting the cottage painted and polished up, now she was going to take herself out to explore. Diana had been over the night before and—over gin and tonics garnished with sprigs of rosemary and slices of orange—they'd discussed what Jess was going to do next. Since the little phone-box library was so successful, Diana suggested speaking to the head teacher at Middlemass Primary about it. The school was just past the pond on the Portneath road and it was high time for her to go and see. At the library in Bourton-on-the-Marsh, she had mostly been too under-confident to get involved with the schools liaison work, but now she actually thought she might steel herself to volunteer. Maybe she could help with administration or reading—or something. Just while she was settling into the village. It might even improve her CV and help with netting a proper job. When it came to that, she had a feeling she was going to need all the help she could get and, although she hated the idea of approaching the head teacher out of the blue, at least she had the library as an excuse for making contact.

There was a fresh, chilly breeze but the lemon-yellow sun was full and cheerful, promising summer warmth one day soon, and in the meantime the spring filled her with optimism. She could see tulips and daffodils blooming in Diana's pretty front garden, and she looked hopefully for signs of the older woman; but the windows of the little red-brick cottage were blank, curtains open, blinds semi-lowered like eyes half-shut. The smart little white VW Beetle Diana drove was gone.

The pond was shaded by willow trees, the branches curving protectively over the green waters and trailing into the chilly depths. The ducks were waddling around importantly, two of them with a string of tiny, fluffy ducklings tumbling in their wake. The white drake was bustling around with not enough to do, organizing them all and nipping at his harem in short-tempered pecks.

The walk to the school took her through an even prettier part of the village than the bit she saw so often on foot, the route to Paddy's shop, which she popped into most days. Houses were larger in this second part of the village, with sweeping brick walls hemming in homes with expansive lawns and circular gravel drives, bearing names like The Old Mill and

The Old Vicarage. The river which fed the pond ran alongside the narrow lane here in a fast-flowing rill, the sound of the water soothing Jess as she walked.

She was getting gradually nervous about the conversation ahead. She had driven past the school on the way to Portneath. The little cluster of flat-roofed sixties buildings was on the far side of a narrow, stone, humpbacked bridge, where the rill widened into a stream, traveling under the bridge and away. Standing at the highest point of the bridge, Jess could see beyond the village, glimpsing in the distance the glittering band of blue that was the sea. Nearer at hand was the school and, just beyond that, the village church with its stone bell tower and slate-gray roof. She never imagined she would live in such a beautiful place, but it was more than that. She was starting to feel at home here. Somehow, she felt Mimi with her as she stood, gazing at the scene, and knew she was smiling.

She couldn't stand on the bridge blocking the traffic for long. As she was nearly there, she wanted to steel her nerve and get to the school as quickly as possible—before she changed her mind. She hurried down the other side of the little bridge, but not soon enough to avoid being glared at by a tiny, blonde woman in a bright blue tank of a four-wheel drive.

Once she reached the road that led to the school entrance she slowed to a stroll, not wanting to hustle the woman walking in front of her. She was pushing a buggy, herding a little schoolboy away from the road and simultaneously cajoling a toddler, who kept holding up proceedings by sinking to the pavement and refusing to get up.

"Please, Angus," implored the woman. "I need you to walk, darling."

He howled in response, his hand in hers. But rather than allow himself to be pulled to his feet, he kept his bottom planted firmly on the ground.

"Becky?" called Jess, recognizing the slight Scottish burr in the woman's voice. "Hi again," she went on as Becky turned toward her. "I didn't realize it was you at first."

"Yep, this is us," said Becky, with a harried smile, as the little boy continued to tug at her hand. "Jess, right? It was so lovely to meet you the other night."

The little boy let out an anguished wail and hung off his mother's hand.

"What, darling?"

"Tiredy legs, Mummy," he complained. "Want a carry," he went on, reaching his arms up to her.

"I need to push the buggy, Angus."

Angus howled louder.

"Can I help?" Jess offered, sensing Becky's patience was fraying. "I could push the buggy for you, maybe?"

"Would you?" Becky said, her voice rising with hope. "I'm not taking you out of your way?"

"I was going to the school, actually. Just to have a look around and maybe a chat. I've done so little exploring, what with sorting out the house and the library."

"The library's great!" said Becky. "Everyone's talking about it. In fact, that reminds me, I must drop in on the way back."

"It's attracting interest, for sure," said Jess, taking the handles of the buggy. "I don't see how you can ever cope. You need at least two pairs of hands with these three." ¯

"I usually have the double buggy, but Rakesh went off this morning with it still in the car." Becky's exasperation was palpable.

"I'm glad I bumped into you then," said Jess, grabbing the buggy handles. "Who's this?" she said, bending forward to see. An adorably chubby baby—about the same age as Hannah's daughter Molly—with brown bubble curls and what looked like strawberry yogurt smeared round her mouth. Hearing a new voice, the little girl tipped her head up and grinned confidently at Jess.

"She's a little smiler, isn't she?"

"This one's Isla," said Becky, sagging with relief. "I've only just fed her, didn't get time to wipe her face."

"She's a poppet," said Jess, glad Isla wasn't one of the children she had met who screamed like a banshee at the sight of an unfamiliar face.

"Angus is a poppet too, honestly; it's just today. And my big boy is Hamish," she said. "We're just about to drop him off." The solemn little boy in uniform, with a big bag slung around his shoulders, looked up at Jess and nodded his acknowledgment.

By this time, Becky had hauled Angus into her arms, and he had flopped his head sideways onto her shoulder, his eyes half-closing and thumb firmly planted into his mouth.

"So, have you and Rakesh been together for long?" asked Jess conversationally, as they continued down the little road together.

Becky nodded. "A looong time. We met at university," she said. "At graduation, we still seemed to be together, so we sort of drifted on. Rak was on the whole junior doctor treadmill thing and—I dunno—I was trying to trail after him while I was finishing my legal training," she said, stopping briefly to shuffle Angus into a more comfortable position on her hip. "So, we spent a lot of time apart in the early days. 'Absence makes the heart grow fonder' and all that. Then, just about the time I finally qualified, I found out I was pregnant with Hamish—and that was eight years ago now, amazingly enough."

"Then this little one came next?" Jess encouraged her on, indicating the tired toddler in Becky's arms.

"Angus. He's nearly three. Quite a big gap," said Becky, dropping a kiss on his head. "Hamish had just started school, and life had started to get a bit easier, so it seemed like the right time to crank things up a level." She pulled a rueful face.

Jess smiled at Angus and was rewarded with a distrustful look.

"And then there's Isla, obviously," Becky finished, over her shoulder. "She's just turned one, bless her."

They were making slow progress wending their way down the lane, on the narrow pavement, with Hamish out at the front, and Jess bringing up the rear. By the time they approached the school, more families had appeared with children in tow, either excitedly chattering or sticking like limpets to legs and hands.

Angus was now asleep in Becky's arms, a sporadic suck on his dummy the only sign of consciousness.

"Thanks so much for this," Becky said. "He was up half the night with a tummy ache, that's why he's tired. Although I'll get criticized for it in a minute, just you watch," she added in a mutter as they arrived at the school gates.

"You've got your mummy where you want her, haven't you? A big boy like you."

Jess turned to see the little blonde woman—the one who had wanted to mow her down on the bridge—giving Becky a patronizing look. Becky briefly shot Jess a meaningful glance.

"He's under the weather," said Becky tightly, turning so she was facing slightly away from the woman.

"Haven't I seen you somewhere?" the woman asked, turning her attention to Jess. "Ivy Cottage." It was a statement, and before Jess had a chance to answer, the woman continued, "Of course, you've got the telephone box to contend with, that'll complicate things . . ."

"It already has," admitted Jess under her breath, pasting on a polite smile.

"Rather you than me. And the house, now *that* house needs

a bit of work. I've got some little men I could recommend if you're looking for reliable tradesmen," Blondie said.

That was kind, thought Jess. She must be careful not to jump to conclusions about people on first impressions.

"We took forever to renovate the Mill," Blondie went on, "but of course it's a much bigger house than Ivy Cottage. A complete nightmare, but it was worth it in the end. It's going to be featured in *Elle Decoration* in the summer, did I say?" This was directed at Becky, swaying gently from side to side with her hands locked together to help support Angus, who was now fast asleep.

"I think you might have mentioned it, yes," replied Becky, tight-lipped.

"So," said Jess, brightly, trying to lighten the mood and casting around for a change of subject. "What's the cunning plan today? Do you need me to help with picking up time too?"

"That would be amazing," said Becky, shooting her a look of relief. "Pancakes for tea. Join us?"

"We had pancakes for breakfast, this morning," said Blondie, smugly. "Such a rush, after school, as always. My two have got G&T, and Mrs. Mount has been begging me to help out with the PTA plans for sports day." Blondie rolled her eyes with self-satisfaction.

"G&T?" queried Jess. "I can't imagine it's what I hope it is."

Blondie was clearly thrilled at having to explain. "It's 'Gifted and Talented.' Both of them. Nightmare!" she said conceitedly, throwing her hands up in the air and giving a little tinkling laugh. "What I wouldn't do for a couple of 'normal' children," she said, doing the air quote thing that always made Jess want to poke people in the eye.

But of course, she knew the Gifted and Talented set from her library work. The library had been begged by a local primary school head teacher to set up enrichment workshops for his own group of G&T children (or the "Grasping and Tenacious" crowd, he had called them, meaning the parents). Brian, her boss, had pushed her to go for it but despite being intrigued by the challenge, she hadn't felt she had the right experience, and he had reluctantly given the job to someone else. She regretted it as soon as it was too late to change her mind, kicking herself for not being prepared to take the risk and stretch herself a bit. She vowed not to turn it down if it came up again, so she was even more disappointed when she heard the scheme had been scrapped after a few weeks. She had heard it was because the children had spent the whole time nagging to play daft computer games or watch unsuitable videos. These were all activities totally forbidden to them at home, alienating them even further from the other kids in the playground than they already were by being singled out for their intelligence.

Jess had been sympathetic. She had felt apart from the other kids at school, too. "Never mind," Mimi had always said. "It's their loss."

"But anyway," Blondie went on, "you'll be picking up late too, surely, Becky? Doesn't Hamish do catch-up maths after school on Wednesdays?"

By now Angus was awake and agitating to be put down. Becky slid him down to the ground thankfully. "He hates catch-up maths," she muttered to Jess. "It's not on this week, because it's the school governors' meeting," she told Blondie. "He's doing very well with it. He even did a little bit of maths with me in the Easter holiday too."

"Goodness, you are brave," simpered Blondie. "I can't follow Monty and Fenella's maths homework anymore, but then they are working at a higher level than most of the children in years four and six. I've decided I'll leave teaching to the experts. One doesn't want to accidentally use an out-of-date method, does one? Must dash . . ."

*

"So," said Jess with careful consideration, once the woman had gone, "she's a monster, isn't she?"

"It's not just me then," said Becky, sighing. "She makes me feel like the shittiest mother on earth."

"I'm pretty sure that's the intention."

"Oh look, they're going in. Darling," said Becky, looking down at Hamish, "have you got everything? Yes? Sure? Off you go then."

She gave the little boy a tight, one-armed hug and dropped a kiss onto the top of his head.

As soon as she let go, he scampered off.

"Thanks so much, again, for all the help," said Becky turning to Jess. "I'll be okay now if you want to peel off, but I meant it about tea after school. Let me give you a proper thank-you."

After waving off Becky and a now more energetic post-nap Angus, Jess summoned up her courage, took a deep breath, and went in through the main entrance of the school. She found herself in a vestibule separated by a glass screen from the main hall of the sixties building. The pinboarded walls were almost totally covered with posters, signs, and children's artwork. Blocking her way into the inner sanctum was a pretty young woman with brown wavy hair, wearing the outfit that epitomized the teacher or librarian—a cardigan and sensible skirt. This must be the head teacher. Jess relaxed a little. She looked as if they would have something in common. The poor woman was nodding and smiling as Blondie—who had annexed her—held forth with lots of self-congratulatory simpering. Off to one side a small knot of parents was gathered, clearly waiting their turn to speak. They were simultaneously listening avidly for a gap in the conversation and politely pretending to be somewhere else. Jess thought she wouldn't stand a chance, but waited patiently at the edge of the group, idling away the time by reading the notices on the boards. They told parents about which days gym kit was needed and which days it should be brought home, what the PTA needed people to volunteer for, and when parents would be expected to turn up for assembly each Friday morning.

Finally, with the poor head teacher now starting to look mildly harried and impatient to get on with her day, Jess stepped forward at last.

The woman summoned up a sweet, patient smile.

At this, Jess, who had had ages to decide what to say, found herself at a loss. "I'm a local," she said hurriedly, "local now, I mean, I've just moved into the village. I'm by the phone box—and I just thought I'd come and say hello."

"Amanda," the woman introduced herself, holding out her hand.

"Jess."

"Hello, Jess," said Amanda, her large brown eyes still patient and mildly amused. "I think I know of you. Do you have something to do with the new phone-box library?"

Jess nodded, feeling she was on solid ground again. "That's my baby."

"I absolutely adore it," said Amanda. "I've been meaning to come and find you. I'd love to get the children down to visit it—in small groups of course."

"That would be fantastic. It's got all my favorite children's books; something for everyone. We could do some activities at the phone box, maybe, like a story-writing competition, or a quiz, for the older ones." Jess's mind was fizzing with the possibilities, but that was not why she was there. "That aside, though, I just thought I might be able to help here in some way. Sorry, it's probably a mad idea, but I'm not working at the moment and I have the time. I'm not expecting to be paid or anything."

"What do you do?"

"I was a librarian . . ."

"You were? How excellent! It's amazing you've popped by today. A few months ago I managed to get a grant to buy some more books for the school reading corner—wonders never cease. I need to research what to buy and get on with it before they take the money back again, but I just haven't had the time. I don't know if it's the sort of thing—?"

"Would it help if I drew up a short list?" asked Jess, her heart soaring at the opportunity. "I know a fair bit about primary school authors; it was sort of my specialist subject in my last job. It would be really nice to talk to the children, too, about the kinds of books they want," she added bravely. "Maybe," she said, gathering her courage, "I could do a few focus groups and get them to tell me what they like to read?"

Amanda's eyes lit up. "Fab!" she said. "Good luck with the ones who don't like to read." She paused. "I have to be frank, Jess, I don't have any budget to pay you. I wish I did."

"Doesn't matter," Jess insisted happily. "I'd just really love to help."

Back at the school gates that afternoon, Jess experienced a definite feeling of déjà vu. There was Isla, sleepily distant, in her buggy with what looked like a chocolatey mouth this time, and poor Angus was—again—in Becky's arms, dozing.

Becky acknowledged her arrival, but her attention was elsewhere. "Here come the sharks. They can smell blood from miles away," she muttered, inclining her head.

The school mums had formed a semicircle around the school gates, like hyenas focused on their prey. There was a token pair of dads, standing a few yards distant; they looked strained as they made conversation, jangling change in their pockets and studiously not making eye contact with the women, or even with each other.

From the huddle of women, the words "phone box" and "library" floated across to them and Jess saw that April from the parish council was in the cliquey little huddle too. When April saw her, she scowled and muttered something to the group, who all turned and looked, making Jess flush to the roots of her hair.

"What's her problem?" she asked Becky out of the corner of her mouth, nodding slightly in April's direction. "Do you think she's anti the library or something?"

"Why would she be?" asked Becky. "What's not to like? I think she's just one of those negative people. And she'll find a willing audience here. Don't let them get to you."

To add to the problems, Isla—who had been placidly watching the scenery and sucking on her dummy with concentration—was starting to make warning noises of a melt-down, waking Angus and drawing further eyes to the little group. Becky, ducking her head, could clearly do without it.

"Why don't you go?" said Jess. "I'll pick up Hamish. He can help me in the library—I'd appreciate his ideas—and then I'll bring him home to you when I've finished. Yours is the house with the green porch with the bike and the scooter on the lawn, isn't it? I saw you go back there after the parish council meeting."

"I really must tidy the front garden," said Becky. "You're right, though. That's us, we're just the other side of the pond from you. Practically next-door neighbors. And yes please, that would be amazing," Becky exhaled thankfully. "There's no rush. These two need a nap and they'll never settle if Hamish is there. I just have to . . ." added Becky, waving at someone, pointing exaggeratedly at the top of Jess's head and then giving a thumbs-up. "There, we're fine."

"What did you just do?"

"Informed Hamish's class teacher that you're the responsible adult taking charge of him today."

"I totally love that this is the kind of school where a wave and a point replaces in-triplicate form-filling and ten years' notice," said Jess. If she ever had a child, this is the school she would like them to go to.

"Hello stranger," she said to Hamish moments later, as the flood of children descended on the waiting adults.

"Where's my mum gone?" he said, without any great concern.

Jess explained. "And also, I asked her if I could borrow you, because I need you to help me sort out the school reading corner."

"Booorrring!"

"No, sorry, not 'sort out' as in put books back on shelves. I need someone who knows what they're talking about to tell me what books to buy."

"How much money have we got?"

Hamish's face showed no emotion as Jess told him the budget, but clearly it was an acceptable sum.

"Go on, then," he said, with such studied nonchalance that Jess had to stifle a laugh.

Chapter Twelve

Hamish, it turned out, was genuinely insightful and Jess was glad to have his input. Once he got the hang of the fact that nothing he said was wrong, he was more than articulate. He told her what he liked and why (history, because it has lots of blood and dead bodies in it), along with what he didn't like and why (nature, because grass and flowers are boring). Because he was there, Jess concentrated on the middle grade book recommendations, drafting a list of suggestions on areas that seemed weak in the existing collection. For example, there were no "choose your own adventure" books, which she knew could really capture the imaginations of reluctant readers. They were also brilliant at showing children that stories can have more than one ending; and this was something some children—especially those with social communication issues—struggled to understand.

She also used "the Hamish factor" to test out her own ideas. Books about vampires and werewolves got a thumbs-up. Some charming stories about ghosts which reminded Jess of old favorites like *Tom's Midnight Garden* got a thumbs-down because they were too "boring," although Jess did sneak a couple onto the list anyway.

By the time they had spent nearly an hour there, Jess had made a useful start and Hamish's concentration was starting to flag.

"Come on, mate," she told him. "You've been brilliant, but

Mum must be starting to wonder where we are, and there's talk of pancakes for tea."

Hamish chatted cheerfully all the way home; in fact Jess barely got a word in. She imagined he rarely had the willing ear of an adult for long. It must be an occupational hazard with two younger siblings.

"Mu-um," he roared as he went through the door. "We're going to have lots of new books in the school and I'm going to read them all."

"Lovely darling, I look forward to you reading a book without complaining," said Becky, pasting on a bright smile but looking, Jess thought, totally exhausted. "Cup of tea?"

"Definitely," said Jess. "It's suspiciously quiet," she added. "What have you done with Isla and Angus?"

"Had them adopted. It was all very quick because I didn't want to give the new parents time for second thoughts. I think I got away with it."

"But seriously?"

"But seriously, Angus is stuck in front of a vintage episode of *In the Night Garden*, with a cheese string dangling out of his mouth, and Isla was sound asleep when I got back so I stuck her in bed with her shoes on because I was so excited at the thought of her napping for an hour I didn't want to risk waking her up."

"Nice parenting," said Jess, with an approving nod.

"I thought so. Actually, sod tea, it's . . ." She looked at her watch. ". . . well, it's getting on for six o'clock."

It was not even quite five o'clock, but Jess could see where this was going. "Let's have a glass of wine," she said obediently.

"Damned good idea," said Becky with a mixture of surprise and enthusiasm, as if Jess's suggestion was a novel but exceptionally pleasing concept.

There was a bottle of white wine open in the fridge and Becky sloshed generous amounts into a pair of large and slightly smeary wineglasses.

"Cheers," she said, clinking her glass to Jess's and then taking a decent slug. With her free hand, she was giving a final stir to a jug of what Jess assumed was pancake batter.

Jess gazed around the well-sized and well-equipped kitchen-diner. It wasn't at its best. There was washing-up in teetering piles in and around the sink. The detritus of breakfast was still on the table, with spilt milk and what looked like yogurt smeared on the polka-dot patterned wipeable tablecloth. The highchair—clearly Isla's—was clean enough but the floor beneath it was encrusted with nameless food remains.

"We need a dog," commented Becky, absently, pushing a toast crust under the cupboard with her foot.

"Can't be easy, with three children," commented Jess. "Could you maybe get a cleaner?"

"I'm thinking, at this point, it might be sensible to just move house," joked Becky.

"Are you planning on moving, then?" Jess said, disappointment at the ready. She would rather know early on if her budding friendship with Becky was going to end prematurely. A warning would be nice, before she got in too deep.

"Rak's just got his first consultancy post in Plymouth," said Becky. "The benefit of that is we can stay as long as we like, at last."

"That's good to hear," said Jess with relief. "So, a cleaner does seem to be the way forward."

"Ha!" said Becky, her wine slopping dangerously as she flipped a pancake. "But that's what's called 'subcontracting.'"

"What do you mean?"

"It's my job to do childcare and running the home, Rak's contribution is to earn the money. If I buy in childcare and cleaning or gardening services then that's me subcontracting my role, and—worse still—doing it with his money, if you see what I mean."

"Is that what he says?"

"Okay, well, no, not in so many words," Becky admitted, "but it's what I'd probably think if I were in his position. Rak's been rising up the ranks super-fast, because the man's got a brain the size of a planet. Someone needs to do the work on the home front and it ain't gonna be him, so guess what," she said, pointing at herself. "Mind you, I'm rubbish at it, which makes me feel bad when he comes home from heroically saving lives to discover he still doesn't have an ironed shirt and dinner's half a grill pan of rejected fish fingers with a packet of cheese puffs. Plus, half the time the kids are still up, creating chaos when he wants to rest." Her voice was rising and rising as she spoke. She got to the end and the sudden silence rang with desperation.

"Sorry," she added, more quietly, rubbing her forehead. "I don't mean to rant." She took another swig of wine, refilling her glass and offering the bottle to Jess, who had barely started hers.

"So, none of this particular division of labor was really planned?" Jess asked, tentatively.

"Don't get me wrong," said Becky, staring into the middle distance. "I love my kids, and I was pretty delighted when we got Isla because secretly I always wanted at least three. And a girl. To be honest, our sex life is so sporadic, she's practically a miracle baby."

Jess gulped. Becky was obviously one of those people who became startlingly candid after a glass of wine. Clearly she needed to talk, though, and Jess was happy to be a listening ear. She knew from her relationship with Hannah how incredibly important friends could be when life wasn't going too well.

"What would you be doing, if you had a job?" she prompted, trying to be constructive.

"I'm a solicitor. I got my SRA registration—Solicitors Regulation Authority, sorry—when I was about four months pregnant with Angus. We moved again the following month, or the firm I was working for at the time would have kept me on. That would have been great." Becky pondered, staring into her wineglass.

Then she gave herself a little shake. "Probably just as well. I'd be a rubbish solicitor anyhow, and even more rubbish as a working mum. I'd constantly be turning up at work with jam in my hair or being late to pick up the kids from school, which would give Natalie a great opportunity to look down her nose. And that's fair enough because I already turn up late with jam in my hair, if I'm honest."

"Natalie being the little blonde woman in the four-by-four with the genius, weirdly named children?" Jess guessed.

"That's the one," confirmed Becky. "And I was always intending to be this single, childless, kick-arse solicitor, righting wrongs and defending the defenseless. I'm not sure what happened, really. Oh God," she went on. "That makes me sound awful. I *am* awful. Like I say, I wouldn't be without the little horrors for the world. Honest," she said, draining her glass and reaching for the bottle to refill it.

There did seem to be a lot of having babies for a woman who declared she only had career ambitions, thought Jess.

As if Jess had spoken aloud, Becky went on, "I appreciate there's a lot of 'accidentally getting pregnant,' and I just want to reassure you we've worked out what causes it now, what with Rak being a doctor and all."

"Three kids, though, and two under five years old . . . It must be pretty intense," said Jess, "especially with Rakesh not around much. How about the weekends? Do you maybe get a break then? Do something together, all of you?"

"Ha!" said Becky. "At the weekends, he's still barely here because he's checking up on his patients, or catching up with his clinic admin. If—miraculously—he's not doing that, he's just out playing golf, doing the clubbable bit with his nerdy little brain surgeon mates. Although that is partly how he got his consultancy gig so quickly, to be fair. That, and being genuinely brilliant at his job."

"How about your family?" said Jess, feeling more and more sorry for her new friend.

"All up in Scotland. You'll no have failed t' notice the good old Gaelic names in the kids," said Becky in a suddenly thick Edinburgh accent. "It amuses me to call them traditional, haggis-loving Scottish names when they have an Indian surname. It confuses people no end."

Jess had to agree, Hamish, Angus, and Isla Persaud would probably not struggle to get their choice of email address.

"You don't have much of a Scottish accent."

"I do when I'm pissed. Which is increasingly often—so that's something else for Rak to be holier-than-thou about."

Jess wasn't sure she could cope with too many of Becky's bad days. While Becky had produced a stream of pancakes with admirable panache (and only one of them stuck to the ceiling) they had demolished a good bottle and a half between them. She had been reluctant to leave Becky in such a despondent mood, but was even more reluctant to stay, imagining how bad an impression it would make if the wunderkind Rakesh arrived home to find his new neighbor cluttering up his kitchen in a state far from sober.

She and Becky were about the same age, but she could hardly imagine herself in Becky's position, clocking up a twelve-year relationship and three children just in the time she, Jess, had been a librarian and little else. She wondered if she would ever have had Becky's certainty and courage, building a whole life together with a man she had met so young.

Jess, by contrast, had for many years stoutly declared no interest in romance. Reading about it was one thing, but engaging in the whole messy, complicated business herself seemed to her to be the height of silliness, whatever Mimi had always said on the matter. And after all, Mimi was lucky enough to have been loved absolutely and unto death by Jess's grandfather. With perfection like that as the benchmark, Jess knew her own attempts at love were doomed to failure.

She hadn't even tried. Far better to deny yourself the chance of love than open yourself up to the very significant possibility of losing someone you've learned to be emotionally dependent on. She knew this. It happened. It had happened to her with her parents after all.

So she had eschewed romance when it was offered and, on reflection, she didn't have many friends of any gender nowadays. The ones she had collected in her journey through school, university, and eleven years at the library had been more like seaweed than barnacles on the hull, easily detaching themselves and drifting off to more exciting places as others moved on with their lives and she did not. The exception was funny, loyal, challenging Hannah, who was far too many miles away. Jess missed her physical presence terribly, despite their Skyping habit. It wasn't the same.

Jess had to admit, with a frisson of shame, that for years Hannah had made all the running, keeping their relationship alive in the face of unforgivable neglect from her, especially during Mimi's illness.

Mimi had implored her, with something close to exasperation, to nurture her other relationships, to be more outgoing. To look for love. But Jess knew better. She had been resolute and unapologetic. When cancer had placed a limit on her time with Mimi, it made her acutely aware of treasuring every moment. There was no room for anything, or anybody, else.

Now, everything had changed and here she was in Middlemass. She seemed to have the possibility of friendship with all these people who were accepting her so easily as one of their own: Becky, Diana, Mungo, even Maisie. Maybe it was a little less impossible to imagine than before . . . Maybe one day, even the romance thing would change.

"What's your impression of Rakesh?" Jess asked Diana as they sat having coffee in Jess's sitting room. She had been thinking about him a lot since her talk with Becky but there was something about Becky's presentation of him that niggled. It would be interesting to get someone else's view.

"He's a good man, I think," said Diana, "but to be honest, I don't feel I know him at all. He's never around, so this probably isn't fair, but I suppose I get the impression he's a bit of a cold fish." Diana put her cup down carefully on the newly cleared floor and offered Jess a biscuit from the packet. "We don't see much of him because he's always working. When they first moved in—of course they just had the two then, with Hamish ready to start school and Angus a teeny baby—I actually thought Becky was a single mother," she said. "She may as well be, for the support she gets from Rakesh. He turned up at Mungo's Christmas drinks last year and it was the first time I'd clapped eyes on him in months. Even then he was drinking tea because he was on call, when the rest of us were on champagne. It was Christmas Day, for heaven's sake! Becky says he's senior enough now that he could perfectly reasonably get his minions to deal with the majority of the out-of-hours stuff, but instead he races back to work at the drop of a hat. You have to admire his dedication," she added grudgingly. "Basically, I get the feeling he's mega–emotionally detached and that's why he's so good at what he does. He's a bit of a psychopath, in that sense. If I had a brain tumor, I wouldn't want to see anyone else. If I was looking for a husband, I think I might look elsewhere."

"Talking of husbands," said Jess, nervous about being impertinent, "have you ever been married?"

"God, no."

"You must have had offers."

"God, yes," repeated Diana without vanity. "I was the archetypal blonde, busty secretary who whips off her glasses, lets down her hair, and finally gets noticed by her boss. 'Why Miss Jones, you're beautiful,'" she hammed. "Cliché alert, the man I was having an affair with was originally my boss. It went on for years. I left the company—got another job—purely because staff relationships were forbidden. I wanted to legitimize our union, I suppose, if I'm honest with myself. I tried everything . . ." Diana looked into space. "I was an idiot. He didn't want our relationship legitimized. He had a nice little compliant wifey at home, keeping house and raising his children, and then he had me, a nice little compliant mistress, providing him with adoration every time he wanted it."

"Why did you stay?" Jess asked, determined not to show her shock at Diana's confession. She didn't want Diana to think she was disapproving.

"I ask myself the same question," Diana admitted. "I knew it was wrong, having an affair with a married man. Even if I only found out a few months down the line that he *was* married—he lied to me at first—but, as always, I'm the baddy."

Jess swallowed and said the first thing she thought out loud, "Actually, you're not. He's the one breaking his marriage vows, not you."

"Ah, but it's the place of the woman to take the blame, isn't it? It's unsisterly, if nothing else, to facilitate a man who wants to have his cake and eat it."

"How long were you with him?"

"Thirty years, nearly."

"What?!"

"I know. You'd have thought I would have figured it out before then, wouldn't you? From the moment I found out the truth he constantly told me he would leave her, but it was never the right time. The children were too young, or in the middle of exams, or her parents were unwell, and it would be cruel to go while she was coping with that. There was always something. Some excuse. And then his children were grown up. They had left home. He was coming up to retirement—he was a few years older than me—and I thought it was my time at last. Eventually, they were selling the family home, they were downsizing, he could have used it as a trigger to get out, take his share, be with me—at last—or so I thought . . ."

"But he stayed with her?"

"Of course he did. He was never going to leave. They've bought a little pied-à-terre in central London for shopping and the theater, and a big old, rambling house in France for the summers. They're off on cruises a lot, I gather. I wouldn't know. I gave him his marching orders about three years ago. Better late than never, I suppose."

"And since then?"

"Seeing as we're 'sharing'"—she did the inverted quotes thing with her fingers—"and—forgive me—I started it," she added. "Seeing as we're on the subject of loss—it hardly compares, but I retired a couple of years ago and—to be honest—I'm finding it really tough."

"I'm so sorry. I suppose I imagine retirement is meant to be amazing," said Jess. "Holidays and gardening and—I don't know—daytime telly. Actually, maybe not the last one."

"That's certainly what I thought. I couldn't wait for all the cake eating and staying in bed as long as I liked, but it turns out it's no picnic. Not for me anyhow."

"Why not?"

"Honestly? I'm lonely. So, I suppose, it's not the retirement as such, it's the fact that I gave so much to my working life. I was committed, successful, smashed the glass ceiling and all that. I think I forgot to do the other stuff."

"Like . . . ?"

"Marriage. Children. Friendships. Saying that, I do have friends, of course I do; and I love having time for the garden too. But Middlemass is quiet; it's not as tight-knit a community as it used to be. So when the curtains are drawn and the fire's lit in the evening, I'm alone."

Jess took a gulp of coffee, thoughtfully. It was a tricky issue, and she could see her own life going the same way. The last thing she wanted to do was to be seen to diminish the size of the problem—to come up with some pat answer, like "take up a hobby."

"Dating apps are the way to go, I gather," said Diana, sitting up straighter.

"Have you tried them?" said Jess, intrigued.

"I don't know how."

"I could maybe help with that," said Jess, "but they're pretty brutal, I've heard. Definitely not for the faint-hearted. There have been these studies. People ghost each other, stand each other up: all these behaviors they wouldn't dream of subjecting the people in their own social circle to. It's better if you could try and see who is already around. Friends of friends and stuff. They behave better." Jess thought for a moment: "What about Mungo?"

"Mungo, bless him," said Diana. "He's never had a serious relationship in his life, at least to my knowledge. He's lived with his mum for decades. All his adult life, I gather. She only died a couple of years ago."

"That's surprising, isn't it? Not that his mother's died—that's just sad—but no long-term relationships?"

"Not as far as I know. But is it really surprising? He's a prize prat, as you saw the other night," said Diana, but her tone was affectionate. "Also—I'm pretty sure I'm not his type, if you know what I mean?"

Jess thought for a moment. "You mean he's gay?"

"Well, yes, I think I've always assumed it, not that he's ever said anything. But he truly was so devoted to his mum. I just don't think he's ever prioritized finding someone."

"It's a shame he's not for you though," persisted Jess. "He seems like a really nice man. And I got the impression you get on really well."

"We do feel very comfortable with each other, that's true," admitted Diana.

"Although, why would he be romantically interested anyway? Even if he were straight, let's face it, I'm a dried-up old hag, and that's on a good day."

"Whaaat?" Jess exclaimed. "You are the most glamorous person I know. Thinking about it, you're the most glamorous person I've *ever* known . . . although granted I don't get out much. Actually, you remind me of my grandmother, and she was always *really* chic."

"I've tried to be glamorous in the past, with varying degrees of success, but I don't know if I'm not losing the will a bit nowadays," admitted Diana.

"What do you mean?"

"Stuff is dropping off faster than I can stick it back on. My makeup takes forever nowadays and even then, I don't look great, I look at myself in the mirror, and I think, 'I wouldn't.' So why should anyone else?"

"You're mad," concluded Jess in exasperation. "If you want a new relationship, I'd say go for it."

"Not sure I do," said Diana. "Too much hassle. On balance, I'd rather let myself go in peace than have to keep up standards against increasing odds."

"Amen to that," said Jess, who had been extremely conscious of Diana's apparently effortless elegance in contrast to the grubby jeans and yesterday's T-shirt she had flung on that morning. It would just be typical if Aidan would suddenly turn up with her looking a mess. Not that she cared, obviously.

"So," said Diana, changing the subject, "the critical question is, how are people responding to the little library?"

"There have definitely been a few visitors," reported Jess. "There's a lovely old man on a bicycle, who wears a flat cap. He stops there. He likes the romantic stuff; in fact I have a tiny inkling he's got *Jane Eyre* at the moment. I've noticed because Joan wants it too. And there's a couple more from the romance shelf missing; I can't think which ones. They're all Mimi's favorites. And so, so precious . . ." she added quietly, to herself.

Diana nodded. "I've got *Great Expectations*, and I'm loving it. Haven't read it for years. Your grandmother was clearly a lover of books and has very good taste—I'm assuming her passion for books inspired yours?"

"Yes, I think it did," said Jess. "I've always read and read and read. Mimi was fabulous about buying books, although we weren't well-off, but she would always shell out for the latest Harry Potter, and that sort of thing. We went to the charity shops for them a lot of the time, too. I have an awful lot of really lovely secondhand books, and we went to the library at least once a week too, of course. You'll laugh, but when the other children were all announcing they wanted to be doctors, firemen, or astronauts, I genuinely already knew I wanted to be a librarian. How sad is that?"

"Not sad at all," said Diana stoutly. "I think it's laudable. And how lovely that you've fulfilled a long-held childhood ambition. How many adults can say they've done that?"

"What was yours?"

"Can't remember, but I definitely didn't end up doing it, whatever it was. I spent decades in marketing, and I'm pretty sure I didn't even know marketing *was* a job when I was little. And then, of course, I was a mistress."

"That's not a career, as such," Jess teased gently.

"You're right. I made it my life's work. Also, in my abject stupidity, I wasn't even a proper mistress. I wasn't a 'kept woman.' I thought I was maintaining my independence, always working for a salary big enough to support myself without having to ask for anything. In retrospect, I was a cheap alternative to the real deal. I let him off lightly."

"Did you ever want children?"

"Yes, there was a long time when I did, but—and here I was even more stupid—I didn't want to put pressure on him to have a love child. It seemed too much to ask. Then—before I knew it—I had left it too late, so that was that." Diana blinked slowly, staring into space, remembering.

"I'm so sorry. I shouldn't ask." Jess felt terrible for lowering the mood with her questions. She had never seen Diana so bleak.

Diana sighed, and pulled herself upright. "You are amazingly brave and generous to put your grandmother's books in the little library. Bravo to you," she said. "And may karma reward you with good things."

"Thank you."

"Like a hunky man," she said, the twinkle back in her eye as she held out her coffee cup for a toast.

"Thank you again." Jess clunked her cup against Diana's obediently.

"Such as Aidan, for example."

"I don't think that's a good idea," said Jess, repressively. "And I'm pretty sure he doesn't think so either—but thanks anyway."

Chapter Thirteen

People were complicated, thought Jess. Not only was she thinking over Becky's, Mungo's, and Diana's problems, she couldn't
help occasionally wondering what was going on at Aidan's
house. Just as she climbed into bed that night, she allowed
herself one last look over the pond to Quince Cottage. The
Land Rover was on the verge, with the sports car back on the
drive. She hoped Lucie's discovery of them both in Portneath—
what she now thought of as Crabrollgate—hadn't caused any
lasting grief for Aidan and also, especially, for Maisie. There
had definitely been something strange about Lucie's proprietary
behavior that day, seeing as they were supposed to be divorced.
Also, given that, why was Lucie still there?

Then Jess told herself firmly to mind her own business and
focus on the little phone-box library instead. There it was,
with its precious contents, safe and sound in the moonlight,
a happy focus for her, providing the satisfaction that she was
doing something good for the community, and binding her
to the village in a way which made her feel that—one day
soon—she might belong.

As the weeks passed and the days lengthened, Jess established
a habit of replenishing and tidying the library at dawn. She
loved being outside in the clear dawn light, with the birdsong
and the cool dew on the grass, ahead of the daytime glare and
bustle. This was her time. Working with the books was also a

time when she allowed herself to think of Mimi a little, and to shed a tear, perhaps; although that happened less often nowadays. The acute pain of fresh grief eased over time, it seemed, lifting a little and then flooding back to overwhelm her like the tide racing in when she least expected it.

The early morning was also a chance to revisit what Hannah had said in the latest of their regular evening chats. She was quite the life coach nowadays, and Jess valued her friend's opinion, even when it was different to her own.

Except when it came to romance. On that subject, Jess was definitely right, and Hannah was well wide of the mark. Hannah's opinion was that now Jess had left her job, bought the cottage, volunteered at the school, and started boozing with various new friends, the natural next step would be to explore the possibility of a romantic relationship. Jess did not agree. The woman was obsessed with the idea that Jess should hook up with Aidan. Come to think of it, Diana kept saying the same. She must get the two women together one day. They would definitely get on. When she was in a more concessionary mood, Jess was prepared to reluctantly allow that maybe the answer to the "finding love" issue was for her to widen her social circle. Perhaps then she could give Hannah and Diana someone more appropriate to obsess about on her behalf.

She tidied the shelves absently, putting the cookery books back on their designated shelf, shuffling all the romances—the most popular section—back into line and making sure the children's book spines were all facing outward. Judging by the disarray, the library was popular with readers of all ages. And she should know, because she spent far too much time lurking at the window watching them come and go.

She was just crouching, pushing a copy of *The Secret Garden* back onto the shelf next to *The Magic Roundabout*, when a polite cough made her leap backward, sending her tumbling halfway out of the door. The tall but slight figure rushed forward to help her up as she flushed at her undignified position.

"Whoa, sorry," the man said as he helped right her. "I didn't mean to startle you."

Jess straightened her T-shirt and brushed her hair out of her eyes. "You're fine. I just wasn't expecting to see anyone at this time in the morning."

"So, we are both insomniacs, it seems," he said, with a little bow. Now she was steadier she took another look at the new library visitor. He was dark-skinned and very handsome, with thick, black hair. She took in the running gear of the serious athlete, all high-tech fabrics with sections of mesh and go-faster stripes. The man seemed to notice her checking him out and sheepishly said, "I like to run at this time of the day. It clears my head." His voice was pleasant, decorous: the kind of voice with quiet authority that makes you do whatever they say.

"You're the psycho—I mean—you're the brain surgeon," Jess blurted. "I mean, you're Becky's husband, aren't you?"

"I am at least two of these things," he agreed pleasantly. "Rakesh, and you're Jess. I'm sorry not to have introduced myself sooner, but I'm not around much, as I am sure Becky's told you."

Jess blushed, remembering her conversations with Becky and Diana. Somehow the man in front of her was just not what she'd imagined, although she could see Angus and Isla had inherited his eyes, and the quirk around his lips reminded her of Hamish's grin.

"I go running at weird times," Rak continued. "I've also been meaning to have a poke around here," he admitted, gesturing to the library. "I don't get much time to read, but . . ." He ran his finger along the row of books reverently. "Ah, I recognize this," he said, with obvious pleasure.

"*Swiss Family Robinson,*" read Jess, peering over his shoulder. "Classic story. They don't write them like that anymore. Why don't you take it out? Enjoy."

"I will, thank you," he said, tucking it under his arm, and holding out his hand to shake hers. "I'm glad we've finally met. I wanted to see this woman who's been such an ally to Becky. I know she hasn't been having an easy time of it being a full-time mum. The school gate parents are a tough crowd to win over."

"You know about that?" Jess said, surprised.

"And she's missing her work. My fault, as I'm sure you know," he replied thoughtfully with a dip of his head.

"I—well—I—" stammered Jess.

"Don't worry!" he waved away her awkwardness with a good-natured laugh. "I'm not taking responsibility for everything, but we've fallen into a pattern where I work all the hours God sends and Becky picks up absolutely everything else. It's an unhealthy balance, I'm well aware." He leaned against the door of the library thoughtfully. "She's a clever woman, and a great lawyer. She loves our kids, I know she does, even on the bad days. But she also needs to have the high-flying career she's capable of."

Jess blinked. "You're not what I expected."

"I get that a lot," he said, with a wry grin.

As she wandered back to the cottage, Jess began to wonder if her new friend's main barrier to work and happiness was less obvious than she had previously thought. Drawing on her knowledge of her own failings, Jess wondered if Becky's problem was at least partly her lack of confidence in herself.

Perhaps a lack of willingness to try something scarily new for fear of failing.

That was something Jess could relate to.

The bicycle man with the flat cap was in the library again. He was definitely perusing the romance shelf and—as Jess watched—he slipped out a book and popped it in his bicycle basket.

Her heart warmed to him, this elderly man she had barely met. She should go and say hello, she knew. That was what Mimi would tell her to do. And Hannah.

It had been another bright, perfect May day, but Jess had missed it. After hours spent inside, sanding the bedroom floor, she decided she would allow herself a moment in the fresh air before she settled down to a bath and then macaroni and cheese in her pajamas. Her critical study of the rear of the house was not encouraging. Despite all her hard work over the last few months, the window frames were still waiting for a fresh coat of paint, which they badly needed. That was another job to be done before the winter, and she hadn't forgotten Aidan's comment about the lack of insulation in the loft either. She knew she should look into that before she worried too much about the aesthetics; in her first few weeks in the cottage she had found the bedroom at night perishing cold, even with the window closed. Now, in the balmy heat of the early summer, it was difficult to summon up vivid memories of that time, but she should sort out the insulation or she would be sorry when the cold weather arrived again. She would get on the phone tomorrow.

Now, though, it was inescapable how thickly the ivy—the cottage's namesake—had encroached on the brickwork at the rear of the house. Experimentally, she tore off a trailing branch which was blocking the kitchen window. It came down, leaving another detached and dangling in its place. She tugged at that too and soon she was tearing at the branches, revealing the brickwork beneath. A thick stem, at least the width of her thumb, clung stubbornly, before eventually coming loose in a shower of mortar dust. Jess leaned back to yank it off the wall, higher than she could reach.

She needed the ladder from the privy—the one Aidan had used to get into the loft. She pulled it out nervously, eagle-eyed for big, hairy spiders, and propped it against the back wall, rattling it experimentally. Secure enough. Soon the ivy was coming down in satisfying sheets of matted root. Her hair came loose from its band and clung to her now sweaty forehead, her face and eyes itching with dust.

The kitchen window was now completely clear, and if she could just reach . . .

Someone cleared their throat politely behind her. The ladder lurched alarmingly in response.

"Christ," said Aidan, as he grabbed it to steady her. "Is this wise?" he asked, as she climbed safely down and waded through the mound of ivy she'd dropped at the base of the ladder.

"I was going to leave it until tomorrow, but I didn't know where to stop," Jess admitted, self-conscious at being so dirty and sweaty in his presence. Again.

She smoothed her hair out of her eyes with grubby hands. What a shame. She had seen Aidan very little over the last couple of months and had hoped she would make a better impression the next time she spoke to him, especially now she knew how glamorous Lucie was. Not that it was relevant.

"It looks like I'd better stick my trailer outside your house, doesn't it? You can chuck all this stuff in there and I'll get rid of it for you," said Aidan.

"Would you do that for me? That's really kind."

"It's what neighbors do. Not a big deal. Now, listen, I need to do a bat count, you remember that, right?" he asked. "It's one of your responsibilities, you know, as the owner of the property."

"I bet it is," she replied wryly, "one of my many onerous duties toward my funny little furry squatters." Despite her initial horror, she had to admit to herself she'd got used to their nighttime antics over the last few months. Not that she was going to tell Aidan that, of course.

Aidan looked mildly disapproving at her irreverence, but said nothing. He also showed no signs of leaving.

"You mean, now?" she said.

"If you don't mind?"

It wasn't really a question.

"Okay, well, if we must, we must," Jess went on, brushing bits of mortar and ivy out of her hair. "Can I interest you in a beer? Or is there a 'no drinking during the bat count' requirement, clause fourteen, subsection 3b?"

"I think a beer might just be acceptable," he said with a facial expression somewhere near a smile.

Jess left Aidan outside and—once in the house—she scampered to the bathroom for a lightning-quick cleanup. She wondered if she should offer him something to eat. Looking at the clock, it was later than she realized, so she decided to assume he had already eaten. She just hoped he wouldn't be able to hear her tummy rumbling as she thought longingly of the macaroni and cheese she had promised herself.

They took their beer bottles and settled themselves on the bench, near the raised beds of the vegetable patch. It had been a warm day—perhaps the warmest so far that year—and even as the sun hung on the horizon, momentarily pausing as if reluctant to leave, the stored heat of it was gently rising from the terra-cotta sets of the path.

"So, let's see precisely how many of our fiendish furry friends we are dealing with here," Jess said, settling in and stretching out her legs.

"Want a go?" he replied, handing her the little clicking device he was holding. "Just push that button every time you see a new one come out," he said, pointing at the apex of the roof.

Just as he did so, first one then quickly two, three, four little shapes launched themselves from what Jess could now see was a gap in the eaves.

She clicked assiduously. "I've seen them before, on reflection. I thought they were birds," she admitted.

"Hard to tell unless you see them up close but look, there they go." He gestured with his bottle, as the little creatures swooped and dipped in the mauve light of dusk, which was slowly deepening.

Jess's stomach gave a growl.

"Two more," said Aidan, apparently not noticing.

"Got them," she said, clicking away as she watched, her eyes starting to water from staring at the same place and hardly daring to blink for fear of missing one. "I'm glad they're going the other way," she commented.

"They're probably off to the pond. Lots of insects there."

"Good. I don't want them getting stuck in my hair or anything."

"You do know that's a myth, don't you?" he said, dismissively. "I can't imagine a bat has ever got stuck in someone's hair. Their radar systems are too amazingly accurate for that."

"They use sound, don't they? I know that much," said Jess. "They're basically making a constant racket to work out where they are?"

"Constant," agreed Aidan, with a wry raise of one eyebrow.

"Just think," said Jess, "if they didn't have high-pitched,

largely inaudible little squeaky voices, we'd probably be reporting them for noise nuisance. I suppose I should be thankful for that at least, but I'm thinking I don't want to store anything important up in the loft."

"Do you need to stick some things in the trailer with the ivy for the dump?" he asked. "Sounds like you do."

"Nooo, don't make me throw away my precious junk," she protested, raising a hand in mock horror. Was that a smile? "Anyway, it's not really junk; it's memories," she admitted uncomfortably, as the silence stretched out.

"I haven't kept my grandpa's junk. Doesn't mean I'm going to forget he existed."

Jess considered mentioning he'd off-loaded his grandpa's house—which, given the state of it at the time, probably counted as junk—but the conversation was so amiable for a change that it seemed a shame to ruin it.

"Do you miss him?" she asked, keeping her eyes focused on the eaves again.

"Yeah," he said after what felt like an endless amount of time. "Obviously."

"I'm sorry."

There was another long pause.

"How is Lucie?" she asked, the words hanging between them to fill the silence.

"She's fine."

"I don't mean to intrude . . ."

"It's okay," he said. He was stretched out now, leaning back on the bench, his legs casually crossed and relaxed. He sighed. "She's just got some thinking to do. About the divorce." He took a swig of beer, looking straight ahead, and continued. "It's been a long time coming."

Jess wondered if he meant the divorce or the thinking.

"How long has it been, Lucie not living with you both?" she asked tentatively.

She held her breath as she felt him stiffen beside her. She shouldn't have said anything.

"She went for the first time when Maisie was two," he went on at last. "She didn't make the adjustment to being a parent naturally. We were young. I don't suppose I supported her particularly well."

Without having been a parent herself, Jess kept silent, tensely waiting for more. After a long, uncomfortable pause, Aidan went on.

"That time, she came back after a couple of months but disappeared again the following year. We got used to it. Her absences were longer every year, until she was spending more time away than here. Nowadays, the deal is I do the parenting—the heavy lifting bit anyhow—and Lucie swans back in whenever she feels like it. She does a bit of hugging and grandstanding, showers Maisie with presents, and then . . ." He took another swig of beer, looking out past the end of the garden and over the meadow. "And then she sods off again."

"You're angry?" Jess ventured, cautiously.

"I'm angry for Maisie," he said, inclining his head in agreement and then leaving it there, examining the hand with the beer in it, which now hung loosely between his knees.

"So, Lucie's been upset? About the divorce?" pressed Jess, living dangerously, but not wanting to reveal her heart-to-heart with Maisie.

"Lucie likes to be the instigator," he offered. "She doesn't like not being the one who's calling the shots. Our marriage was over years ago. The divorce was long overdue, but it was still a shock to her when I filed for it. Ironically, she's been around more since then, mainly to wind me up. So if having her turn up to rattle my cage means that she spends a bit of time with Maisie, I'll take it. I'm a big boy. I can cope."

"Maisie is a great kid," Jess said. "I've told her she's welcome here anytime. I hope that's okay?"

Aidan didn't answer. He didn't even look as if he had heard her. He was frowning away into the darkening sky. Clearly sharing time was over. It was nice while it lasted.

"So, the library's going well, I see," he said, at last, returning from wherever he had been in his head.

"Yes, it seems to be. I'm so pleased."

"I said you'd contribute to the community and I was right."

Jess was nettled. Only Aidan Foxworthy could say something very nearly positive to her for the first time ever and then somehow make it all about a clever thing *he* had done.

"You can't have known I had books—which are very precious to me, by the way—and you definitely can't have known I would be prepared to lend them out."

"Yeah, I did. Okay, not exactly that, obviously, but I flatter myself I'm a good judge of character and you—despite first impressions—have delivered a fairly acceptable result. Considering."

"Damned by faint praise," muttered Jess, sulkily.

Aidan gave a shout of laughter. "Relax. I'm teasing. I'm seriously impressed. In awe. Good job, well done, and all that."

She looked at him suspiciously, but he was grinning as he turned to her, amused at her irritation. He had amazingly even, white teeth, she noticed, gleaming in contrast with his suntanned skin.

He raised his empty beer bottle. "Mind if I help myself to another?"

"Go ahead," she said. "Me too please, although two beers

in one evening is practically binge drinking for me," she admitted. "I'm starting to make a habit of it."

"I hope it isn't your demonic housemates driving you to drink?"

"I'm not loving the whole house-share idea, but I think we can make it work. As long as there's mutual respect. Anyhow, when it comes to drinking, I reckon Diana and Becky are more of a corrupting influence than the bats."

Aidan came back holding two more beers, cold from the fridge, with condensation forming and running down the sides. They drank in silence for a few minutes, the only sounds the birds preparing to roost for the night and Aidan's clicker, counting away. The number of bats exiting the house was dying down now, as the final few left sporadically, intent on an evening of hunting.

"If you buy some insulation for the loft, I'll put it up there for you," he said, not looking at her.

"Really? That would be amazing. I'd appreciate it. I suppose paying you is out of the question?" she asked, suddenly remembering—with a flush—their first meeting when she had tried to press a tenner into his hand for starting her car.

He raised a warning eyebrow in reply. "I've been meaning to do it for years," he went on. "Get it delivered as soon as you can and I'll get onto it, because now's a good time. Nesting season's a quiet period for tree surgeons."

Effusive thanks probably wouldn't go down too well, but Jess tried to show her gratitude through facial expressions. She probably looked a bit mad.

"It's not just the bats—I've got mice, too," she confided, just to make conversation.

Aidan cocked his head, sympathetically.

"I hate the idea of laying traps or poison, though."

"I'm surprised you don't have a cat."

"Ah—I see—I fit the profile for a mad, solitary cat-woman, do I? Thanks."

"You do a bit," he said, teasing again. "Have you never thought about it?"

She pursed her lips at him, but then relented. "I'll let you off, because I've always loved the idea of having a cat, but we really couldn't where we lived before. The traffic on the road at the front was just too heavy. We couldn't risk it."

"Not a problem here. If a cat living here had any sense it would go out through the garden to the meadow. Lots of little mammals there to keep it occupied."

"Ugh, killing! I don't want to think about that."

"It's what they do. At least it's what some of them do. They won't necessarily be good at hunting, but mice won't stay in a house with a cat in—even if it's the laziest, most useless cat in the world. I'll keep my ear to the ground for you. Right," he added, standing up, "come on, let's get all that ivy into my trailer."

"Aren't we counting bats?" said Jess. After two beers she was feeling mellow and not at all like doing more hard work.

"I think we're done with the bats. We're not compelled to count every single one, as such," he added. "I might have slightly over-emphasized that bit." He smiled as he said it and so did Jess, warmed at the thought that Aidan might have simply sought her out for no other reason than her company.

They could even be friends. Or friendly neighbors, at least.

Chapter Fourteen

"It was just really normal, and relaxed," Jess said, proudly relating her encounter with Aidan to Hannah over a mug of tea the next evening. Jess thought she should have a teetotal day, just to show herself she could.

"Go you," said Hannah, when she heard the news. "Although I'm disappointed to hear about the complete lack of tongue tangling. Did you discuss the single-and-available thing?"

"It didn't come up," said Jess, reprovingly. "He's just a single dad, with a complicated ex-wife; the last thing he needs is any extra hassle. And if he was looking for hassle, he'd be after someone a lot more glamorous than me. His ex is seriously gorgeous . . ."

"Mm," mused Hannah. "Best not to get embroiled at the moment then. Even I can see the sense in that."

"Exactly," said Jess, relieved at heading off more totally inappropriate matchmaking. Finally, Hannah had come around to her own way of thinking. "Best not to get embroiled. He's being really nice at the moment. He's even offered—purely platonically—to lay my loft insulation."

"'Lay your loft insulation'?" crowed Hannah. "Not a euphemism?"

"Definitely not," said Jess, firmly. Really Hannah was beyond ridiculous. She knew perfectly well she, Jess, didn't do casual sex. The trouble was—with her fear that daring to love was inevitably followed by loss—she didn't do non-casual sex either, which sort of left her nowhere. Hannah's obsession with Aidan as a potential suitor was becoming annoying. If she was looking for a relationship, she'd be looking for someone . . . well, Jess wasn't quite sure who. But it would be someone else though, that was for certain.

There was a short queue outside the phone box when Jess left the house the next morning to pick up milk and some fresh bread from Paddy's. She didn't know anyone by name, but they were familiar faces by now and all made a point of saying hello and sharing a few words about the weather. Who would have believed that quiet little Jess Metcalfe would have upped roots and moved into a run-down cottage, made friends with her neighbors, and started a popular lending library out of a phone box. Mimi would be proud. Actually, she was proud of herself. Perhaps for the first time she realized that much of her life was exactly the way she wanted it to be. Other than the small niggling worry of a job. But she had friends—or at least people who were becoming friends: Becky and Diana, Mungo, and Maisie too—maybe even Aidan.

"I've been meaning to congratulate you on the fabulous little library," came a voice behind her as she perused the milk selection in Paddy's, startling her out of her musing. It was Muriel. "Such a lovely idea."

"Oh! It wasn't me that thought of it," protested Jess. "It just seemed lucky that it was there. And I had the books."

"It's marvelous," continued Muriel. "I've just had a cookery book out myself. I'm making strawberry shortcake this week and the recipe in the book looks well worth a try. I had a nice chat with a lady who lives down the Portneath road about it. Margaret. We've never spoken before, although I knew her by sight. Anyhow, she puts extra baking powder in hers. I'm not at all sure about that, but it takes all sorts, I suppose. She's such a nice lady, and it's lovely to be making new friends in the village after all these years," she beamed.

"I'm so pleased," said Jess, her heart swelling with tentative pride. How amazing that other people were finding it so helpful for making friends too. Perhaps it would reignite the community spirit people talked longingly about.

"Never mind what anyone else says, for years we've needed another hub in the village, that's what's been missing; we don't all want to hang around in the pub," Muriel added, throwing Paddy a crushing look.

"That's me told," he muttered to Jess, as Muriel stepped up to the till. "There we are, Mrs. Rowbotham, that's your *Daily Mail*, I saved it just for you. Although I don't know what you mean about hanging around in the pub," he told the older woman defensively. "I'm far too busy with the shop all hours to be out boozing."

"Any progress on the post office issue?" said Jess, to change the subject before Muriel could give a rejoinder.

"No news, I'm afraid," said Paddy quickly. "Only the realization that I would need a free member of staff for at least ten hours a week to offer any kind of worthwhile service. That's as far as I've got and—not surprisingly—I've hit a brick wall, unless either of you know anyone looking for an unpaid job."

"Jess is already doing an unpaid job," said Muriel, "being chief librarian for the telephone box."

"And I'm helping out at the school, but that's unpaid too. I'll be needing a real job before autumn," said Jess, glumly, "or I'd offer."

*

Diana turned up with her basket again at six o'clock sharp, this time laden with a purple gin bottle and accoutrements.

"I know it looks like methylated spirit but it really isn't," she explained. They had settled in their customary spot on the little sunny terrace and she was pouring Jess a large measure of dauntingly purple gin. "I haven't stooped that low—not yet anyhow. It's infused with lavender."

"It smells amazing," said Jess, giving her glass a sniff. "More ginger than lavender, somehow." She loved it when Diana turned up like this. It had started to become a habit for the two of them. There were days when she went the whole day without speaking to anyone, not even Hannah. Those were the days when she missed her library job, when she felt a little lonely, and she could begin to imagine how little she would see of people once summer was over and they were closed away in their own cozy homes.

"So, I've been thinking," said Diana, swirling her ice, "we really need to have an opening ceremony for the library. A proper launch."

"It's open already," said Jess, "and people seem to be drifting toward it slowly."

"Sure, but it's a good idea to get the library properly established in the community as quickly as possible. Get more people using it. It'll be less easy to undermine that way."

"What do you mean, 'undermine'?" said Jess, mildly alarmed. "Who wants to undermine it?"

"It's just a turn of phrase," said Diana, looking shifty. Then, seeing Jess's worried expression, she held out her hands in surrender. "Look, there's some boring village politics going on. It's people having a pop at me, not you, so don't worry. I'll sort it."

"Tell," Jess insisted before taking a fortifying sip.

"I suppose you'll find out soon enough," Diana sighed.

"There's a ridiculous situation with April, the parish council clerk. I can hardly credit it, but the woman has sneakily gone behind my back; she's been squirreling around through the statutes and all that nonsense, and she's come up with some failure in process, some accusation that I've exceeded my powers as chairman. In other words, the decision at the meeting about the library wasn't done 'constitutionally,' as she puts it. There was no public consultation."

"That's because I was the only member of the public who turned up."

"Exactly. They never do, here, in Middlemass. No community spirit, although I'll grant you it's changed a bit recently. Anyhow, she's been campaigning around the village getting people to sign a petition, saying the phone box should have a village defibrillator in it," admitted Diana. "Now, I've got a sticky situation because there's this petition—which is, one could argue, the result of a public consultation—in support of the defibrillator."

"People want to shut it down?" Jess said, stunned.

"Yes, I know, ridiculous. And you know precisely what I think about defibrillators—I must get around to drafting my 'Do Not Resuscitate' order. Anyhow, it's not a big deal," said Diana, dismissing it with a swipe of a hand that nearly took out Jess's gin and tonic. "She's only got sixty-eight signatures. I've told her there will now need to be a petition in favor of the library and may the best petition win."

Jess nodded, feeling a tiny bit less mortified, but was still horror-struck at finding herself piggy in the middle of some crowd-baying village dissent. She had thought nothing but sweet, fluffy thoughts of the community up until now.

"So," Diana went on, "you need to put up your own petition in the library. And Paddy's shop, now I think of it. And we should have an event too, like I was saying—not so much for people who already know about it but an awareness-raising campaign leading up to it for people who don't," said Diana stoutly. "To cement it into the village as something positive, that's there to stay. I was thinking we could maybe get the school and the church involved. And the *Portneath Echo*, perhaps."

"Okay," said Jess, doubtfully.

"Good," said Diana briskly. "So, as for timing, I was thinking about tying it in with the Harvest Home at the end of August."

"The Harvest Hoe?"

"Harvest Home," Diana corrected. "It celebrates the August harvest on the August bank holiday weekend. It's an ancient Middlemass tradition. We grow a lot of wheat around Middlemass, so high summer is harvest time here."

"What sort of things happen at the Harvest Home then?"

"Recently, not a lot, but there used to be traditional things like corn dollies on front doors, morris dancing on the green . . . There's usually a cricket match that day too and cream teas in the cricket pavilion; just village stuff. Oh, and a barn dance in the evening, for the youngsters to get together, snogging behind haystacks, that sort of thing. You know."

Jess didn't. Snogging behind haystacks sounded positively alarming, and she was concerned her sudden, disturbing thoughts of Aidan glowering down at her might be obvious to Diana.

"Oh, come on," said Diana, seeing her dissembling. "It's a classic time of year for hooking up, going back literally centuries. They kill a sheep, crack open a keg of ale, the girls wear their best dresses and pounce on the men who've been catching their eye in church over the months leading up."

"It sounds like as good a day for a phone-box library celebration as any other," said Jess, grudgingly, hoping to keep

Diana's mind on the library and off the idea of getting Jess hooked up with anyone. Especially Aidan.

"So," Diana went on. "We've got ages, but what we should do is have a meeting to sort out who does what. And, in the meantime, we need a poster to shove up around the village. You can leave that to me."

"As long as you don't expect me to do a photo call or anything. That really isn't my thing, having my photo taken. I look a mess." Jess pulled fretfully at the hopelessly curly hair she had always despised.

"I love your hair," said Diana, giving her a piercing look.

"What? I hate my hair."

"Don't be ridiculous! You're a beautiful girl. You're petite, you've got curves in all the right places, you have amazing, wavy auburn hair like some Pre-Raphaelite. You're a babe. Why are you dressed in such shapeless clothes, if you don't mind me asking?"

"Don't hold back, will you?" protested Jess mildly. "What do you want me to flipping wear? I've been cleaning all day. Dungarees are perfect for that."

"You look like a children's television presenter. Actually, you look like a child."

"Ouch."

"Sorry," said Diana. "Truce. Seriously, forgive me, I have this nosy habit of shoving my oar in."

"It's fine," smiled Jess. "You sound a bit like my Mimi. I still miss her, but I think she'd be glad I've met you."

Diana raised her glass, with the sprig of lavender still bobbing around cheerfully. "To saving the library and to Mimi."

Jess relaxed. Maybe the whole petition thing wasn't that big a deal. An event to spread the word about the library couldn't be a bad thing; plus wasn't Muriel just saying earlier how it was helping to bring the community together?

*

When Aidan came to put the insulation in the loft, Jess found herself curiously disappointed that he brought with him a young, muscle-bound helper who was introduced as Josh, his tree surgery apprentice. It took no time for the two men to pass the huge rolls of insulation up into the loft space and barely any longer for them to put it into place. She tried to engage them both with tea, cake, and conversation afterward, as thanks for their efforts, but the interaction felt wooden, the conversation seeming far more difficult than when it had been just herself and Aidan counting bats the other day.

The two men praised her lemon drizzle cake—a recipe she had always made with Mimi—and wolfed huge amounts of it as they gulped their tea.

Josh even volunteered that his girlfriend had been using the library regularly to find bedtime stories for their toddler son. He confirmed that they'd both signed the petition in favor of the library, but then spoiled the effect by admitting he had signed the one for the defibrillator as well. This statement killed the conversation, leaving Jess wishing Aidan would say something. The heavy silence seemed to make the room feel claustrophobic with all three of them in there, and Jess couldn't wait to be left alone again. But when they left, the house felt too quiet and still. She couldn't win.

With melancholy beckoning, Jess went out into the garden, where she could never stay sad for long. The tulips and hyacinths had given way to the early roses now, their sweet cinnamon scent wafting toward her whenever she opened the back door. Aidan's grandfather had been generous in his planting. It was early June and the clematis was in full bloom, with honeysuckle burgeoning on the edge of flowering. Despite the many opportunistic weeds, decades of careful, loving care were evident everywhere, like a kindly, nurturing thread of connection between Jess and the man she had never met. She wondered what he had looked like, and whether Aidan had inherited his broad shoulders and his thick wavy hair from his grandfather. She imagined she could see the shadow of him, digging this same soil, walking these same paths. All around her, the living evidence of his decades of hard work remained.

Next year, thought Jess, she might be done with the house repairs and redecorating. Of course, she would have to be working but hopefully she would also be able to take the time to tend the garden better, coaxing out of it the beauty she could see unfurling as her first year there passed. She knew what to do, especially with Maisie showing her what her great-grandfather had put where. As for general gardening skills, Mimi had taught her patiently as a girl, and it was instinctive in her now: when to prune, when to plant, when to harvest. Jess knew these were strange skills for a townie and for a woman her age, but she took comfort from the reliability of plants in responding to her care. Human relationships, she had always found, were much more complex.

The fruit trees espaliered along the old brick wall running down the side of the garden had been frothing with blossom and now had tiny, bullet-hard fruit, where the bees had pollinated. Bees, thought Jess; perhaps she should have a hive? She could ask Aidan: he was bound to know who kept bees locally. It was the kind of thing she would've knocked on his door to ask before today, but he had hardly been able to meet her eye over tea and cake. She didn't think it was the right time to ask for more favors.

The grass in the orchard was thick, green, and shaggy, peppered with clover and daisies. Left long, it was seeding now too, the delicate seed heads blowing in the breeze. She would need to get it trimmed in the autumn. Maybe Aidan would help with that? What with being a tree surgeon, he probably owned all the right tools. Funny how all her thoughts seemed to track back to him.

Beyond the little orchard, the meadow had burst into life, the celandines she remembered from her very first morning having now given way to cowslips, and then to cow parsley and lady's bedstraw, the early summer sunshine releasing the heady scent from the blossom. It was hypnotic.

But today, she fought the inclination to stop and dream. It was getting her nowhere. She sighed, brushing her hands down her jeans to clean them. Without an income—and with the future of the library threatened—her life in Middlemass was far from stable and guaranteed. The fight for this new, exciting future she pictured for herself had only just begun. It was just as she always knew: allowing herself to feel happy and settled was dangerous. As soon as she admitted she was content—happy, even—a cataclysmic act of fate would steal it all away from her, just as it had in the past. No. Happiness was dangerous. It was to be avoided.

Chapter Fifteen

"We're only three days into half-term and I'm already at my wits' end," admitted Becky, who had popped over to the telephone box with Isla and Angus to find a children's cookbook. Jess had gone out to rescue her from a little huddle of school mums who were also there with their children, passing the time of day.

"Listen, if we end up making cupcakes again this afternoon I swear I'll go insane," Becky told Jess. She had Angus perched on her hip as usual. "I need fresh inspiration," she pleaded, "and I know you've got cookbooks. Let me at them, but first I'm dying for a cup of tea."

Angus and Isla were quickly settled in the living room with a selection of suitable books while Jess popped on the kettle.

"I can't even let myself think about the summer holidays," Becky said, when they both had mugs in their hands and were settled around the worn kitchen table. "Rak's being funny about me arranging for us to go away somewhere because his surgery lists are booked up for months. It's a nightmare. I just want two weeks in an all-inclusive deal, somewhere with a spa and a kids' club where I can lie in the sun and read. Or just sleep. Instead, I can see us spending the entire six weeks in Middlemass trying not to kill each other, while he's at work as usual. Anyhow, back to today's problems . . ." Becky slumped back in her chair. "Thank goodness for the library.

April's little interference notwithstanding, how's it all going, anyway?" she asked, moving on to Jess's life with an effort.

"Good, I think. I have to try not to sit here twitching the curtains every time someone turns up. I'm pining to go out and see what people are borrowing and if they're signing the petition."

"Then go and find out. It must be fascinating, being a librarian, getting to see what people are reading."

"No one's ever said that to me before."

"No, but it must be. Other than doctors and priests, I can't think of anyone who gets to see inside the minds of strangers more than a librarian would."

"There are sometimes surprises," admitted Jess. "There's this sweet old gentleman on a bicycle who's rapidly working his way through the books. I think he's taking out the classic romances. I see him there a lot."

Becky smiled, then looked worried. "What will you do when everyone's read everything?"

"I suppose, in the long term we'll need new books to go in. Perhaps people will donate them . . . I just hope the original ones find their way back."

"I am surprised you can bear to let them go out."

"It's a leap of faith, really. I am stamping them all on the flyleaf, just to say they belong to the telephone-box library. Look, I sent away for this little stamp." She showed Becky the stamp and ink pad she'd ordered especially. *The Littlest Library*, it said, in mirror writing with a simple line drawing of a telephone box above.

"Cute," said Becky, picking up the stamp and peering at it. "The books will come back. After all, most people are nice, as I constantly remind myself at the school gates. There's lots of positive chatter about it there, by the way, unlike what we half heard the other day. Ooh, and I was totally thrilled to see the Michelle Obama memoir in the phone box. I've grabbed it, if you're wondering who's got it."

"*Becoming*? So great! Just what you need to inspire you." And it was, thought Jess, the perfect book for someone needing the courage to change. She should probably reread it herself.

"Your grandmother's inscription in the front made me cry," Becky went on.

"I'd forgotten about that," said Jess. It had been the last birthday present Mimi ever gave her, just weeks before she died. "What does it say again?"

"Something about you being stronger than you think, and how you make her really proud and she'll always love you and watch over you," said Becky, her voice breaking. "Do you want it back?"

"No, you read it," said Jess, dabbing at her now dampening eyes.

"Anyhow," Becky went on, selecting another biscuit, "there's loads of us using it. I saw Mungo going back with a book this morning. He took another one out too."

"Should we be worried about those two?" queried Jess, cocking her thumb at the sitting room.

"Quiet is fine," Becky reassured her. "I reckon we're good for another couple of minutes."

"Mungo's such a funny old thing, isn't he?" Becky went on, reaching across the table for the biscuits that Jess had pulled out of the cupboard. "So courteous and droll, but somehow . . ."

"A little bit sad? Lonely?" Jess hazarded.

"Yeah, definitely," agreed Becky. "I know he lived with his mum at the Dower House and she only died a couple of years ago. She must have literally been a hundred, because he's got to be in his seventies, don't you think?"

"Early seventies? He's very debonair, isn't he? He'd make a lovely boyfriend to some older woman. Or man."

"Man, I think we can assume," said Becky. "Unless my gaydar's totally off. Although he'd make a fabulous walker for anyone—you know? A companion for someone to go to things with—the theater or parties, or whatever. He's so polite and kind. I think we need to set him up with someone."

Jess balked at the thought. "I'm sure he can do it himself," she said. "There must be other older gay men around here. Or in Portneath, at least."

"You know what? I wouldn't be surprised if he's never had a serious romantic relationship," Becky mused, munching on a chocolate chip cookie. "Apparently, he's pretty much always lived at home. I think his dad died when he was quite young."

"How tragic. Diana said she didn't think he had ever been with anyone special," remembered Jess. "It seems he's spent his life dedicated to keeping his mum company and now he's missing out."

They both sighed, sadly.

"So, all right," said Becky, "now we've analyzed the poor man to within an inch of his life, who are we going to fix him up with?"

"Diana?"

"Not his type?"

"True, but I didn't mean *that*. What about as companions? But then they're quite crabby with each other sometimes. I have already suggested it to her, by the way. She didn't hate the idea."

"Mm," said Becky, unconvinced. "We'd be rubbish as professional matchmakers," she admitted after a long pause.

"Definitely; don't give up the day job."

"Not that either of us have got a day job," said Becky. "Talking of which, who needs a law degree when you're spending your days changing nappies, wiping snotty noses, and arguing with three-year-olds? God, they can argue, though. Isla's getting to be as bad as Angus, and she's not even two yet. I suppose you could say the arguing is good training for law."

"It's so good to hear you talking about your work ambitions," said Jess, encouragingly. "Did you say you did criminal law? I can see you in a wig, banging the table and asking the piercing questions no one else has thought of."

"You've been watching too much telly," smiled Becky. "No, family law is my thing. Divorces and custody battles. Mind you, that's where the real drama is, I promise you."

"People's marriages are a mystery, aren't they?" said Jess, thinking of Aidan and Lucie.

"Mine certainly is, to me," said Becky, which reminded Jess how unexpectedly lovely Rakesh had seemed in their brief meeting. And yet, if he was really crushing Becky's career ambitions, he couldn't be as nice as he seemed, could he?

She thought about bringing it up, but squabbling had now erupted from the other room and Becky went back in to intervene. Isla was quickly distracted from her battle with Angus and was sitting on the floor showing Jess her own old copy of *The Tiger Who Came to Tea*.

"Your children's book collection is amazing," Becky said, looking fondly at her two engrossed children. "It's all the ones I remember. All the important ones . . . Anyway, talking of jobs, what about you?"

"That's a good question. Libraries are a dying breed, but I don't know how to do anything else."

"The world will always need books," insisted Becky. "And doing stuff with books is what you love. That's important."

"Hmm," said Jess, remembering she still had to draw up the book purchase list for the school. "If only someone would pay me to enjoy myself. But unfortunately reading, in itself, isn't a job as such."

Over the next week Jess found her days went by quickly, full of activity, clearing up the library every afternoon and bustling around the house and garden. During the day, she was purposeful and content, but it was the evenings that dragged, the eventual darkness bringing a pang—not of loneliness exactly, but aloneness—which Jess counteracted with the reassuring rituals of fire-lighting and closing of the shutters. She was gazing into the roaring blaze, thinking about a glass of wine, her supper simmering on the stove, when a sharp rap on the door made her jump. Heart racing, she fumbled with the lock and then opened it to see a familiar broad-shouldered figure standing on the doorstep with the dark surrounding him.

"Good, you're in," said Aidan gruffly.

Where else would I be? Jess thought to reply, but instead she stood aside to let him in, her heart pounding more, not less, now she knew who it was. "More books?" she queried, puzzled, as he stepped into the sitting room and put a large cardboard box down gently on the floor.

Just at that moment, she heard a faint, high-pitched mewing sound. "Oh, my goodness," she exclaimed in wonder. "Is it a cat?"

"Not quite," said Aidan. "Look."

He unfolded the flaps on the top and sat back on his heels to let Jess peer inside. "Two cats," he said, straightening up. "If you want them, that is."

"Not cats, though . . . kittens," said Jess in awe. "Oh, my goodness, they're gorgeous!" She carefully scooped them both up and lifted them out to see. The little balls of fluff, one with orange stripes and one tortoiseshell, continued to mew furiously but, as she cradled them both, high on her chest, one in each hand, they settled and started to purr. The orange one yawned, displaying a tiny pink tongue, and then seemed to settle down to sleep on her palm.

"What are they called?" she asked, gazing up at Aidan in wonder.

"Up to you. Maisie had some weird suggestion, something like Baboo and—what was it? Ladder or something." He scratched his head, trying to remember.

"Batou and Ladriya?" Jess hazarded.

"Yeah, that's it," he raised his eyebrows in surprise. "How did you know that?"

"Classy idea, I love it!" she exclaimed. "*Ghost in the Shell*."

"Wha—?"

"*Ghost in the Shell*," explained Jess. "Your daughter has impeccable taste. Are they a boy and girl? I assume they are, with those suggestions."

"Yeah, ginger boy, tortoiseshell girl, they're a litter a client was telling me about. Just moggies, but healthy and just the right age to leave their mum, so . . . But seriously, ghost in the what?"

"Shell," said Jess. "Absolutely classic manga comic material. Full of empowered women. I'd forgotten Maisie was a fan. I've got my own collection from about twenty years ago in one of these boxes. I've been meaning to lend them to her, they're great reading material."

"Comics, though . . . Do they count as reading?"

"Of course! Manga is a highly respected form of storytelling. Calling it 'comics' doesn't do it justice. I'll sort her out with some other graphic novels too. It's all stories. It all counts."

"Okay, thanks," he said with some reserve. "So, which one's Bamboo?"

"Batou," laughed Jess, "he's the boy." She dropped a kiss onto the little ginger tom's nose, before lifting up the tortoiseshell, "And this little gorgeous person is Ladriya. So . . . It's a bit of a responsibility though. What do they need?"

"Nothing complicated. Right now, a bowl of water and maybe some food? I gave them a tin of sardines earlier, that's why they're a bit oily and smelly." It was true, they were, Jess noticed; but she didn't really care as the kittens nuzzled under her chin.

Jess popped the kittens back in their box just while Aidan busied himself by sorting out a little corner of the kitchen with water, a tin of tuna Jess had dug out, and a newspaper.

While he worked, Jess pottered, stirring the chili she had bubbling gently on the Aga. Having recovered from the initial nerves of him arriving, it felt good to have him there. Comfortable. Or at least a considerable improvement on their first few interactions.

"Will you join me for something to eat?" she asked, diffidently. "It's just chili. I've made a big batch, so there's loads."

"I don't want to gate-crash your evening."

"You're not. Only I suppose . . ." she added with a pang of disappointment, "I suppose you and Maisie have something planned?"

"Maisie's eaten," said Aidan with economy. "And she's out with her mum tonight."

"But you've not had supper?"

"No."

Jess made a gesture to the pot on the stove. Was he going to make her beg?

"That's very kind," he said, inclining his head. "Thanks."

*

The kittens climbed right into the bowl with the tuna and tucked in with enthusiasm. Then, they both peed on the newspaper and turned their attention to exploration. They were a constant menace while Aidan laid the table and Jess made a simple salad, getting under their feet and risking death by squashing at every turn. She and Aidan were both relieved when they could sit down at the kitchen table to eat, cautiously sliding their chairs in and resolving not to move from then on.

"They are adorable," said Jess again as the kittens gamboled across the floor together, intermittently play-fighting and making her laugh. "Thank you."

"You don't want the house overrun with mice," he replied simply. "Thanks again for this," he added, gesturing to his full plate.

"It's nothing special," said Jess, offering the sour cream and guacamole. "Thank goodness supermarket deliveries come out this far. I've been far too grubby and untidy with the garden to show my face in Portneath for the last few days."

"Do you cook like this, every night?"

"I tend to batch cook and freeze," she confessed.

"I'm eating one of your would-be future ready meals," he said. "Sorry."

"Don't be," she smiled. "It's nice to have the company. And no, I'm too lazy to do this every night," she admitted, "although Mimi—my grandmother—wouldn't approve of me using the freezer so much. She was a big one for cooking from fresh—a simple, seasonal meal and a large glass of good French red wine."

"She sounds like a very sensible woman," he said with a nod, and Jess couldn't help but smile. She suddenly had a feeling Mimi would have liked Aidan. Her presence in the room was so strong at that moment, Jess felt it like a hug.

"You've really settled in now," he went on, waving a loaded fork around the now cozy kitchen. "The house looks different. Homey."

Jess looked around the room, trying to see it through Aidan's eyes. It had been hard work, but it did look pretty good now. The Aga was gleaming, the cupboards had their new gingham curtain fronts, the wooden countertops were scrubbed and oiled, and Mimi's old dresser looked handsome against the wall with her familiar Cornishware china on it.

There was an awkward silence.

"We had some of this stripy china when I was little," he said at last, nodding to the dresser. "I wonder whatever happened to it all."

"I probably bought it from your family at a car boot sale," joked Jess, lightly. "Mimi had a few bits of it to start with, but most of what you see on the dresser is secondhand."

"And these are from the garden?" he said, indicating the jug of roses on the table they were eating off.

"Yep," she said. "I could pick armfuls if I wanted. Your grandfather must have planted an awful lot of roses over the years. There just seems to have been wave after wave first of bulbs flowering, and now all these roses. The garden's amazing."

Aidan nodded. "When he was ill, toward the end, he used to fret about not being able to look after it. He'd ask me to help but of course I was useless, always cutting the wrong bit off and digging up plants thinking they were weeds."

"And you a tree surgeon, too . . ."

Once they had finished, Aidan insisted on loading the dishwasher and washing up the pans. Then Jess managed to persuade him to come into the sitting room for coffee. The wood burner was glowing with a heap of red embers now, still emitting occasional tongues of flame. She switched on the two little lamps, adding to the rosy glow of the fire.

The tidying up seemed to have broken the easy mood they had relaxed into over supper, making Jess start to wish she had not insisted on coffee.

With Aidan taking the sofa, Jess sat primly on the armchair opposite, although the room was so tiny that their knees were nearly touching.

At first, they sat in silence. Why did he make her so nervous? It was ridiculous to feel that way. She never felt like this with anyone else.

"So, how are you finding Middlemass?" he asked as if he was at the vicarage tea party, his little coffee cup and saucer balanced on one knee.

"Fine," said Jess, grateful for a safe topic. "Everyone is so lovely. I've enjoyed getting to know people. I can't believe it's been four months already."

"Four months? It feels like longer."

"Thanks."

"No, it feels like the telephone-box library's always been there. A bit like the old days, community spirit and all that stuff," Aidan explained awkwardly, his knees beginning to bob up and down as he shifted on his seat.

Maybe he was nervous too, thought Jess, and the thought made her feel less anxious. "You say that, but it may not be there much longer," Jess said, going on to explain about the defibrillator campaign.

"Typical Middlemass," sighed Aidan. "Try not to let it rattle you. It just sounds like the biggest silly fuss since the last silly fuss. There's always something."

"I'm not sure Diana would agree with you. She's telling me not to worry, but . . ." Jess trailed off. "Have you borrowed any books yet?" she asked, determined to focus on the bright side.

"I'm not a reader," he said apologetically.

There was another clanging silence.

"I like this color." He indicated the freshly painted walls. "It's nice. Warm."

"Thanks."

Silence fell again. Jess desperately wished that the kittens would wake up and cause a diversion, or that she could think of anything to say in reply to being told Aidan "wasn't a reader." What did that even mean? Who didn't read?

"What are Maisie and"—she mentally kicked herself for hesitating to say the name—"and Lucie up to this evening then?"

"Some alternative theatrical thing in Exeter."

"Maisie's a lovely girl," said Jess. "It's nice that they're out together."

"Yeah." Aidan gave a mirthless laugh. "Lucie enjoys playing the role of the beautiful mother with the beautiful child who mirrors her perfection. Maisie's got more of a mind of her own now, which makes it a bit harder for her to maintain the illusion."

"Situation normal for the average twelve-year-old, I imagine?"

"She's great," he said awkwardly, staring at the rug. "The way she's so grown up one minute and just my little girl the next. Lucie is less impressed with all that. She just wants Maisie to be a mini-me." He shook his head. "That said, I don't want it to put her off doing things with her. Maisie would see even less of her if I did."

He was brooding now, staring into his coffee cup as if the answer to the problems he clearly agonized over would be obvious in its depths.

"It can't be easy, having her coming and going like she

does. Surely the divorce gives a bit of certainty though?" Jess ventured.

Aidan sighed. "It's definitely a relief to be divorced. I should have done it sooner. Lucie still tries to get a rise out of me whenever she can. I refuse to engage nowadays; it drives her mad." He produced a twisted smile. "She thrives on it, you see—the drama. So, the marriage is over, as I constantly remind her, but she's still got Maisie. My little Achilles' heel. Talking of drama, that's what she's off doing next, did I say? She's got this theater group based in Bristol. They sound like a right lot of layabouts—wouldn't know an honest day's work if it bit them on the arse."

Jess didn't know how to reply. So she tilted her head sympathetically and racked her brains to think what Mimi would say, if she were here. Mimi was always so wise about relationship things.

"So, yeah . . . We're struggling to sort out the co-parenting to go with the divorce," Aidan went on, looking down into the dregs of his coffee. "Lucie's basically refusing to cooperate with setting up a proper child arrangement plan because she wants to punish me for instigating it all. It's pretty gratuitously destructive, which is Lucie all over. She says she wants to be more involved with Maisie's life, but—the saddest thing of all—she doesn't really. That said, the latest thing she suggested, to wind me up, was that Maisie should go and stay in her Bristol flat with her for a few days. It wasn't an option and I told her so. I need her to see Maisie here, so I know what's going on."

He rubbed his face wearily and looked at Jess. "I'm guessing you think I'm being the heavy-handed father?"

"From what I've seen, you're a really good father."

There was a pause.

"But?" Aidan prompted.

Jess sighed. "It's just," she went on, carefully, "I'm wondering when Maisie is old enough to have a view on all this."

"Not yet," he said, his jaw set.

"Are you sure?" ventured Jess, emboldened by his candor. "She's got to be allowed to have a say at some point, surely? And she seems really sensible. What are you afraid of?"

Aidan's face darkened. "She's too young. She's only twelve, she needs protecting."

"Okay, now you sound like a heavy-handed father," said Jess and instantly regretted her boldness, seeing his face darken further. Yikes, she had really done it now.

"I am not sure I appreciate being told I am not doing right by my own child. Especially by someone who has neither been married nor had a child herself."

Jess recoiled and clasped her hands together, saying nothing.

He sat back too and looked at her wearily. "Sorry," he sighed, rubbing a hand wearily across his face. "That was totally unfair. Look, I surprise myself. I never thought being a dad would change me like it has. As soon as I laid eyes on Maisie, I knew I would always do whatever I needed to do to keep her safe." He seemed distracted, now, his anger no sooner roused than spent. As he spoke his eyes wandered over Jess's face; "So here I am, twelve years later. Her own mother's spent fewer of those years with her than you could count on one hand . . ." He trailed off, his eyes now resting on her mouth until he dragged them away to meet her own. "And now . . ."

There was an endless silence. Jess felt herself leaning in, her heart pounding so hard she thought he must hear it. She was unable to look away. His gaze held hers for long seconds before he closed the last few inches of the gap between them and brushed his lips against her own. The gentle touch made her shiver, and no sooner than it had happened it was over. Opening her eyes, she saw him look at her for a sign and then he leaned in again, emboldened this time, and she could feel his rough, unshaven face, and smell his aftershave—something green and fresh, with musky undertones. She found her hands had sprung up of their own volition to run through his hair, holding him there, his mouth on hers until finally—reluctantly—they slowly pulled away from each other.

The silence felt like it went on forever. A log collapsed into ashes in the fireplace and made them both jump, breaking the spell.

"Listen," he said, brusquely. "I should really get going. They'll be back soon, and it won't occur to Lucie to tell Maisie to go to bed. She needs to stick to her usual bedtime routine, or she'll be shattered for school tomorrow." He stood up, putting his cup and saucer on the little side table.

"Thank you so much for the kittens," Jess said awkwardly as they both stood at the door.

"See you soon, Jess," he replied softly, placing his hands on her shoulders, seemingly as much to hold her away as to embrace her. He gave her a chaste peck on the cheek, his stubble rasping briefly on her face.

Then he was gone, and she was alone again.

Chapter Sixteen

Jess made herself a cup of tea. It was already ten o'clock—past her usual bedtime—but she was wide awake. The kittens, on the other hand, were sound asleep now, piled in a heap on the cushion she had put out for them at the base of the Aga. She checked they still had water, changed their newspaper, and took her tea into the sitting room.

"This is a terrible, terrible idea," she told herself sternly. "Even thinking of getting into a romantic situation with the man who sold you the house, who is your near neighbor, who has complex family issues to contend with, and is—all told—a nightmare waiting to happen."

At the same time, she couldn't help blushing and clutching one of her sofa cushions to herself as she relived the heart-pounding moment their lips touched.

She was still far too skittish to go to sleep. The afternoon felt like it must have been days away. She was now in possession of two cats and the disturbing thought that Aidan Foxworthy might be more than a neighbor. More than a friend. Or not. Checking the time, she dialed up Hannah, but her friend wasn't online. She was probably off doing some family activity with little Molly and her husband, whose name was Dan but who was only ever referred to between the two of them as "the hunky vet." It was probably just as well she wasn't around. Hannah would be all too keen to make too much of it. Far better for Jess to take the time to decide whether she wanted to confess anything at all to her friend on the matter. And figure out exactly what she wanted to happen next. It wasn't clear what Aidan was thinking. And it was this swirling confusion that danced in Jess's mind long into the night.

In no way was Jess's decision to deadhead the roses in the front garden influenced by her curiosity over seeing Aidan again, but she could hardly help hearing when Lucie and Aidan came out of the house, arguing loudly. Lucie flounced to her car, starting it and roaring off, shouting something as she went, which Jess failed to catch.

She was so busy not listening, she didn't notice Aidan had crossed the road toward her and was now standing at the gate.

"Jess?"

She jumped, guiltily, and turned to face him, hoping he wouldn't think she was eavesdropping.

"So," he said through white lips, his eyes dancing everywhere but her face. "I take it you heard all that, just now?"

"Erm, a little bit, sorry," admitted Jess. "Is Maisie all right?"

"Yes. It's about Maisie, but she's fine. She doesn't know."

"Doesn't know what?"

"We had a row, me and Lucie. I was angry with her for drinking and then driving Maisie home last night—"

"So would I be."

"Precisely. But she's just been coming up with some rubbish about me poisoning Maisie against her, and how I thought I was Jesus Christ just because I'm here with her all the time." He shook his head in astonishment.

"Same old, same old, surely?" said Jess.

"Yeah, but . . ." Aidan ran his fingers through his hair and tugged at it, like he wanted to pull it out by the roots. ". . . now she tells me she wants to take Maisie away. Not just to stay with her in Bristol, which was bad enough, but to live there with her. All the time."

Jess gasped in shock. She mulled it over for a moment. "Does she really mean it, do you think?"

"Who knows." He gave a hollow laugh. "It could just be a power play—punishing me for criticizing her. But if she did . . . Maisie's just finishing her first year at secondary school, settling in, making new friends. A change in school now would be really hard on her. Different classmates, different teachers, all that work trying to make sure she's got support in place for her dyslexia, getting her extra time in exams. I've got her local school trained, more or less, but it hasn't been easy."

"Aidan, I am so, so sorry," Jess said, her mind whirling. "I cannot imagine why she would want to do something so destructive."

He shook his head, despairingly.

"Like you say, though," Jess went on, "maybe she's just hitting out? Getting back at you for complaining about the drunk driving thing?" She cast around desperately for a helpful suggestion. "You should speak to Becky," she said, suddenly. "She was telling me her speciality was in family law. She'll know what to do."

"Really?" he said, his eyes meeting hers for the first time. They were full of hope, or was it relief? "Okay, yeah, maybe I will. Look, anyway, also, I'm sorry."

"What on earth for?" Jess couldn't seem to think clearly; his eyes were on hers and all she could think about was that long, lingering kiss. Shaking her head to dispel the disturbingly wonderful vision, she turned back to deadhead more roses, desperate to have something to do.

"About last night," he pressed, as she silently pleaded with him to stop. "That's the other reason I came over. It was completely inappropriate."

"Sure. No problem," insisted Jess, her heart sinking. "It didn't happen."

"Yes, but I owe you an explanation at least. The reality is, there's no way I'm going to expect you to get involved with me with all this stuff going on plus—well, this shouldn't be a factor, I know, but Lucie's jealous of you and it wouldn't be a good idea to give her more reasons to make trouble. I'm really sorry."

"No, no, a hundred percent, sure, totally . . ." she reassured him. Strangely, she felt bizarrely breathless all of a sudden.

"And it won't make things weird between us?"

"Definitely not. There will be zero weirdness."

"Just friends?"

"Just friends," agreed Jess, emphatically, as she pasted a bright, breezy smile onto her face.

Jess went inside, and as she closed the door on Aidan she simultaneously closed the door on her ridiculous aspirations toward romance. As always, love was beyond her reach. Of course it was. Jess did friendship and—if she said so herself—she did it well, at least sometimes. She had Hannah, and now she had precious new friendships in Middlemass—Diana, Becky . . . and maybe Aidan too. She would be content with that. It was enough. It would have to be.

"Ha!" said Diana, popping up at the gate seemingly from nowhere, as Jess used an old kitchen knife to dig weeds out of the brick path. "I've got you exactly where I want you."

"How's that?" she asked. "Also, why have you brought me a trowel and a stack of flowerpots?" she added, noticing what Diana was holding.

"I haven't; they're mine," explained Diana. "I've been waiting to pounce on your digitalis seedlings."

"What? These?" Jess said, standing up and walking over to the rash of tiny green stalks in the soil among the broad, furry leaves of the foxgloves Aidan's grandfather had been so fond of.

"Yesss!" said Diana, in triumph as she hunkered down beside her. "I knew it. At least, I hoped it."

"Help yourself," said Jess, smiling. "You're lucky you came along. I'd have hoed them back in without thinking if you hadn't. I've got no room for more foxgloves here."

"You look distracted this morning," said Diana as she carefully scooped and transplanted the tiny plants into her pots.

Jess sighed. "Just brain ache. Life is complicated, isn't it?"

"Why, what's happened? Are you all right?"

"Sorry, yes, fine, I'm fine." Jess paused. "It's Aidan," she blurted. "But there's nothing to say," she added hastily. *Damn.* Diana was never going to let it lie now.

"Have you two made some progress?"

"Hardly. The opposite, if you mean what I think you mean."

"With hanky-panky of course."

"Good grief," said Jess, diverted from her reawakening distress, "is that seriously what people are calling it these days?"

"They are in my generation. Hanky-panky, nookie, how's-your-father . . ."

Jess laughed, despite herself, but her stomach gave a painful twist as she remembered her last conversation with him—how she leapt to agree with his decision at the precise moment it felt like her heart had dropped like a stone in her chest. "All right, all right, you've made your point. I am sad to have to break it to you that, although Aidan and I did share a momentary frisson, by mutual consent we have decided not to take it any further at this moment in time."

"'At this moment in time,' my foot," echoed Diana. "Really, the two of you are infuriating. He's gorgeous, you're gorgeous, you live next door to each other. Honestly, what does it take?"

"We live next door? Is convenience an actual criterion? Romance really isn't dead in your world, is it?"

"There's a lot to be said for proximity," insisted Diana. "It's a darned good start. I don't believe in missing what's right under your nose."

"Okay, well, thanks for the advice, I'll make sure I give you a minute-by-minute account, the next time a suitable man passes my way and we decide to indulge in 'hanky-panky' or whatever you're calling it."

"You do that. Anyway, why have you mutually decided not to take things forward with Aidan 'at this moment in time'?"

"Ask Aidan."

"Don't worry, I will."

"Oh God, please don't," said Jess, her bluff well and truly called. "Then he'll know I said something—and it's awkward enough as it is."

"Okay, I won't," agreed Diana, victorious, "but only if you tell me everything."

"There's nothing to tell. I'm not interested. He's not available. End of."

"'Not available' never stopped me," said Diana.

"No, well, we're not the same," said Jess, awkwardly, aware the banter had reached dangerous ground.

"I don't suppose we are," agreed Diana, without apparently taking offense. "You're with a lot of the world on that one. Affairs with married men are frowned upon; I get it."

"God, hang on, don't be . . . I would never judge," said Jess, quickly. "Anyhow he's not even married. It's not that."

"You've got a better moral compass than me." Diana went

on, simply. "I was just unable to resist the flattery of a man who said I went in and out in all the right places and never mind if I could type or not."

"Yuck. Nothing you've ever said about him has made me warm to him," said Jess. "And it's the antithesis of feminism, making those nudge, nudge, wink, wink comments. He'd never get away with saying something like that to a young woman now."

Diana put her head back and laughed. She had a full-bodied, sexy laugh that made the other person in the conversation feel they must have said something very clever.

"'The past is another country,'" she said. "'They do things differently there.' It's more of a generational thing than you'll ever know. You wouldn't believe what passed for normal in those days. Anyhow, you don't know how accurate you are. The man was—and doubtless still is—a complete arse. My only regret—and unfortunately, it's a big one—is that it took me more than thirty years to see it." Diana stared into the middle distance, and then shook herself, newly resolute. "Aidan's a much better bet, in my view," she said firmly.

"Now, my other reason for popping over was this," she said, indicating a rolled-up cylinder of card in her basket.

"You did this?" breathed Jess, unrolling the card on the kitchen table once they had both washed their hands and Jess had checked for crumbs and smears of marmalade from breakfast. "This is amazing!"

Lying before her was the most beautiful watercolor painting of the telephone-box library, complete with the shelves of books, the grassy verge, and, in the background, the stone wall, with Jess's cottage just visible. Diana had perfectly depicted the scene and even included a white duck, with a row of ducklings in close pursuit, off to one side and heading for the pond. There was minimal lettering, just the bare details: time, date, and headline about the library celebration.

"I had no idea you were so superbly talented," said Jess in awe.

"Oh well, I don't know about that. I go to this painting group once a week, in Portneath. We're doing an exhibition in the town museum for our sins next summer."

"Wow, I'm definitely coming to that. It is absolutely beautiful," said Jess, poring over it. "So, this is the original? I hardly dare breathe . . ."

"Yep, I just wanted to check it was okay with you and then I'll take it into Portneath and get a few copies run off."

"Brilliant, but let me," said Jess. "Poor old Betsy's been stuck outside with a flattening battery, she needs a good run, and I need to get my head out of here. It's been intense over the last couple of days."

Diana gave her a knowing grin and Jess laughed ruefully. Life was complicated, but somehow having a friend to share it made the little fluttering of unease, and the sleepless nights, not too bad after all. It was the kind of thing she would have shared with Mimi. She knew Mimi would have encouraged her to take risks, to be brave and follow her heart, rather than take the safe path that protected her from possible hurt. Maybe—in Mimi's memory—she would try to be brave more often.

Jess was glad to have an excuse to go into Portneath. She needed kitten food for Batou and Ladriya, as well as prints of the launch poster.

It was a beautiful summer's day, the golden heat of the sun freshened by a gentle breeze. It made everyone—Jess included—feel just that little bit more relaxed.

Going out to the car, Jess waved at Joan, who was just arriving at the library.

The lovely old man in the flat cap had switched to a dashing panama in celebration of the sunshine, and he acknowledged the two women with a decorous raise of the headgear. He'd continued to use the little library often and was now certainly working his way through the classic romantic novels Mimi had so loved. Thankfully, they featured highly in the ten boxes of books Mimi had left her. Mimi was a great believer in love. It was a shame that Jess couldn't quite seem to share her optimism. From everything her experience showed her, romance was better left in books.

Betsy the Mini crawled at ten miles an hour past the pond. Jess was terrified of becoming the reviled village resident who flattened one of the white ducks as they trotted endlessly across the road from the green to the pond and back again. It was particularly dangerous with all the juveniles out and about. Born in spring, they weren't quite full-grown and still had a teenage, kamikaze attitude to traffic.

As she drove, relishing the breeze from the open window, she wondered how she would look back on this time, in the future: the exciting, terrifying weeks of deconstructing her life in Bourton-on-the-Marsh—her job, her home, and then these short months being welcomed into the arms of the community in Middlemass. When she looked back on everything in old age, would she see now as the point her life truly started? She allowed herself a little fantasy where—perhaps ten years on—she was still living in Ivy Cottage; with a perfect garden bursting with flowers, fruit, and vegetables; with some form of work, maybe from home, that was fulfilling and challenging. In her picture of this life, the kittens were fully grown, basking in front of the Aga or sitting sphinxlike on the windowsill, and doubtless surveying the food on the table with an acquisitive gleam. There were friends in her fantasy too: noisy, casual suppers around the kitchen table, summer picnics, hectic Christmases. Yes, there would certainly be friends. She knew them already: Becky, Mungo, Diana, Maisie as a young woman, as she would be by then . . . There might even be a man, one day. At this point, infuriatingly, Aidan's face kept intruding on her otherwise perfectly pleasant daydreams. She saw him, unavoidably, at the kitchen table with the rest of them. There was no glamorous Lucie, just Aidan—older now, more solid, more lined—catching her eye, raising an eyebrow at a comment someone had made, exchanging a glance with her because that was all that was needed for the two of them to share a joke.

Consciously she erased Aidan from her fantasy. He was just messing it up, shoving his oar in. Instead, she imagined another man at the table, any man, and tried to summon up the feelings she might have if that were true. The comfortable ease of a relationship, a meeting of minds, bodies, everything that came with it. Children, even.

What if all of this could be Jess's future? There was a part of her daring to make it happen; then there were the old ways of thinking, the ones that told her to avoid change, to dodge risk and adventure in order to avoid pain . . . But perhaps, perhaps, those old ways were not relevant to her life anymore. What if Mimi was right? Hannah might even be right. Now, there was a thought. The two most important women in her life so far seemed determined to challenge her on her old beliefs. Maybe there was something in it.

Shaking her head to reenter the present, Jess took in the now familiar scenery of the journey. There was the DIY store at the edge of the town—the one she'd been to with Aidan to get the shelves for the telephone box. She sighed in exasperation with herself. It was funny how all her thoughts led back to that man.

She was at the top of the hill now, by the retail park with

an interiors store, a large supermarket, and a place you could get car tires changed. Portneath inhabitants who were keen on their cars, homes, and stomachs were well catered for. There was another cluster of single-story buildings on the way down the hill toward the main part of the town. She now knew this was Portneath Academy and Leisure Centre, the secondary school that Maisie had just started traveling to on the bus the autumn before. There was wire fencing everywhere, and the flat-roofed buildings looked shabby, but she knew that was no indicator of the quality of the school. Aidan rated it highly and thought it was the best place for Maisie. She hoped the poor girl would be allowed to stay there—to stay living in the village with her loving father. Lucie had gone quiet about her plans—as far as Jess had heard. She hoped Aidan had confided in Becky, because she knew Becky was as good as her word: she would do everything she could to help if Lucie tried to make good on her threats.

Poor Maisie. Jess's heart ached for her. And for Aidan.

She parked in the car park at the top of town. Betsy was certainly smaller than Aidan's Land Rover, but Jess still didn't fancy her wing mirrors' chances against the steep twists and turns of the road down the hill to the sea.

Her spirits never failed to be raised by the Georgian and Victorian terraces in ice-cream colors, fronting right onto the steep and narrow road. As a holiday town, Portneath had a good selection of fudge shops, cafés, and shops selling everything from newspapers to shrimp nets. But other retailers probably struggled, she imagined, especially off-season when the holidaymakers—swelling the local population and spending money there—were gone.

As she came out onto the road running along the harbor wall, there was seemingly a vast choice of places to buy fish and chips, cheap, lurid clothes, and burgers. Along the row closest to the sea, there was the little kiosk selling those divine crab rolls; the sight of it made Jess's mouth water. She recalled Aidan's brief carefree mood all those months ago, his weather-bronzed face relaxed and smiling, with a sunburst of creases around his eyes, and his wavy hair tousled by the wind. And then Lucie had appeared.

It was funny how things could change so dramatically, so quickly.

Preoccupied with her thoughts, she must have missed the turning for the printing shop, but miraculously—as if she had magicked it up with the power of her mind—she found a tiny, ramshackle shop, just off the main drag, selling pet equipment. There was a rusty-sounding clang as she pushed the door open releasing a pungent smell of birdseed and sawdust. The kittens needed bigger collars already—ideally ones which could grow with them—and she was desperate to find them a compelling enough selection of cat toys to stop them climbing the curtains. She worried about them being injured when they hurled themselves from nearly curtain-rail height onto the floor. The end of the sofa was also starting to suffer from being a focus of their climbing adventures too. They used their claws as crampons to scale Jess's precious inherited furniture, apparently for no other reason than that—like Everest—it was there.

She loaded up on toys, collars—fluorescent ones to keep them safe outside at night—and a little stack of proper tinned kitten food that had smaller-than-average lumps in. They ate so fast they occasionally choked on the ordinary adult stuff Paddy stocked. Jess would be heartbroken if anything happened to either of them. She took her responsibilities seriously. They were certainly characters. Batou, in particular, didn't seem able to eat without his front paws planted elbow-deep in the food bowl, but Ladriya was more fastidious nowadays. She was the first to be toilet-trained too. They both understood to go out into the garden now; and currently she left the door propped ajar for them, in the daytime at least. As winter came, she would have to see about getting a cat flap installed. Planning ahead, she added an electronic one to the teetering pile of kit she was holding. Maybe she would be able to persuade Aidan to help her install it.

Once she had a full shopping bag of pet supplies, she headed out to find the print shop and off-loaded Diana's precious master poster.

She was just walking back up the street in the direction she thought the printer might be, when she suddenly came to nearly touching distance with a broad chest she instantly recognized.

"Is that lot for Booboo and Leafmold?" Aidan asked, pointing at the bulging bag she was carrying.

"I'm not going to rise to that," Jess retorted, her heart pounding at the unexpected encounter. "You know perfectly well that's not their names."

"Okay, but I genuinely can't remember the real ones. Maisie was really touched you went with her suggestions, you know."

"Remind her she's welcome to come and see them whenever she likes," Jess said, trying to tell herself that this little catch in her throat wasn't attraction. It couldn't be. They'd agreed. "Anytime she likes. They're growing really fast. How is she? I mean, with all this going on between you and . . ." Nope. It was strange. She just didn't want to say the woman's name aloud.

"Lucie," Aidan supplied, his face clouding over. "Not great. Maisie's fine though. Looking forward to the end of term." He paused, obviously wondering how much to say. "I had this fear Lucie had told her about all this shit she's trying to pull off with moving her to Bristol. But I know Maisie: she

wouldn't be able to hide it if she had. So that's something."
He lapsed into preoccupied silence, glaring at the pavement.

Jess wondered if he had forgotten she was there, and shifted
awkwardly from foot to foot.

"The trouble is," he went on, at last, "I don't want Lucie
suddenly popping up and saying Maisie should go to Bristol
for the summer holidays either. They start next week. It would
be the thin end of the wedge."

Jess felt terrible for him. Under his summer tan his face
was ashen, except for the deep shadows under his eyes.

Her forehead creased in worry.

"God, I'm sorry," he said, rubbing his face. "I'm doing it
again, dragging you into my problems. And why should I
expect you to care after—"

"I care," she reassured him, reaching out her free hand to
touch his forearm. "I care about you both, very much. Did
you speak to Becky? About the custody thing, I mean?"

"Yes, I did," he said, the clouds lifting a little. "You were
right that she's up on family law. Anyhow, she tells me Lucie can't file a residency thing—what did she call it, a "child
arrangements" order—in court, until she can prove there's
been mediation."

"Mediation sounds like a great idea."

"Yeah? Well, you say that. But we've had one formal session
so far. It didn't go too well. Lucie's all over the place. I don't
think she knows herself what she wants. We just have to hope
I can persuade her to sort it out with me without going to
court again. That would be a nightmare. Becky's warned me
the judge might order for Maisie to appear. What a thing to
ask of a twelve-year-old kid."

There was a silence. Another shopper pointedly went into
the road to get around them, giving them both dirty looks,
and muttering.

"Listen," said Aidan, putting his hand up to touch her arm and then thinking better of it, "I really am sorry about—well—us."

"It's completely fine," insisted Jess briskly. "As you said yourself—you don't want to explore 'us'—not that there is an 'us'—and can't be an 'us' with Lucie threatening what she's . . . Honestly, it's fine."

"I'd like to tell you how I feel," Aidan persisted.

"Oh God—I mean—oh good," Jess joked humorlessly.

"Listen, hear me out," he continued. "It's true I need to put Maisie first, always, and—as you know—Lucie comes to stay. You have to be wondering why, seeing as we're divorced. And then here I am going around kissing other women . . ."

"You kissed me," admitted Jess. "I don't know about all the 'other women.'"

"I think you know there aren't any 'other women'—and I kissed you because, I admit, I wanted to, and I still want to. All the time, actually. Now, even."

Jess's heart flipped uncomfortably.

"Okay," she said. "So, talk."

"I have to play this carefully, for Maisie's sake. But you deserve to know what gives . . . with Lucie being around for days at a time. So, look," he said, striving for clarity, "when she comes to the cottage she stays in the spare room. She doesn't like it, but she knows that's the deal. It doesn't stop her trying it on, mind you," he admitted, "just like she was doing when you met her on the quay, making out it's more than it is between us."

People were streaming either side of them now, some squeezed up against the shop front and some stepping into the road. Aidan and Jess were oblivious, as if they were in a bubble.

"Okay, so she wants it both ways; I get it," said Jess, impatient now, and feeling braver. "Why do you let her stay with you? You have to admit that is . . . unusual."

"I'll tell you," said Aidan, holding Jess's upper arms gently but firmly, as if to focus her attention as he talked. "Rightly or wrongly, the reason I let her get away with being possessive is because I don't want to do anything that would cause Maisie to see less of her mother than she already does. I'm fully aware Lucie comes back largely to make sure she's still got me dangling rather than to see her own child." He shook his head. "Unbelievable, really. I wonder more and more who I married. But as long as she keeps coming back, I don't care what her reasons are. Does that make any sense at all?"

"Of course," said Jess. "I do understand, honestly, but why did you even go ahead and divorce? Why rock the boat?"

He smiled grimly. "It was selfish of me, but I instigated the divorce because I wanted it and I thought it was safe to. I admit I've wanted to be able to move on. Clearly, I was wrong. Now she's threatening to turn Maisie's life inside out and it's partly out of envy, seeing you and me getting on well. It's extraordinary but I actually think in some ways she wants me to resurrect our marriage, not because she really wants me but because she wants to exert her power. So . . ." He sighed deeply. "I'm not going to drag you into this mess. Out of respect for you. You deserve better."

Feeling hollow and wondering whether respect was everything it was cracked up to be, Jess nodded her acceptance. If Maisie were her daughter—if she were in Aidan's position—she would do the same. At least they had that in common, she and Aidan, she admitted to herself glumly—their matching moral compass.

Aidan showed Jess where the print shop was, and the cheerful girl with blue hair who was running the place helpfully did three A3 and six A4 color copies of the poster, which Aidan dutifully admired on Jess's insistence.

She felt a tug of regret when Aidan made his excuses and went off to complete his to-do list in town, but she could hardly follow him around like a little dog. To console herself, and to pass some time, she lugged her shopping to the seafront and treated herself to a crab roll, eating it on the harbor wall in memory of that all-too-brief carefree time together before Lucie started to mess things up.

As she sat there with the breeze in her hair, her thoughts then filled with worry, mainly around her complete failure so far to look for any form of work. Her holiday from employment couldn't last forever. By the autumn it was essential that she was back earning a salary, as Mimi's little pot of savings was dwindling fast. Public libraries might be on the wane, but librarianship was her skill. She would pull out her old laptop and get down to it. Today.

Chapter Seventeen

The job sites made for grim reading, and her searches through a couple of other recruitment websites weren't much better. Librarians, as a breed, were fighting for survival. There were a few junior jobs which even Jess realized were below her. Many of the positions were not only poorly paid but also part-time. They would not be enough to keep body and soul together. Her heart sank. She knew it was going to be a challenge, but she hadn't expected it was going to be quite this bleak. She wondered about researcher posts, but they all wanted relevant experience which she didn't have, and in any case they were poorly paid as well. All in all, there were just two jobs that were even worth considering and both were far, far away from Middlemass.

Putting it aside for now, she gave in to the call of the garden as a welcome distraction. She busied herself tying in the raspberry canes with new twine, and then checked under the broad strawberry leaves for ripe fruit. There was one gloriously scarlet fruit; the rest were still hard and pale or tiny and green. She picked the single ripe strawberry and popped it into her mouth, savoring the intense, sun-drenched sweetness.

All around her in the garden was burgeoning with vitality and growth: roses unfurling in the sunshine, going blowsy and dropping their petals too quickly for her to even cut them for the house. There was such abundance, she was never without a fat posy of short-stemmed rose blooms in the vase Mimi always used for them: a vivid, barge ware jug with copper luster that sat on the kitchen table, just like it always did.

This was a life she might not be able to enjoy much longer.

"Come and have a cup of tea with me before I murder my children," pleaded Becky, when Jess eventually found her ringing phone under a pile of seed catalogues.

A short time later, Becky's two youngest children were corralled in front of a DVD and Becky and Jess were hiding from them at the kitchen island with large mugs of tea and chocolate brownies.

"He did look a bit down," said Jess, telling Becky about having bumped into Aidan in town.

"I'm concerned for him, and Maisie too, if I'm honest," admitted Becky, picking at her brownie fretfully. "Did he tell you we'd spoken about Lucie's legal challenge?"

Jess nodded. "I'm sure you can't tell me about it. Professional conduct and all that."

"Yeah, I can't say much, although I'm just advising as a friend. For now, at least."

"Could you represent him in court if you needed to?"

"I wouldn't stand up and speak for him. It would be inappropriate with my level of experience and with me not attached to an actual law firm. He could speak for himself—and I think he should—but I can be there to direct and advise him if he wants me to be."

"Could Lucie do this thing she's talking about? Claim custody?"

"Sole residency. Technically, she could—that's the concern. But Aidan's got a lot going for him. They were married when Maisie was born, so he has automatic parental responsibilities and rights. Contrary to urban myth, individual parents absolutely don't have the right to make decisions for their children without the other parent's involvement unless—and it's rare—they have sole residency, which she totally doesn't. At the moment, at least. In any sensible court, it ought to be given to Aidan, in my view, not Lucie."

"Ought?" queried Jess.

"Only that courts can be biased toward the mother," Becky admitted.

As awful as the situation was, Jess felt a little swelling of pride in her chest seeing Becky take control. She was serious, incisive, and totally precise—very different from the mummy-Becky she had seen so far. The idea of her in a severely tailored, wildly flattering suit, with a large corner office—ruler of all she surveyed in a slick city law firm—seemed entirely plausible.

"The mediation meeting last week was sticky, I gather," Becky went on, "but I've told Aidan to sit tight. We'll soon see what her next move is."

"We need a WhatsApp group for the launch," suggested Diana when Jess took the finished posters and a pot of freshly made rhubarb jam over to her the next morning.

"I suppose you want me to download it then."

"You mean you don't even have WhatsApp? You are a funny old stick. Text then?" Diana said as she prized the lid off the rhubarb jam and dipped her fingertip in to taste. "Yum," she said, closing her eyes in blissful appreciation.

Jess smiled, pleased that—between the job and Aidan—something had gone right so far . . . Well, she wasn't going there. "Okay," she said. "I'll just jump-start my steam-powered mobile phone. It's nearly out of battery and I haven't seen the charging cord for a few days. I'm not even sure I've got everyone's number—"

"I can give you whoever's missing."

"Great, so, we've only got a few weeks. You know, I was

thinking I might make Sunday lunch for everyone this weekend. That way we can talk and divide up the jobs. Sound like a plan?"

"Good idea, but are you sure? Who are you thinking of inviting?"

"Pretty much everyone I know in Middlemass," replied Jess. "Becky, Rakesh and the children, Maisie, you, Mungo . . . and Aidan, I suppose," she added, reluctantly.

Diana's eyebrows shot up at the sound of his name but—with palpable effort—she managed to say nothing.

Jess nodded her gratitude at her friend's forbearance. "Yes, so I would invite a few of the other families, and people like Paddy," she went on. "But he'll be working because he's always open. I could invite Muriel and Joan too—they are both absolutely lovely on their own—but I wonder about the atmosphere if I had them here together."

"I wouldn't," agreed Diana. "As it is, you won't have room in the kitchen to sit everyone down, will you?"

"Not even close, but I'm counting on the weather," Jess replied. "What are our chances for a lunch outside?"

"Fair to middling, but you're awfully British for thinking of it," said Diana, getting into the spirit of the thing. "And it is July, for heaven's sake, so you ought to be all right. I salute you. What can I bring?"

Jess got up early to put the lamb in the Aga that Sunday. It was the biggest lamb shoulder the butcher in Portneath could find for her and was nearly too big for the roasting tin. She laid it on a bed of sliced red onions with olive oil and a good sprinkle of salt and pepper and popped it into the oven. It was a simple way of cooking she knew always turned out well. In an hour or so she could chuck in some red wine, cover it with foil, and put it in the bottom oven for as long as she wanted.

By lunchtime it would be cooked to perfection and falling off the bone. The wine and onions, along with the meat juices, made the most amazing base for gravy. Adding in some fluffy mashed potatoes, she hoped she would have created a meal everyone would enjoy.

There was plenty more to be getting on with in the meantime. Maisie had come over with a message from Aidan that she was to help out in any way needed.

Maisie was great company, chatting cheerfully about anything and everything that popped into her head: from what her friend Lola said in the playground, to her imminent summer holidays and what she was going to do with them, to her riding lesson next week and how much she was looking forward to it. Her initial shyness with Jess seemed to have passed.

Jess couldn't help but notice that Maisie seemed even taller than when she had last seen her only a couple of weeks ago. She had her mother's pretty features, endless legs, and thick dark-brown hair. She was going to be a beauty. She was also extremely handy. Together, Maisie and Jess managed to haul out the two foldable tables Jess had unearthed while clearing out the shed. Impressively, Maisie was willing enough to brush them down with a stiff brush, being less frightened of potential spiders than Jess was. They set them up on the grass in the orchard, end to end between two trees, so that the long table they created was all in dappled shade. She wasn't too fussed about them being completely level, but Maisie did a good job finding stones and bits of wood that could be wedged under the legs where needed. Chairs were going to be a problem, though. Jess calculated how many they needed if the children all sat down to eat at least some of the time. There were only six wooden chairs in the kitchen, so Maisie ran backward and forward tirelessly from Quince Cottage to provide another six. That would probably do.

An hour into preparations things looked as if they were coming together nicely, especially after she rummaged in the airing cupboard and found two of Mimi's best cotton sheets with embroidered cutwork tops. Laid end to end, they looked a lot like plain white tablecloths with beautiful lacy edges. Some bright turquoise linen napkins—intermixed with a few pretty green floral ones that Mimi had had for as long as she could remember—complemented them nicely.

Diana turned up in a rush just as Maisie and Jess were hunting in the cupboard for enough drinking glasses. "I'm on my way to church," she announced.

Jess looked surprised.

"I'm only going because I'm down to do the reading," Diana admitted. She exclaimed over the good smells coming from the Aga and handed over a carrier bag stuffed with French beans. "I've got so many I don't know what to do with them, so you'd be doing me a favor. I've topped and tailed them for you. I thought you'd have your hands full. Now please excuse me, I must just go and have a quick pray. Shall I say one for you?"

"I'm past redemption. Say one for the success of the library."

"Will do. I'll be over straight after I've chatted up the vicar. I'll be needing a glass of wine by then."

There was now a high, blue, and cloudless sky with a fierce heat, but the dappled shade and gentle breeze blowing in from the meadow made the little orchard the most delightful place to be. It was a bit of a walk from the kitchen, but worth it, with its flower-studded meadow grass and apple trees bejeweled with small, bright green apples. The harvest was going to be amazing. There was a pear tree too, also laden with soon-to-be-picked fruit.

The chicken coop needed a coat of creosote before the winter and well before she housed any chickens in it. Its silvery-gray appearance rebuked her every time she came down to this part of the garden. She would ask at lunch where she could get some chickens; someone was bound to know. Probably no cockerel, though. With all the noise that would bring with it, her new friends and neighbors would quickly go off her.

Having laid the table, she got Maisie to pick all the raspberries she could find, along with the first of the beautiful cultivated blackberries, which were juicier and fatter than their wild relations. While Maisie was dealing with the soft fruit, Jess took the chance to grab the last two empty jam jars from her rhubarb jam making and used them to do some little flower vases for the table. She wanted something low, so it didn't get in the way of conversation, but that was a given, because the flowers she had in the garden were all on very short stems.

She had just a few blooms in each, but they looked extremely pretty with fistfuls of the fat, marshmallow-smelling roses broken up with some little sprigs of wild carrot from the meadow beyond the gate. She spread the pretty patchwork quilt from the spare bed on a patch of grass near the table in case Becky and Rak's lot would prefer to have a picnic there rather than sit at the table with the adults.

They managed to drum up enough tableware in the end. The ill-matching wineglasses, water glasses, knives, forks, and spoons added to the air of haphazard charm.

"Now," Jess said to Maisie, once they were satisfied the table was complete and had come back into the kitchen, "I'm going to teach you how to make the most amazing pudding. It will sound totally bizarre, and I can almost guarantee you won't have eaten it before, but you're going to love it. Ready?"

Maisie grinned. "Go on then, I've never met a pudding I didn't like."

"Now, you watch this oatmeal in the frying pan, all right?

Keep stirring and turning it and take it off the heat when it's nicely toasted."

"That. Is. Weird," Maisie said, incredulously, stirring as instructed with a furrowed brow. "Fried porridge? Seriously?"

"Ha. That's nothing. When the oats are done, I want you to whip this cream." This part she was delighted to have Maisie for. With no electric whisk, it needed youthful energy.

"What now?" said Maisie, puffing with effort, when the cream was nicely thickened.

"Then, it's in with the honey and Scotch. Folding gently, see? And then we're going to layer it with the raspberries, blackberries, and oats in this glass trifle dish. Trust me, it'll be amazing. At least, if it isn't amazing, Becky will definitely let us know, as she's the arbiter of all things Scottish."

"That's pudding? Are you sure?" Maisie's quizzical look made Jess smile.

"Trust me, grasshopper. Now follow my instructions and, while you're at it, tell me about your favorite manga characters."

Chapter Eighteen

People were prompt in Middlemass, Jess noticed.

Within two minutes of midday the little kitchen was crowded with people shuffling around each other and talking nineteen to the dozen. Jess was busy welcoming everyone and exclaiming over all the things they had brought with them. Mungo had brought three excellent bottles of burgundy plus a couple of bottles of champagne "to get started." Becky handed over the most delectable handmade chocolates from a little shop in Portneath. As well as the earlier French beans, Diana had produced a lavish bouquet of flowers which, she assured Jess, were all picked from her own garden. Aidan turned up with a cheeseboard he had made himself from a slab of a walnut tree he had felled, complete with a selection of locally made cheeses, pressed on him by a grateful client the day before.

The only person not exclaiming and shouting at everyone else was Rakesh, who was standing to one side, calmly avoiding the mayhem. He looked tall, dark, and handsome in a snow-white shirt and black jeans. Noticing his apartness, Jess warmed to him even more. He too preferred to quietly watch, just like her. She saw this now, not as aloofness, but—in his case—the calm reserve of the quietly, supremely confident. They seemed so opposite, Rakesh and Becky, but Jess thought a little of Rakesh's confidence might be just what Becky needed.

With a bit of shooing and encouragement from Jess, who was trying to get on with things, Diana drove the little party in front of her down the narrow brick path through the vegetable garden to the little orchard. This left Jess in peace to get on with the final bits of cooking: boiling the water for the beans, mashing the potato with a shocking amount of butter, and making the gravy. The lamb was now resting on a large oval serving dish, under a lid of foil with a tea towel on top for insulation. The skin was treacle brown and the meat so tender Jess had been able to draw the bones straight out of it. Using two carving forks she pulled the meat into a huge pile of juicy shreds and then—because the kittens were mewing at her feet, driven insane by the marvelous smell—she put some morsels of crispy fat into their bowl for them. She was sure they would make a thorough mess with it, but she would worry about that later.

The open doorway darkened as Aidan appeared. "This is your wine," he said, handing her a flute of champagne. "Also, I've come to carry things out."

"Wow, this is amazing," she said, looking at the glass respectfully after taking a sip. She was painfully conscious of him standing so close in the little room. In just two steps she could slip her hands around his waist and rest her head on his broad chest. Banishing these intrusive thoughts from her mind, she smiled at him brightly and took another sip. Goodness, this stuff could go down far too easily.

"Champagne is such a treat. Mungo is kind."

"He's been telling us it's not champagne," Aidan said. "It's English sparkling wine, apparently."

"Tastes like champagne," said Jess.

"Tell him that, I think he'll be chuffed. There's some family link with the vineyard, apparently. It's in Sussex."

"Oh, that reminds me, talking about wine," said Jess, "I've got red wine in the larder to go with the lamb."

"There's some decent-looking bottles of red out there already."

"Of course, Mungo."

"Yep. Am I taking this?" he said, picking up the large oval serving dish of lamb in one hand as if it weighed no more than an empty plate. "And this?" pointing at the pan of mash.

"Yes, but hang on, I was going to put it in a nice bowl."

"If you must," said Aidan, his face telling her what he thought of such fripperies. "I was going to say, 'Why make more washing-up?' But seeing as Maisie and I'll be doing it . . ."

"Maisie might think differently. She's been an absolute star already today," Jess said, dusting off her favorite green china serving bowl, a molded cabbage leaf design. She had a similar one in white for Diana's beans.

"Right," said Aidan, picking up the huge bowl of mash with his free hand. "Anything else?"

"Just the beans and gravy," Jess said, picking them up. "I hope it's not too hot for people to want hot food."

There were lots of appreciative noises when Aidan and Jess arrived, and it didn't take long to get everyone served, with the usual flurries of "Who still needs mash?," "Yum, amazing gravy," "Where's the spoon for the beans? Oh, there it is on your plate"; with Angus setting up a steady litany of complaint about the things he didn't like—all of it, apparently—and Becky cajoling him to just try.

Mungo's wine was perfect: earthy, full, and unctuous. Even Maisie had a little bit, which she pulled a face at.

"Ah, so it looks like my daughter's not going to be much of a drinker when she grows up," declared Aidan. "Unlike her mother," he added under his breath, too low for Maisie to hear.

"Is this your own crab apple jelly?" Diana asked Jess, scooping more of it onto her plate. "So much better than redcurrant with this. It's the best I've ever tasted."

"Good," said Jess, "because nobody leaves without taking at least one jar of it with them. And I've got jam I've just made too." She looked around the table. "It's so lovely to have you all here," she said, as the conversation lulled while they tucked in. There was a tiny break in her voice.

Aidan noticed and looked up at her swiftly. "It's great to be here," he replied, stoutly, raising his glass and drawing attention away so she could compose herself. "A toast," he declared. "To superb food, fine weather, and friends, new and old."

"Friends," they all chorused.

Jess dabbed away tears with her napkin, hoping no one saw. "And," she said, raising her own glass, "to the telephone-box library."

"To the telephone-box library," they all chorused again.

"Talking of which," said Diana, putting her knife and fork together neatly, "we have work to do."

"Pudding first," said Jess, getting up to fetch it.

The huge, beautiful old crystal bowl turned the layers of raspberries, oats, and honey-laced cream into a work of art.

"Cranachan!" exclaimed Becky, appreciatively. "Food of the gods, everyone, a true Scots pudding."

Maisie piped up and gave them a rundown of how she made it as they tucked in, and it was unanimously agreed that it looked beautiful, tasted amazing but—as a concept—sounded totally weird.

She might have been a tiny bit heavy-handed with the Scotch, thought Jess, as she plowed through her portion. It really had quite a kick to it. It was probably just as well she had bought choc ices for the younger children to have instead. Isla and Angus solemnly ate theirs on the quilt Mimi had painstakingly stitched during her childhood, not dropping as much melted chocolate onto it as Jess had feared. She was pleased to see Becky relaxing over her meal, and Rak being the one to jump up and wipe the kids' faces with his spotless handkerchief when they had finished.

"I'll never eat again," groaned Diana, as she pushed her bowl away. "That was all incredible. I am now going to have to go on a diet for the rest of my life."

"Can we do the library launch discussion lying down, do you think?" asked Aidan, splaying himself flat on his back on the newly vacated quilt. Isla and Angus were now running around the meadow screeching happily as Hamish and Maisie chased them.

"I think we could all do with a bit of a lie down after that astonishing meal," concurred Mungo, joining him, but lounging back elegantly.

"You really look the part, Mungo," said Diana. He was wearing impeccable cream flannels, with a striped shirt and a battered panama. "This whole thing looks like something out of a Merchant Ivory film. I love it. But, inevitably, down to business . . . Jess?"

"Can I just ask a stupid question, though?" asked Aidan, lifting his head from the quilt. "Why are we doing an opening ceremony for the library when it's already been open for months?"

"It's not an opening ceremony," said Diana, "it's a celebration of a fait accompli—an acknowledgment of success. Plus," she admitted, "it's a little bit strategic because of the rumblings over this ridiculous defibrillator idea, which I will not mar this occasion by discussing. So, it's going to be on Harvest Home day, which hopefully means people are already out and about. It makes perfect sense to do it then. We need to make sure everyone who might benefit actually knows that it's there and it's for them."

"It's going really well though, I thought," persisted Aidan. "There was a queue of school mums there just the other day. About nine o'clock, it was. Cars dumped everywhere. It was a complete pain," he added, frowning, and reminding Jess suddenly—with a wry smile—of the first time they met.

"It's definitely busy just after school drop-off," chimed in Jess. "I've been noticing that. And it's not a pain, it's great," she insisted boldly.

Aidan accepted the rebuke philosophically.

"It *is* great," persisted Diana, "but I'm all in favor of making the effort to give it a proper boost on Harvest Home day, for reasons already outlined."

"Hear, hear," said Mungo obediently.

"We honestly don't need to do anything arduous today, or even next week," said Jess, reassuringly.

"Thank heaven," interjected Diana.

Jess smiled. "Diana's already done a lovely poster," she told everyone. "By the way, I've spoken to Amanda at the school and she's going to put the details in the school's end-of-term newsletter. Obviously, the celebration itself is during the school holidays but she's keen to get the school involved in some way during the autumn term.

"Anyhow," she went on, pressing her hands together, "I do need a few volunteers for bits and bobs. First, I think we need to decorate the area, just a bit. Maybe some balloons or bunting?"

"Balloons *and* bunting," insisted Becky. "And a ribbon to cut. Leave it to me. Rak and I had bunting for our wedding which I've kept; I'll dig it out. And I'm pretty sure I've still got balloons left over from Hamish's last birthday party too."

"Perfect, that was easy," said Jess, mentally crossing several things off the list.

"Good, now we'll need someone to cut the ribbon," said Jess.

"Like who?" said Becky.

"Chair of the parish council?" suggested Diana.

"That's you."

"Yep."

"So, that was easy."

"I know, I try hard to stay accessible to my fans and followers, despite my exalted status."

"That's awfully humble of you," muttered Aidan, closing his eyes again and relaxing in the golden sunshine.

Rakesh's bleeper had gone off during pudding and he had been pacing up and down the edge of the meadow talking intensely on his phone ever since. Now, he approached Jess and apologized. "I'm so sorry to rush off, the patient I had in surgery on Friday has developed complications. I must go in. Thank you for lunch, it really was spectacular."

And then he was gone, leaving Becky looking irritated but resigned.

"Doesn't he have some acolyte who can deal with these things at the weekend?" Diana asked.

"You'd think so, wouldn't you," Becky said, sourly. "That was the acolyte on the phone, I suspect. But what we need to appreciate is Rak would rather deal with important, clever things like brain surgery than do his parenting stint. Oh, but ignore me everyone, I can't win. He's God Almighty in scrubs, I know that. I can't expect normal husband behavior. Sorry."

"There's nothing to apologize for," said Jess. "And the children are fine just running around. You can relax."

"Have another glass of wine," said Mungo, reaching to fill her glass. "Now, what's next?"

Jess cleared her throat. "Diana is putting up the posters, but if someone could help with those, that would be great."

"Me," volunteered Mungo from his reclined position. "I'd be glad to."

"Great, and by the way, Paddy has confirmed he's happy to put a poster in his shop window."

"I'll remember that," said Mungo. "And I've got plenty more of that fizz we were drinking. I'll bring some. We should probably smash a bottle against the telephone box like they do with ships."

"That would be a tragic waste of good wine," laughed Jess. "And broken glass everywhere would be a problem, so better not. We'll just drink it, please."

"And we need someone to do other publicity," said Diana. "Not just posters. I think the local media would be interested."

"I'll do that," said Becky. "I listen to local radio; you just phone stuff in. Plus, I've got the local newspaper contacts from a thing we did at school for the PTA. That's no problem."

"You're doing loads, Becky. Are you sure?" asked Jess, concerned, as her friend refilled her wineglass haphazardly.

"It's the kind of thing I can do in between nose-blowing and bum-wiping, it'll be light relief, to be honest."

"Anything else?" asked Mungo.

"Social media," said Jess. "Can we all post on Instagram, tweet, and whatever?"

"Sure," Diana said with a nod. "I've got a few Instagram followers from posting my art. I'll take some photos and share them."

"Twitter's my thing," said Becky. "I'll post on there, for what it's worth."

"Great. If everyone who actually does all that kind of stuff could do that, it would be great. I'm not even sure I can remember my sign-in details for Instagram, but still . . . Actually, I think that's everything," said Jess abruptly, realizing her mental list was now all allocated. "Except to say—critically—that all this publicity is a good opportunity to mention the petition to keep the library open. The petition forms in the library are filling up fairly fast, but we are preaching to the converted there. We need to be sure we are reaching new people too, so don't forget to ask for signatures every time we mention the library to whoever we are talking to from now on."

"Brilliant," said Diana. "Well said, and now I hereby declare this meeting closed," she added, holding her glass out to be refilled.

After everyone else had left, Aidan and Maisie were as good as their word on the washing-up, their banter providing a companionable backdrop as Jess finished bringing everything in from the orchard.

Jess was able to spend all of Sunday evening—when she was finally, thankfully, alone—finishing the job of sticking color-coded labels on books to make it easier for her to tidy the library. She was now needing to sort it out at least once a day—it was amazing how people took out a book and then put it back in any old place. Also, not all the books were stamped with her special *Littlest Library* stamp yet, as it had arrived after they went out, but she decided against doing the stamping herself. It would be a great job for Angus and Hamish next time Becky needed some respite. With the long summer holidays stretching ahead, Jess suspected child-friendly activities were definitely going to be a good thing to provide.

It was lovely to be making plans with her friends for the coming months, but she dared not look too far ahead. There were many reasons why that would be a bad idea. If fate had different things in store for Jess, the pain of leaving Middlemass would be all the sharper for having allowed herself to put down roots too firmly.

*

When Jess came across Diana as she set out for Paddy's shop she was struck by the older woman's serious demeanor, especially when Diana admitted it was concerning news about the library.

"Fill me in," said Jess firmly, but with an edge of anxiety. "I'm right in the thick of this. I want to know."

"I didn't see the point in dragging you into every cough and spit of this ridiculous thing but—well—okay," said Diana, who had capitulated reluctantly and brought Jess into her little kitchen to bring her up to speed. "It's a storm in a teacup, honestly.

"All right, so we had another meeting last night and I've had no choice but to accept April's position that the decision about the library was made unconstitutionally. But"—she held up her hand in response to Jess's squeak of dismay—"even given that, all we have to do now is get more signatures on our petition than on hers. She's only got sixty-eight, so that won't be difficult."

"But what if we don't? What's the worst that can happen?" said Jess, not sharing Diana's confidence.

"Then . . ." sighed Diana. "I don't know, I suppose it'll have to close," she admitted.

Jess sat down, her heart hammering. "Now I wish I hadn't asked."

"But it won't come to that," said Diana firmly, patting her on the shoulder. "And this is why I didn't drag you in. Don't upset yourself. I'm the chairman and I'll not be pushed around by my own traitorous, self-aggrandizing clerk. Leave it with me."

*

"The man in the panama hat," as Jess had now started to call him, arrived at the little library just as Jess was finishing her morning stint of tidying. She usually made herself scarce when people turned up to browse. She didn't want to make people feel she was intruding on their choices, but here he was, in person, his bicycle propped against her garden wall.

"You're Jess, the lady who set up the library, aren't you? I've been hoping for an opportunity to introduce myself and to thank you. My name is Gordon."

They shook hands, formally.

"I am so pleased you're using it," said Jess, smiling. "What sort of books do you prefer?" she asked, knowing the answer perfectly well.

"Don't let appearances deceive. I am a sucker for a good classic romance," he admitted. "Austen, Brontë, all those and more."

"It's so brilliant to hear a man say that."

"Other men don't know what they're missing," he agreed. "My wife was a great respecter of the power of love."

She didn't fail to notice the past tense.

"Yes, I'm afraid our own, forty-six-year love story came to an end two years ago," he confirmed, catching her gentle look of inquiry. "It's been two years, five months, and two weeks to be exact, but the books we both enjoyed are a great comfort," he said, holding up the copy of *Frenchman's Creek*, which he had tucked under his arm. "This was a favorite of hers and, as Ms. du Maurier tells us herself," he said, opening the book and reading, " 'I will shed no more tears, like a spoilt child. For whatever happens we have had what we have had. No one can take that from us.' " He closed the book carefully, keeping the bookmark on the page, and sighed. "And that is what I must do: shed no more tears. Not easy, most days," he said, with a quaver in his voice.

He whisked out a brilliant white handkerchief and mopped his face, self-consciously.

"I'm so sorry," said Jess, putting her hand on his forearm, distraught at his tears. "It means so much to me that the little library is a comfort."

"It is, it is," he said with a sigh. "But I don't know why I'm reading you quotes from your own book, that's clearly one of your favorites, too."

"I do love *Frenchman's Creek*," said Jess, taking it from him, "but I don't remember . . ." The book obediently fell open where there was a delicate pencil underline of the quote. Tears crowded her eyes, blurring the dog-eared page. It must have been Mimi. She adored *Frenchman's Creek* too. Between them, they daringly admitted sometimes they preferred it to *Rebecca*; and at some point, possibly years ago, Mimi had marked out those few words. It was probably long before her death, Jess told herself, and of course, she must have been thinking of losing Jess's grandfather—the great love affair of her life—but she must also have known Jess would one day have to continue life without her too. The words were so extraordinarily apt, in that moment, a shiver ran down Jess's spine.

"Thank you," she said to Gordon. "Really, thank you, you've made my day."

The following morning brought no good news on the job front. She had dutifully gone back through the websites and looked through them forensically. This week there were a couple of new ones to apply for, but it also reminded her she had heard nothing from the two rather lackluster applications she had made online a couple of weeks previously. It might have been for jobs she didn't really want, but not even getting a reply was demoralizing, all the same.

*

"You're not helping much," complained Jess to Hannah that evening.

"Stop applying for such crappy jobs then. You're better than that."

"It's flattering you're so certain I can pick and choose. You don't seem to realize that librarian jobs aren't exactly growing on trees here in the UK."

"Do something else then."

"Not qualified to do anything else," said Jess, sulkily.

"Rubbish. You could do loads of stuff. Hit me with another."

"Fine," said Jess, reading from the jobs she had circled in the paper. "How about 'Senior Supervisory Librarian, directing all aspects of a full-service library program and supervising a team of library personnel'?"

"How much?"

Jess mentioned the salary.

"Not bad," said Hannah, grudgingly. "Where?"

"Birmingham."

"Obviously not then," said Hannah, exasperated. "If it's not commutable from Middlemass, then no way."

"I may have to move."

"Out of the question," said Hannah, dismissing her protests with a wave of the hand. "You've got something really special there. I'm not having you throwing it away."

"Ivy Cottage is special, and I'm pretty sure I've added value to it, with all the repairs and redecorating," said Jess. "If I sold it now, I'd probably make money. You have to be objective about these things."

"Who says you do? Finding Ivy Cottage was miraculous. You don't just chuck that away for a few grand's profit," reprimanded Hannah. "Living in Middlemass is changing you. You're becoming—I don't know—more *you*." Hannah searched for words. "More open, somehow."

"Well, I'm sure that's all lovely," said Jess, matter-of-factly, "but it doesn't matter how 'open' and 'me' I am, if I'm starving to death. I need to work."

"Yeah, okay," conceded Hannah, "but you don't need to earn squillions—unless you've developed a particularly expensive wine habit . . ."

"It is past six o'clock where I am," complained Jess, putting down her glass defensively. "Lay off the wine shaming. And—okay—I don't need to earn massively, but I can't live on fresh air, however picturesque and charming life in Middlemass is. I can always turn it down—and that's if they offer it, which they probably won't."

"Just don't throw the baby out with the bathwater," said Hannah in a more conciliatory tone. "That's what Mimi would say—you know it."

"Talking of what Mimi would say, a lovely thing happened today," said Jess, keen to change the subject. She told Hannah about the quote in *Frenchman's Creek*.

"That is lovely," said Hannah, "but it's your future we're talking about here, not your past. Mimi would want you to reach out and grab yourself a happy future. Be brave. Don't compromise."

"Fine," said Jess, without conviction. Dreams and aspirations were all very well, but she was going to apply for that Birmingham job anyway. It was the pragmatic thing to do.

Chapter Nineteen

"I've never had so much fun being chair of the parish council. Goodness, that's a sentence I never thought I'd hear myself say," mused Diana, who was sitting in the garden, having arrived with gin one evening just after Jess had finished her Skype session with Hannah.

"Really? I assumed the glitz and glamour never stopped."

"Sarcasm is the lowest form of wit, as you know. Seriously, though, I've only been in post for three years, and I've never presided over such dynamic plans for the Harvest Home as we have lined up for next month," explained Diana. "Apparently it was a huge deal in the old days. Before my time. The exhibition cricket match has been revived, for a start. And this is from a cricket club which was so moribund it couldn't muster a full team last summer. I even thought Mungo was going to have to play, at one point. Talk about scraping the barrel. Although actually, that's not quite fair," she admitted. "Mungo's a stalwart of the cricket club. Has been for years, incomprehensible though that is."

"That's really good news though," said Jess. "What else happens at Harvest Home? I can't begin to imagine. There hasn't been a tiny library to launch, I know that for a fact."

"The church usually has a special harvest service. No, I know what you're thinking—it's not that exciting—but actually it's worth seeing the decorations in the church. And who doesn't like a spirited rendition of 'We plow the fields and scatter . . .'? What else? Oh, the Middlemass Women's Institute would have put on a cream tea back in the day, but there isn't a WI here now. They struggled to recruit, and all the members just died of old age in the end. That said—good news—the cricket club wives have decided they're going to do it instead. I had an email just yesterday."

"Fab. I'm a sucker for a cream tea. I don't know much about cricket, but I can think of worse things than watching a cricket match on the playing field on a sunny day," Jess mused, taking a sip of her gin and tonic.

"It's deathly boring," confided Diana. "It seems to go on for weeks, I warn you. But one can always take a hip flask and a good book. That's what I've always done, when Mungo ropes me in."

"What else, this year?"

"Well, there's the morris men coming for the first time in practically decades. Again, lack of interest kept them away for years."

"Is there a sudden interest in morris dancing?" asked Jess doubtfully.

"I know, unlikely as it seems. It's the Portneath group. Our own lovely Gordon—I am sure you know him, he wears a panama hat, rides a bicycle? Anyhow, he has been on at them relentlessly until they agreed to come. There's something in the air, I tell you."

"Yes, I've been sensing that. Is it manure?"

"Cheeky. Make fun of us country folk at your peril, we never forget. And half of us are witches, remember. I know I am, and I have my suspicions about Joan and Muriel."

Jess couldn't help smiling as she remembered their conversation later. It felt great to be part of something, to contribute to a community all working together to create something special. Also, she had not dared ask Diana about the defibrillator issue. There had been no mention though, so probably the whole episode was resolved now.

No, it was all very pleasing and, rather than be sad at the thought she might not be staying in Middlemass, she resolved to enjoy it for what it was—happy memories—or, as Mimi pointed out, "Whatever happens we have had what we have had."

"I've had a thought," Jess told Paddy the next day, as she picked up some milk and a fresh loaf of bread.

"Great! I had one of those once. It gave me a terrible headache, so it did."

Jess tutted, impatiently. "Listen, I know you'd have to have special training to run the post office if you had it in your shop, but I imagine the training to just put things through the till isn't that bad?"

"Ah, you say that," began Paddy, "but operating this old girl"—he patted the till affectionately—"takes a great deal of experience and talent."

"Not really?" said Jess. She was never quite sure when Paddy was joking.

"No, not really," he agreed with a wink. "Why, what's the thought?"

"Just that I heard some ladies in the library queue chatting about how the village really needed to persuade you to take on the post office, and I had an idea . . ."

"Do go on."

"Let's have a rota of volunteers to man—or woman—the till and then you'll be free to do post office stuff. It doesn't have to be all your opening hours. It could just be three hours a week—even that would help. Maybe a bit more, ideally. What do you think?"

"Would people really work for me for free?" Paddy asked doubtfully.

"To help you do the post office, yes, definitely."

"That's a genius idea!" Paddy exclaimed, his face brightening. "You know what? My little shop might survive after all."

"Let's not get ahead of ourselves," cautioned Jess, delighted that he seemed keen, "but I'm glad you think it might work. I'll put up a notice for volunteers in the library. Sorted," she said, squeaking as he swept her impulsively into a hug.

Jess was in the library just before bed, giving it a quick tidy to save her having to do it in the morning. She wanted no distractions from her planned day, dedicated to job-searching. She also wondered how long she might have left to indulge in a little light book-tidy of an evening. How long could they keep the library open, if more people were signing April's petition for the defibrillator? Her own rival petition seemed to be increasing in support very slowly.

She dusted around the noticeboard. It did have a couple more signatures on it, she was relieved to see, but they weren't up to sixty-eight yet, which was the magic number to beat. She only had twenty-seven so far. They were going to have to do an awful lot better than that. Although really, did it matter? If she was forced to leave Middlemass for work, the little library would have to close anyway.

She noticed *Jane Eyre* had been returned at last. Maybe she should drop it round to Joan? If she didn't take it while she had the chance, someone else would borrow it, and Joan had been waiting for ages. Deciding to take it round and drop it off, she tucked the book under her arm and set off in the fading light.

*

Joan's cottage garden was tidy enough, but the door was a dull green, flaking in places, comparing unfavorably with Muriel's house next door, with its shiny brass door knocker and a huge hanging basket.

There were no lights on in the sitting room, just a dull, amber glow from the dim light in the hallway. Perhaps Joan had already gone to bed? If she had, she wouldn't appreciate Jess knocking. Maybe the best plan would be to quietly drop the book through the letter box, she thought. She pushed open the flap and, crouching down, put her hand as far through as she could to lower the book gently onto the doormat. It landed with a dull thud.

As she turned away, she was musing on whether to make cocoa back at home when she froze, belatedly processing what she had just seen; a shoe, no, a foot, on the section of coir doormat glimpsed through the letter box flap. A foot! She turned back and pushed open the flap as wide as it would go. This time, bending right down, she saw the foot again, and, beyond it, several inches of leg. It was completely still.

Jess recoiled, her heart beginning to race. Taking a deep breath, she knocked hard on the wood of the door and then—slightly more carefully—on the glass. Was she dead? There was no movement. Nothing. Damn, she didn't have her phone with her. Not consciously thinking, Jess ran next door to Muriel's house. She rapped the brass knocker sharply, several times.

She heard an exclamation inside the house, and then a rattle of locks.

"What on earth?" said the man, framed and backlit in the doorway.

"Who is it?" shouted Muriel from upstairs.

"There's a body," Jess told him, breathless as though she had been running. "It's in the hall, next door. I think it's

Joan. I think she—I think she might be dead . . ." The last word was a sob. Jess pressed her hand to her top lip to stop it trembling.

"All right, my love," said the man, in a calming Devonshire burr, laying a reassuring hand on her shaking arm. "Let's see what's been going on, shall we? Hold on while I put on my shoes."

As he disappeared with an implacable absence of haste into the kitchen, Muriel came down the stairs wearing a fluffy pink dressing gown, her gray curls encased in a hairnet.

"Is that you, Jess?"

"Yes, it's me, I'm so sorry . . . I think it's Joan. Your husband is going to come and see."

"Leave this to me, pet," he said, pushing gently past his wife. "You wait here."

"I'm Ted," he said as they walked—he calmly refused to run—the few steps to Joan's door. "And you're Jess from Ivy Cottage?"

"I am. Nice to meet you. Look," Jess said, pushing open the flap again. "See?"

"Stand back, lass," he said, turning so his brawny shoulder was facing the door.

"Ted, don't be silly," rapped Muriel, having followed them out. "I'm calling an ambulance."

Ted then clearly thought better of bashing down the door with nothing but his shoulder. "I'll get a chisel," he muttered, "to pry out the lock."

"Typical of my sister—always the drama queen," said Muriel, to no one in particular, but her mouth was working anxiously. Suddenly, she pushed the phone at Jess. "I can't, lovie," she burst out, clapping her hand over her mouth.

Jess was in the middle of giving details to the comfortingly calm lady in the call center when Ted came back, looking like he meant business. He had an old metal toolbox with expandable drawers, which he plonked on the doorstep.

"The ambulance will need to get in," he said, "I'll just have to . . ." he selected a chisel with a fat, wooden handle and wedged it between the door and the frame at about the height of the lock.

"There'll be hell to pay if we damage the door, mark my words," said Muriel in a shaky voice.

"I think your sister's front door is the least of her problems at the moment," Ted said, giving the chisel handle a series of firm bashes with a hammer. It wedged in tighter and he wiggled it experimentally. "Now stand back, ladies," he said and shoved the chisel to the left, as far as it would go. There was a sound of splintering wood and—just at the last minute, when it looked as if it couldn't possibly work—the door inched open by millimeters and then gave way. It flew open so suddenly Ted almost fell into the hallway, and on top of Joan's body, which lay crumpled under the harsh light of a bare lightbulb swinging in the sudden draft.

"Let me in," cried Muriel, as she pushed past them both. "Joan," she said, sternly, "wake up and pull yourself together this minute, do you hear?" She fell to her knees beside Joan's head and grasped her shoulders.

"Is she breathing?" asked Jess, uncertainly as she hovered out on the doorstep. It was crowded enough in the little hall already.

"Of course she is," Muriel replied sternly. She shook Joan by the shoulders again. They were rewarded with a faint groan, and a bubble of spit at the corner of Joan's mouth expanded and popped, leaving a small trail of saliva on her face.

"Joan, stop this," said Muriel, relief flooding her face. "Stop this now."

Another groan and, this time, Joan's right eyelid lifted

and then closed again. The left side of her face was sagging, without muscle tone.

Jess tried desperately to remember the acronym for checks to see if someone has had a stroke. There was something about seeing whether they can smile with both sides of their mouth, and Jess suspected poor Joan couldn't, but she didn't think there was much point asking for a demonstration. The last thing Joan wanted to do was smile.

Jess still had the call center lady on the phone. "Is she conscious?" the lady asked.

"Erm, yes, sort of. She's groaning."

"That's good," said the lady calmly. "Any sort of noise is good. Keep watching her breathing for me and tell me if anything changes. The ambulance is on its way."

An interminable time passed as Ted and Jess stood anxiously over the two women. Muriel talked constantly, harping on at Joan for sins as diverse as keeping everyone up in the dead of night; making a spectacle of herself; not taking proper care of her health (and didn't she, Muriel, say as much?); always thinking she knew best; nothing ever changed . . .

All the while, Muriel was kneeling in the drafty hallway, rubbing Joan's cold, motionless hand between her own.

"I'll find a blanket to keep her warm," muttered Jess, bolting up the stairs. She couldn't find a blanket, so she brought down the duvet off the bed in the front bedroom. It smelled faintly of mothballs.

"Good," said Muriel. "There you go, Joan. Keeping you warm." She tucked the duvet tenderly around the unmoving body.

Joan was groaning steadily now and trying to speak, her mouth contorting with no recognizable sound coming out. She seemed confused by this, her face a mask of consternation.

"Hush now," said Muriel soothingly. "No point in fussing. Ah look, here they are at last."

Once the two burly ambulance men had arrived, Jess felt like she breathed out for the first time in hours, although it could only have been fifteen minutes or so. The men kept up a more positive line of chatter than Muriel, who took herself off upstairs to pack a bag, announcing that only a sister was the appropriate person to be rummaging through Joan's drawers.

If the ambulance men hadn't insisted otherwise, tactfully citing lack of space, Muriel would have traveled in the ambulance with Joan, but even she could see the sense of allowing Ted to drive her. She was also suddenly abashed at Ted pointing out that all these strangers and near strangers had seen her in her nightie and didn't she think she might get dressed before the whole of Portneath saw her too.

"Tell me how she is in the morning, won't you?" pleaded Jess, pressing *Jane Eyre* into Muriel's hands to give to Joan later. She stood back as she watched them drive away, the lights of the ambulance bouncing off the dark windows of the houses in the street as they headed toward the big hospital in town.

Chapter Twenty

By morning, it seemed the whole village knew at least a version of the night's excitements. There was a little group of people outside the phone-box library, sharing what scraps of the story they had. They were thrilled when Jess came to provide primary source information.

"So, the paramedics told us it looked like a stroke, but Muriel's with her and she's promised to update me," concluded Jess, refusing to get drawn into the nitty-gritty of the evening's events—details that had haunted her long after she'd turned off her light that night.

"Muriel, eh?" said one white-haired old lady. "Who'd have thought we'd see the day?"

"It was very touching, seeing Muriel care for her," insisted Jess.

"How long had she been lying there, poor soul?" someone asked.

"Well, I saw her at Paddy's in the afternoon," piped up a voice behind Jess, "so some time after that. But thank heaven you found her when you did."

"Yes, thank heaven," said Jess in a heartfelt whisper.

How awful it would have been if someone had found her the following day or even later. It was hard to imagine she could have survived a long night on the floor of her hallway, so cold and so unwell. Jess was so thankful she had done her tidying in the evening for a change, and so thankful for her spur-of-the-moment decision to take *Jane Eyre* to Joan without delay.

It really did seem that somehow the little library's magic had worked again, intervening in people's lives in the most unexpected but positive ways.

"You're the hero of the hour," exclaimed Becky, who had seen the huddle of people from across the road and come over, with Angus tripping over his own feet and Isla singing to herself in the stroller.

"I don't know about that," said Jess, reshelving the cookbooks that had somehow got themselves completely out of order in the last few hours. "Muriel was a lot more heroic. And what about Ted? I thought he was going to bash the door down with his bare hands."

Then she noticed Becky wasn't really paying attention. "Anyhow, what?" she said.

Becky sighed. "Listen, I've just heard, Aidan's had some bad news. He's had a letter . . ." She took a deep breath, straightening and pulling her shoulders back.

"From Lucie?" Jess supplied.

"No . . . Worse. From the Family Court. Confirmation of the preliminary hearing date to look at the residency arrangements for Maisie. It's next week. Can you come?"

"To court? Of course, but Aidan doesn't need me, he needs you—and I'm sure he won't want me there."

"I need you," said Becky, reaching out a hand. "I really do. I'm so nervous. And Aidan won't mind. I'll tell him, before."

"You'll be totally fine," reassured Jess. "But of course, I'll come if Aidan really doesn't have an objection. Go you with all this stuff, though! It's amazing."

"I have actually done a law degree, remember, even if my Mastermind specialist subject is now Peppa Pig."

"And do you think you can quash this thing?"

Becky pressed her lips together. "It's a worry," she admitted. "Courts have a tendency to take the mother's side in these things, and—even being an essentially absent mother—she could make a convincing case for further consideration, if nothing else. The chances of ending this with the preliminary hearing are low, to be honest."

"Poor Maisie," said Jess.

"And poor Aidan," said Becky. "It would be wrong to say I'm enjoying this—I wouldn't have Aidan and Maisie going through it for the world," she went on, "but having something to do that requires my brain feels good," she admitted. "I'm channeling my new career woman superpower."

"Go you!" encouraged Jess. "There's this steely purpose I can see in you, I don't think I've seen it before."

"That's because I don't need steely purpose to wash the kitchen floor and do the laundry, and all the other tedious, mindless jobs that currently constitute my life."

Knowing how grubby Becky's house was, Jess couldn't help thinking a bit of steely purpose with the cleaning wouldn't go amiss.

Bored, Isla and Angus were now chanting, "Mum, Mum, Mum," in unison.

"But, as we can see," said Becky grimly, "I'm still three kids away from being able to actually join the workforce."

Jess woke a few days later feeling guilty about all the things on her to-do list. She had neglected finalizing her list of books for the school to buy. With September, and the start of term approaching in just a few weeks, she would need to give it to Amanda pretty quickly if there was to be any chance of getting them in for the beginning of the school year. She promised herself she would go down to the school today and see whether there was anyone there. But first she should check the library.

The tidying was a soothing distraction from distressing thoughts about Joan. She had heard nothing from Muriel in the past few days, but she reminded herself to think positive. In the meantime Jess's plan for opening the post office in the village shop was going well. She had Sellotaped a sign, inviting volunteers, up on the door of the library, and just days later there were six names on the list. Checking this morning she was thrilled to see that now nine local people had volunteered to spend an hour a week on Paddy's till so he could run a post office service. That would be enough, surely? No one was asking for a full-time post office service, just enough of a provision to help out isolated people in the community.

Aidan had fixed a noticeboard onto the inside of the door now too, with the vital petition in pride of place. The board was quickly wallpapered with community messages about everything from a new yoga class to children's bikes for sale. There was even a book club starting called the Telephone Box Book Club.

A nominal fee of two pounds a month was requested for each notice and Jess got used to emptying the honesty box every few days. It was heartwarming to see there was always the right amount in there. It quickly paid for the board and for the various bits she had bought for the library herself, although she hadn't minded the expense. People in Middlemass were as honest as the day was long, it seemed.

She was pleased to see there were increasing numbers of reading visitors to the little library too. The children's books had been very popular over the summer holiday. It seemed that most of the local families had come down to see it at least once, and several came nearly every day.

Jess was just finishing her tidy of the library books—and

she had propped the door open to get rid of the stuffy smell—when Muriel drove past, screeched to a halt, parked at an angle over the grass verge outside Jess's gate, and got out, looking purposeful.

"Muriel, I'm so glad to see you," said Jess, rushing over. "How is Joan, do you know?"

"Of course I know. Haven't I been at the hospital night and day?"

"I'm really pleased you have," said Jess warmly, putting her hand on the older lady's forearm. "I am sure it is a comfort to her, having you there."

Muriel looked mollified and a tiny bit self-conscious. "Well, it's just the usual family stuff, at the end of the day, isn't it? You learn what's important when something like this happens. Like I said to you before, they've confirmed it's a stroke. She still can't speak at the moment. She tries, and either nothing comes out or it's not the words she wants. She gets quite frustrated but—like I keep telling her—she'll improve, she just has to be patient."

"It's her left side that's affected, isn't it?"

"Yes, right brain stroke, so left side weakness, but she's getting better already. Thankfully, it wasn't the other side. If it is, language can never return sometimes."

"Wow. You know your stuff," Jess said, looking at Muriel impressed.

"I'm having to pick things up fast," Muriel acknowledged. "It's a steep learning curve. So, she's right-handed, fortunately, but walking is tricky. She's going to need a lot of support. We're just trying to get her home as soon as possible."

Jess was touched. Muriel really was taking charge despite whatever feud the sisters had been battling over. "Are you going to help her when she gets home?"

"Naturally," said Muriel, as if she were astonished at there being any doubt. "Who else but her own sister? The strangest thing is . . ."

"What?" prompted Jess, gently.

"Well, when you came hammering on the door, I was just in bed reading *Little Women*, which I got out from your library, and I'd just got to the bit when Beth dies. It was eerie, because it had just got me thinking that at the end of the day, your sisters are your sisters for life, aren't they? And you just don't know . . .

"I tell you," Muriel continued, "I had a *lot* to forgive that woman for, but then minutes later discovering she was there, lying on the floor . . . The idea she might end up like poor Beth: well, it gets you thinking, doesn't it, if you know what I mean?"

"Blood is thicker than water?" Jess asked, remembering that Joan had also read the little library copy of *Little Women*. How would Muriel have reacted at the time if she had known that they had both read the same book from the little library? Would she have rejected something so recently in her sister's hands? Perhaps Muriel would have decided against borrowing it and might not then have been feeling so conciliatory when Joan was found so unwell. How different it could have been, Jess mused.

Was it too much to feel that the little library was a catalyst for healing and reviving the community in Middlemass? Perhaps that was fanciful, she thought, but—not for the first time since Mimi had died—Jess felt her grandmother's presence, like a warm hug, a sense of safety and love and comfort that flooded her eyes with tears.

"You're right, dear, blood *is* thicker than water," Muriel went on. "Anyhow, I told her this, and I don't mind admitting we both had a little cry. Joan loves *Little Women* too. Heaven knows where our old copy got to, but we knew that story inside out. Both Joan and I read it endlessly. I was Jo, of course. Joan thought of herself as Meg—well, she is the oldest. And didn't she just behave like Meg too, going off and getting married, having children? Full of herself she was too, but where are they now?"

"Isn't she a widow?"

"Yes, and her husband John was a useless individual. Didn't do anything for himself. She waited on him hand and foot, just like she did with the kids. You'll notice they're conspicuous by their absence too, of course. Turned up at the hospital nice as you please with flowers and grapes, but when the real work needs doing, they'll be long gone, you just watch."

Jess couldn't help feeling Muriel wouldn't have it any other way.

"So, when will they send her home, do you think?"

"As soon as possible. Hospital's no place for ill people. The longer she stays the more likely she is to catch I don't know what. I'd have her home tomorrow if I had my way."

"I'm so, so glad you're talking to each other again," Jess said, feeling a rush of tender feeling for the older woman.

Muriel looked abashed. "Yes, well . . . Family's family at the end of the day. There you are. Bygones."

When Jess got down to the school later that day, she was relieved to see Amanda's car. It was the only car in the car park, but then she was the one person Jess needed to see.

"For once, I have a friendly knock on the window," said Amanda, coming round to let Jess in. "Mostly it's grumpy parents wanting to complain about something."

"Do they really summon you by banging on the office window?"

"They totally do. Although most of them are absolutely lovely," she added, hastily. "It's a great job, even with all the boring budget stuff. So, talking of which, do you have my shopping list for all those fabulous new books?"

"That's why I'm here," said Jess, handing over the paper, shyly. "I hope it's what you were wanting." She pointed at the items at the top of the page. "There's been a big uplift in publication of list books. They're great for the boys, things like 'Ten things you never knew about sewers' and 'The twenty deadliest creatures known to man.' They love all that stuff."

"You know what? I have several boys on the autistic spectrum," mused Amanda. "They do love a list! One of them has memorized all the local bus routes, which I suppose could be handy, but I'd love to find a way to broaden his interests a bit."

"I've got him covered," said Jess, more confidently. "There's a perfect book for everyone, for every occasion."

"Talking of which, I hear the little library is quite the hub of the village nowadays."

"I don't know about that," said Jess, modestly. "I'm getting some great feedback, which is amazing. And surprising. I thought people didn't read anymore."

"Not surprising at all. Reading will never go out of fashion, although us teachers feel like some children will never catch the habit. Well done, you, for doing something to bring the village together a bit."

"Do you live in a village?" Jess asked, realizing she didn't know where Amanda was from. She had never seen her anywhere but at the school.

"*A* village? I used to live in *this* village. Middlemass born and bred, that's me."

"Gosh, that must have been incredibly handy for work."

"Too handy. It was a nightmare. That's why I moved to Portneath."

"Really?"

"It might not have mattered if I was doing any other job,

but you get this weird effect where no one treats you like a human being anymore. I'd be in Paddy's shop and grown men would start acting awkward and apologetic when they saw me, as if they'd been caught scrumping or failing to hand in their homework. It was a bit depressing in the end. I felt like I was at work the whole time. I was certainly treated as if I was. At the end of the day now, I can go home and fade into relative anonymity. Everyone's happier. And the children just think I don't exist outside school anyhow; they probably imagine I put myself away in one of my cupboards at the end of each school day. I prefer being anonymous when I'm not working."

"I don't mind not being anonymous," said Jess. "But I'm not sure I'd like people to know *all* my business."

"They will. They do. Especially the juicy bits," admitted Amanda apologetically.

"Do you think you'll make it to the launch, by the way?" Jess said, to change the subject.

"I wouldn't miss it for the world. And I'm really glad Harvest Home is happening in style this year. It's about time it was revived. Talking about the library launch, we'll have to organize some trips to it from school when term starts."

"Yes please! I love that idea. Bring them up a class at a time and we can do storytelling. Only when the weather allows, of course."

"I wish all librarians were like you," said Amanda. "Some of the children in our school come from homes that just don't have books. If families are struggling to feed and clothe themselves, they're not going to buy books, are they? And with the funding cuts here . . . Well, it's so frustrating. I feel if we don't get them reading at primary school, the chances are they'll never pick up the habit."

"I feel the same," agreed Jess. "I'd love to see what else I can do to help."

"So anyhow, I understand you're settling in well," Amanda said, "Getting to know—erm—people?"

After a long meaningful pause, it dawned on Jess what Amanda was alluding to.

"What's being said?" she said in a rush, feeling her cheeks heat.

"Nothing, but . . ."

"But?"

"But I also understand you and Aidan make a lovely couple," Amanda blurted out.

"The greatest love affair that never was," said Jess, aiming for jokey acceptance and ending up sounding a little bit frustrated, maybe even a little bitter.

"Oh really?" said Amanda, clearly unconvinced. "Anyhow, I thought you'd rather know it's out there."

Jess sighed. She knew exactly where she stood with Aidan. Nowhere. And that was genuinely completely fine, she told herself, but it seemed there was nothing she could do to stop people assuming otherwise. Even Hannah, who didn't live in Middlemass, seemed determined to see something that simply wasn't there.

Chapter Twenty-One

"Hi," came a voice, just as Jess was compiling a new stack of books to go into the telephone box. "I've come to scrounge a cup of coffee."

"Run out again?" teased Jess. "I was just going to stop for one."

"Chop, chop then. I haven't got long. Look—I'm embracing life," Diana said, giving Jess a twirl. She was wearing leggings, trainers, and a bright pink hoodie. "I'm off to a Pilates class and then Maisie is going to help me download a hooking-up app so I can find myself some hot, ancient totty for dinner and maybe more. There's loads of them, you know. Apparently, I should go on the new one, it's called Binge, or Whinge or something."

"Hinge," said Jess, trying not to laugh. "I'm not sure you're exactly the demographic for that one. Although goodness knows how I know that. And I'm even more astonished Maisie knows. Are you totally sure that's a good idea?"

"Yep, pretty sure."

"I've created a monster," joked Jess.

"Absolutely, it's the little library and that's all definitely your fault. Talking of fault, by the way, Mungo was saying he's been very much inspired by your comment in the front of that copy of *Maurice* he borrowed."

"Not my comment," said Jess, carefully. She didn't even remember there being a copy of *Maurice* in the ten boxes, although she remembered reading it in college. As a novel on the life of an early twentieth-century gay man not being able to be open about his sexuality, she couldn't even fathom why Mimi had put it in the little collection. "What was the comment, exactly?" she asked.

"Oh, I dunno, something about living life to the full, being true to yourself or something. I think the lilac cravat I saw him in earlier today speaks volumes. Mungo's going to have a go at Maisie's dating apps as well, he says."

"Dear God," muttered Jess, faintly. Portneath had better watch out with Diana *and* Mungo on the dating scene.

"Anyhow, it's part of my new getting-out-there ethos to ask him if he'll take me for a picnic soon. Somewhere lovely to make the most of this glorious weather. He's got an Aston Martin, you know. We'll go there with the top down. Why not. Actually, Cringe might help us *both* hook up with someone new. He can pick himself up a nice toy boy and so can I. We'll go as a foursome."

"It's Hinge," said Jess again, wondering why she was bothering. "He must have a big Aston Martin," she muttered as Diana reached forward to help her restock the shelves, humming a pop song under her breath. Diana's enthusiasm for a life unlimited was a little bit alarming. What had she started? Also, she couldn't help feeling a bit left behind. If Diana could put herself out there, find some happiness and not be put off, then what was Jess waiting for? All she had managed to achieve in terms of romance since Mimi died was an unsuitable crush on a man who was completely emotionally unavailable. Again, her familiar feelings resurfaced—the fear of reaching out for happiness, the certainty that devastating loss would shortly follow . . .

Perhaps that was why she had feelings for Aidan. How convenient to fall for a man she couldn't have.

*

Popping up to Paddy's for some milk later in the week, Jess was still in a contemplative mood. It might not have been her original plan when she moved into Ivy Cottage, but Mimi would have been delighted to have seen her books being read and loved by others. In a flood of fresh grief, Jess felt blindsided yet again by the loss of her grandmother's presence, her voice, her capable hands over Jess's own as Mimi taught her to sew or bake bread. Mimi had been her everything, she had taught her everything . . .

Jess thought about the underlined quotes in *Frenchman's Creek*, the strength Becky was drawing from the inspiration of Michelle Obama, the perfect timing of *Little Women*'s story for Muriel and Joan. Mimi was still spreading her wisdom.

However, while Jess could share Mimi's words and thoughts through the library, could bring the community together through the magic of books, and could even come up with an idea to bring the post office back to the village, when she looked around she realized that no one was doing that for her. She might have moved into Middlemass, embraced the village and her new neighbors, even found some friends to drink gin with, but ultimately, somehow, she was still alone.

Was this what Mimi had wanted?

Exchanging easy banter with Paddy as she picked up her meager groceries—the main purchases were three more tins of cat food and the newspaper—she was disconsolate on her walk home with her basket on her arm.

The August sun was fierce today, bleaching out the colors and browning the lawns. The roses, past their first flush, looked bedraggled, and the hollyhocks towering in Joan's front garden were rusty-stemmed.

The summer had reached its weary zenith and now the

season was in dry, tired decline. Jess felt fatigued too. Her sabbatical, these months of settling into Ivy Cottage, were drawing to a close and she had no idea what the future held for her. She had to earn money, but it was clear from her conversations with Amanda that the career prospects for trained librarians locally were no better than they had been in Bourton-on-the-Marsh. If anything they were worse.

Back at the cottage, Jess scrolled through her search results. This site had most of the public-sector library posts worth looking at. She pored over her laptop with a cup of tea in hand, pen and notepad ready to highlight anything likely. There weren't many. Mostly they were too far away. A couple more might have been worth looking at, but they were not only a big commute, they sounded deathly dull. She tagged a couple more uninspiring jobs disconsolately.

Revising and updating her CV, trying to pad it out to make her seem more dynamic than she actually was—having stayed in the same role for eleven years—by lunchtime she had managed to complete a total of three applications for jobs she didn't want.

Even a spell in the garden, tying in the beans and picking raspberries, couldn't lift her mood. It was not only the dispiriting job hunt but also the realization that this could be the last few weeks of the library—and even of her time here in Middlemass. It was the same old group of people using the library now. They had all signed the petition, Jess thought, and she still only had fifty-one signatures. Whether she stayed in Middlemass or not—and that looked unlikely work-wise—the library would close in just a few weeks and the defibrillator would be installed in its place. And who was Jess to say some old books were more important? She had seen with Joan how life-threatening health catastrophes could happen. How could she live with herself if someone died unnecessarily just because the library existed?

Feeling hopelessly down now, she spent the afternoon cleaning the house and watching the comings and goings at the telephone box. There was a book to cure every ill and solve every problem. That was what Mimi had always thought. It was like a tiny sanctuary providing a balm for all of life's challenges, but it couldn't fix things for Jess. Her problems were starting to look insurmountable.

"Misery likes company," Mimi had always said and—still feeling low—Jess wandered over to Diana's house to see if she could persuade her friend to come to the cottage for an early G & T.

Instead of Diana, it was Mungo who came to the door.

"Oo, sorry," said Jess. "I thought I might lead Diana astray with a sneaky sundowner."

"Too slow," he said with a grin. "She's on her second already. Quick, you had better come in and catch up."

"I was going to ask you to join me, not invite myself in," she told Diana when Mungo had escorted her through to the garden.

"I like your thinking, but I'm too lazy to move," admitted Diana. She was draped languidly on one of two steamer chairs on the little wooden veranda in the back garden, a novel splayed on the table and, in her hand, a long glass of something with ice cubes and what looked like mint.

"Mungo makes a mean mojito," she explained, giving her glass a tinkling shake. "Ah, get me! I'm a poet and I didn't know it."

"Alliteration is the lowest form of wordplay," said Jess mock-sternly. "Will he make me one if I ask nicely?"

"Already have," called out Mungo, joining them from the kitchen, handing an identical glass to Jess.

"Wow, cheers," said Jess, taking a large gulp and then spluttering slightly. "Wow," she said again, giving the glass a respectful look.

"I know, and it's only Tuesday," said Diana happily.

"On the hard stuff at—what?—barely six o'clock, on a school night," chided Jess unconvincingly.

"It's her second, as well," Mungo reminded Jess eagerly.

"And yours," said Diana, "if we're dobbing each other in."

"It's all very well for you retired people," said Jess. "Some of us have got to get up for work in the morning."

"Do you have to get up for work in the morning?" asked Diana disingenuously.

"You know I don't, because—and this is a key and pressing issue—I don't have a job."

"Jobs are overrated," said Mungo as he stretched back in his chair and took a long sip.

"Says the man who has never had to have a proper job," rebuked Diana, tipsily.

"How cruel, but a fair point, well made. Now, what could you do?" he mused, giving Jess an appraising look up and down.

"Not much. Being a librarian has become sadly unfashion-able," said Jess. "There's hardly anything out there, even if I was prepared to commute vast distances."

"We are a bit out in the sticks," agreed Diana.

"It's a really gnarly problem," fretted Jess. The last thing she wanted to do was burden her lovely new friends with her concerns—they had issues of their own—but here, in the fading light of a hot August day, surrounded by the warmth of good company, Jess's eyes brimmed with tears. Had she been idiotic moving here? Buying the cottage? How on earth did she think it was going to work out?

By Christmas, at the latest, she would have to be putting

the house back on the market and getting real about how and where she could get work. She had been deluded to think she could live this charmed life. What if the cottage wouldn't sell? Just the other day she'd discovered a patch of damp on the chimney breast in the spare room. And several of the window frames were badly rotted. Aidan had been generous with the sale price, she conceded, but it could sit on the market for months while she starved to death with no income. All of these issues flooded into her head as she stared pensively into the sunset, blind to its beauty.

"Come, come," said Mungo, noticing her distress. He whisked out a spotty handkerchief and pressed it into her hand.

"Darling, I'm so sorry, what have I said? I'm such a clumsy oaf," Diana exclaimed, pulling herself upright and reaching across for Jess's hand.

"No, you're lovely, both of you. It's just . . . I've been kidding myself, taking my time to unpack, doing the school library stuff, the books, doing up the house." She sighed. "The reality is, I can't stay." She dabbed away tears with Mungo's handkerchief. "I really, really want to be here, but it's not realistic. I see that now.

"Mimi and I, we always talked about moving out of town, to a little cottage with an open fire, a vegetable garden, the village pond. We had this fantasy world, and then I came here, and—I realize now—I fell in love with the dream."

Mungo and Diana nodded, their faces creased with concern.

"I'm in my early thirties," Jess went on. "I'm alone in the world, so I have to be a grown-up and find a way to earn a living. The cottage isn't for me. Not now. It's somewhere I might retire to one day, when I've earned, and strived for a few decades . . ." She trailed off, shrugging.

"That sounds miserable," said Diana frankly. "Don't fall into the trap I did—putting my life on hold, not living for now."

"You? Heavens, me too," said Mungo, nodding enthusiastically at Jess. "Me even more so."

"You mean you're unfulfilled too, Mungo? Even now?" asked Jess, sadly.

"I am, or at least I was," said Mungo, eagerly.

"That's so sad," Jess said, her chin wobbling.

"Come, come," he continued, smiling gently as Jess began to sob into the handkerchief. "It wasn't so bad."

"What about your father?" Jess said, her voice muffled as she sniffled.

Sitting back slightly, Mungo took a sip of his mojito and looked thoughtful. Somehow, he sensed Jess was looking to hear his story, to be diverted from her own worries.

"Well," Mungo went on, "he died when I was really very young, hence my being an only child. I don't think I could have left my mother to live alone with barely a backward glance. No matter how much time passed. It just never felt right."

"So, have you lived with her always?"

"Always. And while I was judged for it, mocked for it sometimes, I didn't care. She and I were happy. It really isn't a great tragedy that I've not had a significant romantic relationship," he said firmly. "My mother would never have stood in my way, but it just never seemed important. Truly. I admired her so much for bringing me up on her own. There was family money later, when she inherited from my grandparents," Mungo said, with a wave in the general direction of his house. "The Dower House was theirs. Initially though, she had to work. That was partly why I was sent to boarding school. She had quite a high-powered job, you know—I mean by the standards of the day in any case. She was personal assistant to the chairman of a large metal company. She stayed in that role with him for thirty years."

"She sounds like you," said Jess to Diana without thinking, her tears now drying on her cheeks, forgotten.

"More than you know," commented Mungo, then he gave himself a little shake. "Anyway, who would want an old queen like me?"

"I would," said Diana, loyally. "At least I would if I could be bothered with all that. And if I was gay. And a man. Then I most definitely would . . ."

"Never mind about romance. I think we ought to pal up and have fun," said Mungo. "Just like we're already doing, really. We could even get together to go on the *prowl*, if you felt like it."

"Good plan," agreed Diana, raising her glass. "Relationships are more than just finding a romantic partner. What ever happened to a 'partner-in-crime,' eh? Portneath would never have seen the like . . . And the good thing is, if we find some old codger we jointly like the look of, there are reasonable, statistical odds he'll fancy one of us."

"We have it covered," laughed Mungo, toasting Diana with his near-empty glass.

"Are you really going to go out together looking for sex?" Jess asked uneasily.

"Nah," they said in unison, wide grins spreading across their faces. "Can't be bothered."

"I think I'm quite relieved," Jess admitted.

"So, I've applied for a job in Birmingham," Jess said, a second mojito in her hand. "I'm qualified for it. Just about."

"Birmingham? But you'll have to move! Surely not . . ."

said Diana, her eyebrows arching with concern. "What's it to do, anyway?"

"It's what I was doing before, only slightly more senior. Responsibility for managing budgets and provision for a group of libraries in the Birmingham area."

"Sounds dire," said Diana truculently.

Jess didn't reply. Diana was right. Suddenly an image of Brian, her boss in Bourton-on-the-Marsh, popped into her head. He was gray by the time it came to an end and he must have only been in his forties. His hair was gray, his suit was gray, even his skin was gray—his health ground down by years of pen-pushing and cuts. The Birmingham job would be that. A step up but not a step forward. More of a step back, in fact—just when life in Middlemass, with the little library and her new friends, was starting to open up.

"I've never hoped for a person not to get a job before, but there's a first time for everything," said Diana, firmly.

"Hear, hear," agreed Mungo.

Jess was none too steady on her feet when Diana and Mungo reluctantly let her leave, and that wasn't until after Mungo had tried out his experimental espresso martini on her. She was now not only drunk but so wired with caffeine that she would probably never sleep again.

The dew was falling after a sultry day, and the night had a welcome chill to it. Autumn was just weeks away, and with it the need for Jess to make a future for herself. Drinking with her new mates until she was falling around drunk was going to achieve nothing.

Aidan and Maisie's house was dark and silent as she went past. Jess tried not to think of his difficulties with Lucie. She had enough problems of her own to worry about, without being drawn in to his and Maisie's dramas. She couldn't afford to care. There would only be hurt for all of them if she allowed herself to get involved. Mostly, she should concentrate on getting a new job. That needed to be the priority.

The email was crouching in her inbox like a large, unwelcome spider in the bath as she gulped down her first cup of tea, wishing she'd remembered to drink more water the night before. The title was *Senior Librarian—Job Application* and the sender was Birmingham City Council. She skim-read the body of the message and her heart sank. They wanted her to attend for an interview as one of a shortlist of applicants. Rather than feeling optimistic and excited, she felt encumbered, like the world was closing in again. The comfort and security of life in the library at Bourton-on-the-Marsh now felt hopelessly stifling.

Jumping into the shower, Jess tried to talk herself around. It's not like she had a lot of other options and anyway, it was only an interview. It would probably come to nothing. The chances are she wouldn't find anything for months, she thought, feeling her spirits lift at the thought of being forced to stay for longer. It didn't have to be too soon, she thought. Maybe she could rein in her spending a little more to eke out Mimi's savings just a bit longer.

Chapter Twenty-Two

The day of Aidan's hearing seemed to come around so quickly Jess nearly forgot. Just as she was getting dressed in yesterday's grungy jeans and T-shirt, it suddenly popped into her mind.

Glancing at her watch, her heart thudding with stress—what time had they said?—she peeled off her jeans and, to create an air of respectability, jumped into an old brown skirt she found tucked at the back of the wardrobe. It would be so lovely to have the kind of job where she didn't have to dress like a civil servant, but it felt like the right dress code for court appearances. Mrs. Winter, in the library, had always made a point of telling Jess how much she approved of her wardrobe. "Now that's what I call a sensible skirt," she would say. "And good quality too. You'll get a decent amount of wear out of that."

Jess had occasionally wanted to turn up to work dressed like a children's TV presenter, with stripy socks and brightly colored dungarees. But then was that really her? She might like it to be, but no, sensible brown skirts and little cardigans in dull colors had been her uniform. That was what librarians wore.

She pulled her unruly hair back into a scrunchy and smoothed her skirt in front of the mirror. She was so nervous for Aidan—and for Becky, who had been throwing everything she had into preparation for the day. She had called Jess frequently to check how something appeared to her, or to just talk it through, her voice gradually taking on a crisp air of authority and strength. Jess was so proud of her friend, Becky seemed to be taking more and more charge of her life, and she couldn't think of a better person to help Aidan.

Jess hurried over the road to Aidan's house, skipping breakfast. She was too worried on Aidan's behalf to eat.

Becky was already there.

"You are child-free?" Jess observed.

Becky raised her arms out from her sides. "I am indeed. The lengths I will go to, just to be able to say that. They're all with Diana for the morning. I'm worried one of them might not come out alive. Probably Diana."

Aidan was monosyllabic and stern, barely acknowledging Jess's arrival. He was looking handsome in a dark gray suit. His hair was uncharacteristically swept back and smooth. He looked as if he was going to a wedding. Or, more like, a funeral, Jess thought.

"So sorry, am I late?" she asked, giving him an apologetic look.

"Not at all." He summoned a smile with visible effort.

"Are you all right?" she pressed, touching his elbow.

"Yeah," he said, but his eyes said something else. He didn't look as if he had slept. "Yeah, fine," he repeated. "Nervous."

"No need," said Becky crisply, snapping shut the clasps on an expensive-looking brown leather briefcase.

"By the way, you look amazing," said Jess, noticing Becky's conker-brown hair, precisely cut and glossily blow-dried into a smooth bob, with wings grazing her jaw. She was wearing a jade-green trouser suit with an impeccably ironed white shirt and shiny brown loafers.

"You look really amazing," Jess said again, when she had fully taken in Becky's dramatically altered appearance. "Posh briefcase too," she added. "New?"

"Old," admitted Becky. She fiddled nervously with the clasps, a flash of the old Becky resurfacing. "But barely used. Rak gave it to me to celebrate getting my first legal gig after I was fully qualified. We didn't know it at the time, but I was already pregnant with Hamish. Best-laid plans, and all that."

"Shall we?" interrupted Aidan, shooting his cuff to check his watch, a chunky brushed silver number with a black dial Jess had never seen him wear before.

"Fancy watch," observed Jess.

Aidan looked at it again, as if he had never seen it before. "Lucie gave it to me," he muttered, as if he was talking to himself. In the next second, he was struggling with the clasp, before wrenching it off. "I'll wear my normal one," he said, rifling around in the detritus on the kitchen dresser and pulling out his old, scratched watch with the worn brown leather strap.

"That's more like it," he said in a determinedly more positive tone of voice, as he strapped it on his wrist. "Let's go."

"Don't tell Aidan," Becky whispered urgently, as he strode ahead of them to the car, "but I'm absolutely bricking it. What if she turns up with a barrister, or something, and I'm left trying to help him fight that?"

"You're going to be great," Jess murmured back to her. "Hold on to that thought. You've prepared, you've worked so hard, and more than anything you know that. Think *What would Michelle Obama do?*"

The law courts in Exeter were in a bright, white-rendered building like a wedding cake. As they went into the glass atrium, a wave of warm air enveloped them. Aidan's face took on a sheen of perspiration.

"This is not my natural habitat," he muttered.

There was a short queue and Becky gave the security guard

at the entrance a professional tight-lipped smile as he ran the handheld scanner over her. Jess, too, got through without incident, but Aidan set off the alarms repeatedly. He emptied his pockets, dumping change, keys, and a Swiss Army penknife into the tray.

"Can't let you keep that, laddie," said the guard, a tubby, balding, middle-aged man with the world-weary gaze of someone who had seen too much over the years. "That's a knife. I'm instructed to confiscate all knives. Get 'em off the street and all that."

Aidan blanched. "I'm so sorry. I forgot I even had it with me; it's just there all the time. I need it for work. Please don't take it away. I'd be really grateful . . ."

The man gave him an appraising look and, clearly finding what he saw to be tolerable enough, sighed and said, "I'm not supposed to, but I'll let you off just this once. I'll have to keep it with me while you're in there, mind, or—for all I know—you'll go into court and go berserk with it."

"I can't very well go berserk with a two-inch blade and a gadget for getting stones out of horses' hooves," reasoned Aidan.

"Collect it on the way out," said the man.

Aidan smiled his thanks, relieved not to lose it completely. "Thank you," he said, picking up the change and keys.

The little conversation seemed to have distracted him from the enormity of what he was facing, and he looked more relaxed as Becky checked the list to see where and when the hearing would be held.

"So," she said, turning to Aidan with a reassuring smile. "It is possible that Lucie will be in there, with her own legal representation, so don't let that shake you. Okay?"

Jess was keen to get Aidan into a waiting room out of Lucie's way, but just as they were going into a small room with chairs around its perimeter, Becky was distracted by a shout from the foyer.

"Rebecca McCallum?" called a slick young man with a sharp suit and a shiny briefcase. "Rebecca!" he called again.

"Oh, my goodness," said Becky looking around and then locating the source. "That never is . . . Sorry, guys, hang on, I'll join you in a sec."

To distract Aidan, who seemed to be getting increasingly nervous, Jess procured them two cups of truly awful vending machine coffee—sneakily selecting decaffeinated for Aidan, as he seemed jittery enough as it was. They had nearly finished drinking them in a tense silence by the time Becky returned.

"Sorry about that. The weirdest thing! I haven't seen that guy since uni, so the chances of him ending up in Exeter and being here today . . ."

"He's a lawyer?" Jess said, seeing that Aidan was clenching his takeaway cup and staring into the middle distance.

"Yes. And he's done really well for himself," Becky continued, with a flutter. "Alistair was always going to do well, though. He graduated with a first, as far as I can remember. And now he's at Eaglestones, of all places."

"I've heard of them," supplied Aidan, rousing himself with visible effort.

"They've been involved in a couple of pretty high-profile cases," agreed Becky. "They're amazing on family law. It's sort of their speciality, along with medical ethics. Alistair's an associate in the family law division, so he's definitely climbing the ladder."

"Well, what a small world," Jess said, as Becky lapsed into silence.

Jess noticed Aidan's hands begin to quake and resisted the urge to reach over to him.

"Anyway, that's wonderful," she said to Becky, "and so nice that he remembered you too. Plus, this could be your breakthrough high-profile case. You'd blow them all away—it would be great to make your mark in the legal world," she added, confidently.

Becky gave her a grateful look. "I hope it won't go high profile," she said, and then, seeing Aidan's face get paler, "Listen, Aidan, don't worry. There's practically no chance of this being noteworthy in any way—I wouldn't be doing a very good job for you if it was. We should be the only ones in the courtroom. Preliminary hearings like this are bread-and-butter stuff. Honestly."

"They're not going to let me into the actual courtroom, are they?" asked Jess.

"It's usually a closed court," admitted Becky. "Parents and their legal advisors only."

"I don't mind you being there," said Aidan. "But I think it might wind Lucie up. Would you mind . . . ?"

"I'll stay outside," confirmed Jess. She didn't want to do anything that might hinder Aidan and Maisie's chances in there. Plus she had a feeling that they didn't really need her. Becky was looking even more professional and confident since she'd bumped into Alistair. They would be fine.

"Aidan!" came a sultry voice from behind her and suddenly Lucie was ushered in alone, managing simultaneously to throw a beguiling look at Aidan and one of disapproval at Jess. She ignored Becky altogether.

Far from the sex-kitten glamour she remembered from their brief encounter in Portneath, today Lucie looked like the archetypal girl next door. She had a pretty polka-dot dress like something worn by a teen on her prom night, with a sweet little pink cardigan resting on her shoulders. Her makeup was that "no makeup" look that takes forever and thirty separate products to achieve—with rosy cheeks and dewy skin, speaking of blameless living. Today, her artfully streaked blonde mane was tamed into a simple ponytail.

"Lucie," said Aidan, giving her a curt nod.

"What's *she* doing here?" Lucie asked accusingly, glaring at Jess.

"She's here with Becky," said Aidan stiffly. "Becky is being very helpful with legal advice."

"How nice," said Lucie. "I can't afford legal support myself. Not on my tiny maintenance."

Aidan didn't respond and instead walked away from Lucie toward the window. Unabashed, Lucie pulled out a mirror to check her face.

"You could cut the atmosphere in here with a knife," murmured Becky to Jess as she led her to the doorway. "The judge is not going to be thrilled Lucie doesn't have legal counsel. That could make this hard work."

"But you've got this," she reminded Becky. "You have the upper hand—right? You know what is going on and how to help Aidan, and Maisie. Just remember that."

Becky nodded and gave Jess a grateful nod.

They were all relieved when the usher came to summon them in.

The hearing seemed to be over very quickly, and Jess didn't know if that was good or bad. Back in the car, on the way back to Middlemass, Becky filled Jess in. "As I thought, the judge wasn't very impressed with Lucie having turned up without legal representation," she said.

"Are you supposed to?" Jess asked. She couldn't help but notice how tense the back of Aidan's neck looked as he navigated through heavy traffic.

"You don't have to," Becky explained, twisting around from

the front passenger seat to look at Jess. "But Lucie didn't have a very good grasp on what was going on, and judges are generally patient but he did get a bit fed up in the end. Lucie kept insisting she was there because Aidan was denying her right to parental responsibility."

"Which he isn't?"

"No, as the birth mother she's already got that, but Aidan has it too, so it isn't the same as having carte blanche to decide where Maisie lives."

"So, what happens now?"

"We've been sent away to have another go at trying to agree how much time Maisie spends with Lucie—which, I'm starting to think, should be less than she does now," said Aidan, grimly.

Becky looked worriedly at him. "I thought the judge gave you a fair opportunity to tell him how things work now though—that you're Maisie's main parent. You came across really well. That was good."

"I am her key parent. And I can't understand why that—apparently—stands for so little," he said, suddenly banging the steering wheel.

"It stands for something," Becky reassured him, laying a supportive hand over his arm. "Don't despair."

"What happens if Lucie doesn't agree with you remaining as Maisie's main carer?" asked Jess.

Aidan shot a look at Becky.

"At worst," said Becky, "we'll be back in court for the judge to decide on Maisie's behalf."

Aidan was frowning, "Lucie isn't going to let this lie. I know her too well. She's lost face and she can never cope with that. She'll be back with a solicitor—her father will probably bankroll it. But I'm not going to let this issue get back into court. I'm not going to let that happen to Maisie."

"Ah yes. The judge also made an order that if Aidan and Lucie can't agree out of court, then he wants Maisie to come into court next time," Becky told Jess.

"I'm not going to let Lucie do that to her," said Aidan. His jaw was set. "This is not going to turn into *Kramer vs. Kramer*. Hell will freeze over before I let that happen."

"Don't let her know you feel that way," advised Becky. "That's just the kind of leverage she needs to get you to agree to her unreasonable demands."

"Isn't Maisie too young to be forced to go into the courtroom?" said Jess.

"She's young, but the judge can order it from eleven years old so . . . it could happen," said Becky, flashing an anxious look at Aidan.

"Over my dead body," he growled. "I hate the thought of Maisie having this hanging over her. I'm not going to tell her, and I hope Lucie won't, either. She's got so much else to cope with. She's not had a particularly easy first year at secondary school, for a start," he said to no one in particular.

Jess was silent. It was a privilege watching Aidan's devotion to his daughter, but it was clear that—whatever he and Jess had together, or could have together—protecting Maisie from the fallout of his battle with Lucie would always take precedence. She knew that already, of course she did; but a small part of her, she realized now, had been hoping this issue with Maisie and Lucie could be settled today. If that had happened, what could that have meant for her and Aidan? Was it reasonable for her to have hoped? It went against all her instincts to dare to wish for something like this. She was just opening herself up to be hurt.

*

"Sounds like you were brilliant," Jess said to Becky encouragingly, once they were alone and settled into her cozy kitchen, mugs of tea on the scrubbed table.

"I was all right," admitted Becky. "It was kind of weird; actually it was good to be back. Although I'd do anything for Aidan not to be facing this awful thing, obviously—God, that Lucie! But, yeah, it does light a little tiny fire in my belly. I'm not gonna lie."

"So, when is the great legal career renaissance going to begin then?"

"Whoa, hang on a minute, barriers to work being numerous, not excluding no childcare and no job," Becky half-joked, though she looked briefly crestfallen.

"I reckon that Alistair bloke would give you a job," Jess suggested cautiously.

"He sort of offered me one, actually," admitted Becky, averting her eyes. "I mean, he didn't, but he said we should have lunch to discuss the possibility. He's just about to start recruiting for a new role in their family law team, but he said he'll hold off until we've spoken properly."

"There you go, then!" exclaimed Jess.

"Childcare, the lack thereof, being the other small obstacle," Becky reminded her. "A slightly insurmountable issue."

"Really? Insurmountable? You've got Hamish at school and Angus starting preschool in September, remember. Not long to go now."

"It'll be easier then, of course, but I still have Isla at home. It would only really work if I could sell her, or something," Becky added with a wry grin.

"She is very cute," said Jess. "I reckon she'd be snapped up."

"Isla's more sussed than either of the boys. She could probably bring herself up, to be fair. I just can't imagine Rak going for it though . . ." Becky trailed off, thoughtfully.

"Actually," she said, sitting up straighter and taking a deep breath, "it's not him really. It's me."

Jess nodded, encouragingly.

"I just feel so daunted about it all," Becky went on. "I know if I presented Rak with a fait accompli, he'd accept it. If I managed to actually get a job with a half-decent salary, we could pay for someone to clean the house. I could do our grocery shopping online, set up one of those standard lists where they just deliver the same things every week, so you don't have to think . . ."

"There you go, then," said Jess. She was thrilled simply to see Becky being open to the possibility of returning to work. The sojourn in court had obviously worked wonders on her confidence.

"Isla, though . . . Plus not many employers would be impressed at me leaving early for the school run."

"Are there really not childminders or a day nursery nearby?"

"There is an after school club here," admitted Becky, glancing in the direction of the school. "But that's not for Isla's age group. The childminders in Middlemass are all fully booked—I asked around when Isla was born—and there's a day nursery in Portneath that I wouldn't send my dog to. Even Isla wouldn't cope there. Honestly, I just couldn't."

"It's such a shame your parents aren't nearby," Jess mused.

"Oh, I dunno, it has its upside," said Becky, dryly. "But yeah, if we were in Aberdeen, I'd be fine. Mum and Dad would love to see more of their grandkids."

"You need a locum grandparent, that's what you need," said Jess thoughtfully, an idea beginning to emerge. Could she make it work? Seeing how happy Becky had been in the court, how confident, well, she couldn't let her friend give that up for anything.

*

Jess felt honored Diana was with her for a change and not with Mungo. The two of them seemed joined at the hip these days.

"I've finished *Great Expectations*," said Diana, sitting in Jess's kitchen with yet another wacky, artisanal gin for them both to try. "I'm loving it and—to be honest—it knocked me when I got to Miss Havisham. Too close for comfort, that was. Someone's underlined that bit. 'The broken heart. You think you will die, but you just keep living, day after day after terrible day . . .'"

Jess nodded, her head drooping. It was so sad.

"It's how I felt when I finally realized the true situation with Michael," Diana went on, "finally accepting that he was never going to leave his wife for me." She gave a heartfelt sigh. "If only I'd read it sooner." Then, she sat up straighter, and held up her glass. "Onward!" she proclaimed. "That's my motto now. Although I'm not going to stop being sad that things haven't worked out differently."

"In what way?" Jess asked, feeling a strange bubbling of emotion at the thought of her grandmother underlining that particular quote. *Great Expectations* had been one of Mimi's favorites, and that haunting line . . . How sad it made her feel to remember how Mimi had pasted on a smile to cover her endless grief at widowhood. She had never allowed Jess to see her pain.

"Oh, don't get me wrong; I can live without a man in my life," Diana went on. "What have men ever done for me? Given me grief, that's what. But I do regret one thing, desperately."

Jess looked at her, concern snapping her out of her own reverie.

"I do regret not being a mother," Diana admitted. "Of course, at my stage in life, it's not the missing out on being a mother, but knowing I'll never be a grandmother. I think

I'd be excellent, personally, so it's a waste not to have any grandchildren to spoil and lead astray."

"I have a feeling I'll be ending up on the same path," Jess confided, but she was distracted, her mind racing as she wondered if indeed maybe she might actually have a solution for her two closest friends in Middlemass.

"Now, you're far too young to be arriving at that sort of conclusion," reproved Diana. "And anyway, you've got the delectable Aidan ready, willing, and—well, we know he's able because of Maisie," she added naughtily.

"You are a wicked old woman, but you know it's just not possible. I think it's best to leave that particular storyline to books and dreams," Jess replied. And then, partly to distract Diana from her obsession with a nonexistent relationship between her and Aidan, she told her about Becky's problem and Jess's potential solution.

"I bloody love those children," declared Diana, when Jess had outlined the issue. "Especially Isla, I'd look after her in a heartbeat. She reminds me of me and—you're right—it's a great opportunity to do the whole grandparent thing. But surely you shouldn't be telling me this?"

"I know. I'm interfering unforgivably," admitted Jess, "but I can't resist. It's just so solvable, and she really needs this. Of course, it's mostly during the school holidays because Hamish is at school most of the time, plus Angus will be starting preschool this autumn too. That's nine o'clock until three sorted with the boys . . . Really, it's just Isla, but I think from what Becky said it might only be a part-time job, so it won't be every day." Jess trailed off. "You should offer. She'll never summon up the courage to ask."

"Sounds like you've given it a bit of thought," said Diana admiringly.

"It seems meant," Jess said. "Becky was amazing in court,"

she went on, remembering. "Aidan was really impressed. She gave him so much confidence, just by being there."

"So, I offer my childcare services?" said Diana, earnestly.

"You do," said Jess with finality.

"Then I will. Now for sorting out your problems," said Diana, pouring them both another gin.

Jess was beginning to think one of her main problems was the amount she was drinking nowadays. Diana was a terrible influence.

"Please tell me you haven't got that ghastly Birmingham job you applied for," Diana went on.

"They've asked me for an interview next week," admitted Jess. "But I probably won't get it—and that's bad, not good," she added before Diana could speak. "I'm going to run out of money in a few weeks if I don't find something soon. It's too much of a miracle to hope for that something suitable is going to come up in Portneath or somewhere. No"—she drew herself upright—"we have to be realistic."

It was increasingly clear, thought Jess, that her own dilemmas were harder to solve than her friends'.

Chapter Twenty-Three

Diana had persuaded Jess to join her in church on the morning of Harvest Home. "I'm not really into God-bothering myself," said Diana, "but there are times when these things matter, and Harvest Home is one of them. Plus, there's going to be a big contingent of defibrillator supporters there. I'm relying on you to put the case for the library."

The little church, at the center of a pleasantly cool, shady graveyard with a monumental yew tree, was humming with anticipation by the time she and Diana arrived. Mungo had saved them a pew about halfway up the aisle and Jess slipped in gratefully, her head bowed. The last time she had been in church was for Mimi's funeral, and suddenly her recollections— the starkness of that morning—had blindsided her. To distract herself, she looked around her, taking in the echoing chill of the building with the smell of incense and damp heavy in the air. She brushed away quick tears and steadied herself with a breath. Mungo patted her arm comfortingly. The church, as Diana had promised, was bountifully decorated with corn sheaves and meadow flowers. There was a cornucopia of fruit and flowers flowing across the wide steps to the pulpit, artfully arranged to echo nature. Here were blood-red poppies, delicate petals already wilting, alongside purple mallow, yellow buttercups, all the delicate wildflowers Jess had seen in the meadow at the end of the garden—great swathes and washes of delicate color like a Monet painting.

"It's beautiful," she said to Diana.

"There's one thing I'll say about this vicar," she said, nodding toward the skinny, colorless-looking man in the dress who was standing in the pulpit, "he gives good Harvest Home."

Diana was right. Jess enjoyed the service in the end, joining in lustily singing the familiar hymns and taking comfort from the homily and readings. Renewal and reward was the message. If you sow generously and toil in good faith, then—come harvest time—you will be repaid with good things, intoned the vicar.

Jess was feeling distinctly more positive when, without warning, he indicated for Jess to stand up during the reading of the notices to tell the congregation about the library opening. Jess shot a furious look at Diana, who nudged her encouragingly. She might have warned her. Jess got to her feet, her heart hammering, and blurted out something about the library and the opening ceremony later that day. She was vaguely aware of banging on about the library's value to the community, bringing comfort and cohesion, the poetry of there being a perfect book for each person at each time they visited . . . before realizing, all of a sudden, that she had been talking for too long. She abruptly shut up and sat down.

She had no real sense of what she had just said but she saw several of the congregation nodding and smiling at her, so perhaps it was all right after all. She was all too aware of the need for the launch to be well supported. And it was a great chance to get a few more signatures on the petition too.

By the time Jess came out of church, she was fretting about getting the decoration of the library done in time, but Becky had already come with armfuls of decorations and quickly transformed the phone box and the area around it on a garden-party theme. There were balloons tied to the lamppost nearby, bunting was on absolutely everything, and there was a stunning ten-inch-wide gold sparkly ribbon which she wrapped around the telephone box. Once it was finally positioned to Becky's satisfaction she tied a big, multi-looped bow on the front of the telephone box and warned everyone on pain of death not to touch it.

Jess, with little else to do, had been sent off to make sure there were scissors for cutting the ribbon. That was her only job.

Mungo brought several bottles of the delicious English sparkling wine plus a couple dozen wine flutes. Jess's paste tables and bedsheet tablecloths were getting plenty of use, being pressed into service for the wine along with some jugs of elderflower cordial for children and those not drinking. In pride of place was the most amazing red telephone box cake—only slightly wonky—which Becky and the children had made together.

It all looked so pretty, Jess thought, surveying the scene. She was glad they had decided on midday. The afternoon itinerary for the Harvest Home festival was packed, with the cricket, cream teas, morris dancing, and then a barn dance in the evening. It wouldn't have done to be competing with any of that. As it was, she wasn't at all sure who would come or how many. But Diana's posters seemed to have attracted a lot of attention and a good number of villagers Jess had never seen before materialized as the moment of judgment arrived. There were a few from the church that morning too, she was satisfied to see.

"I'm not going to have to give a speech or anything, am I?" Jess fretted.

"I definitely think you should, and you'll do brilliantly. You were great in church," Diana replied. "But look, if you really hate the idea, you can just introduce me, and I'll come out with some old nonsense myself. It doesn't have to be much. Quick intro, few words, cut ribbons, drink a toast, bish, bash, bosh, job's a good 'un."

"I wonder if I even have to introduce you?" Jess fretted. "I mean, people are far more likely to know who you are than who I am."

"Fine," Diana conceded. "I'll introduce you, and then—honestly—it would be best if you say a few words."

Jess didn't think so at all, but just as she was wondering how to argue the point, Becky rushed up to them holding her mobile. "Quick. It's Stevie Brompton on *Devon Talk*—he wants to interview you live."

Jess's face dropped in panic. "I don't know what to say."

"Just say something about 'everyone needs books,' you know . . . That thing you said the other day—solace and inspiration, blah, blah."

Jess could barely remember her own name, let alone what-ever top-of-the-head stuff she might have been spouting sev-eral weeks ago, probably after a couple of glasses of wine. She stood, transfixed, clutching the phone in a death grip. She had it planted so hard against her ear she could feel it pressing against her skull.

"And next," came the voice over the last bars of the song, "we have Jess Metcalfe, librarian extraordinaire, to tell us why good things come in small packages. Jess, tell the listeners what this is all about."

Jess gave Becky the evil eye as she started to tell the story, but as she got going the words began to flow, and soon she was laughing with Stevie over some of the worst librarian clichés and assumptions, and he was commiserating with her over how library services were being cut. He made the community of Middlemass sound cute, dynamic, and warm-hearted—which, on the basis of her own experience, they were. In the end, she was sharing her passionate belief that the right book can be the cure for everything from fear to loneliness; and just as she was getting into her stride, he cut in with, "and that's all we've got time for from Jess in Middlemass, but check out the county's smallest library next time you're passing, and here's the next number," before launching into the Beatles and "Paperback Writer."

She handed the phone back to Becky, who handed her a glass of fizz in return. "You were brilliant! That's some amazing coverage we've got there. Everyone nearby listens to Stevie's show."

"You did a great job getting it," said Jess, smiling in spite of herself. She needed to stop saying no and learn to push herself, to take risks. Mimi was right. She had always been right. Jess wished she had appreciated it sooner.

"Look, we've got quite the crowd forming," said Diana, rushing up to them. "I'm going to take the petition around and get signatures from everyone." Jess noticed there was a gaggle of around twenty people, ranging in ages, chatting and enjoying the cakes and wine laid out, with Mungo behaving as the most gracious host. Some of the visitors looked familiar to Jess and some she had never seen before. Muriel and Joan—Joan with her walking stick—were there, standing amiably next to each other with Muriel fussing over Joan's cardigan, making sure the sleeves were pulled down, and Joan tolerating the interference well, as far as Jess could see.

Becky dragged Jess into the thick of it and she looked up to find herself next to Aidan. Together, amused, they looked in the direction of the two older women.

"It's a miracle," he murmured into her ear. Jess could feel his breath caressing her neck and her knees turned to water.

"Sisters and next-door neighbors," Jess said, gathering herself together, "and yet they didn't speak to each other for more than thirty years, I've been told. What on earth did happen between them? I've heard so many things . . ." she rattled on, before deliberately stopping herself.

"Nobody knows for sure. There are lots of rumors," Aidan said. "My favorite one is that it was something about the seating plan at Joan's wedding—apparently Muriel was offended, in some way that history doesn't relate."

"I heard it was something about sweet peas."

"That too, probably," said Diana, joining them and picking up the gist immediately. "Anyway, shall we?" she added, pointing at the scissors laid out for the ribbon cutting.

"Help yourself," said Jess, handing them over.

"We are extremely lucky . . ." said Diana, her voice suddenly loud and carrying surprisingly far. The little crowd that had been bubbling with conversation turned toward her, and everyone stopped talking. Diana waited until they were all paying attention.

"We are extremely lucky," she repeated slightly more quietly, "to have in our midst a newcomer who totally understands and values community—our community—and has been generous enough to donate time, effort, and an extraordinary library of books in pursuit of community cohesion."

Jess started to shrink. She wasn't sure she'd quite done that, and definitely didn't feel she had been given a lot of choice in it by her new friends. But it would be churlish to quibble, so she listened obediently, hoping her head wasn't swelling too noticeably at being praised and singled out.

"Jess Metcalfe," Diana went on, putting her arm around Jess's waist and pulling her toward her, "is an absolute star, and has surpassed herself to our considerable benefit. To Jess," she finished, raising her glass so enthusiastically that some of Mungo's delicious sparkling wine sloshed out.

"To Jess," everyone chorused, and then quietened, waiting expectantly for her to say something.

"It's—I don't know—it's such a privilege to be here . . ." she started, haltingly, wondering what on earth had been left unsaid. And then, without even a conscious decision, she started telling them all about Mimi—how Mimi had instilled in her an abiding love of books, showing her the way they could magically guide, inspire, and even provide an escape from life, especially when life was painful and difficult, as it was after the loss of her parents. She told them, honestly and from the heart, how Mimi had supported and encouraged her through school and university, assuring her the world was her oyster but also understanding when Jess preferred to retreat to safety rather than spread her wings, when she chose the little library job in Bourton-on-the-Marsh; respecting her need to stay close, to minimize the risk of loss.

And then, of course, she had to tell them all how she had lost Mimi too, leaving her rudderless, until she landed in Middlemass, where people had been kind and welcoming, taking her to their hearts. Here she faltered. How could she go on to tell them all how—probably—she would be packing up her books and leaving them again. It didn't make sense. How could it be the next step in her story?

She stammered to a halt. The silence stretched before them, and people, their smiles faltering, began to turn to look at each other. Diana, with the experience born of a lifetime, swooped smoothly in, made another toast, and then, brandishing the scissors, chopped through the gold ribbon and waved them dramatically in the air.

"I hereby declare the telephone-box library officially launched," she proclaimed.

"Hurrah!" the crowd cheered and then the general chatter rose in volume once more.

Jess found herself shaking hands and being clapped on the back, and ended up squeezed up next to Muriel near the cake, which Becky was now beginning to cut into generous slices. Seeing Muriel's friendly smile, Jess felt instantly guilty about her little gossip session with Aidan and the others.

"You are a lovely, sweet, girl," said Muriel. "Thank you for telling us your story. That was so brave, and we are all so lucky to have you. If you don't get told that enough then here's me saying it now."

Jess was so mortified at the praise and attention she was getting that—feeling guilty about her plan to leave—she was just about ready to do a runner there and then. Also, she was acutely aware that lovely Gordon—the man in the panama hat—was hovering at Joan's elbow, just yards away, decorously attempting to engage her in conversation. Joan was ignoring him either deliberately or accidentally and Jess was just wondering if she should go over to provide introductions when Joan softened and turned to him. He said something to her, doffing his hat, and she demurred, a little coquettishly, in response.

How wonderful it would be if the little library could play a role in a new relationship, thought Jess.

". . . my absolute favorite is *Jane Eyre*," she heard Gordon saying, and Joan gushing in reply that it was her favorite, too.

"Those two look as thick as thieves," Diana remarked, looking over, when she rejoined Jess with a fresh bottle of bubbles ready to refill her glass. "I reckon you've started something there. I've got loads of new signatures, by the way," she added, waving the clipboard.

"We didn't do the bit about borrowing books and taking them back," said Jess, refusing to be diverted from the matter in hand.

"It's a library, darling, they know how it works," said Diana.

"Okay, well, we didn't do the bit about being able to donate books of their own."

"Ah, no, we didn't do that bit, to be fair. But that's boring. Let's just put a note up. People can read, can't they? At least people using the library presumably can."

"Fair enough," chipped in Aidan, who had woven through the crowds to be near Becky as she handed out the cake. "Although I basically can't."

"I've got ideas about that if you're looking for recommendations," said Jess. Aidan was the prodigal son of librarians. She could hardly resist the temptation to create another convert to reading.

"It's about time you entertained ideas about each other," needled Diana but Jess and Aidan both gave her a quelling look. "Okay, okay, just saying," the older woman grumbled unrepentantly.

"Well done, you," said Mungo as they were clearing up. "I should think your ears were burning with all the gratitude and praise I was hearing about you."

"People have been really kind," said Jess. "I also"—and here she looked meaningfully at Diana—"took the opportunity to tell everyone how it wasn't just me. Diana and Becky have been amazing in helping to organize everything. And I'm really grateful to you, Mungo, for this," she added, waving her now empty glass.

He took it from her gently. "We rather dumped it all on you, though. I'm sure it's the last thing you had in mind to do when you came to Ivy Cottage," smiled Mungo, squeezing her arm. "We love having you here."

"I love being here," responded Jess politely, and then realized, quietly, that she meant it. "Your speech was wonderful," Mungo went on. "I had no idea about your parents—such a tragedy—and then Mimi. She was obviously an incredibly special woman."

"She was," said Jess, with a lump in her throat. And what would Mimi say about the challenges she faced now? About the realization, as she talked to the villagers, that she had finally found her confidence and her direction in life only to have to give it all up, because she couldn't see how she could continue without her career? At thirty-two, it was too soon to give up on that. She sighed.

How sad that she should discover this just at the time it was probably all going to come to an end.

Jess managed to persuade everyone to let her finish tidying up, sending them all on their way to the other multitude of events starting that afternoon. It wasn't too difficult, as Mungo was starting to anxiously check his watch and mutter about the cricket match.

"I'll see you down there," Diana instructed Jess. "I'll save you a place on the touchline."

"That's rugby, dear heart," said Mungo. "With cricket you just sit and enjoy a large Pimm's anywhere you're least likely to get bonked on the head by a cricket ball. And frankly, with me bowling, I'm afraid nowhere is safe."

The village street was preternaturally quiet by the time Jess was ready to join Diana at the playing field. It felt strange to be walking there alone; the now familiar landscape deserted and bleached out by the baking sun. Even with her sunglasses on, Jess was feeling dazed and a little light-headed in the heat, not helped by the glass of sparkling wine Mungo had insisted she drink at the launch. She hoped there would be some shade where Diana was sitting. She would never survive the afternoon otherwise. She dawdled as she walked, in no hurry to arrive, happy to be alone for a brief moment. She spent so much less time alone nowadays and it went against her nature a little. Mimi had always respected the need for solitude at the same time as gently pushing Jess to expand her circle of friends. "I won't always be there, *ma chérie*," Jess could hear her saying, but—until it was true—she had never let herself believe there would be a time when Mimi was not there. She definitely never believed there would be a time when Jess would feel comfortable in a new place with a new set of friends around her. It was the strangest thing that had happened in Middlemass. Over the last few months she had become the type of person who had friends—real friends who you could rely on and turn to in times of trouble, who she wanted to help and who wanted to help her.

Even if she had to leave—and, of course, she almost certainly would—Jess felt, for the first time, that these changes she had made were something that might happen again, something she might just be able to take with her, wherever she went. That was a comfort, at least.

Before she rounded the last corner, she could hear the murmur of the spectators, and the *thwock* of leather on willow. And there it was, the tableau which conjured up this quintessentially English scene: a village cricket match on a summer Sunday's afternoon. Aidan was bowling, with his back to the sun. The thick shock of wavy hair and the broad shoulders were unmistakable. He bowled with authority, but also with a palpable level of restraint, given that Mungo was at the wicket. Mungo hit the ball confidently and began shambling gently up and down between the wickets.

Someone wolf-whistled their approval. It was Diana, of course. Jess crossed over to her, nodding to the people she recognized from the library event, who smiled in recognition.

But it was surprising how many unfamiliar faces there were in the crowd. Where did all these people come from?

"Do you approve?" asked Diana gesturing around her. "Have I thought of everything?"

Diana had placed herself strategically halfway down the pitch to give the best view, with deckchairs, cushions, a sun umbrella, and a cool box. She held a large gin and tonic in her hand and looked utterly at ease.

"How did you cart all this lot over?" asked Jess in awe, settling herself on the blanket and cushions at Diana's feet.

"I didn't, Mungo did," she explained. "This match is going to take hours, apparently. I needed to make it survivable. Look, I've even got my book, just in case it gets too boring. Actually, it's been fine so far. Your man's doing a sound job picking off the opposition," she said, indicating Aidan, who was loping in to bowl again.

"Not my man," said Jess, automatically.

"Whatever," replied Diana, unrepentant. "He's bowled out half a dozen already, although Mungo's giving him a run for his money."

"So, what do we do?"

"We just sit and applaud decorously whenever anything exciting happens; and that's really not too onerous, as it's pretty dull most of the time. There's tea soon, though," she said, brightening.

"I've just seen you polish off a huge slice of cake at the launch."

"That was forever ago. I happen to know they've got cucumber sandwiches and scones."

"Scones!" said Jess, wanting to be enthusiastic. Having been far too nervous about the launch, she had had nothing to eat all day except for a polite forkful of cake; but the idea of eating in this relentless heat made her feel queasy. It was probably just as well. She would be the size of a house if it was Harvest Home every weekend.

"Cream teas," elucidated Diana with an approving head nod. "Devonshire cream teas, obviously."

"Not Cornish, naturally," agreed Jess, "one wouldn't dare. But still, clotted cream, I imagine?"

"Absolutely."

"And what is your position on the jam and cream debate?" asked Diana. "Think carefully, mind, a wrong answer in this environment would be shocking."

"You mean, which one first? Jam or cream?"

"Yes, that debate. Is there another cream tea debate I'm unaware of?"

"Of course, there is. Seminars—nay, week-long conferences— have been held to determine whether the scone in a cream tea should have raisins in it," said Jess.

"And that's after the heated controversy as to whether it's a 'scon' or a 'scoan,'" Diana said.

"Of course, it's a 'scoan,'" echoed Jess. "I'm not even going to give that issue the oxygen of discussion."

"Shall we have one?"

"A cream tea? It's a bit hot for eating," admitted Jess. "I'd love a cup of tea though."

Once the cricket match had finally wound up and Jess had managed to nibble on a corner of a cucumber sandwich, she was ready for a little lie down, hoping it would soothe her increasing headache. The overall plan was for the village inhabitants to have a short break before meeting at the flint barn on the Portneath road for the barn dance that evening.

"A tiny snooze before tonight, I think," said Diana, folding away the blanket and the umbrella. "When do you want to go down there? Mungo and I can collect you on our way."

"Oh, I don't know about the barn dance," said Jess. "I'm pretty knackered, and anyway it's a couples thing really, isn't it?"

"Certainly not, it's a family thing."

"Whatever, I haven't got one of those either."

"Don't be ridiculous, you have us. Also, you have to go," said Diana. "Doesn't she, Mungo?"

"It's definitely not to be missed. I'll dance with you."

"So, will I," said Diana. "I refuse to accept a refusal."

Chapter Twenty-Four

In the end, it had been easier to agree to go than to keep saying no, but Jess felt weighed down by the heat and her sadness at the thought of leaving.

She tried to perk up by splashing her face with water and changing into a pretty floral dress she had had for years and which Mimi had always liked to see her wear. It was sleeveless, so she paired it with a long blue cardigan. It would get cool later.

The last thing she was in a mood for was several more hours of polite conversation in a noisy environment, having to pretend everything was fine. If only a suitable job would come up locally. She didn't need to earn a fortune, just enough to keep her going; but realistically it wouldn't, she had to accept that. Also, the pain of her unrequited feelings for Aidan was something she wouldn't miss when she was gone. It was all for the best, even though—at the moment—it felt like the worst thing in the world. In the meantime, she may as well try to enjoy Diana's and Mungo's company while she still had it.

They were as good as their word on collecting her, and she closed the door behind her reluctantly. Their constant, gentle bickering kept her amused on the walk down. The dusk was already deepening, reminding Jess it was nearly autumn. Maybe it was just her, but even the sunset had a mournful, elegiac atmosphere. Walking through the darkening village, it felt like the end of things. It was—very nearly—the end of things. Her first Harvest Home, and her last.

The bright lights inside the barn were exposing and harsh. That, along with the wall of chatter that assaulted them as they went inside, deepened Jess's headache. She really was feeling rough now and thought longingly of being in bed with Ladriya and Batou curled up behind her knees.

Mungo soon found them a table and went to get drinks. The volume of conversation around them was so high that by mutual consent she and Diana sat without speaking, taking in the atmosphere. Diana's insistence that it was a family event seemed to be right. Children were everywhere, running around the tables and around the big open space in the center of the barn, where the dancing would be.

The band, setting up on the raised area at the end, were tuning their instruments: two guitars, a fiddle, and an accordion. The caller—an amiable man who introduced himself as Phil—soon got people organized to start the first set. Jess point-blank refused, as she always had two left feet when dancing. But Mungo and Diana gave it their all, enthusiastically galloping up and down the middle as the others clapped, twirling each other vigorously and charging around the outside in the wrong direction, earning them a special mention from Phil, who applauded their deeply individual interpretation. It was all hilarious and good-natured. Jess laughed so much, just from watching, she was nearly as breathless as Mungo when they came back to take their seats with relief.

"I think we've shown them how it's done," said Diana, with satisfaction.

"Absolutely," agreed Mungo. "We can leave it to the young ones now."

"Thank goodness for that," said Diana, as she snapped open a fan.

Jess was starting to enjoy just watching people having fun, but it was Paddy who eventually persuaded her to dance.

"Go on, go on," he cajoled. "My lovely wife Deb had to go and put the little one to bed. You'd be making an old man very happy. Plus I've been wanting to talk to you."

Paddy was clearly experienced at dancing ceilidhs, as he managed to remember and execute a complex series of moves while informing Jess in snippets every time they were close enough for him to be heard.

"The sign-up list in the phone box was inspired," he gabbled, while briefly facing her for a do-si-do. "Half my customers signed up, by the look of it," during a clockwise, linked arm turn. "Getting together on Tuesday to sort out a timetable . . . easily ten hours a week," while galloping up the middle with her. "Post office training next month," he panted, during an anticlockwise linked-arm turn, and then a triumphant "So the post office will be open in-store by October!" as they thankfully found themselves back in their starting formation for the final chord.

As low as she was feeling, Jess couldn't help being thrilled for him. How wonderful for him to see just how loved and valued by the community he was. Everyone wanted to help, and now Paddy was going to be at the center of a vital post office service. This was how communities should work. She felt proud to have made a tiny contribution to it.

"Now *that's* a family!" exclaimed Diana as Jess sat down with relief. Jess followed her gaze to see Rakesh, with Isla in his arms and Becky beside him, trying to get Hamish and Angus to stand opposite to make up a four for the next dance. Jess thought it was optimistic of them both, but she was impressed at their resolve.

"He's not working, for a change," observed Jess, in amazement, realizing she hadn't seen him at any of the other events that day.

"Better than that," shouted Diana, into her ear, "observe the teamwork. Rak even looks like he's enjoying himself, bless him," she beamed in approval. "They make a lovely couple, don't they?"

It was true, thought Jess. They did make a lovely couple. Rakesh was having a whale of a time, lifting Isla up on his shoulders, then handing her back to Becky and swinging Angus in a circle until he squealed with excitement. Jess had never seen Becky so relaxed. And it was a pleasure to see both Becky and Rak not just tolerating but enjoying the chaos that was their family.

Tears sprang unbidden to Jess's eyes, and she dabbed them surreptitiously. She needed to stop this crying but she could hardly help shedding just a couple of tears for her friendship with Becky, which had sprung up so strongly and rewardingly in the short months she had been in Middlemass. Jess had always been so cautious about new relationships in the past, but the times with Becky, in her kitchen, drinking wine or tea (mostly wine) and feeding the children, had felt so easy, so effortless. The only other person she enjoyed that degree of acceptance and casual ease with had been Hannah. Her best friend Hannah, who was so far away. Hannah, who she hadn't spoken to in a week, she had been so wrapped up in her life in Middlemass. Jess felt bad about that. Something else to feel bad about. She didn't want Hannah to end up being just a foul-weather friend, someone she only bothered with when the chips were down. Maybe there would be more time for Hannah again when she moved. If she moved.

Jess realized she had been looking out, since she got there, for Aidan and Maisie.

"Lover boy's not shown up then," said Diana, as if she had read Jess's mind.

"You see," she replied. "People *are* allowed to not go."

"I wouldn't have allowed it if I had known he was going to play hooky. How about Maisie? She might have liked to go."

"I don't know if Lucie's around at the moment," said Jess. "They've got a lot to sort out."

"I wish they'd hurry up and sort it then," shouted Diana impatiently over the music. "No one knows where they stand. It's ridiculous."

Diana didn't mean no one, of course. She meant Jess.

It was just then Jess saw the two of them: Aidan and Maisie, at the drinks table. Aidan was handing Maisie a glass of orange juice and she was looking glum. Jess tried to read his expression, but his face was closed and blank as he watched the dancing dispassionately. Maisie was tugging at his sleeve to attract his attention over the din. He summoned a smile and looked down at her. That was when Jess saw she was pointing in their direction. Aidan followed her gaze, caught Jess's eye before she had a chance to look away. Next thing she knew he was coming over.

"I've been instructed to ask you to dance," he shouted into Jess's ear.

"You put it so persuasively," she teased him, but smiled to show she accepted.

Diana and Maisie looked on approvingly as Aidan and Jess took their places.

"I hope you know what you're doing," she shouted into his ear.

"Not a clue," he shouted back, but he executed the dance with clockwork precision, manhandling Jess so effortlessly it might even appear—to a casual onlooker—that she knew what she was doing too. His expression was completely deadpan, marking him out among the smiling and laughing faces, although Jess had eyes for no one else. Mentally, it was quite relaxing dancing opposite Aidan, but physically it was draining. After only a few minutes Jess broke out into a cold sweat, her heart pounding.

"Are you all right?" he asked, looking at her sharply as he twirled her around, steadying her as she spun to face him.

"Fine," she panted, gathering herself to carry on.

"No, you're not," he said, taking her around the waist in a way that Jess hoped others didn't realize was as much about holding her up as guiding her around.

Increasingly, she felt she could barely keep her balance as they swung, clapped, and wove their way through the dance, going on and on through all the permutations until finally, thankfully, they reached the end, to whooping and applause.

Jess stood, swaying, letting the noise and color wash over her, the music, the shouting, the excitement. It was all exhausting.

"Jess?" came Aidan's voice, seemingly from a long, long way away.

She felt the ground tilt beneath her feet. "I feel a bit queasy," she admitted. It came out so quietly he can't possibly have heard, but somehow—after checking that Maisie was happily chatting with Mungo—he propelled Jess through the wide barn doors and outside. Once out of sight, he swept her up into his arms and carried her effortlessly away from the noise and the crowds.

"I'm fine," she protested. "I can perfectly well walk."

"You're white as a ghost," he told her, setting her down carefully on a hay bale and sitting next to her. "What have you had to eat today?"

Jess did a quick run through her memory banks; nothing for lunch; nothing for supper. No wonder she felt rough. She *had* had a glass of champagne and two gin and tonics though. They counted as calories. She thought she probably shouldn't mention them.

"It's been a bit busy," she admitted.

"Hm. So nothing, in other words."

Their arms brushed.

"You're cold," he said, putting his arm around her waist and pulling her to his side. She leaned gratefully, the sudden shock of warmth from his body raising goosepimples. It felt right, just sitting, slumped against him. Comfortable.

They sat, companionably for a few minutes. Jess was relieved that her heart rate slowed and her stomach steadied. She would never have recovered her dignity if she had fainted or—even worse—thrown up in front of him.

"Did I tell you? I borrowed a book from your library," he said quietly, stroking her hair away from her face as she imagined he did for Maisie when she was ill.

"You did? Which one?" she replied, feeling like she was floating as she leaned her head onto his shoulder.

"You'll laugh . . . It was a Doctor Seuss one, *Horton Lays an Egg* or something."

"*Horton Hatches an Egg*? I love Doctor Seuss."

"Yeah, I mean—I know it's a kid's book—I only got it out because it reminded me how much I loved *Green Eggs and Ham* when I was little."

"What's it about, remind me?"

"Basically," he said tucking her snugly into his side, his arm around her waist, "it's about how being a good father comes from nothing more than doing the everyday stuff and always being there. It was amazingly comforting, what with everything that's gone on."

"I'm surprised Mimi chose to put it in," said Jess. "You've reminded me. I liked it when I was little, but—to be honest—it wasn't a huge favorite or anything."

"I think she might have chosen it for what it meant to her," said Aidan. "There was a little note in it, at the end, in pencil. It said something like 'Parenting is about being there, not about being conventional.'"

In her mind Jess could hear Mimi saying the words, in her strange accent, a mix of phlegmatic Northern and exotic Parisian. "She was always there for me—and she definitely wasn't conventional, but I wonder why she wrote that?"

Maybe even brave, confident, reassuring Mimi had doubted herself sometimes.

"It was definitely appropriate for me," said Aidan. Pressed up against him, she could feel his voice rumbling from inside his chest. "I feel for Maisie, sometimes, that she's ended up with me as her main parent. It can't be easy for a girl having her dad be the one who's around all the time. I'm sure she'd much rather have her mum."

"Really?"

"Okay, maybe not *her* mum," admitted Aidan. "Lucie's definitely not winning any parenting awards."

"Where is she, by the way?"

"Back in Bristol. At last."

"Is everything all right?"

"Not really. Nothing that involves Lucie is ever all right."

After the sultry heat of the day, the temperature was finally dropping. Despite basking in his body heat, Jess shivered in the chill night air.

Aidan slipped off his jacket and put it on her shoulders before pulling her back into his side.

This would be where he would kiss her again, she thought. Round the back of the haystacks in true Harvest Home tradition. That was if the malignant shadow of Lucie wasn't still casting an evil spell over their would-be relationship.

"Is she saying she wants to go back to court for sole custody?" asked Jess, determined, for some masochistic reason, to subject herself to further pain by dwelling on the issue.

Aidan stiffened.

"She is, isn't she?" That explained the bleak look in his eyes.

He hung his head, sighing.

"I had a letter this morning from this hotshot lawyer she's gone out and got for herself. She's saying"—he laughed mirthlessly—"she's saying she has concerns about Maisie being in a household where her father has girlfriends coming and going, and that it creates a chaotic and destabilizing influence."

"Unbelievable," said Jess, breathless from shock.

"Believe it," said Aidan grimly. "Although I hope you realize, I *don't* have girlfriends coming and going."

"I think I did," said Jess, with a wan smile. "Which is worse in a way, because you and I both know she means me. I suppose the best thing to do is for me to stay clear."

Jess paused, waiting for him to disagree. But, of course, with a little additional twist of pain, she realized he wouldn't. Of course not. He would always put Maisie first.

"You'll think I'm a complete bastard, and this is totally unfair to you, but for Maisie's sake I just need to keep Lucie sweet, not give her any reason to rock the boat. She knows the judge wants Maisie to speak next time, and she also knows I'll do anything to avoid her having to go through that."

They sat in silence, listening to the music and the dancing feet still thumping away in the barn. Keeping her and Aidan's "just friends" agreement hadn't got any easier. Jess felt utterly crushed, but she willed her tears not to fall. The last thing he needed, with everything he was facing, was to have to take responsibility for her misery as well.

Before she had a chance to change her mind, she detached herself from his side, slipping off the jacket and handing it back to him.

"I'm so sorry," said Aidan, his eyes filled with anguish.

"It's fine," she said, brightly, with only a tiny wobble in her voice. "There's a good chance I'll not be around much longer anyhow," she said, briefly explaining the Birmingham interview and—if not Birmingham—then the financial need to find work somewhere. He looked at her nonplussed.

"It sounds awful. And you're not convincing me. You've not even managed to convince yourself, from what I can see . . . But if it's really what you want?" Aidan said, pausing for a moment when she stood up. He gazed up at her. "Good luck with the interview, if I don't see you before. I'm sure you'll get it. Now, as Maisie's with Diana and Mungo, at least let me walk you home."

He wouldn't take no for an answer and they walked back, arm in arm, not speaking. There was no pretending now that they didn't want each other. No pretending they didn't need to be close, even though they couldn't. What they did have was these few moments, and Jess made the most of every second.

The silence stretched between them as they reached Ivy Cottage. The pond was empty and smooth now, with the white duck and his harem all tucked up for the night on the island in the middle, safe from the foxes.

Their eyes met. In the end it was Jess who tore her gaze away.

Reaching up to plant a kiss on the corner of his mouth, she gathered her cardigan around her—why was she always cold, these days?—and she slipped away without looking back.

Chapter Twenty-Five

Jess had never felt so bleak. September had always been an exciting time for her in the past. She loved the brisk chill of autumn, the fresh challenges, the pencil case filled with newly sharpened pencils, the shopping for winter boots . . . It was generally a good time to look for jobs too. She should be relishing the challenge. And as for Middlemass and all her new friends, it had just been a summertime dream, coming to a close as the leaves started to fall from the trees. It was sad—sure—but inevitable. She knew that now.

There were moments in the days that followed when Jess managed to forget about the impossible situation with Aidan and her need to move away from Middlemass. Those were the happy moments.

Since the radio interview on Harvest Home day, summer tourists up from Portneath had been posting about it on social media, with the hashtag #TheLittlestLibrary. Hannah had taken to following it on Instagram in New Zealand, most evenings giving Jess exciting updates on the Littlest Library's increasing fame. It was still odd to see people—strangers—queuing up outside, chatting and posing for selfies. One day, there was even a Japanese film crew. The petition, pinned to the noticeboard on the back of the door, collected so many signatures that Jess took it down once it had got to five hundred, deciding that should be more than enough to give Diana the firepower she needed to vanquish April's defibrillator campaign. So that was something. The stream of people from outside the community was a huge help to Paddy's business too. He found himself doing a roaring trade in snacks and ice creams.

If the little library was the beating heart of the community, then the school, the church, and the parish council were the limbs. The whole village was buzzing with energy; volunteers were falling over themselves to do their bit. Litter was picked; bulbs were planted on the verges and around the pond; and parish council meetings in the cricket pavilion were packed.

On a golden, early September morning, Jess went out to the library before she had even put the kettle on. She wanted it tidied up early before the crowds arrived.

She jumped when Rakesh, in his running gear, appeared silently at her side just like he had the first time they met.

"I wanted to let you know," he said, in his soft, precise voice, "I've loved *Swiss Family Robinson*, and you're absolutely right in your comment. I was so touched to see it."

"What comment?" Jess asked. Was it too much to hope for another little something from Mimi?

"I've just put it back in this morning. Look," he said, reaching past her and plucking the book off the shelf. He riffled briefly and passed it to her.

"*Family is everything, children grow up fast, so don't miss a minute,*" someone had scribbled on the back page in a broad cursive. Now it was Jess's turn to swallow a sudden emotion. "That's not my writing," she said with a sigh of recognition. "That's Mimi's. I was hoping . . . I think that's another message from my grandmother."

"She's a wise woman," said Rakesh. "Her advice certainly works for me," he added, staring unseeing past Jess toward the pond. "After I read this, I just had a feeling I might've been missing out on something. Becky and I had a chat; probably one we should have had years ago. We're happier as a family now. We understand ourselves better. If I'm honest, I just thought she was doing a better parenting job than me, that she—they—didn't need me. But I realize now I've been cheating myself. Also, if I'm allowed to say it about myself, I was cheating them too."

"You're allowed to say it," smiled Jess, remembering how he was with his family a few nights ago at the barn dance. "Like the Swiss Family Robinson—they totally need you with them on this adventure. You're their dad, so be their dad."

Rakesh nodded his agreement. "I also see that Becky needs to get back to work, just like I do. I've been allowed to concentrate on myself, career-wise, and I've got my consultancy position, thanks to her support. It's still intense, and that won't change, but it's Becky's turn now, and I am going to support her any way I can."

"All you need to do is tell her she's good enough," Jess said, simply. "That's what she needs to hear. Often."

Her positive encounter with Rak made Jess feel brighter than she had done for days. Whatever happened next, she had the satisfaction of knowing the library had helped people. Perhaps, even if she had to move, a way could be found to keep it open and keep helping the community. She just needed to figure out how.

Jess gave it some thought while she showered and dressed, and was sitting idly at the kitchen table, deleting junk emails and letting a mug of tea go cold, when there was a knock at the back door, which then opened.

Diana looked stern, which was so unlike her friend that Jess rose to her feet in alarm.

"What is it?" she asked, her eyes widening.

"Sit down, darling," said Diana, wearily. "I'll tell you."

Jess sat.

"I'm so sorry . . ." said Diana.

"Say it," Jess beseeched her. "You're scaring me now."

"April's ridiculous campaign. We've had the two petitions handed in, and ours was amazing, as you know."

"But?"

"April sneakily had a last-minute rally and she's beaten us."

Jess clasped her hands to stop them shaking. She needed clarity. "She can't have done! We had five hundred signatures. How many did she get?"

"It hardly matters, really."

"How many?" Jess insisted.

"There are five hundred and two signatures to support the defibrillator going into the phone box," Diana said, reluctantly.

"Five hundred and two?" Jess felt like she had been punched in the stomach. "Five hundred and two people want the library to close? So, we've just had the celebration, with the ribbon-cutting, and the speeches, and the press, and all along there have been more than five hundred people, living in this little community, who specifically want me to close down the library?"

She pulled her cardigan around her even tighter, but nothing could counteract the queasy chill of knowing that so many local people actually, actively, thought the library was a waste of space and it should go.

"You can't take these things personally," said Diana, robustly.

"You say that, but how can I take it as anything other than personally?" cried Jess. "It's horrible. I began to feel like this is finally somewhere I can belong, be accepted . . ."

Diana looked at Jess and sighed. "I'm so sorry."

"And it has to be done? It has to be shut down?"

"Unless I can wangle something."

Jess looked hopeful.

"In all honesty," Diana admitted, "I'm probably going to have to say yes, it will have to close."

There was a silence, broken only by the relentless drumming of the September rain.

"Well, if it does, it does," said Jess, matter-of-factly, brushing nonexistent creases out of her skirt. "That's absolutely fine, Diana, please don't worry. It was lovely while it lasted." While she spoke, she was ushering Diana out of the door, desperate to get rid of her before her composure broke.

Jess rubbed away angry tears, her stomach clenching with tension and what felt like dread. The thought that people in the village, people she didn't even know—actually, worse, there were probably people she *did* know—had signed a petition specifically to say that her precious library of books was not welcome! And of course, the community didn't need the library. What hubris it had been to think it did.

She would pack up her books, back into their ten boxes, and let the phone box be used for something that mattered. It was only right. She had begun to feel she belonged—which had been lovely—but all evidence was increasingly to the contrary. The reasons for leaving Middlemass were piling up now. The library didn't matter. Any relationship with Aidan was clearly never going to happen. She certainly didn't want to demand he do anything that might rebound negatively on Maisie. And in any case she, Jess, badly needed to find an income and this would necessitate moving away. These answers might not be the ones she wanted, but that was life.

*

Becky was horrified when she saw Jess's face peering through the front door window.

"What on earth?" she said. "You look like shit."

"Thanks," grumbled Jess, and briefly filled her in.

"God, villages, I bloody hate them!" Becky said, furiously. "Where is this petition? I will personally go and beat up everyone who signed. What ignorant, double-dealing, nasty, backstabbing idiots."

"You can't blame them," reasoned Jess, Becky's outrage somehow making her feel calmer. "They have a chance to have the defibrillator, and I can quite see . . . Anyhow, it really doesn't matter. Frankly I'd be lucky to get a job near enough to stay here anyway, and I wouldn't have left Mimi's books behind. If I don't get this Birmingham thing, I'm going to have to keep looking. There's another one in Hull come up this week that's probably worth a go."

Becky looked dumbfounded. Jess didn't feel like she could survive an interrogation over that last statement just at the moment, so before her friend had a chance to react she added, "It was great to see you all at the barn dance. You seemed"— she swallowed to overcome the sudden urge to cry—"you all seemed to be having a great time."

Becky gave a sigh of happy contentment, her friend's problems momentarily forgotten. "We are," she said, simply. "We just are. Rak's amazing, the kids are amazing . . ."

"You're amazing," interjected Jess.

"I am, aren't I?" said Becky, and then laughed at herself. "I mean, I just feel . . . I can do this working mum thing. If it's good enough for Michelle Obama, it's good enough for me."

"And you know Rakesh will be supportive, of course?"

Becky gave Jess a sideways look. "To be honest," she admitted, "Rak has always been supportive of my career really. I just couldn't see it. I was putting these barriers up, making excuses. It was me, not him. I was scared to try, and fail. And I used the kids as a bit of a reason not to. I remember being secretly relieved when I got pregnant with Isla, because it meant I had longer before anyone could reasonably expect me to try and get a job."

"Ah," said Jess. "Sometimes we play tricks on ourselves. We find excuses to hide from our feelings because we don't want to see the truth for what it really is." Which was what Jess had been doing too. Time to stop and get real.

"I talked to Rak, a few days ago," Becky went on.

"He mentioned that," Jess told her. "It sounds like you had a really good discussion. I'm so glad for you both. He seemed really supportive about work."

"He is," Becky sighed happily. "And it was all the stuff about him not being around for the children, not doing family things together, and not pulling his weight in the house, putting us last on his list of priorities all the time. It was a major talk."

"So, the going-back-to-work thing?" Jess pressed gently. "Is this more than a cunning plan now?"

Becky nodded slowly and gave Jess a delighted grin.

"Go on, then, spit it out," said Jess, summoning up an answering smile with difficulty.

"I had lunch with Alistair and one of the partners yesterday," Becky confided.

"Did you now? And what about the kiddiwinks?"

"Aha, well they spent a bit of time with Grandma Diana. Also, I've got to tell you, I'm thanking God it was the beginning of term this week. It's been a looong summer."

"So, Diana stepped up," said Jess with admiration. "She moves fast; we were only talking about it a couple of weeks ago. How did they all get on?"

"Brilliantly, apparently. They all arrived back filthy and exhausted, Diana included. They had a whale of a time."

"And Alistair?"

Becky smiled like the cat that got the cream. "They really, really want me!" she said in wonderment.

"Course they do. What have they offered?"

"Part-time—at my request—junior solicitor in family law with a pretty decent starting salary, plus contracted review of salary and role after six months. *And* I can work from home two days a week out of three. It's a biggish commute, but just once a week, plus it's a shorter working day when I'm in the office, so I can avoid the rush hour."

"That is one sweet deal!" Jess exclaimed.

"It is. They pride themselves on being family-friendly; and half the partners are women, which makes a nice change, so it's not just a politically correct veneer. They really mean it."

"You'll be a partner within the year," teased Jess.

"I've got some catching up to do. After all, I've been out of the job market for eight years. They've actually been really, really generous. We even had a conversation about me working up to being offered a partnership in a few years, so you're not far off. Obviously, there are no guarantees, but it's nice to have had that discussion at such an early stage. And things will get easier as the kids get older. Isla will be starting preschool in two years. It'll fly by, if the last few years are anything to go by."

"It would look pretty bad if the family law team itself wasn't family-friendly," Jess pointed out. "But that all sounds amazing. When do you start?"

"They want me to start at the end of this month, which will give me a couple of weeks to get Angus settled into preschool and give Diana a trial run wrangling Isla for full days. I don't want to burn her out. What if she can't cope?" Becky chewed her lip anxiously.

"I think Diana's got the measure of Isla," Jess reassured

her. "My only worry is what mischief they'll get up to. They'll be a right pair—like Thelma and Louise—if you ask me."

Autumn term, thought Jess, the lead weight still in her stomach weighing all the heavier at the thought of the children at the school enjoying the new library books she had chosen. And how sad that there wouldn't be the little trips out to the phone-box library that she and Amanda had planned! A class trip out to see a defibrillator just didn't have the same appeal, she was guessing.

"So, what did Rakesh say?" asked Jess. "About Diana and everything?"

"Funnily enough, he was much more positive than I thought he would be. I wasn't sure if he approved of Diana because— let's admit—she is a bit wild. But he loves the idea of Diana filling in the childcare gaps, with me doing something mean-ingful and not feeling guilty about using childcare. I'll be in a much better frame of mind to enjoy my children when I *am* with them. He's even suggested we pay for a cleaner!" Becky gave Jess a high five, then added wryly, "Provided I'm the one who finds them and sets it up, of course."

"You can't expect a leopard to change its spots overnight," said Jess.

"No, true," said Becky. "But to be fair, I don't know why I thought I had to do the cleaning myself, when Rak wasn't even assuming I would. It was all me, putting it on myself."

For a moment, Jess had forgotten her own job situation, which was not nearly as joyful. She half hoped the interview would be a disaster, that she wouldn't get the post, wouldn't need to take action. But then if she didn't, there was slim to no chance of anything local coming up, and the pressing need for employment would remain.

*

On the way back home, her mood lifted by Becky's good news, Jess was thrilled to see Joan making slow but steady progress along the street. She had a walking stick and her leg dragged slightly, but she was walking independently and doing very well.

Jess was just about to hail her but decided not to when she saw Gordon, of the dashing panama hat, coming toward Joan from the opposite direction. He was holding in his hand a short-stemmed bouquet of beautiful pink and yellow roses. He stopped and lifted his hat to Joan as he approached; and as they met, Jess was thrilled to see him offer her the flowers.

"Well!" thought Jess as she watched the delightful tableau. She couldn't hear what they were saying, but she could see a girlish blush rising on Joan's cheeks as she looked out from under her eyelashes flirtatiously. All her hopes had been fulfilled. Joan and Gordon really were the library's first bona fide romance. And its last . . . ?

Feeling glum again, Jess decided to distract herself by feeding the ducks. She had nearly half a loaf from Paddy which had grown too stale to eat.

The ducks were thrilled with her offering. The white male—who, by the looks of the adolescent ducks, had impregnated pretty much all of the females that year—barged his way to the front. He quacked noisily, even with his beak full of bread, at anyone who dared to get too close. Once he had eaten his fill, Jess broke up the rest of the bread and scattered it on the ground for the girls and the young ones. She was just brushing the crumbs off her hands and her shirt when a loud *parp* made her jump. Half thinking it was the white male duck, she turned and saw Mungo and Diana in Mungo's open-top sports car. Diana was waving frantically at her.

"We're off for a champagne supper at the open-air opera," Diana explained. "It's *Fidelio*. I've always loved it."

"She made me," joked Mungo, straightening his cravat and smoothing his hair.

"You're both looking very distinguished," said Jess.

"Thank you, darling," said Diana. "I do love a reason to dress up, and a man to dress up for." Her face was suddenly serious. "This is all down to you. Mungo is the best 'husband' I never had. We would never have been having so much fun if you hadn't intervened."

"I'm glad," said Jess, suddenly tearing up and not wanting Diana to see. Damn, she should have worn her dark glasses.

"So, what are you up to tonight?" queried Diana, looking at her sharply.

"Oh, nothing much," said Jess, wondering whether to remind her friend she had to spend the evening preparing for an interview the next day with a view to being recruited to a job she didn't want. "Nothing, really. Early night."

"You should come with us," said Mungo, gallantly.

"I really shouldn't. Thank you though. Have a fabulous time."

Chapter Twenty-Six

"Don't go!"

"What do you mean 'don't go'?" retorted Jess. "How can I not go to a job interview?" She had felt lonely after Diana and Mungo left, but she was beginning to regret dialing up Hannah for a bit of company with her early evening glass of wine. It had been a while, and she had been feeling bad about neglecting her friend. "I've got to go," she said. "They're expecting me. And anyway, I need this job."

"Ridiculous," grumbled Hannah. "Bloody ridiculous."

Jess gulped. Hannah never swore. "What's so difficult to understand about 'I need a job'?" she asked defensively. It was like her friend had gone mad. She was making no sense. She took another large gulp of wine in irritation. And Hannah was driving her to drink.

Hannah took a deep breath and plonked her coffee down so violently it sloshed over the side. "Listen," she said heavily. "How do you think I feel, watching you build this amazing life for yourself, making friends, creating a beautiful home"— she waved her hand expansively—"I've seen you taking risks, putting Mimi's books into the library, I've seen you open yourself to the possibility of romance, even . . ."

"Yeah, and see where that got me," interjected Jess.

Hannah growled in frustration. "You've made so much progress though! Mimi would have loved to see you being so brave, so open to change, to happiness. It's what she wanted. It's all she wanted, was for you to be happy and fulfilled."

"But I don't understand why you don't see I need to get this job," said Jess, doggedly.

"I think you're scared," challenged Hannah. "I think it's all going too well, and it's the same old thing with you. You just can't allow happiness to happen, can you? And it's understandable," she said earnestly. "I get that terrible things have happened to you, Jess. You know I've never been able to imagine how awful it was to lose your parents."

"And Mimi, remember," said Jess, defensively. "I lost Mimi too. I'm just— All I'm saying is bad things happen and it doesn't do to be . . ." She waved her hand in frustration, searching for the words.

"It doesn't do to be happy," Hannah filled the gap for her. "You have to sabotage it before anything else happens, because at least if it's you destroying things, you're still in control. And that's the thing that matters, right?"

Jess blinked. Was Hannah really right? Did she really destroy everything that was good just to beat fate to the punch? No. Why would she be so blind? So destructive?

"You're wrong," she said, with a tiny wobble of uncertainty.

"Fine," sighed Hannah, defeated. "Go."

"I will," Jess replied, reaching forward to kill the screen.

The alarm inserted itself into her brain like a cattle prod, seemingly only minutes after she had finally slept.

She looked out of the window and smiled, in spite of herself, at a lady in the little library looking at the cookery books shelf. She didn't know her—and probably never would now. She wondered when the news would get out about the library needing to close. Perhaps the best thing would be to just go ahead and do it. In fact, that was what she should do tomorrow. There was no point letting things drag on. She needed to face facts. That was another thing: her relationship that never was, with Aidan, was just like a fantasy from one of those romantic novels; they could never make it work in the real world. The timing was wrong. The situation was all wrong. They were star-crossed, or something. And anyhow, she—a childless woman—was ill-equipped to be a stepmother to a complicated young girl like Maisie.

Who did she think she had been kidding?

Heavy with sorrow, Jess made herself some scrambled eggs and then couldn't face eating them, so she put a little bit in a saucer for the cats, only for them to turn their noses up at it and squall for their normal food.

"So ungrateful," muttered Jess, not minding really, as she opened a can of tuna for them as a special treat, seeing as she would be out for most of the day for her interview. She was probably going to have to give them back to Aidan if she was moving to the city. They were country cats through and through. They would hate being cooped up in some high-rise Birmingham flat. So would she.

When she set off, downhearted and exhausted from lack of sleep, the countryside around Middlemass mocked her by being more beautiful than she had ever seen it. The valleys were swathed in a soft, heavy down of mist, but driving up from the valley to the top of the tor that led her to the main road, she burst out above the low cloud into brilliant yellow sunshine, the landscape laid out before her in every shade of green and—here and there—the painterly dabs of yellow and orange that promised autumn glory to come. The highest rooftops of Portneath, in the distance, were poking above the mist, like a fairy-tale land. And it had been enchanted for her. It had been an enchanted summer.

Anxious about the long journey, she had set off so early the traffic was light at first. She made good time, getting onto the M5 and settling down, depressed, to the endless drone of motorway driving. It may have just been her mood, but the daylight seemed to dim as she headed north. Angry gray clouds formed on the horizon as she drove toward them.

She was due at the Birmingham City Council's libraries division offices at midday. Despite arriving at the outskirts of the city only just after ten o'clock, the one-way system and the dodgy zip code meant she still had a panic over finding the right building. Then she had another panic over parking. Eventually, she found a space for Betsy in an anonymous concrete multistory parking lot, costing an exorbitant amount an hour.

She just about had time before the interview to find a sandwich bar, where she bought comfort food—a hot chocolate and an almond croissant, stuffing them down to calm her nerves. Her appetite roared back to life after the long drive, and then, draining the dregs of the hot chocolate, she felt a bit sick. She went to the loo to wash the stickiness off her hands, discovering bleakly that the room had a blue lightbulb so crack addicts couldn't find their veins.

Accepting she would look ghastly in the mirror there whatever she did to her face, she just slapped on some blusher and lipstick and hoped for the best. She was wearing her favorite work suit, a moss green skirt and jacket with a nipped-in waist. She knew it suited her—Mimi always loved her to wear it—but today she felt frumpy, colorless, and very alone.

The three other candidates smiled at her wanly as she joined them in the waiting room. There was a mumsy-looking woman, an extremely thin young woman who looked even more nervous than Jess, and a beaky, balding man in his fifties. Jess immediately felt she had overreached herself. Who did she think she was to apply for a senior librarian's job, with her limited skills? The job would clearly go to one of the older, more experienced candidates. Thinking this, she was surprised to find she was relieved. Okay, so her savings were dwindling to nothing, but she could still eke them out for another couple of months, still draw the tattered remnants of her dream life in Middlemass around her as she looked for something else. She would savor every moment.

Feeling now as if she was just there for the ride, Jess settled in to enjoy herself. First there was an aptitude, personality, and skills test. She had never been asked to do anything like it before and she raced through the multiple-choice, before persuading herself, at the last minute, that they were all trick questions and not one was the obvious answer she had previously thought. It was too late to change her mind by then.

Straight after that, she was in the panel interview with three formidable-looking people seated behind a long table firing questions at her about disability inclusion, funding rounds, and education proposals. She came out thinking she had managed to hit the target with a couple of her off-the-top-of-the-head ideas and had even found herself waxing lyrical on the need to reach disadvantaged parents who can't afford books for their children. She couldn't possibly have done enough to earn an offer though. Of that she was reassuringly certain.

It was still only three o'clock, but the rush-hour traffic was already building. Jess wondered about getting something else to eat; she felt starving again now her nerves had died down. But she decided to get straight back in the car and face the journey home. With so little time left to enjoy living there, she didn't want to miss a single moment in Ivy Cottage.

She found a garage to fill up and grabbed a bag of wine gums at the checkout. Mimi would be spinning in her grave at such shocking dietary habits. *Not how I brought you up*, she would say. Jess desperately wished she could hear her now. "Not how I brought you up," she said aloud, into the space. Silence was the reply.

The first part of the journey, getting back onto the motorway, was easier to navigate than the journey in. Jess switched off the satnav and just followed the green and yellow signs out of the city, but it seemed half the working population of Birmingham had decided to go home early and that—coupled with the end of the school day—slowed her exit to a mixture of stationary waiting and first-gear crawling.

Every song on the radio seemed to remind her of happier times: making jam in the kitchen in Bourton-on-the-Marsh with Mimi; celebrating Hannah's engagement with too much Prosecco and laughter. Suddenly—and most painfully of all, it turned out—was the song that had played on the radio when she and Aidan had been bat watching, shooting the breeze in the garden at Ivy Cottage with beers in their hands.

In her time left in Middlemass, she would have to steer clear of Aidan and Maisie to avoid further damage to her already bruised heart. Aidan knew she was going now, and with everything that was going on there was no point seeking further contact. It would only cause more pain.

Her heart ached for them both. And for herself.

Jess's mood lifted as she finally made it onto the smaller roads that led to Middlemass. She would be home by nine. Even after she sternly reminded herself this wouldn't be home for much longer, it was still an immense relief to turn down the little slip road she had spun off onto just months earlier.

The car was stuffy, and she opened the window a crack as she drove down the steep, narrow lane. As she passed Paddy's shop, a tendril of smoke wafted into the car and she sniffed appreciatively. The evenings had become chillier in the last few days and the village inhabitants had retreated to the warmth of the hearth. Perhaps she would light the woodstove when she got home and then—after supper—sit by it with some cocoa until she felt sleepy. She would be glad of her bed tonight.

Chapter Twenty-Seven

In her dream, she was wheeling a cart of books around a huge, gray library. The endless corridors of shelves seemed to close in on her claustrophobically. The cart, its wheels drumming on the floor as she pushed, got heavier and heavier, teetering precariously from side to side. No matter how many books she put back on the shelves, the more there seemed still to do.

When Jess woke, the rumbling of the book trolley wheels became the drumming of the rain which was beating down monotonously.

Sitting in her usual place at the kitchen table, Jess was listlessly scrolling through the job sites when the email alert sounded and there, in bold, was a newly arrived email from Birmingham City Council. Her hand shaking, she went to open it and skim read it:

. . . a field of excellent candidates . . . pleasure in offering you . . . Please return your confirmation . . .

She got up and walked away from it into the sitting room. Motion seemed imperative, even though it didn't have purpose. To add to her misery, looking across the pond, she could see Aidan and Maisie's house. Then she looked away and saw the little library at the end of her front garden. Everywhere she looked there seemed to be painful little reminders of the life she could have had.

It would be a relief to leave the village in many ways. Or at least that was what she told herself.

Jess sighed. This was it. The next step. All the signs were there now. She should sell up and go. The trouble was that her head was telling her to accept the job and get on with it even as her heart was still telling her something else. Agonizing, she jumped when there was a knock at the door.

"Mungo and I are the bringers of good tidings," announced Diana. "That's got to be worth at least a cup of tea. In fact, I feel, it's so good it's worth a choccie biccie or two, if you happen to have such a thing."

Jess laid a tea tray despondently, while the two friends sat in the little sitting room. She wasn't sure any good tidings could overcome her gloom at having to dismantle the telephone-box library.

"I think I ought to get some sort of award for the most stateswoman-like chair of the parish council. You will be wildly impressed."

Mungo nodded eagerly. "You will," he said.

"Go on then," replied Jess, trying to inject some enthusiasm into her voice. She was exhausted after her trip to Birmingham and then not being able to sleep for hours. She didn't see how there was anything that Diana could tell her that would make her feel less depressed.

"The library will live on!" said Diana, flourishing her teacup and spilling a fair bit onto the table in the process.

"How?" asked Jess, astonished.

"I've knocked the defibrillator nonsense into the long grass, done a shady deal with the village hall committee chair . . ."

"Can the defibrillator go in the village hall?" Jess asked in a rush, her mind buzzing. "Isn't it locked most of the time? The defibrillator has to be accessible, I thought."

"They've agreed it can go in the porch, on the wall next to the door," said Diana triumphantly. "Bish, bash, bosh, job's a good 'un. The inhabitants of Middlemass can now electrocute each other with impunity."

Jess nodded slowly, letting it sink in. What a simple solution. Why had it not come up sooner? It was great for the community, of course, but a pity it didn't matter to her anymore.

"You're an amazing negotiator," she said without energy.

"I know! Next stop, world peace," Diana replied exuberantly, making Mungo cackle in approval.

Jess needed to tell them about Birmingham, of course, but she didn't feel able to do it without crying; and she had spent so much time tearing up in front of her two friends recently, she thought she would spare them more blubbering and let Diana revel in her victory for a while longer. There would be time enough to tell her in a few days.

When Diana had been suitably praised for her genius, she and Mungo were setting off to get ready for lunch in some fabulous new brasserie in Portneath they were wanting to try, having failed to persuade Jess to come with them.

"Ah yes, by the way," Diana said, remembering at the door, "Amanda, the head teacher from the school, came around looking for you yesterday. I was passing when she knocked. She said she needed to speak to you urgently about something. Seemed quite excited."

"It'll be about the book order that's going in for the school library," replied Jess listlessly as she cleared up the mugs. "I'll pop down there later." She should make sure her work there was all tied up properly, or the effort would be wasted. That had to be what it was. She couldn't imagine what Amanda wanted from her though. She had listed the titles, authors, and ISBNs of everything she recommended.

She had been so looking forward to the plans they had

for the school and the little library; the storytelling sessions and story-writing competitions; there could have been author talks, perhaps, themed reading weeks . . . Jess kicked herself again for not doing all the fabulous school liaison work Brian had encouraged her to do in Bourton-on-the-Marsh, but she had stupidly declined because she was sure there was someone else who would do it better. Now she finally, belatedly, had the confidence, she was going to end up working full-time miles away, drawing up ever-decreasing budgets and identifying funding gaps in a job she didn't even want.

Because she was going to accept it, there was no doubt about that. Just not now. Not yet.

Aidan was out when Jess went over with her stash of manga comics for Maisie, but it wasn't him she had come to see. In fact, she had made sure his Land Rover was gone before she set off. There was such a long pause after she knocked, she began to think Maisie wasn't in either, but eventually she heard the fumbling of locks and the door opened to reveal a pale, somber Maisie. Her hair was tousled and none too clean. She was wearing what might have been joggers or might have been pajama bottoms, along with a Grateful Dead T-shirt with a gruesome image on the front.

"I admire your taste in T-shirts," Jess said.

"Dad gave me it," she admitted. "It turns out he does have some cool clothes, but not many—mostly he dresses like a boomer. Actually, he is a boomer."

"He's only in his thirties, you horrible child!" laughed Jess. "And what does that make me?"

"You're not a boomer," Maisie conceded, good-naturedly, breaking into an engaging grin, possibly over the memory that her dad had not, in fact, "given" her the T-shirt. "Do you want a cup of tea, or something? Dad's out at work."

"No tea, thanks, lovely, I just came to drop these off." Jess handed Maisie the carrier bag she was holding.

"Manga! Thank you!" she said, peering inside and then giving a little hop. "And these are the ones I've been dying to read."

"I've got more," said Jess. "You should come and see. Come soon," she added. *Or it will be too late*, she thought, but didn't say. The child didn't need to know that. Not yet, anyhow.

"Oh, I don't . . ." Maisie blushed. "I don't want to disturb you."

"You wouldn't be. You know you can come whenever you like. But I tell you what, I'm having a clear out so I'll bring them all over for you. It's great to see them going to a good home."

"These are so seriously cool," Maisie said, walking through to the kitchen with Jess following. She put the stack of comics on the kitchen table and spread them out.

"I thought you'd probably have read the *Ghost in the Shell* ones, so I chose different, but I've got those too," said Jess, as they pored over the magazines.

"How are the cats?" Maisie asked, shyly.

"They're getting big. Like you," Jess said, thinking the child must have grown at least an inch over the summer holiday— probably more like two. "What have you been up to since I saw you last?"

"I dunno . . . back at school. Boring." Maisie shuffled her feet, twiddling her hair.

"Everything okay with you and your dad?"

Maisie nodded, reluctantly. "He's all right, Dad, most of the time—for a boomer—but he's been weird recently. I can't talk to him."

Jess bit her tongue. It wasn't for her to explain why Aidan had been preoccupied. She thought he was wrong to keep the potential court hearing from his daughter, but it wasn't for her to tell him that. That said, she thought, he should know Maisie felt this way about talking to him. But again, Jess felt it wasn't her place. They had agreed she would keep her distance to help protect Maisie, and that's what she was going to do.

"Mum's here a lot at the moment, too," Maisie volunteered. "That's weird too. She basically hates being here and she doesn't normally do anything she doesn't want, so I don't get that, either."

"I'm so sorry you're going through this," said Jess, impressed at Maisie's insight into her mother's motives.

"They think I don't understand what's going on, but I do."

Jess sighed. Of course, the child knew. She was bright. Having something being kept from her was the worst way for Aidan and Lucie to manage things.

"Tell them," suggested Jess suddenly. "Tell them you want to know what's going on, and you want to have a say."

"I will," said Maisie. Her face was pink, and her eyes were suspiciously moist.

Impulsively, Jess reached over and gave her a hug. At first Maisie was stiff, but after a moment, she relaxed into Jess's embrace, wrapping her arms briefly around her waist.

"Mum and Dad need to sort themselves out," Maisie said, detaching herself.

She was withdrawing and Jess knew when to beat a retreat.

"Look, Maisie," Jess said, "make your dad happy by taking a bit of time off the computer. Read your manga stuff. Come and get the rest of them from me too. Soon. Okay? While I'm still here," she said out loud at last.

Maisie's head snapped up.

"You're leaving?"

"Maybe. Probably, yeah."

"Don't go!" Maisie said with anguish in her voice.

"It's for a job, sadly, I have to work. But I'm going to miss you more than you're going to miss me, Maisie. You've got exciting stuff ahead of you. It's all going to be okay. Just make sure your mum and dad know what you want, okay?"

"I will," said Maisie as she walked Jess to the door. "And thanks, Jess," she added, sadly.

Back in the cottage, Jess didn't expect to speak to anyone else that day, but just as she was picking the last roses of summer in the front garden, she heard an exclamation.

"You're here," said Amanda. "I just thought I'd come up from school on the off chance," she said to Jess. "I tried you yesterday, but there was no reply."

"I know, I'm so sorry. I'm not avoiding you; I was out all day yesterday. How can I help?"

"Make me a cup of tea and I'll tell you." Amanda grinned.

"Look," said Amanda in the kitchen, wasting no time as she watched Jess fill the kettle, "I hope you don't think I'm going off on something totally insane, but I had a meeting with my school group yesterday morning, and we were kicking around this idea—"

"School group?" interjected Jess.

"Sorry—all the schools locally are in this group where the heads meet regularly. There's six of us primary schools in and around Portneath. We share ideas and resources. We're all quite small, so it's great for getting discounts from buying in bulk, that kind of thing. Anyway, we were talking yesterday about our reading and literacy programs for the next academic year. I told everyone about the phone-box library, by the way; they were all really envious. Anyhow, there's real pressure on budgets but we would all like to be doing more, organizing book days, author visits, all these amazing things, but we just don't have the time and the money, not as individual schools. But then, we had this brilliant idea . . ." She looked at Jess for an invitation to continue.

"Go on," said Jess, summoning up a smile.

"We pretty much wrote the job description there and then, but the bottom line is, we have agreed to club together to pay the salary of a kind of books czar for all the schools: someone to organize events, create competitions, run (say) poetry workshops, all the good stuff. The pay's not great, and we can only afford it to be part-time . . . But that's you," she finished, looking at Jess expectantly. "We want you to apply for the job. And between you and me," she confided, "it's a shoo-in. Oh, and we need to come up with a better job title, obviously."

Jess was lost for words. "That's so miraculous and wonderful," she said at last. "Damn, crying again!" she went on, wiping her eyes for the umpteenth time in the last few days. "I'm going to have to stop doing this."

"You are. Now, it's ridiculously short notice, I know, but we've already posted the advert, we're interviewing you next week and want you to start in six weeks—actually, we're saying that, but really we want you to start straightaway. Are you in?"

Jess thought.

It was her dream job, in a beautiful place; it was just enough money for her keep. It meant keeping Ivy Cottage, which seemed too good to be true. In not being available to her, Aidan might as well be miles away; but Jess knew that with her other friends—with Mungo, Diana, Becky, and all the others—she would at least be able to stay.

"The only thing I was worried about—the reason I was rushing," admitted Amanda, "was that Diana told me you were going for a job interview in Birmingham and I'm sure they'll have offered it to you . . ." She looked at Jess inquiringly over the rim of her mug.

"They did," said Jess.

Amanda sagged. "Damn," she said. "Am I too late? Have you said yes? Of course, silly me, of course you have. You wouldn't have applied for it if you were going to say no."

Jess took a deep breath.

"No," said Amanda, holding up her hand. "Don't say it. Don't say anything. Just promise me you'll think about it, okay?"

Jess nodded. "I will," she said. "And thank you. Really, thank you so much."

Jess felt bereft at being left alone with her increasingly complex dilemmas. It was too much to think through on her own, but it was too early to call Hannah in New Zealand, where it was still the middle of the night.

She wandered out of the back door of Ivy Cottage with her mug of tea, and let the kittens out into the garden. They were spending more time outside now, but Jess had not yet fitted the cat flap. She had wanted to make sure they had no interest in going out of the front garden and into the road before she gave them completely free rein. She sighed. The last few days had been exhausting, and a heavy languor washed over her as she sat in the garden and contemplated her future.

Chapter Twenty-Eight

Aidan found her dozing in the afternoon sunshine.

"Hey, Jess," he murmured, not to wake her up too abruptly.

"Are they supposed to be doing that?" he asked when she opened her eyes.

The first thing she saw was both kittens swinging by their front paws from the top of the bird table. They had scaled the bark-covered post but were not quite succeeding in summiting over the lip of the table itself.

"Certainly not," she exclaimed, leaping up.

He pushed her gently back onto the bench and reached out a long arm to detach the kittens one by one, popping them gently on the ground.

She found she couldn't look at him and didn't know what to do with her hands. She wondered if the ease they had shared between them would ever come back. Not likely.

"They're monkeys," she said of the two little cats, relieved to have a diversion. "Clearly bird tables and these two are mutually incompatible. Although I think they'll find it even harder to get onto the top of it when they're heavier."

"It's good to see them being adventurous."

"If you say so," said Jess, determined to keep the conversation light. "I must admit, I've had no evidence of mice in the larder since I got them."

"They saw the writing on the wall," Aidan said with a laugh as he settled down next to her on the bench.

"Sensible mice," said Jess. "Shame the bats don't have the same sensibilities."

"You love the bats really."

"You're right; they're okay," she admitted. "It would have been handy to have some loft space I could actually use, though."

There was a comfortable silence.

"How's Lucie?" blurted Jess. "Maisie tells me she's been around quite a lot over the last few days."

"She has," said Aidan, "but I was coming over to say that she's just gone back to Bristol at last. I thought we'd never get rid of her. Me and Maisie thought we'd fire up the barbie tonight. It's such a beautiful day; might be the last time before the autumn. We'd both really like you to join us. It's nothing fancy. I've got some sausages from the butcher in Portneath."

There was a pause.

Jess was suddenly overwhelmed by the impossibility of spending any more time in close proximity with him, let alone an evening socializing politely as if everything was normal.

"Aidan," she said, squeezing out the single word from an impossibly tight chest. Her body felt like it weighed a ton. It was too much.

"I know, I know," he said. "It's been . . ." He made an exasperated gesture with his hands.

"To put it mildly," she agreed.

"But I remember once you said there would be 'zero weirdness' between us."

"I lied." Jess slumped, her hands over her face.

"Okay, listen," he said, intensely, peeling her hands away and demanding eye contact. "Will you just trust me on this? I know I'm not entitled to ask, but I need you to come tonight. Just come, okay? Maisie needs to see you. And so do I."

Jess sighed. "Okay. I'll bring some veg—a nice salad or something." That was what she had been planning for her solitary supper anyway, so it wasn't a big deal.

"That'd be great. If you can get salad into my daughter, you're a better person than me."

"I wouldn't bet on it, but I'll give it a go."

There was something Jess needed to do before she went to Aidan's house. Both job offers required a polite, thoughtful reply and Jess didn't rush with either when she sat down at the kitchen table with her laptop. First, the Birmingham job: the obvious next step up the ladder in her librarian career; a new start in a city far away, no complicated relationships to navigate, no tumbledown house to maintain, no community demands to tug at her heartstrings and eat into her time. Then there was Amanda Martin's invitation: to work ridiculously hard, for half the money, bringing reading and the joy of books to the little Middlemass primary school and a handful of other local, village schools besides. The funding was probably precarious; the job was low budget and big aspiration. She was sure she would have to give many more hours than she was going to be paid for. She wasn't sure when she would find the time—or the money—to stop Ivy Cottage falling apart.

It felt like the very first day, when she had arrived at the village pond and sat in her car looking at the forks in the road not knowing which way to turn. Should she return to something like her old life: familiar, safe, dull? Or should she pursue the possibility of the new life she had glimpsed in these few short months here in Middlemass: risky, aggravating, exciting and—as far as romance was concerned—potentially, so, so painful?

*

Emails sent, Jess resolved to dig up the now straggled and mildew-speckled plants in the bit of the vegetable garden she had yet to tackle. In one small section there were the vegetables and salads grown from the seed that Jess and Maisie had sown. She was coming to the end of some easy-to-grow radishes, coriander, and rocket, along with a small row of cut-and-come-again salad leaves.

In the vast, still uncleared section she found a bizarre-looking squash hiding under a rambling canopy of leaves and cleaned it off, carefully. It looked a bit like something from outer space. She wished she could show it to Maisie. Presumably it was edible, as it was clearly the love child of deliberately planted ones in a previous year, when Maisie's great-grandpop was still alive. Once, she and Mimi had had an outbreak of renegade pumpkins and squashes of all shapes and sizes when they used compost full of pumpkin seeds that were determined to sprout.

The best part of the haul in the Ivy Cottage garden was some beetroot and little potatoes. With her prize squash, they gave her some good ideas for a dish that might tempt a twelve-year-old not keen on fruit and vegetables.

She carefully peeled and chopped the squash and beetroot, dyeing her hands bright red and orange in the process. She cut them all into little cubes and chucked them in a roasting tin along with the little potatoes which went in whole, peel and all. After a drizzle of olive oil, a sprinkling of balsamic vinegar and some sprigs of thyme, she shoved them into the Aga, confident that the old stove would work its magic.

Obviously, it wasn't a date or anything like that, Jess told herself firmly. That said, she was still in her old, muddy gardening clothes, so she should at least have a bath and get changed.

Soaking in the warm water, she scrubbed at her nails to

get the garden out from under them. She slipped down in the water so her hair was submerged, spreading like seaweed, a frondy halo, framing her freckly face. She had caught the sun while she was gardening that afternoon, and her limbs felt pleasantly heavy and achy from the digging.

She dressed in her trusty favorite jeans with a scoop-necked teal top. The color worked well with the turquoise and silver necklace Mimi had once given her for Christmas after she admired it in the secondhand shop window. Mimi had always been good at presents.

She tied up her still-damp hair into a tight ponytail to straighten out the curl, but it looked too severe, so she let it loose again. It would dry into ringlets, but never mind. It was overdue for a cut, but the tight curls it formed when left to its own devices at least stopped it trailing quite so far down her back. Even so, the mass of fluffy hair obscured much of the necklace and a good amount of her face. She looked like an unclipped poodle. She found an old silk scarf of Mimi's, a paisley pattern with all the shades of blue from periwinkle to deep navy, and twisting it into a rope she used it as a hairband, tying it at the nape of her neck. *There, better*, she decided, looking at herself impassively in the long, heavily foxed mirror on the back of the wardrobe door. Jess wasn't vain—she was too short and easily overlooked for that.

Grabbing her favorite green cashmere cardigan because, if they were outside barbecuing, it would be cold later, she took one last look in the mirror. It was futile making any effort anyhow, knowing how polished and glamorous Lucie was.

The vegetables had roasted beautifully, going soft and luscious with caramelized edges. She picked out the strands of thyme, which had done their job, and crumbled a block of feta cheese into the tin before returning it to the oven for a few more minutes. She would have to use her oven gloves to take the tin over the road to Aidan, which meant she wouldn't be able to carry the wine. While she was waiting for the feta to warm through and melt a little, she grabbed her leather rucksack and popped the wine inside it, shrugging it onto her back.

"You had better be good, you two," she told the kittens, who momentarily gazed at her as if butter wouldn't melt and then carried on boxing each other's ears. She examined their favorite arm of the sofa ruefully. The material had taken on an ominously fluffy character, having been pulled apart by their tenacious little claws, as they continued to ignore the toys she'd bought them earlier in the summer, in favor of wrecking the furniture. She must go back to the pet shop in Portneath and see if they had any good scratching posts—if it wasn't too little too late.

She carefully removed the tin of vegetables from the oven for the last time and popped some foil over the top to keep it all warm. She was set.

Chapter Twenty-Nine

Laden with her hot tin and backpack, Jess could only knock at Aidan's door by kicking it, which failed to rouse either of the two inhabitants. It didn't even get Carter barking, which would have been useful for a change.

After two attempts, she gave up and went exploring around the side, where she found a waist-high gate into the back garden. She couldn't see Maisie or Aidan, but she knew they were nearby, as a billow of smoke from the barbecue drifted across to her and delicious smells wafted her way.

Then, perfectly timed, little Carter shuffled around the corner and—seeing her—let out a volley of sharp barks before ambling toward her, snuffling interestedly at the base of the gate.

He looked up at her and then back at Aidan, who had now appeared, in a smart blue and white striped chef's apron, with a pair of tongs in his hand.

"Sorry," he said. "Have you been there for ages? I thought I heard a knock at the front door, but when I went to see there was no one there."

"That was me," said Jess. "I should have had faith and waited longer."

"Are you staying the night?" he joked, spotting the backpack.

"I am absolutely not staying the night," Jess said, pinking up uncomfortably. "I fully intend to stay in a sufficiently sober state to make it back across the road. It's the stuff I didn't have enough hands for, that's all. And also, don't joke. It's too soon."

"Sorry," said Aidan, contrite. "I'm really, really glad you came. Now, this smells amazing," he said, pecking Jess on the cheek and waving his tongs at the oven tin Jess was holding.

"Roasted veggies. I thought they'd go."

"They'll be perfect."

"Amazingly enough, they're out of the vegetable garden. Nothing I can really take credit for. I was just clearing up and there they were."

"I hope you didn't dig up the asparagus?"

"God no, I was eating tons of it earlier this year. I'm just letting it grow now, though, obviously."

The mundane gardening talk helped distract Jess from any potential awkwardness and Aidan ushered her into the garden where Maisie was waiting, smiling and relaxed. It was a relief to see them both in such a good mood.

"I brought veg," said Jess with a smile.

"Yay!" said Maisie, not entirely without irony. "Sweet."

"Take the tray, could you Maisie, and stick it in the oven to keep warm?" suggested Aidan. "I urgently need to get this woman a drink. What will you have? I've got most things, except white wine—"

"Aha." Jess handed him the bottle from her rucksack.

"—And now I even have white wine. Is this what you'd like?"

"Yes please." Jess gave herself a mental pat on the back. Here she was, making polite conversation with Aidan as if he were just a neighbor she got on well with. Which was all he was.

"And we need to get you fed," Aidan told Maisie, "so you can get to bed at a reasonable time. School tomorrow."

"I hate September," she groaned.

*

As well as the sausages on the barbecue—and seeing how Jess had brought roast veg rather than salad after all—Aidan had chucked some salad leaves into a bowl and dressed it with balsamic vinegar, olive oil, and a sprinkling of rough sea salt, just like she used to do with Mimi. He had also put a large loaf of crusty bread on the table. With hunks of that, soaking up the juices from the meat and the roasted vegetables, they all ate hungrily in a relaxed, companionable silence. For Jess, it was the first time she had eaten properly for days. *I can do this*, she thought. *Get me, doing this . . .*

"Gorgeous beetroot," Aidan said, helping himself to more.

"This is a feast," mumbled Jess through a mouthful, glancing up at Maisie. The two of them locked eyes and grinned at each other. She felt so relaxed. She was doing this. She was being Aidan's friend, hanging out with Maisie, and there didn't need to be anything else between them.

Once they were replete, Aidan detailed Maisie to do the dishwasher and then take herself off for a shower and bed.

The barbecue was still radiating a good amount of heat, so they went back outside, but Aidan insisted on wrapping the sofa throw around Jess's shoulders. She snuggled into it gratefully and waited on the bench while he made some coffee—decaffeinated at Jess's request.

Nearly dozing off, she felt rather than heard someone behind her.

"Don't jump," he said softly. "It's just me."

She turned, and Aidan handed her a mug of coffee just the way she liked it, as if it was something he had always done. Taking a deep swig from his own, he sat down beside her and together they watched the starlings' aerobatic displays, wheeling and flowing and tumbling endlessly.

He seemed in no hurry to say whatever it was he wanted to say, and Jess was in no hurry to hear it. She just wanted this. This moment. The sunset cast a golden glow over the horizon, and woodsmoke curled into the sky from a dozen cottage chimneys, scenting the air. The starlings swooped and dived in formation across the skies above the big willows by the stream. They would roost there tonight because they knew it was a safe place, just like Jess knew that Ivy Cottage was her safe place. It was a vibrant place too, where she could build the life Mimi wanted for her: good, interesting, worthwhile employment, a vegetable garden . . . Here Jess smiled, thinking of what Mimi would do with such good soil and the luxury of space: everything would be grown, frozen, bottled, or turned into gin. Mimi's sloe gin was legendary. Perhaps Jess's would be too. Here was a community she could plant herself in, and grow. As the years went by, who knew what the future would hold? One thing Jess did know was that she was home and life was full of nothing but possibilities.

"So," said Jess, feeling shy again for the first time since she had arrived there that evening.

"So . . ." said Aidan, doing that hair-tugging thing Jess now knew was his signal for feeling awkward.

"I'm really . . ." he tried again. Then he took a deep breath and let it slowly out. "Listen," he said. "Me and Maisie have been having some good talks lately. Proper talks. And I've been doing some pretty straight talking with Lucie, too, you'll be amazed to hear. Long overdue."

Jess nodded, infinitesimally, not wanting to interrupt his flow.

He went on. "Maisie's none too impressed with my cunning

plan to keep her out of court at all costs. Essentially, she told me it was a rubbish plan and that nothing—not even I—would prevent her from standing up in court to say what she wants. And she's told me"—he took a deep breath—"she's told me she wants to live here. With me. She is basically refusing to be away from me. And Lucie's legal counsel have told her she's got close to zero chance of getting sole residency against Maisie's will."

He sighed deeply, and Jess felt the tension leaving his body as he sat beside her, their thighs touching. She resisted the temptation to reach over and put her hand on his leg.

"She's too sharp for her own good, that girl," he added, with obvious pride. "Anyhow, she's been telling me in no uncertain terms that she fully expects her mum to stop causing trouble. She said the same to Lucie. That was quite a conversation," he said with masterly understatement. He stopped, gulped his coffee, and then carefully continued, "So, it's been settled now. In fact it's gone back to court already, with all of us discussing like grown-ups—and Maisie's the most grown-up of the three of us—how things are going to be. She'll spend term times with me. And maybe she'll spend a portion of the holidays with Lucie in Bristol. It's up to her. She decides.

"Lucie was desperate to get herself back to Bristol full-time, after all this," Aidan went on. "That's where her life is now, she's happy to admit; it turns out she's got a boyfriend up there and everything. She kept that close to her chest, didn't she? She understands now—at least I think she does—that what she's been doing isn't right." He sighed, looking at his hands. "It all seems so simple now. There's no game-playing. I'm properly free from her and—I've got to tell you—that's a pretty amazing feeling."

Jess's heart leapt, but she said nothing.

"It's long overdue, frankly," he went on. "I've been feeling like I had to pretend, for Maisie's sake."

"So, what happens next?" Jess asked, her skin fizzing with anticipation, but she wasn't quite ready to look over at him.

"We all move on with our lives," he said, spreading his hands. "I'm just sorry I've made it so complicated."

"No one goes into a marriage—and parenthood—expecting to divorce," said Jess gently.

"No, sure. I so wanted that same thing for Maisie, I was hanging on to a kind of pretense of that for dear life. It allowed Lucie to play me, but now I've called her bluff. Maisie's called her bluff. And it feels great."

"I'm glad you've decided," said Jess.

"Because the *other* thing Maisie has been expressing her opinion quite forcibly on . . . This is why you're here, if you haven't guessed already." She looked up and watched—his eyes ranging over her face, his gaze settling on her mouth.

Neither of them moved, for a long, yearning moment. Then, Jess slowly leaned forward to press her lips against his stubbly cheek. He turned as she did so, and she found her mouth colliding with his. Rather than pulling back, Jess stayed, as he gently wrapped his arm around her waist and pulled her close, deepening the kiss as he did so. Eventually Aidan pulled back to look her straight in the eye.

"I feel terrible for having messed you around these last few months," he murmured.

"It doesn't matter anymore."

"And, even now, I don't want to rush you—so . . ." he went on, settling her against his chest with his arms around her, "I'm thinking, me and Maisie are here in the village— where we belong—and here *you* are, in Ivy Cottage, where *you* belong. But what I want—what I *need* to know is: are you here to stay?"

Jess sighed. For a long, long moment she let her eyes rest on the starlings settling in the trees to roost.

"I'm here to stay," she replied, nodding, a deep peace stealing over her as she thought about her earlier replies to the job offers: the polite decline to Birmingham and the full-hearted, joyful yes to Amanda Martin.

"And us?" He looked at her with a steady gaze.

"Let's just see how it goes," she said with a smile and she leaned in to kiss him once more, knowing it was just the beginning.

Acknowledgments

What a pleasure and a privilege it has been to write this book about books. Who could resist a chance to name-check, and even quote from, some of their dearest favorites?

This has been a book begun in the real world and finished in a world few of us could ever have imagined. It has been a solace and a touchstone during this time and it brings a lump to my throat to know it will soon be out there, taking its chances in a book universe that has changed immensely. What never changes though, is—I hope—the appetite for stories that encapsulate the best of human nature. I don't think I will ever lose my appetite for creating them.

My gratitude as always to the inimitable Julia Silk for the cheerleading and arse-kicking, to my husband for those impeccably timed glasses of wine, to my children for the laughs and my dog for insisting the writing day should be punctuated with bracing and head-clearing walks.

I couldn't do it without my friends and readers—often one and the same—and I salute you all for being there, buying the books and rarely rolling your eyes at my numerous crises of faith.

Acknowledgments

Finally my enduring thanks to the fabulous team at William Morrow/Avon books in the US; Tessa Woodward, Alivia Lopez, Lisa McAuliffe, Sophie Normil, Jane Mount for the stunning cover design, and all the bloggers and reviewers who do such generous and amazing work to help writers' stories find their way into readers' hearts.

About the Author

POPPY ALEXANDER wrote her first book when she was five. There was a long gap in her writing career while she was at school, and after studying classical music at university, she decided the world of music was better off without her and took up public relations, campaigning, political lobbying, and a bit of journalism instead. She takes an anthropological interest in family, friends, and life in her West Sussex village (think *The Archers* crossed with *Twin Peaks*), where she lives with her husband, children, and various other pets.

Poppy Alexander is always happy to chat with readers on social media. Search for Poppy Alexander Books on Facebook, Instagram, and Twitter. Her website is Poppy-Alexander.com where you can also sign up for her author e-newsletter.

If you enjoyed *The Littlest Library*, you'll fall in love with Poppy Alexander's heartwarming festive romance . . .

You can't plan for the unexpected. . . .

Kate Potter used to know what happiness felt like.

A few years ago, she was full of energy,
excited by every possibility. But that was back
when everything was different, before Kate's husband
went away with the army and didn't come home.
She can't even remember what it felt like to be in love.

Then Kate meets Daniel. Recognizing her loneliness
reflected in his eyes, Kate vows to try to help bring him out
of his shell. But as Kate plans to bring life back to Daniel,
she might have stumbled on the secret to happiness. . . .

Can one chance meeting change two lives?
Available in paperback and e-book now